Lexington Glory Days

By Steven Reak

Lexington Glory Days

To my beautiful mother Bessie Reak
Travis, my nephew. And my dad
May all your days be glorious

Lexington Glory Days

This book is a work of fiction. Any references to historical events, real people or real places are used fictitiously. Other names, characters, places, and events are products of the authors imagination, and any resemblance to actual events or places or persons, living or dead, is entirely coincidental.

Cover designed by Tommy Jonq, an award winning graphic designer living and working in Chicago, IL. You can find him on Elance.com

All rights reserved, including the right to reproduce this book or portions thereof in any form whatsoever. No part of this book may be reproduced in any form without express written approval by the author.

Copyright pending.

Lexington Glory Days

Lexington Glory Days

Table of Contents

Chapter One: The 1940 County Fair......................................1
Part 2: The Reckoning...16
Chapter Two: The Villagers of Lexington........................ 30
Part 2: Hobo's and Gypsies... 40
Chapter Three: Betty and Edward Move Back Home..... 53
Part 2: The Struggle 62
Part 3: In With The In Crowd 87
Chapter Four: A House On A Hill On A Lake 101
Part 2: Neighbors in The Country 112
Part 3: The Anniversary Waltz..135
Chapter Five: The Fire 147
Chapter Six: A Cold, Cold Winter 161
Chapter Seven: Times Gone By 173
Chapter Eight: A Farm House and Eighty-Acres 207
Part 2: Angels Among Us 218
Chapter Nine: Running Bulls.. 234
Part 2: Among The Harvest 241
Chapter Ten: Quiet Footsteps... 253
Chapter Eleven: A Home in Town 270
Part 2: Living Without Edward...................................... 287
Part 3: Harold And Laura Get Married 309
Chapter Twelve: Is It Cold In Here, Or Is It Just Me?...312
Chapter Thirteen: Spring In The Country..................... 325
Part 2: A Styrofoam Bell 341
Chapter Fourteen: Tickets, Get Your Tickets!............... 355

Chapter One

The 1940 County Fair

Young Edward speeds to the southern Minnesota, Le Prarie county, fair in Centerville and stops the car so quickly that the tires slide and the whole car lurches forward on the old, loose dirt road before it comes to a complete stop. Inside the gate, he meets Betty, his date. "Let's go over to the carnival rides and games after were done here," Betty says happily from the horse stables and sitting on a fence. Her sister, Kimberly, looks up at her and smiles with ice cream on her cheek making Betty throw her head back and giggle.

"That's a great idea," Edward tells her, eagerly, wanting her to like him.

Kimberly looks at Betty and notices something different in Betty's expressions. "Betty, what's wrong?" She looks at the ground then back at Betty.

"Oh, nothing, I'm getting a little tired I guess. Maybe from all the people and commotion or too much sun." Her eyes are squinting.

"You still want to walk over to the rides with us, don't you?" She asks her talking quickly, unsure whether she wants to or not.

"Yeah, I'll walk over," she tells her. Feeling a little better now Betty runs a hand through her thick, black,

Lexington Glory Days

shoulder length, naturally curly hair, and holds up her other hand to shield out the hot sun striking her face.

While the three teenagers walk through the busy crowd to the carnival on the other end of Main Street, Edward notices the same change in Betty's attitude. "You're kind of quiet," he tells her, turning to look at her, playing with his fingers.

"She's a little tired," Kimberly quickly answers for her.

"You getting tired Bett?" Edward asks her directly.

"Just a little," she tells him, appreciating his concern, "But I'm okay. I still wanna go on the Ferris wheel and to the carnival."

"Well, yeah, sure whatever you want," he reassures her, trustingly.

Kimberly interrupts them again, matter-of-fact like, "The community leaders have organized two carnival rides for the townspeople, the Ferris wheel and a merry-go-round, and also three booths with games of chance in them, nearby," she snickers a little.

"I'll pay for your ticket, Betty," Edward tells her, and hands the man behind the gate two quarters.

Larry, Edwards brother, joins them and says, "Lets get on, he's motioning to us, were next." He starts poking Edward in the back.

The big Ferris wheel jerks forward and another empty car appears, and they get on. "Oh, it's moving, I'm scared!" Betty giggles loudly, turning her head around to tell Kimberly, making her laugh. The machine starts to turn. "Look how high we're getting," she tells Edward more calmly, "I'm a little scared."

"It's getting pretty high," he admits, a little uncomfortable himself.

"We can see the whole town from up here! It's so pretty," Betty says.

"It's nice, isn't it?" Edward agrees, watching the

ground swell up and fall again, looking around the town from the high distance.

"Look at all the people, they look like ants," she looks at him and smiles.

He smiles back at her and points, "I think I recognize some people."

"It's hard to make them out, they look so small," she tells him laughing.

Five times around and the ride slowly comes to a stop and the four disembark from the swinging cages. Betty turns to her left, and sees some high school classmates and with Kimberly by her side walks over to them to say, 'hi.'

"She's a pretty girl," Edward tells Larry, catching his eye then quickly diverting his own, with a smirk on his face.

"Ask her to dance, maybe she'd like that," Larry tells him in his slow, deliberate manner.

Larry thinks and speaks very clearly.

This gets Edward grinning. "I might just do that," he tells him.

"For that matter, let's all go out dancing," Larry, tells him. "I'll be right back."

He disappears into the crowd.

Eyeing the people over, Larry, a very tall, and large man, sees Betty and Kimberly's two brothers and earnestly approaches them, "Let's all go out and dance," he tells them, with one of his arms outstretched wide in the air. He spots two of his own sisters, Mamie and Rita nearby, walks over to them and says, "We're all going out dancing, if you want to, find a partner and we'll meet you out on the dance floor." Carrie, another sister of Edward and Larry's, is elsewhere at the fair enjoying herself with friends of hers.

Mamie's full figured with dark short hair and an easy smile and quick temper. Rita's somewhat thinner than her sister and has a serious quality that comes naturally to her, but loves joking around and having fun.

As Larry walks back to find Edward, Mamie and Rita look at each other. Maimie, looking a little dumbfounded, says to Rita, "I don't wanna go dancing."

"Me either," Rita tells her, "but let's go anyway," she says with a nasal laugh and toothy smile.

The large happy crowd lining the streets is high spirited and anxious for the band to play its next song. The dancers that are already on the dance floor talk and laugh with one another between selections as small, well dressed children run and play around them, or sit quietly and eat ice cream cones.

"The band is playing a quick, lively polka!" A young Betty turns and exclaims excitedly.

Jumping up and down, clapping her hands together.

Hearing her, Edward walks over to her, "Would you care to dance?" he asks her, sparing no charm.

A couple walks out onto the dance area that is covered with sawdust. Betty and Edward are the first of their group out, followed by most of the others. The men yell at one another as they pass each other. "You're out of step!" "Hey! I didn't know you could dance!" "Look out for that pothole!" They tease one another. The couples have a wonderful time skirting around and the young women smile to each other as they make the next round.

The men and women in the crowd who are either watching the dancers or listening to the music, smile and tap their feet and easily engage in light hearted conversation with whomever happens to be nearby. Enjoying the day and fellowship of their neighbors and community members.

"Edward has shown a great interest in Betty, his enthusiasm is showing by the wide smile on his face," Kimberly tells Larry, and shucks her shoulders with a smile and a giggle. Kimberly is short and to the point with

Lexington Glory Days

people, but also endearing.

"I see that," Larry tells her in his deep voice, smiling.

Edward and Betty laugh and talk as they make their way around and around again. "You're quite the dancer," the fourteen-year-old Betty tells him.

"You make it easy," the nineteen-year-old Edward says, trying to flatter her. She smiles at him and looks away. "You know I'd be happy to give you a ride home tonight, or whenever you're ready to go," he says loud enough into her ear for her to hear him, trying to impress her.

"I'd like that," she turns her neck to look at him, answering him with a smile.

This is Betty's first date with a boy.

"That's just what I wanted to hear," he answers her back with a smile. Edward was having a dashing time with her before she agreed to let him take her home, but he's now dancing more loosely and with a sense of confidence in his face and posture.

"This is so much fun," she tells him, dancing around together.

The band plays more lively polkas for them, and then plays the 'Chicken Dance'. A popular dance that gets people out on the dance floor, because it makes everyone look equally silly. They walk around each other, elbows in the air flapping like a chicken. They snap their fingers twice then clap their hands together again that many times, and put their hands on their waists and flap their elbows in the air again. Mamie and Rita, two of Edward and Larry's sisters, scratch the dirt with their feet like chickens, and burst out laughing.

"I'm parched, I'm gonna get a bottle of beer, can I get you one?" Edward asks Betty, posturing to move to get the beers.

"No, I'll just have a sip of yours, if it's all right," Betty tells him still smiling. He comes back with two bottles and hands her one. She accepts it from him reluctantly.

"Here you go." He hands the bottle to her, and clinks his bottle against hers, "cheers." She raises it to her mouth and takes a small sip. She looks around with her eyes and begins to feel a little self-conscious. She notices some of the others behind her and takes a step back from Edward, to blend in, and looks at him to see if he noticed.

"Wasn't that fun Betty?" Kimberly, whose two years older than Betty, asks rushing up to her, back from the dance floor. She notices Betty's holding a beer and asks her, "Oh, can I have some of your beer? I am so thirsty."

Betty lifts her hand, smiling, "yes, you can," and hands her the bottle, "I'm having a wonderful time," Betty boasts to her, suddenly giddy.

"It's been a lot of fun today, I have to say," her sister agrees.

There are hundreds of people on Main Street enjoying the warm, sunny day walking around and getting to know one another. Friendly 'hi's' and 'hello's' are heard throughout the day on the street, at the food booths and carnival rides.

People walk by and stand between Betty and Edward, separating them even further. The crowd is getting larger and the group starts to get further and further separated by the sudden influx of people, when suddenly Edward bursts through the crowd with a pitcher of beer and glasses.

"Why don't we go to the outside of this mob?" Edward tells Betty. "You tell Kimberly and your brothers if you want, Betty, and I'll tell Larry and my sisters."

"Well, yeah... Okay," Betty tells him stuttering for words over the sudden change of events.

"Let's meet right over there," he tells her, pointing toward the mercantile, behind where his old car is parked.

"Okay. We'll meet ya's over there then," she tells him,

feeling confused as to why his sisters must come along, or her brothers for that matter.

The group makes it over and Edward is there already pouring glasses of beer from the pitcher, next to his car, and then sets the pitcher on the hood after most everyone's glass is full.

"No thank you Edward," his sister Rita tells him in her nasal voice.

"I'll have some," Mamie, Edwards other sister adds in a voice deeper than his own. She slowly walks over to him with a regal walk.

"Betty you're so dressed up, are you going to a wedding?" Rita jokes, but Betty fails to see into her humor and ignores her.

"Kimberly, Betty, anyone want a beer?" Edward offers.

"I suppose," Kimberly tells him curtly, "and I'm hungry too," Kimberly announces forcefully.

"Anybody else hungry?" Edward asks, "Maybe we should find and see if they have a hamburger stand or something."

"I'll go get them, if somebody helps me; but I'm not paying for them all," Larry says seriously not wanting to part with the money.

"I'll help you," Rita tells him looking for something to do since she's too young to drink, and is getting bored.

"Get one for everybody Rita, here's three dollars," Edward tells her.

Ten minutes go by and Larry and Rita return with the hamburgers. After everyone is done eating, Betty and Kimberly are both tired and ready to go home. "I've had enough for one day," Betty tells them, tiredly, not particularly liking the company of Edwards's sisters.

"I'll give ya's a ride home now," Edward volunteers, "I mean if you want me to and you're ready. I'll see if I can get Larry to ride along."

"That'll be just fine," Kimberly tells him curtly. Betty is quiet and Larry agrees to ride along and the four walk back over to where the car is parked.

Edward opens the front passenger door and says, "Betty, you can ride in front." He's glad to get her alone again, even if people are in the back seat.

She blushes and smiles again, "oh, thank you," she tells him, flirting, and gets in. Edward closes the creaking, heavy black metal door and walks around to the other side. Betty stretches her legs and bounces in the seat.

They slowly drive past the crowd of people on the street to the outskirts of town and into the country. "There was quite a lot of people there," Larry tells them, his hair waving in every direction from the open windows.

"Yeah, there was," Edward agrees, "Betty did you have a good time?"

"I had a real swell time," she tells him, relaxed and feeling comfortable.

All four talk and laugh constantly on the ten-minute ride home and Edward drops the sisters off, and says to Betty, "thanks for the good time, and the dances." He looks at her across the car through her open door.

"Thank you," she tells him genuinely, looking at him like a good friend.

"See you soon maybe?" Edward asks her, hoping for an opening to see her again. It seems like minutes go by before she answers.

"Maybe," she waves to him, still smiling broadly, teasing him.

The two brothers drive off, Edward a little put off by her ambiguous answer, but still happy. Kimberly turns to Betty, "you like him don't you?"

With a little laugh she tells her, "I do. He seems nice," she admits, beaming, pleased with the whole afternoons' events. "He seems very, oh, down to earth." The two sisters turn around talking, and walk towards their house.

"Betty and her brothers and sisters have school all week, at least for those who haven't finished going," Larry tells Edward in the car on the way back to town, the lack of rain spitting up thick clouds of dust as the car moves fast along the gravel roads. "That's what Kimberly told me. When they come home from school they have to do their chores and school work." Larry suddenly sneezes from the dust coming in from the window.

"They all seem well mannered and polite," Edward tells him watching the road and occasionally glancing out at the fields. "Nice family."

"The older girls help with the cleaning, gardening and cooking, and the older boys with the outside chores, milking and feeding the four cows and the pigs, the younger ones the chickens. And everyone helps with the harvest in the fields, which isn't quite ready yet, she told me." Larry looks at him.

"She told you all that, huh?" Edward asks him surprised.

"Yeah, she did," he answers, looking puzzled.

The next day, a bright, sunny afternoon in the early part of fall, Betty and one of her older brothers Brian, an average sized young man with dark hair and an easy smile, and Kimberly decide to walk the short distance from their home, over to the lake and go swimming. The waters a bit cold, but for fun they jump in, and once their bodies get acclimated to the cool water temperature, splash around. "Euw, it's cold," they shiver and walk in.

The three joke, and splash the cool water on each other, "Brian don't do that!" Kimberly yells at Brian, mad, as he splashes her again. "Oh! That's cold!" She screams. "I'm gonna get you," she threatens.

Brian laughs, "Ha ha ha, it's cold, right?"

Kimberly submerges herself in the water to avoid being splashed and walks around the sandy, mucky bottom of the lake. The three near each other and begin talking. "I like fall, it's my favorite time of the year," Brian tells them.

"I know, it's so pretty with all the leaves changing colors," Kimberly responds smartly. "And all the fresh vegetables from the garden, yum."

"I like the hunting," Brian tells them. "I like being outside."

"I like going back to school, but I don't like the cold that's coming," Betty admits, waving her arms around in the water.

Brian splashes lake water on both of them again and laughs when they flinch. "Brian!" They both holler at him. Betty, smiling, takes a few steps back in the murky water and begins sinking in the sand.

"Oh, I just stepped in a really soft spot in the sand," she tells them, startled. "I can't get out!" Suddenly, she screams. "Help me! I'm sinking! I can't get out!" Betty is helpless and starts to panic.

Both Brian and Kimberly rush the few yards away she is to them, "grab one of her arms Kimberly!" Brian yells at her, "and pull her out!" Brian wades through the water as quickly as he can to get to her and reaches her other arm and the two struggle to pull her free, "pull harder Kimberly!" he pleads.

Betty stops sinking, but they struggle to pull her out. "She's stuck!" Brian hollers. "Don't let her go! She might start sinking again!"

"Get me out! Get me out of here," Betty screams, becoming hysterical, helpless. Her hands flail against them, and Kimberly loses her grip on one of her arms as Betty splashes in the water, trying to stay afloat and keep from sinking further. "Help me! Help me!" She screams, terrified, as Brian and Kimberly pull, trying to release the vacuum that's holding her down.

"Be careful Kimberly, so you don't go down too!"

Brian pleads to her.

The sand loosens up enough around one of her ankles and legs and the two are able to pull her out enough, where her foot can get a better grip and she can help them push herself out. "Oh, my God! Oh, my God!" Kimberly screams, "Come on Betty! Try harder! Pull!!"

Betty is frantic, "Pull! Pull harder!" She cries. Brian and Kimberly fight the soft sand themselves, but are close enough to shore to hope the ground underneath them won't cave in and suck them down as well.

"Pull Kimberly! Pull!" Brian encourages her.

The quicksand gives in under Betty's other leg, and in a split second she sinks even further but gains even more footing with her other leg and with Brian and Kimberly pulling on her, she lurches forward, her head getting dragged underwater. They pull her further towards them. Brian helps her up out of the water as she coughs and feels disoriented. She doesn't know where they are leading her. Kimberly helps her keep her balance as Brian guides her to shore.

"Here, sit down, Betty. Sit down." Brian tells her panting. Once they get her to dry land, and help her, she collapses to the ground.

"You're safe now!" Kimberly tells her, a bundle of nerves and adrenalin pumping wildly through her veins. "Sit down and relax! Breathe Betty! Relax and breathe! Relax and breathe! Oh, my God!" Kimberly exclaims, "That was so close!" All three sit down together. "Lie down," Kimberly tells her, relaxing a bit, "lie down, Betty."

The three lie down next to each other, afraid and exhausted. "Are you okay Bett?" Brian asks her.

"I'm okay," she tells him, breathing heavily, her chest heaving and falling quickly. Lake water is streaming down from her nose.

Kimberly rolls over to face her, and wipes her face

with her hand, "you're all right now, Betty, you're all right now." Betty's chest is quickly rising up and down, as she struggles to catch her breath. She's able to relax a little bit and her breathing slows just a little. "You're all right now," Kimberly tells her, "your all right now. Relax," she keeps telling her, her own heart racing fast, "just relax."

The three rest for a few minutes, then Brian followed by Kimberly sit up. "You want to sit up, Betty?" Brian asks her.

"I suppose," she tells him still dazed. They help her sit up.

"How do you feel?" Kimberly asks her.

Betty hangs her head down facing the ground, "I'm okay," she tells her, still breathing hard. She's trembling uncontrollably.

"You'll be okay now," Brian reassures her.

The three look up, staring at the small waves in the lake, that just about took their sister's life. Brian takes a deep breath, "let's go home," he tells them. Brian lets her sit for a while longer to get her bearings straight.

They get up, helping Betty to her feet and stagger back through the marsh field, the short distance back to their home. They tell their parents and other brothers and younger sister, Gertrude, what happened.

Everyone tries soothing them, and tries to keep them comfortable. "Let's get you's in some dry clothes," their mother tells them.

"I never heard there being quick sand in the lake before," their dad tells them, surprised. "Don't go down there anymore," he orders them.

Betty is quiet, feeling like she has done something wrong. "I'll never go in the water again," she tells them, still in shock and trembling.

Her mother tries comforting her, lightly rubbing her forehead with her hand, "lie down for a while, Betty, you'll feel better. You're okay now."

The next day is Sunday and Blanch, a sister of Edward's, and a school friend of Betty's, comes over to visit her, after hearing about the near horrific drowning the day before.

"I'm better, but now I'm deathly afraid of the water," Betty tells her friend, still shaken by the events. "I'm trying to put the awful experience behind me, but it's hard. It seems like something's changed, but I don't know what exactly. Like everything's more clear, even more colorful."

Blanch tries explaining this to Edward after she arrives back home.

"She's begun to have a new appreciation for the people around her, and herself I think, you know that happens sometimes when something like this occurs. But she's now more fearful of life in general, I think. She's trying to get past it all, but she has to retell the story of her almost drowning over and over and over again."

"Is there anything else different you noticed about her?" Edward asks her.

"She's a little quieter...she seems more peaceful, but more decisive somehow too, I think," she tells him.

"I hope she's going to be okay," Edward says, showing his concern.

"I think she'll be okay," Blanch tries reassuring him.

Monday morning, with the sun shining brightly down, Betty walks the quarter mile hike to school with her brothers and sisters as usual, almost as if nothing happened.

Across the lake, Edward enthusiastically is heading off to work as a young farm hand, thresher and mechanic for some of the local farmers in the area. With the corn, wheat and beans in the fields turning a golden yellow as they ripen, it's almost time to harvest the crops and there's plenty to do around the farms to prepare.

"Hi Kenny, What work do you have for me today?"

Edward asks the string bean lean, old farmer.

Stopping to think about it, the nearly bald man in tattered and dirty bib overalls speaks, nearly toothless, "I got a few things I needs to get done. Part of the fence needs fixin anyway. I want to run the picker and make sure all the parts are workin and make sure it's runnin right. Yeah, so go ahead and make a pass around the whole outside of the fields I guess. I'll help you set up for it."

Edward does as he's told and makes one pass around the very outside rows of the fields with the tractor and picker to make sure the equipment is in working order. He turns back to look at the picker and wagon and notices the beautiful golden hues of color in the rows of corn and he watches the picker and listens to it working for any odd noises, but so far everything seems to be running okay.

He begins thinking about Betty and her nearly drowning and what Blanch told him, as he charges up and around the rows of corn, and this makes him sad and a little afraid, and even mad. The tall, dark-haired, rugged young man shakes off the thought and tries to think of more positive things. He remembers the town celebration a few weeks ago and smiles thinking about the whole bunch of them together having so much fun. With everyone riding on the Ferris wheel and merry-go-round and playing the games of chance and dancing, and how he and Betty were getting along so well. He realizes he has feelings for her, and wants her now, and wants to spend more time with her.

He finishes going around the outside rows and drives back into the farmers yard and parks the tractor and picker and wagon off along the side where it won't be in the old farmers way.

"Everything seems to be working all right," Edward tells him respectfully.

"That's good. I'm gonna take it out myself this afternoon and make another pass with it so I can check it myself and be sure."

"I can do that for you if you want me to, that is," Edward says, hoping to work more hours for the farmer, shifting his weight from side to side.

"No, I'll do it. See those wagons over there? There's a couple of wood slabs come off, that need to be re-attached. Check the other slabs and make sure they're strong and won't come off while were filling her. Check the bottom ones too; I think there all right though. I'll be fixin this fence."

The farmer doesn't look at him as he talks, and he begins working on the fence, leaving Edward to wonder for a moment if the old timer is done explaining himself. He doesn't say anything more, and without speaking, Edward walks off to check the wood slabs on the grain wagons.

After fixing the wagons, Edward's job for this old farmer is done for the day. He gets in his car and drives down the road to another farm and another job.

Part 2

The Reckoning

"This coming Saturday night there's a dance down at the bar and pavilion in Lexington," Betty is telling her mother, a large, loving woman, "I'd like to go if it's okay." Betty's looking forward to meeting her friends, and perhaps Edward.

"It's okay as long as Kimberly goes with you. Some of your brothers have been talking about going down too," her mother informs her, "I know it's a popular spot for the young kids, and us older folks alike, for that matter. I'd just feel better if you didn't go alone. You're only fourteen, you know."

"Okay," Betty tells her happily satisfied, "I'll ask Kimberly."

"That old, country dance hall with all its old, worn woodwork and high ceilings, next to the lake like it is, brings people in from all over," her dad explains to her. "Gotta be careful down there. If the band is particularly good, or well known, you can easily expect a packed house that night. Hell, we might even go." He looks at his wife whose looking back at him, thinking it over.

It turns out to be one of the local bands, but the turnout, as usual is good. People begin arriving in their cars and trucks. Several 1925 two door black and gray

Chevy's, big square four door gray Fords, 1926 and1927 green pickups with small back seats, 1928 and 1929 Dodges, 1930 four doors, with long noses and wide fenders.

"Everyone has shed their workaday clothes for their going out bests. Look, all the girls are wearing their light colored skirts and dresses, and the boys' are wearing black and tan pants and white shirts, some even have their hair slicked back. Everyone looks so nice," Betty tells Kimberly as they near the end of their half-mile walk to the dance hall from their home.

"Lots of the neighbors are here. I see Edward and a few of his brothers and sisters and parents, Lloyd and Evelyn, are here." Kimberly tells her. Betty shrugs her shoulders, not seeming interested.

"Looks like all the neighbors have come out to enjoy a night out in the cool air, before the long cold winter comes back again," Edward's dad is telling a neighbor friend of his, leaning on a hand railing.

"Look at the bright lights from the dance hall reflecting off the lake, it looks magical and so romantic," Kimberly's so excited she squirms to finish the words.

The band begins to play and people begin having a wonderful time dancing around the floor, doing the polka and the waltz, the Two Step and the Fox Trot, and all the current dances.

"Edward is at the bar talking wildly with his friends," Blanch, Edward's sister, tells Betty and Kimberly, as they meet each other outside the pavilion. "They've been drinking and laughing a lot. Occasionally they stop someone they know to talk, or give them a hard time. I think he's drunk."

A neighbor is talking to Edward at the bar, after Edward asks him to keep an eye on Betty for him. "Betty is with her friends and family. She's been spending the evening around the dance floor, dancing with them or talking and laughing in one of the old wooden booths."

"The girls have to pass by us when they want to get another soda or beer or make their way to the restroom, at the other end of the bar," Edward tells him. "I wanna see if she'll stop and talk to me. She looks so pretty with that full head of dark black curls and smart round glasses. She has a happy outlook and confident, easy walk that I like," Edward goes on, teasing and makes a grunting noise. Edward notices her several times and his eyes lock on her figure and face as she appears and disappears in and out of the crowd.

"I can't help but look at him at the bottom of the stairs from the dance floor, at the bar, he's such an imposing figure," Betty tells Blanch.

His eyes follow her as she walks further down the bar, to an opening to get to the restroom and back again. Their eyes meet and they both smile, their gaze lingers for a moment, then Betty goes back up to the dance floor to rejoin her friends and family. She wants to talk to him, but she's shy and waiting for him.

"Nope, aint gonna come talk to me," Edward groans, "I guess I'll have to do the chasing." He turns and looks at the wall behind the bar.

The floorboards in the old country dance hall heave with the weight of all the dancers as the evening stretches on, with the band playing its fox trot's and polkas. Edward makes a point to be in the area that Betty is hanging out in, hoping to bump into her. They talk, and have a good time playfully teasing each other and dance a few polkas together, on and off throughout the night.

"It was nice to see you again," they both agree.

The following week, Betty hears that Edward was seen driving his big, wide, black four-door 1932 Chevy, with a long hood in front, around the dirt roads in Lexington and around the lake, killing time and looking for something to do, after work. He loves his car, the motor, the speed and everything about it.

He's a rebel, and guns the motor to spin the tires as rocks and dust spark up behind him, as the rear end of the car fish tales from side to side. He drives past Lexington and the pavilion and the other bar in the village, on the road along the lakeshore, and wonders if he should drive into town, but instead makes a quick right past the neighbors further down the road.

With a hint of mischief in his eye, he hangs another quick right and begins to slow the car's speed down as he drives past Betty's parents' house. He drives by, his arm resting on the open window ledge, as he looks up their driveway to their yard and house and raises his hand in a famliar gesture, and smiles and waves to Joseph, Betty's father.

Joseph's alone outside, dressed in his work coveralls picking something up out of the lawn, or maybe it's their garden, Edward is unsure. Joseph is facing the house and turns sideways a bit to see Edward, and raises his arm at the elbow in return, a look of curiosity and uncertainty on his face.

The place is nice with lots of blooming flowers, Edward notices. Instead of going anywhere further, he decides to make another right and go home, where he spends the rest of the evening with his parents, brothers, and sisters.

"Edward, something's come in the mail for you. I'm afraid it looks pretty official, and it looks like the same letter Larry received," his mother is telling him emotionally, when he gets home from his drive.

Edward is immobilized, momentarily frozen in his own thoughts. "The same type of letter Larry received?" he responds, his eyes welling up with tears. "I'm afraid so, here, you better open it." He looks at the envelope stamped October 1942. He opens it and mumbles the words to the letter and says, "I just received my draft

Lexington Glory Days

notice from the army, for the war against Germany and Japan. I leave right away."

The news makes him sad inside but he tries not to show it.

"I'm sorry Edward," Evelyn, his mother, tells him. Softly, she adds, "You better start thinking about all you might want to do, before you have to leave."

"I want to spend time with you and dad and the kids....And Betty. I have to see Betty," he tells her.

Together as a family, they spend the rest of the day and night at home. The following evening he sees Betty. "I leave next week," he tells her, putting his arm around her, the two sitting in his car, overlooking the lake near the boat landing. "I don't know what to make of it all really."

"You must be frightened. Going away, so far from home," she asks him, holding onto his fingers, sitting next to him in the car.

"I'm a little scared, not too bad though. I'm gonna miss everyone around here, I can tell you that much though, mom, dad and the kids, and you. I'm not the only one from Lexington that's going either, Larry's going, and some others I heard about. Maybe I'll know some of the other guys."

"Joseph junior, my oldest brother, is already there. I'll be sad to see you go. It won't be the same around here without you," she cuddles closer to him, burying her head in his neck.

Edward gently rubs her shoulder, and stretches his neck down to kiss her, "I'm going to miss you the most," he tells her, and kisses her again. She responds, not wanting to let him go.

In the army, Edward becomes a truck driver and rifle marksman in the Northern Solomon's, in the Asiatic Pacific Theater and Guadalcanal, trying to fight off the Japanese in the British owned islands and trying to defend the Allies' communication and supply lines, far off the southern coast of China nearer Australia in the Pacific Ocean. He finishes boot camp and gets sent to the front lines. The fierce battles have already started and have been going on since before he arrives. He gets there just as two divisions team up to battle the Japanese. There's heavy fighting all around him.

"We gotta keep them bastards from getting any closer," Edward, in full military gear, shouts over the loud crashing of the bombs exploding around him. "Keep shooting! Keep shooting!" The man next to him in the foxhole falls back against the dirt then quickly stands up and turns around and continues firing and yells back at him, "Here they come!" "There's a bunch coming from the left!" Edward screams, "shoot!" But the Japanese keep coming. "Keep firing!" he screams again, his heart pounding wildly in his chest. Round after round of ammunition gets unloaded at the Japanese fighters, striking some as their arms flail out and they fall, dead in their tracks. The battle enrages and goes on for hours. "Keep watching!" Edward tells him, "There's more out there somewhere ready to storm us! Keep watching for 'em!" Though it's daylight, the smoke and dust and flying shrapnel in the air, make it seem like it's later than it is. The blasting noises of the bombs going off become mute to the men, stuck in their own mind zone, focusing on the battle, watching, waiting, alert. "There they are! Shoot!" Edward yells, as some of the Japanese fighters have narrowly approached a foxhole nearby, and the deafening screams of American soldiers in pain are heard.

"What the hell was that!"

"I don't know, someone got hit!"

"Watch 'em! Watch "em!" Edward screams.

"There they are! Keep shooting!" All of a sudden, it seems there are Japanese soldiers everywhere. Bullets are flying past them, they don't know if they were being shot at them or at someone else and they can sometimes hear

Lexington Glory Days

the sound of the whizzing bullets flying past them, some barely missing them. Tanks are driving around to where they're needed the most to help the men.

Boom! They unload their arsenal of ammunition into a mass of Japanese soldiers, hitting their target.

Boom! The tank delivers another hit. Edward hollers, "Keep shooting! Don't let them in! Shoot!"

The men in the foxholes peer just above the ground surface and unload their guns on the enemy. There is chaos everywhere as the battle rages on.... and on.... and.... on.

Back in the states, by her mothers' bedside, Betty is talking with her mom.

"Betty, you seem out of sorts, is there something wrong, dear?" Her mother, Elizabeth, has been laid up and sick in bed for two months.

"Everything. Everything is wrong mother," she tells her sadly.

"Tell me what's bothering you, what has gotten to you so?" Elizabeth asks her weakly.

"You being sick mostly. I wish you weren't sick!" She screams and breaks down, her eyes welling up with tears. "When are you gonna get out of this bed?"

Her head hanging down, she wipes the tears from her eyes.

"Betty, please don't be mad or sad. The Good Lord takes care of his children. All of his children. He'll take care of me, and he'll take care of you too. Come here Betty," she tells her, trying to strain to see her as she painfully turns her neck towards her. Her motherly instincts make her want to hold her.

Betty goes to her mothers' bedside, and slides in next to her, as her mother tries rocking her.

"My poor Betty, my poor beautiful Betty. What should I say to take away these anguished thoughts? Mmm? I love you Betty, that's all you'll ever need to know. I love you." She tries holding her tightly.

"But mama you're so sick all the time, when are you going to get better? I want so much for you to be better," Betty sobs.

"Child, we're trying, we're trying, you know that. The doctor gives me medicines he hopes will cure me. I want to get better too. I love you so Betty. I won't let anything hurt you," she tells her, holding her close.

"I love you too mama," a frightened and confused Betty tells her.

After months of pain and suffering and trying the doctors different medications without success, Elizabeth succumbs to the ailments that had kept her bedridden.

"This is the worst thing ever that's ever happened," Kimberly sobs to Betty, who is also openly weeping. "I can't, I can't believe she's gone."

Once again, she clasps her head in her open hands and cries, grief stricken. Betty stares in shock at their deceased mother in the casket, in the living room of their home, tears streaming down her face. "Poor Gertrude and Peter, our poor little sister and brother, their just kids. They, they, can't stop crying either. What are we gonna do without mother?" Kimberly cries, questioning the situation facing the entire family.

"I don't know," Betty tells her, heartbroken, searching for a moment of calm. "I...just don't know," she whispers. She stares at her mom in the cold grey casket.

The shades are pulled closed in the small living room of their home, blocking the light, and the room is dark. Callers come by to pay their last respects to this wonderful woman, Elizabeth, one last time. Friends and relatives come and visit throughout the two days, bringing with them food and words of comfort for the family.

'She was a wonderful neighbor.' 'What a giving woman.' 'You have my sympathies.'

Lexington Glory Days

These are phrases repeated by many friends and family who file by the casket.

The whole family is shaken and continually cries. "I loved her so much," a grieving Joseph, her husband, says to friends.

"She was so sick, for so long, I'll miss her an awful lot. She passed away right here ya know," he tells them. "In her bed and in her sleep. She was only forty-seven."

The body of their beloved deceased wife and mother spends the night in the living room in the casket and will be taken out tomorrow morning for the funeral at the church. Family sadly come and go throughout the evening.

Her grieving husband is finally able to speak: "She was such a devoted wife and mother, her whole life's interests centered on her family, and she worked diligently, diligently for us. She was a good neighbor and friend to all who knew her. During her long illness she bore her suffering with patience and without complaint." He breaks down and cries. Her passing is deeply grieved by all her family, neighbors and friends.

For many months afterwards the children are withdrawn and sullen. Peter barely speaks at all, and the rest of the family can barely lift their heads up high enough to look at each other in the eye. 'If only we could talk to her again,' they constantly think, sadly missing her.

A year later, from what seems like a million miles away from home to him, in the army, one evening Edward sits down to write a letter; "Dearest mother and all, I received quite a few of your letters in the last month. I did not answer any of them because I was on the move. When I first got to Guadalcanal I didn't like the damn place, these islands down here are no damn good. I got a letter from Larry yesterday. He said he is in the Philippine Islands. I guess he doesn't like it so good over there. I wonder who in the hell would like it over there. Not me! I am sending you a picture I had taken. When you look at it don't laugh! I felt kinda sad when I heard Mrs. Joseph Pike died. I feel sorry for them. But there isn't anything I can do about it. I am glad to hear that the kids like school.

You say you've seen my son? Glad to hear that Betty's son is good looking. Yes, I know Larry is a sergeant, the lucky guy. I hope he gets to be a master sergeant. I am going to put in for a furlough. But I don't know if I'll get it or not. I am really going to try for one. If I get a furlough and go back I really don't know if I'll get married to Betty, if she would want me she would write to me. I am fine. I hope this will find all of you in the best of health and happiness. I have a bunch of letters to write. So I'll close for now. Bye now, Edward. Write soon."

The idea of not being able to help Betty with their son, and help her cope with the loss of her mother plus the stress of the war forces Edward into trouble overseas. He's charged with driving a cargo truck wrecklessly down a highway.

To help manage the pressure, Edward's forced to sum up more inner strength than he knew he needed. Betty isn't any happier at home.

"The nurses told me I should put the baby up for adoption. It's unfit they said, for a woman to be a single mother," Betty tells Blanch, imitating the nurses in a snarly manner. "People look at me like I committed a crime, or I'm filthy dirty."

Betty feels like people are watching her when she's out in public.

"It 'is' frowned upon," Blanch sighs, telling her honestly. "It's a big deal. People wonder how you're going to work or get the money to feed and take care of the baby at the same time. Some are shaming you, but don't worry about them. Some are concerned about you."

"I'd like to take some of their smug looks and tell 'em

what I think of them."

'Oh, Betty," Blanch says, "Don't stay mad, that won't do you any good."

Two years pass by and the pain Betty feels from the stigma and ridicule, from strangers and friends alike, of being a single woman with a newborn baby, and from the recent loss of her mother, is lessened in the Fall of 1945 when Edward is honorably discharged from the Army. He's awarded one Asiatic-Pacific Theater Service Medal, five Overseas Service Bars, one Lapel Button, and four Discharge Emblems.

He's matured in a way only the army and war can make a man, stronger, but with his strength came awful memories of battles, seldom talked about.

He arrives back home in Lexington hoping to pick up the pieces of his life before he left for the war. He wants to settle down, and decides to propose his love to Betty. The two get married in a small church wedding in November 1945, of that same year.

Their son Harold is two.

"Let me read the wedding write up in the paper to you," Kimberly eagerly tells Betty, lying on her bed in their dads home, days after the wedding.

"Miss Betty Pike and Mr. Edward Reich were wed on Nov. 28: On Wednesday morning, November 28 at 8:30 o'clock, Miss Betty Pike, daughter of Mr. Joseph Pike was married to Mr. Edward Reich, son of Mr. And Mrs. Lloyd Reich in St. Mary's Catholic Church at Centerville. Rev. Father Minea read the nuptial mass and performed the double ring ceremony. The bride was gowned in a floor length dress of white lace, fashioned with a sweetheart neckline and three quarter length sleeves. She wore a fingertip veil, held in place with orange blossoms, and carried a bouquet of white carnations and roses with orange blossoms tied on the streamers. Her jewelry consisted of a locket and bracelet, a gift from the groom.

The bridesmaid, Miss Kimberly Pike, a sister of the bride, wore a floor length gown of blue, fashioned with a lace bodice and a skirt of alpaca, with matching headdress. For her jewelry she wore a locket, and carried a bouquet of yellow and white chrysanthemums, with yellow chrysanthemums on the streamers. The groom wore a blue tailored suit and was attended by his brother, Mr. Tom Reich, who wore a brown tailored suit. Both wore boutonnieres. The bride attended school at District 93 and at Centerville High School. The groom attended schools at Belle River and Le Prarie. He received his honorable discharge from the army just a few months ago, after spending 35 months in service, 32 of which were overseas. A reception was held following the ceremony for about 40 guests, which included the parents, brothers and sisters of the bride and groom, the bride's grandmother and a few close friends. Out of town guests were Mrs. Stanley O'Patray and Miss Mamie Reich of St. James and Kenny Hartwith, who just received his honorable discharge at Camp McCoy, Wisconsin. They will make their home in St. James after Dec. 1."

"What a beautiful write up, but it makes me sad knowing your leaving us," Kimberly whispers to her wistfully. "I don't want you to go," she tells her firmly.

"I wish you weren't leaving either," Gertrude, their younger sister, adds sitting on the edge of the bed, "we'll never get to see you." Gertrude is trying to be mature for her age.

Betty is cleaning out the last of her drawers and looks in the mirror at them, saddened, "I'll miss you two an awful lot," she tells them and murmurs, "sometimes I wish I weren't going either." She puts her things in the box next to her, "I'm a little worried, but Edward has a good mechanic's job lined up and a place for us to live, and we'll be in the city. With all the people, and commotion and things going on, we'll never be bored, it

Lexington Glory Days

might be exciting."

"You can take the girl out of the country, but you can't take the country out of the girl," their dad, Joseph, reminds them fondly, walking into the room with Peter, their youngest brother trailing behind him, as both sit on the bed. "You'll be fine sweetheart, and so will we. Won't we girls?"

His three daughters all begin talking at the same time.

"Now, now stop your caterwauling," their dad interrupts them, "I know it'll be hard for a while, and we'll all miss each other, but Betty will come down as often as she can to visit us, won't you Betty? And we can go visit her from time to time. It won't be so bad, you'll see."

"Daddy, you always know just what to say," Kimberly tells him in her forthright manner.

"Gertrude, you're kinda quiet, is there something on your mind child?" Her dad asks, looking sideways at her, while folding his hands in his worn coveralls.

"There is daddy. I've been down in the dumps ever since mama died, Kimberly and especially you, Betty, have become my best friends..."

"And we always will be," Kimberly seriously interrupts her.

"I hope so," Gertrude says sadly, "I don't know what I'd do if I ever lost either of you two. With you moving away, Betty, it seems like I'm losing you now." She stops talking, looking to each of her sisters for a satisfactory response from them.

Betty responds, "I'll always be there for you Gertrude, and if there's anything at all you need, or just if you want to talk. You can come up and visit and stay as long as you like, and I'm sure we'll be coming down pretty often."

"Is that okay, Gertrude?" Her dad asks her, with a kind hearted grin.

"I guess it'll have to be," she tells them, not sounding very convincing.

"Oh, Gert, don't be that way!" Kimberly chides her, "besides, I'll still be here for you, and daddy, and Peter and Brian will be too."

"And don't forget your older brother Wayne, your aunts and uncles, and grandma," their dad adds, trying to make them all feel better.

"How about you, Peter, anything you got to say before Betty leaves?"

Peter shakes his head, "I'll miss you." He seems to have more on his mind but can't find the words.

"Oh, come here," Betty tells him and walks over to him, embracing him, as the others stand to hug her good bye. "I'm gonna miss you all so much."

Chapter Two

The Villagers of Lexington

"We gotta letter in the mail today addressed to ma," Joseph is telling Gertrude and Peter, his only two children left living at home since Betty moved away. He's sitting in an over stuffed, comfortable chair in the living room of their small home.

"Addressed to ma? Why would they send it to ma? Don't they know she died a few years back?" Gertrude exclaims, still angry over losing her mother.

"Now hold on, it's about Joseph Jr." He explains tenderly.

"What about him daddy?" Peter says, "Is he coming home?" He asks excitedly.

Joe places his hand on his youngest sons' shoulder. "The letter's from the United States Army. It says Joseph's been seriously hurt in the war with the Japanese, in the Pacific. That's all it says."

Gertrude slowly walks towards her father as he's reading the letter, wiping her hands on her apron, "hurt? That's all it says? Oh my word. I wonder how badly?"

Noticing Gertrude's worried look, Peter asks, "did the Japanese shoot him? Is Joseph Jr. gonna die like mama, daddy?"

"No! I don't think so," he tells him loudly, hiding his

disturbed feelings. "I don't think so, son," he repeats softly as his eyes begin to well up with tears.

"How are we supposed to find out how he's doing?" Gertrude asks him, "Is there someone we can contact?"

"No. That's all it says," he tells her, shakily handing the letter to her.

She reads the letter out loud: "Mrs. Elizabeth S. Pike, Route 2, Centerville. Regret to inform you your son was seriously wounded in action in the Pacific, Nov. 12. Until new address is received address mail for him, "Pfc. Joseph E. Pike, serial number (Hospitalized) Central Postal Directory APO 640, care of Post Master, New York, N.Y." You will be advised as reports of condition are received. Witsel, Acting Adj. Gen."

"Oh my God. Brian's over there too someplace," Gertrude mumbles, "I hope he didn't get hurt too," she tells them, seriously concerned. Looking up at her dad, she lets her arm fall to her side, and the letter falls out of her open hand to the floor. She couldn't bare to lose another family member.

Looking back at his daughter, speechless, he stares back at her knowingly. Just like many of the other families in Lexington and nearby surrounding areas, the bad news of the war has come home to them.

Down the road and across the lake, Edwards mother, Evelyn asks her husband Lloyd, disdainfully, "Lloyd, is that all you gonna do all day is read the paper?" She stops what she's doing and watches him, waiting for him to react.

"War, war, war, everything's about the war. Buy war bonds," Lloyd mutters as he continues reading. "Corporal Singer held hostage by the Japs gets released after twelve weeks. Brown outs and curfews, can't even have the lights on or be out after midnight now. Blood drives, rationing reminders. Can't buy meat, butter, cheese, gasoline, canned goods or shoes without a ration book. 'All stamps must be attached to books when presented for commodities.' There are actual pictures of men overseas fighting in the war. Real pictures of 'em! Seems we live our lives for this war. Small price to pay, I suppose. "

"Damn those Nazis and Japs and this war. I wish it were over and they'd send all the boys home already. I don't want to think about it anymore! I'm tired of reading about our neighbors' sons missing in action, getting wounded or held prisoner, or killed. I could just yell sometimes I get so damn mad. It was all I could do, not to worry about Edward and Larry when they were overseas. It was all I could do. I don't know how poor Joe," Betty's father, "does it. He's got two sons over there now, and no mother to help raise those young ones, I don't know how he manages. I just don't know. I'm a wreck sometimes and I have you and the kids to keep my mind off it," Evelyn tells him.

"There's a lot of folks' sons over there from around here, not just Joe's. He manages, just like everyone else has to, like it or not. We all do," he tells her.

"Manages? What do you mean? Worrying about them? Trying not to wonder if their still alive or lying in some battlefield somewhere wounded and hurt or worse? The papers full of stories like that, every week."

"I know they are. There's more in todays; 'Ted Erickson wounded in action,' 'Gordon S. Bryzsmoceck wounded in action in Germany,' we know both those families. That's just two off the top front page."

"I wonder how Joe's boys are doing over there," Evelyn remarks, still standing nearby and getting antsy.

"I suppose we should buy another war bond," Lloyd tells her, still reading.

"We should buy three or four of them," she counters. "If that's what it takes to help our boys win this thing, we should buy all we can to help. We can afford to buy more than just one, don't be so cheap."

Lexington Glory Days

He looks up at her curiously wondering what she means, "I know, I agree with ya. But it says here the Red Cross is having a fundraising drive, and the paper's always telling us to donate more to reach our goal, for the seventh War Bond Drive. It says Lexington is behind the way it is, and if we don't give more, or raise more, there's gonna be some inspector coming out, knocking on doors, personally asking for more donations. That's a Washington fund drive that quota is, I don't know what would happen if we couldn't reach it. We can only spare so much. We're not rich."

"Give 'til it hurts, that's what they say," she says, put off by her own words. "Since the Nazis surrendered a few weeks ago, they're telling us we can't stop donating now. We got to finish off the Japs. 'Almost done,' their telling us. 'Buy bigger bonds!' We'll all be in the poor house before too long."

"It aint so bad," Lloyd tries convincing her, "at least there's work to be had so a man can make a living. People are looking for help all over, and they're willing to train 'em. Right here in the paper it says, 'men and women needed now, production jobs, tool and die, final assembly, sheet metal, mechanics, engineers.' Here's another one, it says 'the War Manpower Commission is looking to fill ten thousand jobs. 2,100 harvest hands, 1,025 corn detasselers, and 5,400 canning factory workers." He rattles the paper as he reads it to get the wrinkles out of it.

Jim, six, their youngest son, walks in the room and announces he wants to go swimming.

"It's sweltering hot out today, must be close to a hundred degrees. A swim would feel mighty nice I'm sure," his mom tells him, "ask Rita, Carrie and Tom if they want to go with, and you's can all go. Maybe I'll even drive ya's down, be nice to get out of this hot oven for a while."

Excited, Jim goes to find his sisters and brother.

"Think I'll even tag along, a dip in the water sounds pretty good," Lloyd tells Evelyn.

"I better find some towels," she says, and hurriedly scurries away in search of fresh towels.

When they get to the lake, the water is tepid and light blue with very small white caps, and a group of thirty kids and adults are splashing around, some with old inner tubes blown up from truck or car tires, at a popular beach just off the main road. "Look at all the people," Evelyn remarks.

The kids hop out of the car and run into the water across the hot sand as soon as the car comes to a stop. Once the waters' drag slows them down, they dive head first into the cool, refreshing water. Long legged, Lloyd gets out of the passenger side of the car, taking in the picturesque view of the lake and swimmers. The hot, brown, wet sand squishing between his toes.

"Are you goin in? Cause I'm just going to take a towel and sit on the beach and watch the kids and look at my paper," Evelyn tells Lloyd.

"I'm goin in," he tells her light heartedly, trying to be playful.

The outside temperature is ninety-eight degrees but the air near the lake is cooler. There's a small breeze catching the waters temperature and cooling the air around it. You can almost see the water evaporating and there's a haze in the air. The sun is bright off the water and against the clear blue sky. From the sounds of the kids' laughter and yelling in the lake, it's a perfect day to be in the water, to go swimming.

Evelyn lays her towel on a slight slope in the grass and struggles to sit down, sidling next to another woman.

"Can it get any hotter?" She says to her fellow sun bather. The lady is a regular at the beach.

"It's not bad here by the lake," the lady replies, keeping her eye on the water. Evelyn looks at all the people and her kids in the water and takes the folded up newspaper out of her purse and begins to glance through it.

"I see the grocery store has catsup, coffee, lettuce heads, oranges, onions and apples on sale this week," she says out loud, not speaking directly to the lady. Evelyn keeps looking over the ad items on sale this week.

"How much are they?" the lady enquires.

"Which ones?" Evelyn asks, as she straightens the paper.

"All of them," she replies and laughs nervously, glancing at her quickly.

"Well, the catsup is nineteen cents, three pounds of coffee is fifty-nine cents...two heads of lettuce are twenty-nine cents, oranges are nineteen cents a dozen...for ten pounds of onions they want thirty-seven cents, and two pounds of apples are a quarter."

"Twenty-nine cents for two heads of lettuce, that still seems like a lot to me," the lady says, "Hi, I'm Katherine Leacher. We just live about two miles down the road." Evelyn responds as if she is reading from her own personal list.

"Hi Katherine," Evelyn says, turning to look at her, "I'm Evelyn Reich, nice to meet you. We live that way about a quarter mile," she points her thumb over her shoulder behind her, "were kinda new to this area."

"My folks been here a long time already. My dad and ma both came from Bohemia nearly fifty years ago. It's a shame about that polio disease that's going around, aint it. I hope and pray all these kids get spared. It cripples the children's legs," Katherine sighs, shaking her head. She watches the kids in the lake.

Not knowing the lady, Evelyn doesn't know what to say, but tries to be polite, "there's a new medical drug that's come out, they're calling it, 'the new wonder drug.' Penchillum? Or something like that." She scratches the top of her head.

Penicillin," the lady corrects her. "I've heard of it. It still scares me."

"You have family in the military?" Evelyns asks her curiously and compassionately.

"I do," she replies ambiguously, "or did." She crosses her legs and holds them intertwining her arms around them while gazing off into the distance at the peaceful lake.

"I'm sorry," Evelyn empathizes, growing to like this lady more and more.

"It's okay. He was my uncle. My only uncle, on my pa's side."

"Damn war already," Evelyn chastises. The two women sit and watch the kids frolic in the lake quietly for a moment, listening to their antics echo hollow from the water. The happy frolicking of the kids makes the war seem even more pointless. The subject of death makes their minds wonder.

Katherine interrupts the peaceful quiet, "they're saying now since Germany's surrendered, the Japanese shouldn't be far behind."

"I hope and pray every night for an end to this God forsaken war," Evelyn tells her, "my two sons were in it and their home now, right where they belong."

A small child runs up to Katherine dripping wet, laughing and smiling. "Did you have enough now?" Katherine asks the youngster, wiping her with a towel. The small girl nods her head up and down, "It was nice and warm, you should have come in." Katherine gets up and tells Evelyn, "Nice to meet you, but I'm babysitting and we gotta get back now," and starts walking away.

Older children are lying on the beach, sunning themselves and gossiping nearby. Evelyn hears them as a man frantically begins shouting at someone in the lake. Fearful for the safety of her own children she struggles to

Lexington Glory Days

get up and walks to the waters' edge, shielding her eyes with her hands, looking for her kids.

"Where is Adam?" The man is suddenly shouting, desperately. "I don't know!" comes a shrill cry from the water by a little girl. "Where is he?" the man shouts again. "I don't know!" the little girl screams, crying hysterically. The man quickly gets up and goes sloshing through the water to the girl.

"He was just here!" the little girl screams, "I can't find him!"

The man is beside himself with fear for his child.

"Jim? Rita? Carrie? Tom? Where are you?" Evelyn calls out into the crowd in the water. They don't hear her and she can't distinguish them from the other kids. "Jim? Rita? Carrie? Tom?" she hollers again, louder this time.

"Adam! I can't find Adam!" The man in the water is shouting, looking everywhere at once, as he begins to drag his foot on the lakes sandy bottom. "Adam!" he desparately screams again, as people quiet down their laughter and their play and stand and watch him, wondering what's going on.

"Adam! Has anyone seen Adam?" he hollers again, desperate for news of his son. A few of the people shake their heads, suddenly realizing the seriousness of the situation.

"Jim!! Rita!! Carrie!! Tom!!" Evelyn shouts again, "come here this instance!!" She stands at the waters edge, one hand on her hip.

"Help me find Adam!" The man is screaming in a desperate panic.

People begin looking around, not wholly sure who they are looking for. A little boy floats up to the man, holding onto a piece of flat wood with his hands and arms.

"Adam! Oh thank God! Where were you?" The man asks him calming down. "I was over there," squeaks the boy, pointing further down the lake, "looking for a piece of wood so I could float on it." The boy doesn't have a clue of the worry he's caused.

Four kids come close to shore in shallow water, one is crawling on the mushy lake's soggy bottom with her hands, her legs floating idly behind her. "We're here," Tom tells his relieved mother. They slosh through the water closer to shore.

"Where's Rita?" Evelyn suddenly wants to know, after taking a mental head count of her children.

"She's behind Carrie," he tells her. "Do we have to go already?"

"No, we can stay longer, but I want you's to stay closer to shore for a while so I can see you's, okay?"

She looks over to the man searching for the boy.

"It's no fun in shallow water, ma," Tom protests.

"Don't go above your waists, I want to be able to see you's," she insists. The four kids turn around and go back into the water complaining. Finally their dad walks out of the water, wringing wet. Water pouring out from his shorts.

"Who were you talking to earlier?" Lloyd asks her.

"Katherine Leacher, or something like that," she tells him, "she lives down the road that way a couple of miles, near Joe. How was your swim?"

"Nice. The waters just perfect," he replies. "Near Joe, huh? Family?"

"Not that I know of," she tells him.

In the distance they can faintly hear the sound of men hollering and occasionally cheering and sometimes the crack of a bat. "The Giants must be playing ball," Lloyd says, "Maybe we should go to the Green Lantern and have a few beers and watch them play for a while."

"Not without Jim," Evelyn tells him, "the older ones are old enough to be down here by themselves, but not Jim. I don't want him down here without anyone watching him. I don't think they've had enough time in the water yet anyhow. Wait a little while, then maybe."

"I'm gonna walk down there," Lloyd tells her, "I'll be back in a little while. Pick me up if you leave before I get back."

"Don't be long," she tells him, "and don't forget, the church's Fall Festival is tomorrow." He looks back and smiles.

A family with young children in the back of a black 1939 Chevy truck come down to the beach and spread their towels on the warm sand near Evelyn. "Hi," they greet her warmly, and she returns the greetings. "Nice day for a swim," the mother tells her.

"Isn't it though," Evelyn replies rolling her head to see the lady, face the sun and look back at the water, all in one motion. Soon after them a group of older boys, full of horseplay and antics, show up at the swimming hole and head straight for the water, enjoying the last few dog days of summer.

Part 2

Hobo's and Gypsies

"Should we get sugar, or some canned goods or coffee this week? Joe asks Gertrude, " or maybe some cheese?"

" I know you like coffee, I don't drink it, and we don't really need the sugar, but we might not be able to get it the next time we're here," she replies, trying to anticipate what she might need.

"Can't buy sugar this week," the grocer tells them, "sorry, I gotta post it, but I sell what they give me to sell. No sugar and no meat this week. I got cheese and canned goods though. You can get that if you got your ration books and stamps, without the stamps I can't even sell it to you."

The grocery store, with its gray wooden slat floor, has lots of food items on off-white metal shelves that sit no higher than five feet off the floor, for easy reaching. The aisles are narrow, and the carts are small to fit through the rows.

"No meat again? Damn," Joe looks at the grocer disappointed. The grocer returns his look and shrugs. Familiar now with the shortages Joe ignores the grocer and starts talking to Gertrude.

"We need canned goods more than we need cheese, but maybe we could get a half pound of cheese," Gertrude suggests looking up and down the shelves in the store, "for a treat." She thinks over the price, unsure about the purchase and the choices rationing has forced everyone to make.

"Get whatever you think," her dad tells her leaving her in charge, "you do the cooking. You know what we need and what we don't."

They buy three pounds of coffee that's on sale for fifty-nine cents and a dozen oranges for nineteen cents, butter, eggs, flour, and canned goods.

"Town is busy today," Joe says to his daughter, carrying their bags of groceries and walking out of the market onto the sidewalk. Cars cruise by in both directions.

"A lot of strange faces. I know there's a lot of people from town I don't know, but seems like there's a lot of people around that don't look like they belong here," eyeing them from the corner of his eye.

Surprised, Gertrude replies, "Maybe more folks have moved here."

"Maybe. Why they just hanging around though?" He wonders.

There's a half dozen vagrants in tattered, dusty and dark colored ragged clothes, a few with caps, scattered around town, leaning on buildings and loitering. A man walking past them bumps into Joe. He reaches his arm out and looks at them, excuses himself for the incourtesy, and keeps walking, smiling, swinging his arms widely at his side.

"I need to stop at the bank before we go back home," Joe tells Gertrude, "and after, we can stop for a beer and a soda at the saloon. I'd like to talk to some of the men and kinda see what's going on in town a little bit."

They cross the dusty Main street and walk into the bank on the other side. At the teller window Joe fumbles for his wallet from out of his worn back pocket.

"My billfold! My billfold's gone!" he tells Gertrude puzzled, as he reaches into his other pockets. "Damn!" he exclaims, stomping the floor with one foot.

"Gone?" Gertrude repeats. "You just had it daddy. You must have dropped it coming out of the grocery store. Let's go back and look."

"It aint nowhere here!" Joe says sullenly, looking all around the dirt road, "I'll check inside the store. Maybe the grocer found it. You keep looking."

"I saw you out the window after you left," the merchant tells him, "that man who bumped into you, you know him?" The shopkeeper waits for an answer.

"Never seen him before far as I know, why?" Joe asks him.

"I don't know him either and I know just about everybody who comes into town. I think you might a got robbed. You been pick- pocketed."

Joe looks him the eye without any hint of suspicion, still kind hearted and naïve in his worn blue bib overalls, feeling a little foolish. "I shoulda known," he tells the grocer disheartened, "thanks for your trouble," and turns to leave to find Gertrude. He places his thumbs behind the straps on his overalls and walks out with his head down.

"No trouble," the merchant tells him kindly, looking at him and out onto the street. Placing his hands on the counter he shakes his head discouraged as Joe leaves.

"Did you find it?" Gertrude asks eagerly, as her dad approaches her.

"Nope. I think I was pick-pocketed by that man that bumped into me. He might be one of these men that ride the trains and get off wherever there might be work. They call 'em hobos. They aint got a home or money and they're desperate, and hungry. Gotta be a little more careful around folks I guess. Be wary of 'em Gert, especially if you don't know them, he solemnly warns his daughter. I was gonna buy a war bond with that money too, I had twenty-five dollars in there."

Without talking the two look around at the people walking and standing around the streets and street corners as they walk back to their truck, feeling like a stranger in their own town. He suddenly feels like people are watching him.

"Come on daddy, let's go home where it's safe," Gertrude tells him disappointedly. She walks closer to him, by his side.

"All right," he says simply, getting in the truck. "These men make it out to Lexington too, ya know" Joe tells his daughter, "some of them anyway. Make sure to be careful if you see any of them around."

The two drive out of town back towards their home. "How would I know if they were the hobos?" Gertrude asks him as they drive along.

"Oh, they're strangers for one. Second, they just gotta look about them like they don't belong. Like they aint got anyplace to be, or anyplace to go."

They pass a dozen people in a field working and harvesting grain.

"Those people out there in that oat field are Japanese prisoners of war," Joe informs her. "The Jap's are our enemy in the war."

The Japanese workers are shorter in size than the men watching over them, and their eyes have a markable difference about them.

"Those people are?" she asks quietly, suspicious. Joe turns his attention from driving and eyes the men and women in the field, not sure what to make of them himself. "Are they really dangerous?" Gertrude asks him.

"I reckon," Joe tells her, "they got men right there watching 'em making sure they don't run." The images of the strange men and women working in the fields looks out of place to them, like something from another world, out of a movie or a dream. A truck that's coming towards them on the dirt road suddenly loses control and swerves off into the ditch, away from them on the other side. Part of the drive shaft that's attached to the wheel broke. Gertrude looks in horror and Joe briefly turns his head.

"There's a whole camp of them over near Montonia," Joe says.

"Where near Montonia?" Gertrude asks, afraid.

"The other side, outside of town a few miles, there's quite a few of them. They work at the canning factory too," he tells her.

Gertrude can't shake the eerie feeling that has come over her. Lost in her thoughts she reminds Joe, "don't forget we have to pick up Peter from grandmas," she mumbles.

"I didn't forget," he tells her.

"What ever happened to grandpa?" Gertrude suddenly asks him, still dreaming of the POW workers in the camp near Montonia.

"He died a long time ago, along with my folks. Grandmas your ma's ma."

"How long ago did they all die?" Gertrude is suddenly filled with a curiosity about death.

"I was a young man of about...thirty, when both my folks passed. So say about thirty years ago, I'm sixty-two now. You weren't even born yet. Your ma's pa I don't know. He died before my folks I remember. Yer ma and I were married for a while I know." Joe tries thinking back so long ago.

"I like how grandma and uncle Tom live in the country, but still close to town and still close to Lexington too," Gertrude tells him, looking out the truck window, still thinking about the men and women prisoners of war.

Uncle Tom is outside when the two arrive. The grass is long and the place looks unkempt, though the two aren't desperate for money. Tom is a friendly man and not very tall, "Hi Joe, hi Gertrude," he greets them with a wave and a smile, "Peter's in the house with ma."

Gertrude walks into the house and Joe stays outside to talk with Tom.

"How's the threshing going Tom?" Joe asks him, working on a tractor near one of his small sheds. "Oh, pretty good, just about done. The wheat seems dry though," he tells him smiling, "almost ready to plow, now."

"Hi grandma," Gertrude greets the hard-working seventy-four year old immigrant woman. She walks into the house without knocking.

Grandma's been able to maintain a likeable disposition despite losing her husband very early on in their marriage and having to raise her children by herself, and keep the farm running. She's sitting in a tattered dark tan easy chair wearing a long weathered dress. "Place needs dusting," she says.

"Where's Peter?" Gertrude asks her, taking in the house and its contents.

"He was outside," she tells her getting up, "Peter?" she calls out in case he came back into the house, "Peter! Did you's get all your shopping done?" grandma asks her, looking at Gertrude.

"We did. Daddy got pick pocketed in town from a vagabond," she tells her, "he bumped into daddy, and must've reached into his back pocket and took his wallet." Her arms swinging back and forth.

"Did you get it back?" Grandma listens, trying to understand.

"No. Daddy was gonna buy a war bond with the money he had in it. He lost twenty-five dollars." She walks further into the house, looking at her.

"He shoulda been more careful," the old woman says with little expression on her face. Her Bohemian accent is still noticeable even though she came to America over fifty years ago, by ship and sails, with just her mother.

"Lots of Indians use to be around these parts more, they'd walk right into a house and take whatever they wanted. I guess white folks is just as bad now days. Wasn't used to be like that," grandma tells her.

"I remember one time, the Indians came in and took a little baby girl, right out of her mother's arms. Happened not to far from here. When the babies pa found out, he walked right into the Indian's camp and took the child back."

Gertrude listens to her with fascination and horror both at the same time.

Joe walks into the house, the screen door slamming behind him, with Peter by his side, "thanks for having little Peter over for us, Agnes," he tells the old woman.

Joe walks in with Peter, his hand around his shoulder.

"It was no trouble. He was outside following Tom around most the time. Oughta be thankin Tom I s'pose." She raises her hand and points outside.

Joe sits down in a wooden rocking chair. "Tom says the crops look good," he says to her politely, rocking in the chair, "just about got all the threshin done and pert near ready to start plowin. Guess the grasshoppers weren't as bad as they were predicting." He lets the thought linger.

"They were bad 'nough," grandma tells him, "seems like they were everywhere, couldn't make a step without seeing a couple. They was better at your place, Joseph?" Grandma sits down in the worn out easy chair.

"People made it sound like they'd be coming in, like a dark cloud during a storm," Joe tells her, "we sprayed like the county agent said too, didn't have much trouble with 'em after that."

"That's what he tells me, yup," she replies, the wrinkles on her face giving her character, "a good crop.

Lexington Glory Days

Tom does a good job with the little help he gets. I used to be out there myself roping those oxen around to plow. Can't do it no more. The oxen's stronger than me now," she says with a short rough laugh. "The tractor and plow now days makes it easy, we didn't have that back then. We were lucky to have a horse."

"Hear much from your daughters?" Joe asks her loudly, being polite.

"Rose Ann and Margaret? Once every blue moon one of them'll come out to see their old ma, not often. Most the time it's just me and ole Tom here. Margaret's over in Killarney and Rose Ann lives in Prague. A little too far to drive often with the government rationing the gasoline. What do you hear from Betty?"

"She calls us and we call her," Gertrude tells her, "sometimes she doesn't sound happy, I don't think. We don't see her a lot, at all. She'll be home for Kimberly's wedding though." She looks at the things in grandma's china hutch.

"Hard to be happy all the time," grandma tells her wistfully, looking off into the distance.

Thinking over seventy years of life and living.

"I don't think she likes it in St. James," Gertrude explains to them.

"Give her my best, when you hear from her next," grandma tells her.

"We will grandma," Gertrude tells her sincerely.

Joe lightly slaps the sides of the rocking chair he's been sitting on, "Well Peter, what say me, you and your sister here head for home, almost time to do chores." He looks down at his son, sitting on the floor.

"We gotta milk the cows and feed and water the pigs and chickens," Peter says, nodding to his pa, showing his obvious affection. Peter loves his pa dearly.

"You're growing up fast. We won't have any butter if we don't have any milk," he tells his youngest son straightforwardly, "let's get a move on then, say good bye to your grandma." Joe gets up out of the rocking chair.

"Good bye, Peter, come over anytime you want," grandma tells him.

"I will. Bye," he tells her and waves, and starts walking out of the room.

"Joe, just a minute," grandma says approaching him and placing the fingertips of her right hand on his chest, "I heard about Joseph in the army getting wounded and want to say I'm sorry. I'll say my prayers for him tonight."

Joe looks at her and responds quietly, "thank you Agnes. I think he might need them about now." The two lock eyes for a few moments, tears welling up inside. Grandma remembers all too familiar stories about war from her mother.

Meanwhile, Lloyd and Evelyn are at the Green Lantern bar in Lexington, a square little wooden building with a low ceiling, up on a hill, just down the road a quarter of a mile south of the church, and that same distance east of the bar and pavilion.

"What's with all the beat up old campers parked alongside of the road?" Lloyd asks Jacob, walking through the doorway of the bar by the pool table, later that week. Jacob, the young bartender, shrugs his shoulders as he dries a beer glass with a clean white towel, "Hey Lloyd. Gypsies, I guess."

"Gypsies!" a shorter, slightly overweight elderly woman with short, curly gray hair, sitting with her husband on the far side of the bar with a wooden support beam behind them shrieks. Starting to frown, she turns to her husband and says to him surprised, "We got gypsies now?"

As they enter the bar, a young man puts a dime in the jukebox near the entryway, and plays a lively instrumental number with slow verses sung by a man that croons to the music. The man is a stranger in Lexington.

Lexington Glory Days

"I'm sure the ladies in the basement of the church, making enough food to feed over three hundred people for the small parishes' annual fall festival, would like to hear they got gypsies just down the road from 'em," Evelyn says, with a smile and teasing laugh, sitting on a round black swivel bar stool with six other patrons, also sitting at the bar, and ordering two bottles of beer.

"Their festival is today? I didn't know that," the short, curly gray haired lady inquires, as she turns to her husband and says to him, "Did you know that?"

"Some knucklehead just about ran us off the road while we were driving here."

Lloyd tells Jacob, whose limping and appears in discomfort, bringing the beers. Aware that a shady looking young man, with a scruffy black five o'clock shadow, ragged, dark colored clothes and black hat tilted to one side of his head, leaning on the bar is listening to him. "Dang near just about ran into us, then drove into the ditch." He quickly glances at the stranger, and then looks away.

"Lotta people been having trouble with parts on old trucks breaking down," the tall, dark haired bartender tells him, still looking uncomfortable. "Especially the ones made in the nine-teen thirties."

"Are you's gypsies?" the young man in the black hat listening to Lloyd asks him precariously. He looks and doesn't take his eyes off of them.

"Hell no, we aint the gypsies," Lloyd tells him, calmly.

"Do we look like gypsies?" Evelyn asks him condescendingly, eyeing him over.

The man stares at them, and doesn't look away.

"Well, I am. We just got drove off a pasture and looking for another place to camp. We got fifteen trailers," he says, as if this were perfectly normal.

Evelyn stares at Lloyd, surprised, and mouths the

word silently, 'gypsies?

"Did I hear you's say there's a festival today?" the gypsy asks them.

"Where were you's camping?" Jacob asks him getting suspicious, not wanting to tell him the whereabouts of the church festival.

"Near the big bridge and river about twenty miles that way," he raises his arm and points, then smiles, "'bout sixty of us."

"Where's everyone else?" Jacob asks him.

"They was campin with me," he tells him, the expression on his face makes him look as if he were talking to a child.

"No, I mean now," Jacob, explains.

"Now? Oh! They all just hangin around their trailers alongside the road down here yonder," he lifts his chin to point in the direction, "waitin to see where to go next." The gypsy is friendly and talks openly with them.

"Why'd ya's get chased off?" the short woman, with curly gray hair, asks him loudly. Her husband is eating peanuts, and listens.

"Don't reckon I know. Aint had any trouble the four weeks we'd been there, then some men bout my age showed up out of the blue and said to leave or they'd be trouble. Later that night, a big cross, six feet tall burst into flames a small ways from where we was campin. Scared everyone, so we packed up and rode on." He tells them in a way that makes them all shutter.

"Winters a comin, maybe you should pack up and ride south, where it's warm," Evelyn tells him, "what are ya gonna do when it turns cold out? What are ya going to do then? It gets cold here," she exclaims.

Nimbly, he walks over to her. "I's sure could use a shot of something, if you's would be so kind. I can't pay in money, but I's can dance for you."

Before anyone else has a chance to speak, the sly

young man steps back with his pointed black boots, raises his arms and twirls around, then twirls again. He moves his body around slowly for a few seconds, then stomps one boot down, further out than the other and claps his hands once at the same time, and puts his arm out, palm up, and smiles.

"I aint buying you a shot for that," Evelyn tells him then smiles at Jacob, watching him, along with the other customers in the bar.

The gypsy gets a pouty look on his face and charmingly, says, "you don't like my dance?" He lowers and tilts his head, looking at her.

"I didn't say I didn't like it, I said I wouldn't buy you a shot for it," she tells him sternly. She looks over her shoulder at him.

They distrust the new stranger, but let him humor them anyway.

He walks up to the bar, and stands next to the black swivel barstool next to her and strikes up a conversation with her and Lloyd. Minutes later the three are laughing over a simple coin trick he has shown them. He turns around and for a few seconds slowly dances around behind them. Amused, Lloyd tells Jacob, "Get him a shot of something."

The young man walks with an arrogant sway towards the shorter, elderly couple on the far side of the bar and puts his arms around them. He talks with them and smiles, and then a short while later walks in a sophisticated manner back towards Evelyn and Lloyd. He takes his shot, throws it down in one motion and sets the shot glass down on the rustic wooden bar, and walks towards the door.

"I must depart now. Thank you for your time." Before leaving, he theatrically tips his black hat at the crowd, bows, and says, "adieu."

Evening is setting in and when night comes the moon

is full, with a few lost clouds drifting in and around it. It's that kind of evening and brisk, the kind where the tops of the leafless tall trees look like some sort of strange animal.

Evelyn looks to watch him leave, as do the others, then turns and tells Lloyd and them, "He's a charmer."

"A snake charmer," another man there tells her.

"Hey! Where'd my money go?" The shorter, elderly man quickly turns and says to his wife. "Did you take the money I had sittin here?"

"What money?" she asks him, not knowing what he's talking about.

"I had six dollars laying here on the bar, now I only got three," he tells her.

"I suppose the gypsy took it when you weren't looking," she tells him, rubbing her mouth with the back of her hand, looking at the ceiling away from him. Waiting for him to say something.

"Well, God damn. I can't believe that," he tells her.

"What can't you believe? He's a gypsy! He aint got nothin. How do you think they get their money to buy food and booze?"

"God damn," he repeats, "I can't believe that."

"Well believe it," she says looking at him, tapping the bar with her index finger, "You better believe it."

Chapter Three

Betty and Edward Move Back Home

"God damn it, I think we got a flat tire," Edward says, as they pass the row of gypsies heading for parts unknown a month later. On their way home from St. James, back to their roots in Lexington, Betty bristles from side to side and her head shakes as the tire loses all of its air, forcing the car to swerve quickly.

"Damn it," Edward says again, steering the car off to the shoulder, "now I gotta get out and change it." He opens the car door and gets out.

The caravan of gypsies meets up with them and Betty watches them, with her newborn baby on her lap. The wooden boxes on wheels stream along one by one, next to their car, at a pace slower than the regular traffic. Some of the campers have no sides and are not enclosed and Betty can see pots and pans dangling from the ceiling, swinging from side to side from the bumps in the road. Trucks twenty years older than Edward and Betty's 1940's car pull the campers, 'some of the first trucks made,' Betty thinks to herself.

"Look at the campers, Harold," she smiles at the two-year-old sitting in the back seat, making him look. Harold's a well behaved child for his age.

Betty can see some of the faces of the children and a

few of the adults looking out of the windows. 'The children look confused and hungry,' she thinks.

The backs of the trucks are oddly empty, "I'd have thought they'd have more belongings as long as they have the room to move them," she says aloud.

The wooden frames look sturdy and well-built but are faded a rustic gray from the elements and the weather. They look poor and destitute.

'The adults look like anybody else,' she thinks, 'they don't look much different than other people, maybe a little more observant even.'

"See the gypsies?" Betty turns her head and smiles at Harold again, making him laugh. Edward walks back to the car.

"You couldn't wait to call your father could you?" Edward tells Betty reentering the car, mad, making the baby cry. "Just because he wasn't home and you wanted to tell him we were coming, I had to go out and change the tire practically in the dark." Edward hates it when things go wrong.

Betty's smile disappears and unemotion and apathy cross her face. "I mean it," he continues badgering her, "we could have left earlier and been there by now, but because you had to wait and talk to your dad, I had to go out and change the tire practically in the dark."

"Oh, poor thing," Betty frowns at him, "it's not even dark out yet."

With the tire changed, they soon come into a tiny village with a large Catholic church, where the Germans settled when they migrated, about five miles north of Lexington. Edward keeps an eye on the bar and dancehall ahead of them.

"Should we stop and see whose there?" Edward asks her.

"I thought it was too dark to go outside," she tells him, getting even.

"You don't have to be like that," he tells her, more calm.

"Be like what?" she asks him, getting offended.

"Never mind," he tells her looking out his side window, "do you wanna stop or not? Let's stop for one." He knows by now when to stop talking.

"Stop if you wanna stop, I didn't say nothin."

He pulls the big nosed four door black car into a parking space right next to the road in front of the big two-story building.

"Let's go in then," he says and quickly opens his door.

Betty lets herself out, carrying the newborn and follows Edward and Harold to the door and walks in as he holds it open for them.

"The place is busy and crowded. It's loud, people are talking and laughing and having a good time," Edward notices and tells her.

"Where are we going to sit?" she asks him, looking around.

They know a lot of people and have a nice time socializing, but after Edward has a beer, Betty wants to go and see her dad and siblings.

"You want to go already? We just got here!" he tells her mad again.

"What, were you planning on staying all night?" she questions him.

"No, but we haven't even been here an hour yet," he retorts.

"It's too loud in here for the baby, she keeps fussing, besides I want to go and see my dad yet tonight," she tells him softly.

"All right," he reluctantly agrees.

On their way back they stop to look at a house that's for rent, in the country, in Lexington.

"The place is kinda small, but we don't need much," Edward tells Betty pulling into the driveway. "It looks nice," he says, shining the cars lights on it.

"Who did you hear about this place from, anyway?" Betty asks him.

"One of ma and dads neighbors told me about it at the bar," he says with his face starting to get flush and turn red.

"I shoulda known," she says reluctantly, "your ma."

"Well it won't hurt to look at it," he argues.

"I suppose," Betty tells him letting out a sigh, "where are we staying tonight?" Edward was in charge of making all the plans.

"Ma said we could stay there if we want."

"Oh good," Betty replies sarcastically, "I'd just as soon drive back home."

"Well you wanted to come down and see your dad and sisters and Peter, so I bought you down. I thought we were gonna have a nice weekend looking for places to live. I can't win," he says frustrated.

"I didn't say I wanted to stay with your folks' though."

"Where else would we stay? There's no room at your dads!"

They walk up the steps to the house and go in. "It's nice, don't you think?" Edward says, looking around the house.

"There's no running water!" Betty exclaims.

"It'll do until we find something nicer," he suggests to her.

"No, No, no. I've seen enough already. I'm ready to go."

"There's not a lot of places for rent out here, ya know."

"I've seen enough, I wanna go," she tells him, not wanting to give in and walking towards the door. She hates the idea of living without indoor plumbing.

They drive the short distance to Evelyn and Lloyds

and Edward walks into his parents' house while Betty takes the car and kids to visit her family.

"Edward there's a house for rent just down the road you and Betty should look at," Evelyn tells him, after a hearty welcome home.

"We already seen it and Betty doesn't like it cause there's no running water," he tells her matter of fact. "I thought it would do, for now."

"Oh it's fine," she tries convincing him, "there must be a hand-pump in the kitchen sink? That's all you need." Evelyn's trying to be helpful.

"Yeah there is. But she wants hot and cold running water and a working bathroom too," he tells her straightforwardly, admittedly seeing her point.

"She wants the moon and the stars too, I suppose. A bathroom makes the rent higher and you's don't have a lot of money to begin with. I think you's should take it. Call the guy and tell him you'll take it," she pressures him.

"How come you's wanna move back anyway?" his dad asks him, "aren't things going good up there?" His dad isn't readily involved in their lives.

"Betty doesn't like it, and I guess I'd rather be down here too," he confesses, wiping his eyebrow, getting put on the spot.

"I see. Gotta do, what you gotta do I suppose," his dad remarks plainly.

Betty makes the short drive to her father's home, three miles away.

"You don't know how wonderful it is to see you," Joseph tells his daughter, as Betty wraps her arms around him.

"Hi daddy," she says, beaming with delight, then greets her sisters Kimberly and Gertrude and brother Peter with the same kind of enthusiasm.

"How are my grandchildren? Harold you're growing like a weed!" he says rubbing the boys hair, smiling. "And the little one, aaw... just as pretty as her ma."

He gives the little girl a little pinch on the chin.

Betty sits down along with everyone else around the living room, noticing the dust on the antique wooden hutch with old glassware inside and says, "Daddy how have you been? Kimberly how are the wedding plans coming? How is everyone?" She hasn't seen them in months and wants to know everything.

Suddenly everyone starts talking at once and they all burst out laughing.

"One at a time I guess," Joseph says smiling.

"We saw prisoners of war in the fields, and daddy got pick pocketed in town a while back," Gertrude announces, not wanting to be left out.

"Have you's found a place to live yet Betty?" Kimberly asks her.

"Not yet. We're gonna do some looking tomorrow," she replies happily. "I don't really want to live in town, but some of the houses are nicer, the ones in the country can be kinda run down. We looked at one tonight around here, but it didn't have any running water."

"We don't have any running water," Gertrude tells her, "and we get along just fine." She says this, even though she'd rather have it herself.

"What have your heard about Joseph Jr? Is he out of the hospital in France yet?" Betty wants to know.

"No, he's still in the hospital. What they're all doing to him I don't know. He's alive that's about all I can tell ya. He was hit pretty hard," her dad says seriously. Their son and brother was wounded so badly he's lucky to be alive.

"How about Brian?" Betty asks, still upbeat, "What do you hear from him?"

"Brian was wounded too, but he's okay," her dad informs her.

"Oh, no!" Betty screams. "Is he all right?"

"He's coming home on furlough sometime in the next few weeks," Joe informs her. He looks forward to seeing at least one of his sons again.

"Really! Oh, I wanna see him!" She reacts excitedly, then turns dour, "poor Joseph Jr, though, I wonder how he's doing."

"This wars sure taken its toll on our boys," Joseph tells them, hurt.

"He's doing okay," Kimberly, tells her sympathetically, "at least he's alive."

"Any news on the Reich's and what they've been up too?" Betty asks her father inquisitively. "It seems they're always up to something."

"Lloyd and Evelyn and them? I haven't heard nothin. They're a wilder bunch than we are. We go to church, the neighbors nearer by here and home and that's about all. They like to spend their time at the Green Lantern bar and down at the pavilion." They're more a party group than the Pikes.

Betty listens intently, curious, nodding her head.

"Kimberly, tell me about your wedding plans then," Betty tells her buoyantly, changing the subject. "Is Peter going to be in it?"

"Gertrude is going to be in it and I have my dress. It's so beautiful, I'm so excited and Clays been just wonderful. We're having a reception out here after the church," she tells her, "you better come, or I'll be mad," she tells her strictly.

"You know I wouldn't miss it for the world!" she says, over exaggerating, "Daddy, will you play the fiddle for us? I miss hearing you play it, and I bet the kids would love it too," Betty tells him. Joseph taught himself how to play.

With all eyes on him, Joe reaches beside his chair and picks up the instrument off the floor and begins to play. Soon his feet are tapping along and his whole upper body is swaying as the small home, illuminated by

Lexington Glory Days

kerosene lamps, is filled with the sound of the sweet music.

Gertrude hollers, over the music, from the kitchen, "Betty! Phone! It's Edward." Gertrude has an unlady like side, boisterous and quick to the point.

Betty gets up to answer it and listens for a moment then says angrily, "What are you doing at the pavilion? I thought you were visiting at your folks?"

'I was, but ma wanted to come down for a beer, why don't you come down and join us.' With the Reich's, there's always room for more at the bar.

"What am I supposed to do with the kids?"

'Bring 'em with. Say, I told the guy we'd take the house we looked at tonight.' Edward's been dreading having to tell her the news.

"You told them we'd take it, are you crazy? After I told you I didn't want it? Oh, I'll be right down, stay there. And I'm not staying all night either."

Betty walks in to a smaller crowd of people, than was at the bar they were in earlier. Carrying her newborn Carol, and with Harold by her side, she fails to get a warm greeting from her in-laws, they look up to see her and keep talking.

"Did you hear about the president?" Evelyn is telling a friend of hers, "He died earlier today at his home in the south."

"I heard. That's so sad. There'll never be a president like Mr. Roosevelt," she replies, "or a first lady like Eleanor. He did so much for the country, after the depression and all. He got us through the war, and helped the country out when nobody else seemed to be able to."

"Lexington will be a booming town if the railroads come by," Lloyd is telling two older pioneers of the small village, with his son Larry, who's back from the war overseas, nearby.

Their ruddy faces, on the two old pioneers, are filled

with lines crisscrossing everywhere, and their spoken English is broken with words mixed with Polish, their native language.

"I like it how it is," one of the old timers tells him, in broken Polish, "we got everything we need now. I don't want it to get any bigger."

"You made it," Edward greets Betty with a smile when he sees her, then adds coyly, "don't be mad," after he sees her expression.

"I told you I didn't want it," she immediately tells him, bouncing the baby in her arms up and down to pacify her. "A place would be so much better with running water. I've lived without it and it would be so much easier if we'd get it."

"I know, but it's nice enough for now, and we can afford it. We need a place and we can move in anytime we want," he tells her, hoping she'll agree.

"I don't know about you sometimes," she says, shaking her head, "get me a chair to sit on, the baby's getting heavy...I haven't even had a chance to take a good look at it," she tells him, protesting, having not gone beyond the kitchen.

"It's nice," he tries convincing her, "come on," he pleads.

"Oh, all right. I guess I don't have much say in the matter anyway."

After the move, Betty likes being home, close to her family, but Edward doesn't turn out to be the perfect man she had hoped for. Within a few years the young couple will have another baby, a second girl, and they name her Theresa.

Part 2

The Struggle

"You're not going any place today, you were out yesterday and you got all shined up. We got grandma's funeral tomorrow, and I don't want you all hung over again," Betty tells Edward, not looking at him. "You want eggs and toast?" she asks him working around the kitchen in the old farmhouse they rented.

"And coffee," he tells her, "and bacon if we got any."

The next day, sitting next to Edward on her left, alongside Betty in the church are Kimberly, Gertrude, her father, Peter, and Brian, whose home on furlough from the army, and her eldest brother, Wayne. On the other side of the aisle are grandma's two daughters Rose Ann and Margaret, their husbands and kids, and uncle Tom. Betty was fond and close to her grandmother.

"Mrs. Agnes Kulik, who lived on her farm just east of Centerville for half a century, passed away at her farm home in Lexington Township Friday morning, following an illness of about four months. Her age was seventy-five years, three months and twenty-one days," the pastor is acknowledging at grandma's funeral.

"Agnes Stepan was born October thirty-first, 1871 at Themaline, Bohemia. There she received her education and grew to young womanhood. When she was sixteen years old she came to this country with her mother and made her home in the Veseli community until her marriage to Mathias Kulik on January twenty-eighth, 1896. To this union were born three daughters and two sons. She is preceded in death by her husband, Mathias, who died in 1905, one son in infancy, and a daughter, Mrs. Joseph Pike. Mrs. Kulik was a devoted mother, a true neighbor and friend. She worked hard throughout her lifetime, and following the early death of her husband she managed the farm and brought up her family despite the many problems that confronted her through the years. She was a member of St. Mary's Catholic church here from the time the church was built. Interment will be at Calvary cemetery."

Two dozen red roses adorn the top of the dark brown casket in front of the church. In the pews behind Betty are Joseph's three sisters and his brother, and scattered about the church are numerous cousins, neighbors and friends.

"It's sad to lose people," one of grandma's friends is saying to another woman outside of the church. "Heaven knows I've buried my share of people."

"It sure is. Whether they move away or pass on. Why don't some people stay in one place, ya suppose?" Sounding like she's missing somebody.

"Family obligations I reckon. Some, a need to see new things, meet new people, see what's out there in the world. Aint for me anymore."

"That's what I like about it out here, and out at Lexington even more, people come here and stay. My daddy and your daddy were friends, and maybe even our granddads too, for all I know. They both come from Bohemia."

The casket is brought out, and the pallbearers place it in the hearse. It's a short drive out of town to the cemetery, out in the country.

Lexington Glory Days

"How are you doing, Tom?" Betty asks her uncle at the graveyard.

"I'm doing the best I can. I'm gonna miss her, Betty," he says with a smile and tears in his eyes, walking to her plot.

Betty intertwines her arm with his, and walks with him, "you'll be alone now," she comments sadly. "For the first time."

"Ma's alone now too," he says, his eyes darting in every direction.

They walk the rest of the way to grandma's resting place slowly, in quiet, taking in the sunny, brisk, chilly winter air.

A little while later, a heavy set woman in a black dress and black hat with black lace covering her eyes, walks up to Betty and Edward.

"Rose Ann and I are going over to look through some of ma's things," Margaret says to Betty after the service, "you're welcome over too."

Betty thinks it over for a moment and sighs, "I'd like to, but we gotta pick up the kids. Edwards sisters are watching them for us," she tells her touching her arm in a gesture of love, "It was nice to visit with both you and aunt Rose Ann again," she continues.

"We'll have to make plans to visit again more, Betty. Come over sometime."

"I'd like that," she tells her warmly with a hug, then fondly watches the woman walk away.

"Let's go home," Edward tells a teary eyed Betty, feeling her loss.

"There's a peculiar feeling a person gets when someone dies," Betty observes quietly to Edward at home. "It's like a person is only seeing half of what they normally see. Like you can't see further than the end of your own nose, or think clearly. Like your brain is trying to take over your eyesight. Oh, Harold, now where did you get that from? Edward I've been telling you for two years now, to fix that handle, now look."

"Don't look at me, I didn't break it," he tells her, purposely being a smart ass to get some attention. "It's worked for two years," he tells her.

"I didn't say you broke it! I said I wanted you to fix it! The windows and doors are letting cold air in. I told you I wanted all that junk off the porch, from the last people who lived here, and the railings about ready to rot off. And you gotta find out where the mice are coming in. You haven't fixed anything! All you wanna do is go someplace all the time."

"Why should I fix up somebody else's house?

I don't even own it," he tells her defending himself, thinking this is perfectly reasonable.

"So we can live in it! Isn't that reason enough?" she counters emotionally. "So your kids can have a decent place to grow up in without getting sick or bit." She adds as an afterthought, "We never should have moved here in the first place. It's too small already." It's barely adequate for the size of her growing family.

"Your never happy, are you?" he rides her, tired of her complaining.

"When the kids come down with a cold or the flu from the drafts coming through the windows, whose gonna take care of them, you? Then you'll see how happy I am," Betty tells him, still upset from losing her grandmother and attending the funeral this morning.

"I don't even know if there's anything I can do to fix them," he tells her, not wanting to upset her any further.

"Well try something, for goodness sakes," she encourages him, hoping for some results.

"I'll get to the windows," he says, appeasing her. "You got what you need for Harold, Carol and Theresa?" He asks.

"Except help from you, I guess, why?"

"Oh, I don't know..." he starts to say before she cuts him off.

"Why, where do you have to go now? If you think your going down to the pavilion or to the Green Lantern, you can just forget it. We got no money the way it is, and your not gonna waste what we do have down there on that piss water. We can barely afford to pay the rent on this old shack the way it is."

"You know I don't make much money in the winter time and I was gonna find someone and ask them what I can do about the windows and doors," he tells her, rationalizing, hoping to override her suspicion.

"Can't you just call somebody?" She asks him.

"Who am I gonna call?" he asks smartly.

"Well, where were you gonna go to find somebody? Besides, I wanted to go over to uncle Tom and grandma's for a little while."

"And have me watch the kids? It's okay for you to go, but not for me, I see."

He thinks his coming and going is just part of a routine day and necessary.

"God forbid you should watch the kids once. I'll just take them with me. Maybe I'll try and find a babysitter for Theresa. You can drop us off and pick us up when you're done."

"All right then," he tells her, satisfied.

Edward drops Betty off at grandmas and picks her up a few hours later.

A week goes by and Betty's at home looking through the mail.

"We got a letter in the mail today," Betty is standing in their small kitchen with a white apron on, looking mad, one hand on her hip and the other holding out the letter to Edward as he walks in the door. "It says if we don't pay the rent we owe or move out, the sheriffs gonna come out in two days and evict us! I thought you paid this? Now what are we gonna do?" her voice gets higher and tense, "what did you do with all our money?"

"It's gone," he tells her plainly, walking into the room.

"Gone? Gone where?" She wishes he would give her a better answer.

"Just gone, spent it on food for you and the kids, gas for the car...Gone."

"Now what are we gonna do?" she says getting upset.

"I don't know," he tells her, frustration seeping into his voice. "We might have to split up for a few days before I can figure something out."

"Split up? What do you mean split up?" She can't believe he's suggesting this.

Betty is torn apart about having to divide up her family, and explains it to her father. Knowing it's only temporary doesn't relieve her of her misery.

"You and the kids can stay here," her father, tells her at his farm, after hearing her story about the eviction notice. "Where's Edward gonna stay?"

"At his folks," she tells him, looking like she'd been crying. "I don't know what we're gonna do. We don't have 'any' money," she tells him, "and Edward doesn't get his unemployment check for another three weeks."

"It'll be okay sweetheart, lotta folks have trouble first getting started," he tells her lovingly. "I got word today, Joe Jr.'s gonna be comin home," he says to her brightly. "They're finally releasing him out of the hospital in France, he should be home in a week or two," he adds, trying to be positive.

Edward gets a different kind of reception at his parents' house.

"You better find a place," Edward's mother is telling him at her home, "anyplace, even here, if that's what it comes down too. Those are your kids and your wife and you need to take care of them!"

"I need a place to stay myself for a couple of days, so I can make some phone calls and talk to some people about where we can go," he tells her, not wanting to prolong the conversation. He knows these aren't good circumstances.

"Stay here, if you have to."

"But you keep looking until you find something or make a decision. I don't want those kids without their father for any longer than absolutely necessarily or has to be."

"You can stay here and look for a place to live. Maybe you should get cracking at it right now," she orders him, angrily.

The following day, Edward talks with Betty on the phone.

"I found a place in town," he tells her humbly. "It's an apartment. It's just one bedroom and my dad said he'd loan me the money to cover the rest of the month until I get my unemployment check."

"A one bedroom? We all can't fit into a one bedroom! What are you thinking?" She's frustrated with his poor decision.

"It's all I can afford, what else do you want me to do? Rents too high on the bigger places!" This is the only solution he has.

"Won't your dad borrow you more? How are us and three kids gonna live in a one bedroom apartment?" She's eager for him to come up with a better alternative, and a bigger place.

"We'll make it work. We can throw a mattress on the floor for the kids, put the crib next to the bed..." He starts to say, but she interrupts him.

"A mattress on the floor!" she repeats him and groans. "Well, if that's the best we can afford, I guess were gonna have to make do. What kind of place is it?" She hates giving in, but she doesn't have a choice.

"It's got a bathroom and shower down the hall," he tells her.

"That'll be nice at least," she says, starting to relax again. "How big is the kitchen and living room?.........you still there?"

"There isn't one," he tells her, not wanting to hear what she has to say next.

"It's a hotel room in Montonia. It's just for now."

"It's just a room? Are you crazy, Edward?"

"It's just gonna have to work until I can come up with some more money," he says demandingly. "We can't afford anything else," he tells her, desperate.

"When are you going to come up with more money, next year?"

A few days later they store most of their things in sheds at Betty's dads' farm, and move into the tiny one bedroom hotel room with just what they need, in a small town, five miles east of Lexington.

"Home sweet home," Betty remarks, already feeling claustrophobic. "Bring in the bed, I guess and set it up, and lay the smaller mattress on the floor next to it. I don't know how I'm supposed to warm up milk for the baby...Bring in the chest of drawers and the rest of the boxes just stack them up along the wall," she tells Edward and Larry, lacklusterly.

After the bed is assembled and Larry leaves, she says, "Might as well lie down," and sits Carol on the bed, who starts fidgeting, and lies baby Theresa next to her. "Stop jumping!" she snaps at Harold, "and sit down."

Edward lies on the opposite side, "See? This isn't so bad for the time being." He flips his shoes off, and crosses his feet.

She looks over at him and feels strangely contented. The smallness of the room makes her feel close and connected to him. Fewer outside distractions enables her mind to weed out clutter and focus on what's important to her; her kids and her husband.

In the old, three-story hotel a radio is playing in the next room and they can hear the music coming through the wall. The floorboards in the wide hallway outside their door creak whenever someone comes or goes. Most of the other rooms are rented to single men with enough spare coins in their pockets to treat themselves to a warm bed and a shower for a change.

The illuminated sign, hung high outside, on the corner of the brick building reads, "Alba Bar and Hotel' and in smaller letters below that, 'on and off sale.' A few weeks go by.

Betty and Edward park their car next to the big brick building.

"What a nice afternoon. I'm worried about daddy though. He hasn't been feeling good lately. What do you think? Did you have a good time?" Betty asks Edward, walking up to the building and their home, after Kimberly's wedding reception in the country at her dad's farm.

"It was all right," he confesses, having wanted to behave. "I like Clay. He seems like a real good guy." Down home and real.

"I've never in my whole life seen Kimberly so happy," Betty admits.

"Should we stop in for a beer or a drink before we go up?" Edward asks her. He drank sodas all afternoon.

"Yeah, let's go in. We don't have to pick the kids up until tomorrow. Let's kick up our heels a little for a change," she tells him happily. "I loved spending time with my family today. It's so nice to sit down and spend time talking with them again. It makes me sad now in a way, I guess I miss them already."

In their Sunday best, they walk up the steps and enter the well-kept bar, decorated to look classy. Edward in his dark blue suit, white shirt and multi-colored tie,

Lexington Glory Days

black overcoat and fedora hat, and Betty, smiling, in her tan skirt and shoes with black tips, and white blouse and long, dark tan winter coat, sit at the bar near the door by the barbershop. They walk in easily and comfortable.

"My, don't you look pretty this evening, Mrs. Reich," the heavy bartender notices and tells her, wearing a white apron wrapped and tied around his waist.

"Thank you," she tells him, embarrassed, but still smiling, her head and eyes darting up and down at him, feeling self-conscious.

"Hey, Edward, you're looking real sharp tonight. How are you folks? What can I get ya's." The bartenders a chubby man with a twisted mustache.

"Whiskey and beer for me, and beer for Betty, he replies, "or did you want a soda?" Betty's a social drinker and never has more than one or two.

"No, I'll have the beer," she tells him, happily.

It's been two years since they've been able to be alone together without any of the children around. They sit and enjoy their beer and talk, and later walk from bar to bar outside, enjoying running into old friends and reconnecting with them. They go to bed late, happy, a glimpse into the way they used to be.

Later the next evening, someone shouting startles them.

"If you don't like it, you can just get out and stay out!" a spry fifty year old woman with short blonde hair is hollering at a gentleman, whose staying in one of the other hotel rooms, the following afternoon, at the far end of the hallway, near the staircase. "This is my apartment! And I'll have whoever I want, whenever I want, in here," she's telling him.

"I know Mary, I didn't mean to imply you couldn't. I just thought we had a thing going. Just the two of us," he tries explaining to her.

"Well you thought wrong," she tells him, more

calmly.

Betty is sitting with Theresa, laying on the floor on a blanket, out in the wide rustic hallway outside of their hotel room, as Carol and Harold play with one another and their toys, suddenly startled by the commotion.

"Well, what do 'we' have then?" the gentleman asks, holding his arms out to her.

Scared, Harold and Carol cling to their mother.

"This isn't a good time," she tells him, not wanting to be bothered.

Edward comes out of his room dressed in a security officers' uniform.

"Are you leaving?" Betty asks him, hardly noticing or looking at him.

"Dance starts at eight," he tells her, closing the door to their room.

"Daddies a copper! Pow! Pow!" Harold screams, running up to him, shooting him in the leg. "Can I come with you, daddy?" he asks energetically.

"Daddy's gotta go to work," he tells his son, rubbing the boys hair. "I'll be back about midnight," he tells Betty. "See you later."

She doesn't respond, so he starts walking down the hallway to the steps that lead to a foyer, then either to the bar, or to the outside, or to a separate room that someone opens a restaurant in every few years. Harold and Carol chase their dad down the long hallway laughing until Carol falls and starts crying. Edward turns around to look at Betty, who's in another world with the baby. He turns around and picks up the three year old, holding her in his arms.

"It'll be okay. Your okay," he whispers to her and kisses her cheek. He brings her back to where Betty and the baby are and sets her down on the blanket, her eyes full of tears, gasping for tiny amounts of air and whimpering.

Edward walks back down the long hallway with Harold following him. "You gotta stay here, buddy," he tells him, looking at him. "I gotta go to work. Go back by momma and Carol." Harold runs back down the wide, tall hallway, listening to the echo's of his own shrieking bouncing off the walls, as the steps creak with every step Edward takes going downstairs.

"Can't you keep that kid quiet?" the woman with short blonde hair comes out of her apartment complaining. "Jesus Christ, put him in your room or something," she tells Betty. "He shouldn't be playing in the hallway anyway......Hey!....You okay down there?" The woman looks, but it's too far for her to see.

Betty looks half way up for just a moment, then just as quickly looks back down, and hears the woman close her door.

"Mama, I wish you were here," Betty says whispering, looking at Theresa. "Where are you? Daddy's sick and I'm afraid of losing him now," she laments aloud, as the baby holds and pulls her little finger, and she lets out a sigh. Carol walks over to her and sits down and snuggles up close to her. Betty wraps her arm around the child and pulls her in even closer, and lays her head down next to the babies. "Oh, daddy, I hope your gonna be okay," she whispers.

"Hi Edward," says the owner of the dance hall, a little old lady with thin white hair, "how are you tonight?" she says with a smile.

"Oh, so so," he tells her glumly, thinking about Betty.

"Is something wrong? You're not your usual self." she says, concerned.

"A little trouble at home," he tells her honestly. "Betty misses her ma, and's kinda sad, and now her pa's sick." Edward wishes she felt better.

"After her grandma just passed not long ago, I don't doubt it. Didn't her grandma help Joe raise the children after Elizabeth passed on?"

"I guess so. I don't know what to do about it," he tells her, prompting her for advice. "She's so God dang down in the dumps all of a sudden."

"Let her be, Edward, and be a little kinder," she tells him, "she'll come around to you. Things like this need to be handled with care. It's for the best."

"I hope so," he tells her, heartfelt, "I hate seeing her this way."

The dancehall begins filling up with people out to have a good time. Their laughter and gaiety go unrecognized by Edward.

"Edward, hi," Brian, Betty's brother, happily greets him.

"Brian. You made it back. Are you on furlough now?" Edward asks, surprised to see him. Edward had no idea Brian was coming home.

"No. I'm home for good. I got my release papers," he smiles and laughs, then introduces Edward to his companions. "This is Nancy, Katherine Leacher, and Oliver, friends of mine. Nancy and Oliver are from Montonia, and Katherine is from Centerville. They nod their heads and say 'hi,' and 'how do you do.

"How's Betty?" Brian inquires anxiously.

"Oh, she's all right," he says downtrodden, "not feeling well. Not like her old self. She's a little depressed to be honest with ya."

"Something wrong? Are the kids okay?" Brian asks him, looking serious.

"Kids are fine. Just down in the dumps, I guess," he says looking down at his shoes, unsure of his thoughts or feelings.

"That's too bad. Tell her I said 'hi' when you get home, will ya? Tell her I'll stop in and see her either tomorrow or Friday. Where ya's living at?" he asks, suddenly becoming coy. "Maybe I can cheer her up

Lexington Glory Days

some."

"Above the hotel in Montonia," he tells him.

"The Alba? All right. Well good to see ya. Tell Betty I'll be over soon," he finishes talking as he's walking away with his friends.

"All right," Edward replies, loud enough so Brian can only see his lips moving. He hopes Brian coming over will help lift her spirits.

Edward finishes being a rent-a-cop at the dance without any occurrences. He goes home at midnight and slips quietly into bed, next to Betty. He can tell she is awake. He lies there quietly for a few minutes.

"How were the kids tonight?" He asks her in a low voice, so not to wake them, lying on his back, facing the ceiling with his eyes open.

"They were okay," she says, turning on her side to face him. "How was the dance? Did you have any trouble?" She wants to talk.

"No," he tells her, wondering if now is a good time to tell her Brian is home from the war to stay. He doesn't mention anything more about the dance.

After a few moments of silence, she senses he does not want to talk to her, and rolls over to her other side, facing away from him.

He breaks the silence, "Brian was there. He's home for good now."

"You talked to Brian? She asks him, not moving.

"Said he was gonna come over tomorrow or Friday and see you." A few more moments of silence go by. He doesn't know if he should talk or let her.

"I'm glad you didn't have any trouble tonight," she tells him.

"Me too," he tells her, then a minute later adds, "I'll get us out of here, Betty, promise I will. It might take a little while, but I will."

The two sleep restlessly, and begin the next day with

breakfast at the café down the street. It's a small local diner with everything homemade, from scratch. There's twelve booths that have red leather upholstering on the seats and back rests and there's a cluster of small round and square tables in the middle with chairs around them. The long counter, near the kitchen, has round stools with red leather seats and there's a glass plate under a glass dome where fresh pie is kept.

"Betty, I'm so sorry, to hear about your pa passing on," a thin, older waitress with a slight hump in her back tells her, pouring them two cups of coffee.

Betty suddenly goes into shock, and is speechless until she walks away.

"Did she say daddy died?" Betty looks at Edward, with a worried look, tears starting to come to her eyes. "I can't believe I didn't find out sooner."

"I'm afraid so," Edward tells her. "I'm sorry Betty."

"Why didn't someone come and tell me? That damn hotel and no phone service in our room!" she says, her voice suddenly getting loud. "We have to get out of here right away!" She picks her purse up off the table, stands up and picks Theresa up out of the booth. "Poor Gertrude and Peter." Tears begin streaming down her face. "Pay for the coffee and lets go. Come on kids."

Edward looks up at her shaking his head, disagreeing, "Now, come on now, let's feed the kids first or they'll be crabby all day. We gotta eat anyway. We'll eat first, and then we'll go out there." He tries talking sense into her.

"I can't be here right now," she tells him sobbing. "Feed the kids, I'm going back up to the room." She takes Theresa and leaves.

When Edward, Harold and Carol get done eating and walk back up to their room they find Betty in bed, weeping. "You okay?' Edward asks her quietly.

"Find, find a baby, babysitter for, for the kids will

you?" she asks Edward, sobbing. "Atleast for Theresa."

She continues lying there.

Edward goes down to the lobby to the payphone and calls his sisters. Blanch and Carrie agree to watch the kids while he and Betty go out to the farm.

"Peters taking it really hard, why don't you go talk to him," Christina, Joseph's sister, is telling her husband, "I wanna stay here with Gertrude, poor thing can't hardly talk she's so upset." Christina has Gertrude, holding her around the neck and shoulder, rocking her.

Betty and Edward arrive and upon seeing Kimberly, Betty walks to her and the two hug one another and cry. "Do you want to go see him?" Kimberly asks her. "The mortician hasn't come out yet," and Josephs' body is still in his bed. "Come on." Kimberly takes Bettys' hand and leads her to the room.

"Oh, daddy," Betty whimpers and cries uncontrollably, touching his face. "I, I, I miss you already," she says. They look lovingly down at their father who'd taken such good care of them since their mother passed away, six years ago.

"He's with mama now," Kimberly says loudly, watching Betty begin stroking his hair, kneeling at his side and crying.

"Poor daddy," Betty says, in between gasps of air, "Oh, daddy..." she says, her voice high and cracking. She stays kneeling there for ten minutes when Edward walks into the room and places his hand on her shoulder, looking at his father-in-laws remains.

"He was a good man," Edward tells her, barely affected by seeing the dead mans body, having been witnessed to so many deaths during the war.

"Joe Jr.'s here," Brian tells them in a low voice, from the doorway.

Betty gets to her feet and turns to walk into the living room to see him, but he's hugging all the family members who've been so worried about him for long.

"Who's making the funeral arrangements?" Edward asks Brian.

"I guess we are," he tells him with a slight shrug.

"The kids?" Edward says.

By now quite a few of Josephs' relatives have assembled in the small home, and the kitchen is filling up with the food they've generously brought over to share. They speak in hushed tones, not knowing what to say.

"How's Peter doing?" Two of Josephs' sisters are asking.

"He's pretty upset. They were pretty close ya know, they spent a lot of time on the farm, and fishing and hunting. But boys are different than girls, they're brought up to take care of things. Gertrude's the one I'm worried about. Thank God Brian and Joseph Jr. are home again to help take care of things."

Gertrude's looking out of the old windows, the unclear glass inside the window frame is distorted from age, so that it appears things are longer and thinner than they really are when you look out of them. She sees the small tin sheds outside where her father used to repair things. She imagines her father in his old bib overalls, in there working, fitting horseshoes or fixing one of the tines on the plow, unable to escape the pictures of him in her mind.

She constantly keeps a watch on Peter, now more like a son to her than a brother, and he's crying almost all the time now. Betty listens in silence to the low voices and mumbled talkings among her aunts and uncles, while Kimberly carries on, talking with her relatives, and asking them if they need something to eat or drink.

"It's sure good to see you, Betty," Joseph Jr. tells her, sitting on the couch next to her.

"I was beginning to think you forgot about me," she tells him, and wraps her arms around his neck, embracing him. "I'm so glad your home," she tells him in his ear, and lets the hug linger. But the hug begins to feel odd, like she's hugging a stranger and quickly lets go. She stands up and walks into the bedroom where a group of people has gathered around her father.

"Brian and Joseph Jr. are moving back home," Christina is saying, to the others' relief. "I'm glad someone will be here to help out."

"Gertrude won't have to be out here alone, with Peter," Kimberly adds.

"He'll like having the guys around," Christina's brother, Harold, tells them.

"Betty, everybody, the mortician's here," Brian walks in the doorway and tells them quietly. Quickly the mortician walks into the room.

In a short while, the mortician has Joseph in a body bag, putting him on a cart, and pushing him towards the door, as his loved ones look on, anguished in their loss and crying in pain. "Daddy!" Peter screams, "Daddy!!"

Two of Betty's aunts, sisters of her dads, enter the Alba bar with their husbands two weeks later. The two sisters married two brothers, from the same family, and each have the same last name.

"We're looking for Betty, Betty Reich, and Edward her husband. We're Betty's aunts," one of the ladies says to the bartender there.

"Randy, run up and see if Edward or Betty are here. Tell 'em they got company down here," he tells a young lad of twelve. A few minutes later, the wide wooden staircase is creaking with the weight of people walking down them.

"Antoinette and Josephine, hi, what brings you here?" Betty greets them with a hug, looking tired. "It's so nice to see you. What a surprise."

"August. Emil." An unkempt Edward greets them with a nod of his head in a dirty white t-shirt, looking like he just got out of bed.

The men quietly mumble something to one another and suggest they sit down.

Edward notices them whispering to each other, and feels awkward.

"Hi Edward," August says to Edward as the bartender asks them their pleasure. "Four beers," they say, looking around at each other, nodding their heads in unison. Emil leans into Augusts' ear and tells him something.

"What brings you folks around?" Edward asks them, curiously.

"We thought we'd come in and take a chance you'd be here," Josephine tells Betty, "This is pretty nice," she comments looking around curiously, her beige hat with red flowers in it, flopping up and down as she speaks.

"What are the rooms like, are they nice?" Antoinette asks her.

"There okay," Betty tells her, "small," she admits with a lazy smile.

"Edward, Emil and I and the wives were talking about your situation..."

"Situation? What situation?" Edward asks offended.

"Not having a big enough place to live," August tells him. "So we were talking and decided we got extra room, and if you's want, your welcome to come stay with us for a while, til you get better on your feet."

"No, no, but thank you," Edward quickly dismisses the notion. "We're doing fine here," he says, and turns to walk away from them, back upstairs.

"Edward, the bar is no place to raise a family!" Antoinette scolds him, as he walks past her, making him stop and confront her.

"This aint gonna be permanent," Edward declares to her, starting to turn away, "We're doing the best we can," he says, embarrassed.

"We know you are, dear, we just wanted to make you

the offer," Josephine tells him. "You wouldn't be any trouble," she says trying to convince him.

"They would enjoy the extra company," Antoinette adds.

"No, no thanks. Thanks anyway," Edward tells them from the foyer, starting to walk back up the stairs. Not saying any more.

"I suppose you told those guys to come over here," Edward tells Betty angrily, later upstairs in their room.

"Well what are we gonna do?" Betty asks, "You surely don't plan for us to keep living here do you? We got a little money saved up now, let's use it to get a bigger place. We need more room so the kids can have a place to run around!"

"Use up all the money I got put away? Do you know how long it took me to save that little bit?"

"What good is it doing us in the bank? We might as well use it!"

"You planned those guys coming over here, didn't you? Just so you could nag me about moving again," he tells her putting on a pair of worn boots.

"I'm tired of living like this," she tells him, "I want a bigger place, one small room for five people is crazy!" She turns to him argumentative.

"You're a sly one, you are. Setting this up, so you can get your way. I know this is too small for us. Don't you think I know that?"

"If you know it, why haven't you been looking for some place else? It's time you did something about it!"

Edward leaves feeling mad and foolish and comes back a few hours later.

"You got your wish," he tells her with a pissy attitude, announcing it as soon as he walks in the door, "I found us a bigger place to stay."

"Where? With whom?" Betty asks him, suspiciously.

"Tom said we can stay with him,"

He tells her forthright.

"Not your brother Tom?" Betty asks, hoping he means a different person.

"No, Tom, from downstairs at the bar. You know who I mean, he lives in the country, out at Lexington," he tells her. "Twenty dollars a month."

"Doesn't he already have people living with him?" she asks him, skeptical.

"Yeah he does, but he still has an extra bedroom, and we can use the kitchen and living room all we want," he tells her, satisfied.

"I suppose," Betty tells him, thinking it over. "It's better than what we have here." She wonders about living with so many other people.

By the end of the week, the young family is packed and all moved in.

"I thought it'd be nice if we were all here, so everybody'd have a chance to get to know each other," Tom says to all of his renters, who are sitting around the kitchen table, or standing nearby.

"We all know each other," Edward says.

"That's what I thought. That's what I thought," Tom says. A friendly, short, balding middle-aged man in glasses, with a horseshoe hairline.

Two of the renters, a young man and a slightly older man are talking and laughing and smoking a joint near the doorway to the living room, listening to a younger middle aged woman tell them about her sex life, "I might as well slap a mattress on my back and go lay out by the street corner!" Lily, the third renter is laughing and telling them. Lily is good natured and very friendly.

"Hey you guys, you guys!" Tom says, in a nasal voice, "I want to introduce everybody. Betty this is Lily, Junior and David. Lily, Junior and David this is Betty and Edward. And their kids." Tom has a quiet exuberant way about him. "Let's all talk and get to know each other now."

"Hi!" Lily, a full figured woman, greets them enthusiastically with a smile.

"I know Edward and Betty," the younger man tells him, "I've known Edward for a long time. How are you Betty?" Junior, tall and strong as a horse, asks them. "Been up to the bar lately Edward?" Junior laughs.

"David do you know Edward and Betty?" Tom asks.

"We've talked I think," David, with a lot of facial hair says and starts laughing. "Yeah, I've talked to Edward before, I'm almost sure of it," he says in a rough voice, wearing an orange stocking cap on his head.

"Well good, good then," Tom says, "this was a good idea after all. I'll start the grill and in a little while we'll have something to eat. Help yourselves to any refreshments you might like."

Without any further candor, Tom enthusiastically goes outside to light the grill.

"Can I get you a beer, Betty? Edward?" Lily asks them, being the friendly woman she is. She crosses the kitchen and walks towards the refrigerator.

"Yeah," Betty responds, "I guess one won't hurt," she says smiling.

"Don't forget me," Edward tells her, smiling at her.

"Oh, okay," Lily, says, acting suddenly as if it were a chore.

"Junior, what've you been up too?" Edward asks his pleasant young friend.

"What's new at the bar?" He smiles at him.

"Drinkin. Drinkin and screwin," he replies, then quickly smiles a nice smile and laughs a strong coarse laugh. "How about you?"

"Drinkin and Screwin; me too," Edward agrees smiling.

"Everybody's drinkin and screwin..." Lilly says and starts laughing. "...So Betty, what do you like to do for fun?" Lily asks her, handing her a beer.

"I don't have a lot of time for fun, I have the kids to watch," she tells her, in a good mood, holding two-year old Theresa in her arms. "That's what I do."

"Well, we'll just have to fix that, then now won't we?" She tells her with a big smile and a belly laugh. Lily likes to know what people are up to in their lives.

Betty is beginning to like Lily's easy, carefree way.

"So what does everyone else do?" Do you have kids Lily?" Betty asks.

"Junior works road construction and David works in the city and comes out here on the weekends. And no, (ahhh, ha, ha, ha)," she laughs, "I don't have kids. Not yet anyway, (ahhh, ha, ha, ha)," she laughs again. "But ya never know...." She lets the sentence linger, and looks at Betty, whose smiling at her. "And you've got three? Oh, my goodness, I couldn't handle three small children," she tells her.

Lily loves having sex, and likes talking about it.

"David comes out on the weekends to see me," she adds.

"They can be a handful...." Betty starts to speak but Lily interrupts her.

"They're so well behaved! They're like a little gentleman and ladies."

"They're a little timid. They're like that anytime we go someplace new," Betty explains. "I wish they were like that more often!"

Lily laughs, "Yeah, I suppose. So what does Edward do? I mean besides you?"

She smiles at Betty and laughs again.

"He helps farmers out around the area and works out as a security guard for dances and different events," Betty responds.

"Do you have any other family? Brothers or sisters?" Lily asks her.

"I have two sisters and four brothers. My brother, Joseph Jr. is getting married in a few months, he just came back from the war."

"Really, well that sounds good," Lily tells her, "That oughta be fun."

Tom comes back in from outside and lighting the grill, "the coals will be ready shortly, anybody wanna make the potatoes? Anyone? Anyone?" he says pointing a finger around the room, looking at each of them.

"I'll make them," Lily finally gives in.

"I'll help you," Betty volunteers quickly, "Edward move that toddler chair over so I can set Theresa down. Edward!" She says again louder, smiling.

Edward's in the middle of talking to Junior and David and finally hears her and moves the kids' chair without stopping.

"So your still on road construction, huh? I've thought about going on that," Edward tells Junior, "but I'd have to be gone too long. I mean I might not be able to make it home every night," he says, emphasizing certain words with his hands. "I don't think Betty would like that." Everyone's eyes quickly turn to look at Betty, then back to Edward.

"Is everyone good with their beer, or can I get anybody one?" Tom offers.

"I'll have one as long as you're getting them," Edward tells him.

"Get everyone one," David tells him seriously, "what the hell."

The six new housemates eat their supper from the grill and have another beer while Lily and Betty wash and dry the dishes in the sink afterwards.

"So what are we gonna do tonight?" Lily asks everyone, hating idle time and always looking for the next thing to do.

Betty enjoys the extra company of the others at the

new house, especially the company of another woman. Edward feels the same towards the men.

Part 3

In With The In Crowd

Betty, Lily, Junior, Jigger and Shirley are all at Jigger's camper trailer in the trailer park, with other camper trailers, at the campgrounds along side the pavilion at Lexington. Lily walks into the small kitchen to the table to play cards. "Come on in the kitchen everyone, lets play cards," Lily tells them, and sits down at the small table. "Betty, come play cards with us," Lily tells her, looking for more people to add to her fun.

"Betty already knows we're playing cards," Jigger tells Lily. "You asked her already." Jigger is thirty years old and a large, imposing man with shoulder length, dark curly hair and unkempt clothes. "You asked her to play once," he says and quickly laughs like a horse whinnies. "Did you forget already?" He laughs again, making fun of her.

Jigger lives in a small trailer house. The camper and everything inside of it are pint sized with small rooms, small furniture, and small windows. There's room in the bedroom for a bed, and nothing more.

"I don't know what I'm doin," Lily responds to Jigger and starts giggling. "Who needs a beer? I know I do," she says walking over to a small refrigerator.

"I want one," Shirley says, a pretty, petite twenty-five

year old who talks with a lisp. Shirley lives nearby with an elderly couple that took her in and has been taking care of her since her parents died in an automobile accident several years ago. "I haven't had one all day," she tells them with a quiet laugh.

"I'm not having any beer," Betty tells her, "I've had an upset stomach. Besides, Edward wants me to meet him at the pavilion at eight o'clock, and I better get going or he'll be wondering what happened to me."

"Is your stomach upset because your pregnant, Betty? Shirley did you know Betty was pregnant?" Lily tells the young woman.

"You've got to be kidding me?" Shirley responds, letting the words draw out slowly. "And you already have three?" She laughs at the thought of it.

"Jigger, you should find a good woman and have one!" Lily kids him.

"Right," he says sarcastically. "The only baby I want is a hot mama, and I haven't met her yet." He looks at her and starts to giggle.

There are twelve trailer campers lined up in a row a short distance from the pavilion, next to the big lake, with a dirt road separating them from the water. The road goes past the trailers to the boat landing, and to the other way past the pavilion to the main road. Next to the lake, it's a popular spot.

The trailer campers are from eight to twelve feet wide and twenty feet long. The ends and corners are rounded and most are a silver metallic color, though a couple are tan, and one was painted white, and another dark green.

It's after dusk and people have metal chairs outside to sit on. Most have a burnt out fire pit, though a few are lit tonight. Some have attached canopies outside their entry door, overhead to block the sun during the day, or the rain. The occupants sit out there with kerosene lanterns for light, and share stories in the evenings about

Lexington Glory Days

their lives.

The sound of someone walking and dragging something along with them, or behind them, is heard outside down the road.

An odd figure is seen walking along the dirt road that separates the campers from the lake, walking from the boat landing towards the pavilion.

"Where's he coming from?" one of the campers, a man, asks a woman suspiciously, both of them sitting outside.

"Nuthin over there but the lakeshore and an oat field," the woman says helpfully. She listens to the rustle of the footsteps, unconcerned.

The shadowy figure is limping, slightly dragging one foot and walking with a cane. It appears, as he gets closer, to be a young man.

He says nothing as he struggles to walk pass the elderly couple sitting outside and walks up to another camper trailer two spaces away from them. The couple hears a screen door being slam closed, as he must have gone inside.

"Jacobs here," Jigger says looking up from the small kitchen table and card game. Jacob's one of the bartenders at the Green Lantern bar.

"Hi everyone," he greets them wheezing and out of breath.

Everyone greets him kindly, "Hi, Jacob," "Come on in," "Grab a beer."

"Jacob, hi," Betty greets her cousin, surprised, "I was just about getting ready to leave to meet Edward, Lily's watching the kids for me here."

"Why? What are you's doing tonight?" Jacob asks her, wheezing.

"They're gonna go to the pavilion and have a few beers, and then they're gonna go do it!" Lily says starting to giggle. "Oh, I forgot you're pregnant. Well, you can still

89

Lexington Glory Days

do it when you're pregnant," she adds as an afterthought.

"I think he just wants a night out without the kids," Betty tells him. "How have you been? Are you still bartending at the Green Lantern?"

"When I'm feeling good. Which is hardly ever lately."

He and Betty talk a while and Betty soon leaves and Jacob sits down, taking out a pouch of grass, and rolls a joint.

"That looks good," Jigger tells him giggling, looking mischievously at him.

"How're you been feeling, Jacob?" Lily asks him.

"Hurt all over," he tells them squirming in his chair. "This damn rheumatism had me down. I been laid up in bed for two weeks, I wanna get out and do things, but I can't. Lucky I made it this far. I was gonna go to the pavilion for a few beers until I saw all the people in here through the windows, and thought I'd stop in." Jacob has severe rheumatism and only infrequently does the pain subside enough for him to feel good, and then it's not for very long.

"We're glad you did," Jigger tells him, honestly, trying to be kind to him.

"You're welcome anytime," Shirley says.

"At our place too," Lily tells him, "You're always welcome."

They continue playing cards in the small camper trailer, this time with Jacob, and light up the joint, while Betty meets Edward at the bar.

"I think we might be in trouble," Edward tells Betty, sitting at the bar and having a beer, looking disturbed, like something's on his mind.

"Why, now what happened?" She quickly questions him, a look of fear appearing on her face. She stares at him, waiting for an answer.

"We're behind on the rent money. I just talked to Tom," he continues, folding his hands on top of the bar,

Lexington Glory Days

"he says if we don't come up with it, we have to move out. We can leave our stuff there and move back in, once we clear our debt with him, if we want, he says. We got till the end of the week." He sits there, quiet and motionless, looking down at the bar, feeling bad.

"What are we gonna do?" she whispers to him, her eyes big like saucers. "No one will lend us any money. Everybody we know, knows were always broke!"

"Most of our money goes to doctor bills for you and the kids, car repairs and food. I don't know. God damn it, I was hoping he'd let us ride a little while longer. He said three months was long enough to come up with at least part of it, and I aint got it." Tom is easy on the renters, but only up to a point.

Laughter is heard outside through the open window, and all of a sudden the door opens with Junior, Shirley, Jigger, Jacob, Lilly and Edward and Betty's three kids walking in, talking and laughing.

"Fancy meeting you guys here!" Lily says laughing. "I bought you some little people."

Lily decided to cut her babysitting job short, to Betty's dismay.

Suddenly the place is alive with voices, pool balls cracking into each other, a pinball machine with its bells and whistles going off and the jukebox playing.

"So what are you two talking about so seriously?" Lily asks Betty and Edward. She stands there, appearing to demand an answer.

"Money," Betty tells her easily, her face showing concern. "We owe Tom three months' rent and we don't have it."

"Well, be happy and merry anyway," Lily, tells them, walking away.

"I suppose we could stay at the farm with Gertrude, Peter and Brian. Now that Joseph Jr.'s married there's a little more room there," she says, trying to figure

Lexington Glory Days

something out. She looks at Edward, judging his reaction.

"I know, but I don't want to stay there," Edward tells her. "Maybe Joseph and Katherine can take the kids for a week and you and I can stay with Jigger," he suggests. Jigger's kind hearted and would do anything to help most people.

"Leave the kids? Oh, I don't know...that wouldn't be right," she tells him lowering her head and peering into his yes. "He doesn't have room for us."

"You could use a break from the kids," he tells her. "You're four months pregnant, it's gonna be awhile before your gonna have another chance to take it easy again." He tries enticing her, thinking she might like a break from the kids.

"I don't know," she replies sadly. "I don't want to leave the kids, but if they have to stay with someone else, I guess Katherine and Joseph would be okay. There's no harm in asking I suppose. Just for a week."

Over the course of the following weekend, the kids go to Joe Jr. and Katherine's, and Edward meets his brothers and sisters at the Green Lantern bar without Betty. It's a reason for his family to get together and hold a small family reunion. As they get older and marry and start having families of their own, they move further away and see each other less often.

"Edward you don't have a beer in your hand, is everything all right?" His sister Mamie, twenty-nine, ribs him. Sitting outside at a picnic table, she's talking in a low voice, smoking a cigarette and coughs.

"Maybe he's had enough already, are you shined up?" Carrie smiles at him. Carrie, one of their younger sisters, who recently got married, walks by them nonchalantly. "Are you shined up?" she repeats, still smiling.

"This was a good idea, I'm glad you guys came down and rented these cabins," Larry tells Mamie.

Mamie just smiles and grunts a laugh.

Lexington Glory Days

The Green Lantern has six small ramshackled cabins next to the bar with an outhouse far enough away where the rank odor doesn't bother them.

"Who all got cabins? Larry asks them, not wanting to be left out of the whole circle of information. "I'd have got one too if I'd have known sooner."

"Ma and dad, us..." Mamie starts.

"I got one for me and anybody else that wants to use it," Tom jumps in.

"Someone else is in the other three, I don't know who they are. A family with kids is in one, the other two have some old bums in it," Mamie chuckles at this. "That's what they look like anyway."

"One of em's not Edward, is it?" Larry quips.

"It might be," Edward replies, getting a laugh out of them.

"Has anyone seen Jacob Kulik? I hear he's missing," Larry says, turning serious. "One of these days that boys gonna wonder off and not come back."

"Not that I know of," Edward says, "he probably just took off again. Once his rheumatism starts feeling better he's not one to stick around."

"I'm surprised ma and dad rented one," Mamie says to them.

"They only live a quarter of a mile down the road, they coulda walked and saved themselves the two dollars," Tom jokes.

"Maybe they were afraid they weren't gonna be fit to walk back home later," Mamie says, making them all laugh again. "How's that keg of beer doing, is there any left?" The keg of beer is sitting in a round metal tub covered in ice.

"There oughta be, we just tapped it over an hour ago," Rita tells them with a snort. Rita, the youngest sister, is eighteen. "There better be, I'm thirsty."

The contents inside the keg of beer slowly disappears

Lexington Glory Days

in the forth coming hours of the afternoon and evening. The more they drink, the faster they drink.

"I think I need to go lie down for a while, already," Mamie says lightheaded and inebriated. "I think I'm toots'd up now," she says in a low coarse laugh.

"You don't look so good either," Edward, teases her.

"Lie down? It's only four o'clock," Evelyn, their mother, tells her surprised.

"My legs feel like rubber, I'm afraid I won't be able to walk. I'll be like Jacob, and have to use a cane," she snickers.

"Don't stand up then," Edward quips, making her smile.

"Who's that lying on the grass over there?" Rita walks up to them, asking.

"I don't know. Is that Larry?" Mamie says, "It is," and laughs, "he's out!"

"What do you mean he's 'out'? Who's 'out'? Carrie asks, smiling, following behind Rita. "You mean he's passed out? Drunk? Schnockered?"

"Out like a light," Mamie says, chuckling again.

"Let's go do something to him," Rita tells them, mischievously. Suddenly, out of the blue, a strange voice is heard.

"Hey, hey! We're here to party with ya's," Lily suddenly appears, smiling, with Junior and Shirley. Lily doesn't like to miss a good party.

Mamie lowers her head and rubs her forehead, "Oh, no..."

"Lily, come help me rouse Larry," Rita tells her.

"Okay," Lily replies giggling, "what should we do? Oh, I know! Let's put grasshoppers on him, they seem to be everywhere anyway."

"Yeah, yeah," Rita laughs, scrunching her face.

Larry feels the grasshoppers crawling on his arms. "I'll put one on his face," Rita says, almost stumbling over the top of him. She catches herself, standing, and ends up straddling him. She leans over and puts another grasshopper on him.

Walking up to the picnic table with Shirley, Junior tells Edward, "We saw Betty earlier at Jigger's. Jigger's got some other woman over there..."

"Is she good lookin?" Edward interrupts him, making him laugh.

"She just came back from Katherine and Joe's and seeing the kids. She didn't want to stay there with those two fooling around, so she went over to Gertrude and Brian's." Junior stands there with his arms crossed.

"Who did? Betty?" Edward asks. Junior nods. "Oh, okay. Good place for her," Edward says, looking off into the distance, picturing her in his mind.

"We brought a couple of guys over who like to play guitars, should I tell 'em to come over?" Junior goes on, asking him.

Everybody chimes in at once, "Yeah, do it." "Tell 'em to come over." "We're gonna have music!" Mamie pipes in.

Over in the grass, Larry's starting to sit up, swaying from side to side, barely conscious, drunk and hung over at the same time. Wondering what the hells going on, as Rita and Lily are bent over in laughter, at the grasshoppers they put on him, making his skin crawl.

Lloyd walks over with his son-in-law, Mamie's husband, Ted, from behind one of the old cabins. "Looks like there's a party going on," Ted says, smiling.

"Let's find a couple of chairs to sit on," Lloyd tells him.

By the time they get back, Tom has lit a campfire and the two guitar players are strumming and singing to the tune of, 'You Are My Sunshine.' Everyone sings along, clapping. "You are my sunshine...my only sunshine...you make me happy...When skies are gray..." The song ends,

'Please don't take, my sunshine, away...' But the family sings the end of the song another time, slower, 'Please don't take, my sunshine, a-wayyyy,' letting the ending linger.

The two guitar players strum a second song, a favorite, by Hank Williams Sr., 'Jambalaya.' Blanch gets up and starts interlocking her arms toward Rita, who takes her arm and starts twirling around, dancing. The others clap their hands and sing along merrily. "Good-bye Joe...me gotta go...me oh my oh," the guitar players sing, "Son of a gun, were gonna have big fun, on the bayou..."

People from inside the bar come out and visit them around the campfire, seeing them have so much fun. "You look familiar to me," Evelyn tells a woman against the glow of the flames. "I'm Mrs. Joe Kulik, Katherine is my first name. I used to be Katherine Leacher. We lived down the road." She points to the south with her finger. "My husband Joe is Betty's brother."

"I remember now," Evelyn says boisterously. "We talked at the lake a few summers ago, you had a child with you and my kids and husband were swimming...I remember very clearly now."

"Yeah, yeah, that was me." Katherine's giggles are like soap bubbles that rise, drifting in the air for a few moments then burst.

The evening passes by and soon it's after midnight, with the revelers getting louder and louder, and by now having gotten stinking drunk.

"I gotta go squeeze a mop," Rita says getting up to go to the bathroom in the wrong direction. Her choice of phrases is sometimes a bit risqué.

"Where's she going?" Evelyn laughs at her.

Rita walks aways away from the crowd, behind a tree, lifts her dress, squats down and pees. The others laugh uproariously at her.

"My, God," Evelyn says, still chuckling at her. "Makes

a mother proud."

The next morning Betty arrives purposely early to see how bad everyones hang over is and to pick up Edward. As she predicted, he's not feeling well.

"You're still sleeping?" she says to him acting surprised. "How much did you drink last night?"

"The whole keg," he moans, turning on his side. She laughs at him.

"Are you gonna get up or do you want me to come back later?"

"I'll get up. What time is it?" he asks her waiting for the room to stop spinning. "What are we gonna do today? God I'm hungry."

"Find a place to live, is what we should do," she tells him.

"What happened to Jiggers? I thought we were staying there?"

"We all can't keep staying there. There's barely enough room for you and me. Besides, we might as well start looking for a place where we can all be together. I wish we would just stay with Gertrude, Peter and Brian for a while."

"I guess so," not having the wherewithal to argue with her. "Is it all right with them?" It's a quick fix to difficult problem for him.

"They said it was. Anytime I need a place to stay, I can stay with them, they said." She walks over to a chair, picks up his shirt and hands it to him.

"You, yeah. What about me and the kids?"

"They wouldn't hardly think I'd stay someplace without the kids and you."

"You 'think' it'd be okay? Maybe you should find out for sure."

After talking it over with Gertrude and Brian later that day, Betty tells Edward it's okay for all of them to stay there. The following day, they move in.

"It must be nice to have Brian home from the war, to help out," Betty tells Gertrude. She's glad her sister and Peter aren't living out here alone.

"With the farming especially," Gertrude tells her sister. "They think something might have happened to Jacob. His dad found his money and watch at home, but he hasn't seen him in three days. If he were to go off someplace, he would have taken those things with him they figure."

"What? Oh, I hope he's okay, poor Jacob... Edward's been trying to work more hours for the farmers to make more money, so we can move back in with Tom. He doesn't make much working for them." Gertrude looks at her and then looks off to the side.

"Jacobs' dads' been out looking for him in the woods and fields in case something's happened to him. I hope Edward finally finds a good job so you'se don't have to be moving around all the time."

"I don't know which one I'm more sick of; moving all the time or not having a place of our own," Betty tells her dishearteningly. "How's Peter been doing?"

"Pretty good," Gertrude tells her pleased. "He likes school, and goes out hunting and fishing now with Brian. He listens when I have to tell him something. He loves having Brian home, he follows him around like a little lost puppy sometimes. He likes playing baseball. They've been trying to move a big old barn from the Louie Glitinsky farm, so he's been over there quite a bit watching them lifting it up and trying to move it. He hasn't talked about daddy much lately. He's really been no trouble at all."

Brian walks into the house looking for Edward.

"Edward, you wanna come out and help Peter and me with chores?" Brian asks, testing him to see whether or not he plans on lying around the house or helping them. Brian can be sly that way.

"What do you all need done? I'll come out." Brian has

him chop wood for the heat stove for the upcoming winter.

Satisfied he'll pull his weight, Brian feels better about him staying. "Thanks Edward," Brian tells him, and goes to find Peter.

"He might as well help us out. He's not paying us anything for living here," Brian tells Peter, helping him feed the cows.

Back in the house Brian says energetically, "It's nice to have small kids in the house again. The place seems more alive!"

Harold, Carol and Theresa are running around chasing each other.

"Go get him!" Brian entices Theresa to catch Harold. "Get him!"

She hesitates for a moment, not sure what to make of the man so much larger than she is, then quickly turns and goes off running, smiling and laughing.

"There ya go!" Brian cheers her on, laughing at her antics.

"I can't stay here much longer," Edward confides to Betty later that night. "I feel like a kid having to be told what to do."

A week later, two of Betty's aunts and their husbands come over with good news for them.

"Josephine, Antoinette, hi," Betty says surprised, 'how nice to see you."

"Hello dear, we can't stay long, how are you?" Antoinette affectionately kisses her on the cheek. The two look dressed up, as for an occasion.

"The men have something to tell you," Josephine says with a smile.

"We were visiting with some friends of ours a few days ago and they mentioned a place is gonna be coming up for rent in Lexington. Josephine and Antoinette wanted Betty to know, but didn't know how to get a hold

Lexington Glory Days

of her. I suggested we stop in here and see," Emil tells Edward.

"We lost track of where you were living, dear," Antoinette tells her smiling.

"A well off farmer out by Lexington owns it, and he's looking for a farm hand too, if you're interested. I don't know if you are or not. We know you do farm work. Maybe you could even work off the rent, or part of it anyway," August tells him. He knows this is a good opportunity for him to get on his feet.

Edward looks up, suddenly interested. "Who do I talk to? Where's he live? I can go over there today and talk to him if he's around."

"Josephine talked to his wife and told her you worked for farmers before," August tells him. He said to go out and talk to them."

Josephine turns to look at Betty, "We hate to intrude, and maybe you like it here, we're just trying to help...." Her aunts are kind women.

"We just thought it would be nice to have a place of your own again," Antoinette says clearly. "It's a nice place. Three bedrooms, a living room, dining room....There's a root cellar for potatoes and such. A kitchen, of course."

"And it's got running water and an indoor toilet," August adds.

Chapter Four

A House On A Hill On A Lake

"The moon is full over the lake tonight," Edward tells Betty, admiring the view, "look how it shines off the water." They're outside walking along in their new backyard, renting from the farmer Betty's aunts and uncles had told them about. Feeling content she tells him, "It sparkles. It's like there's no other place in the world here. It makes me feel secure and safe."

"It does have a peaceful feeling about it, doesn't it?" he adds.

"Mmm, look how the light shimmers off the water."

"It's pretty," he tells her, "look at the moon, it looks bigger than I ever remember seeing it before. And orange! Have you ever seen the moon that color before? It looks like you could almost reach up and touch it."

"I love living here," Betty tells him, "so close to our families and friends, on the lake. I wouldn't want to live anyplace else in the whole wide world. It sure beats those old shacks we were living in. Remember staying in Jiggers little camper trailer?" she laughs at the thought of it.

"Someday this'll all be ours. I'm working for the farmer down the road for free to pay for it. He's not paying me in cash, but once I work enough hours for him, he's gonna sign the title over to us, then it'll be ours, free and clear."

"I know, and it's all just what I wanted. The kids love it out here. Harold and Carol and Theresa can run around and play all they want. We're gonna be so happy here. A place of our own!" she suddenly gets excited, her voice getting louder, then subdued, "a place of our own."

"Mommy! Mommy!" Theresa shouts, reaching for her. Edward lifts the three year old out from under his arms and hands her over to Betty.

"She wants you," he tells her with a smile, and then says caringly, "I'm glad the kids are gonna have another a little brother or sister to play with."

She stops walking. Hesitantly, seriously she replies, "I don't know how I'm gonna take care of these three, plus another one." She looks at him and sees he's looking at her, "Four kids," she tells him nodding. "Four kids! And I'm five months pregnant! I must be crazy," she tells him and laughs.

A wide smile comes across Edward's face, "We'll make it work. Another one to add to the brood!" he calmly tells her, putting his arm around her. "You're having another baby!" he repeats, making sure she heard him.

"I know," she answers him. He lets out a big burst of a laugh.

"I'm gonna be a dad again!" His reaction surprises her.

Relieved and humored, Betty lets a big smile come across her face, and slowly starts walking again. "It's so peaceful out here," she tells him.

"I think we should invite a few people over and celebrate," he tells her seriously, "you know, so I can brag a little bit."

"Brag," she repeats him smiling, questioning his response. "I guess we could invite Brian and Kimberly over, and Gertrude and Peter, and I guess your folks and Blanch. That would be all right, wouldn't it?"

"And maybe Larry," he adds, as she eyes him curiously.

They talk to with their families when they see them, within the coming weeks, and invite them over to announce the news.

"Come on in," Edward tells the whole crew. His mother walks in, followed by his dad and most of his brothers and sisters. Larry, Blanch, Tom, and Carrie are all in their twenties, and Rita, 19 and Jim, 13. The only one missing is Mamie, who lives in St. James now with her husband and daughter.

"Hi everybody," Edward greets them. He invites everyone into the living room, and a short while later Betty's sisters and brothers, Kimberly, Gertrude and Brian and Peter arrive. Both families have met before on a number of occasions.

Edward's mom and dad, Lloyd and Evelyn, and all of their kids besides Jim are each having a bottle of beer, talking and laughing loudly, celebrating the news of the new baby. Betty's two sisters Kimberly and Gertrude, 27 and 22 respectively, and brothers Brian and Peter, 28 and 14, sit quietly together, and politely decline any sort of drink, only occasionally talking to each other.

"Are you's sure I can't get you's anything?" Betty asks her family, "Kimberly? Gertrude? Brian? Peter? We have sodas too, are you sure you wouldn't like something?" Betty wants to make them feel comfortable.

"We're okay Betty, stop waiting on us and sit down and relax," Brian, a little uncomfortable, tells her, while Edward and his family continue talking and carrying on. "If we want something we can get it, we're okay."

Evelyn, with her big frame and high blue hair, is sitting on the edge of a soft easy chair listening to her children talk.

"You should have seen it," Rita is telling them animated in her high nasal voice, talking with her hands, "the car came around the dirt track and bang! Another car ran right into it." Rita likes to talk and act up.

"You went to a demolition derby? Who did you go there with? Where was that?" Larry asks her with a little grin, showing a nice smile.

"Betty, I can't believe the news, you're having another baby! How exciting is that?" Blanch tells her. "I haven't even had my first one yet."

"It's exciting now," Betty reassures her, smiling.

"Wait till later."

"Gertrude, maybe the boys would like to go outside and play," Evelyn says.

She has more fun when the younger kids aren't around.

"I don't care. Peter you can go outside and play with Jimmy if you want to," she tells her brother, looking at him as he's sitting quietly in his chair, leaving it up to him. He looks at Jimmy who doesn't move.

"What have you been up to, Lloyd?" Brian asks Edwards father.

"Tryin to make a living, like everyone else," he responds.

"I heard you's moved closer to Lexington, How's the new place?" he asks him trying to be friendly. They moved five miles closer.

"Better than the old one," he tells him. "I like it better."

"Closer to the beer joint for ma," Edward chimes in laughing.

Jimmy adds, "This ones got running water, a tub and a toilet, and hot water. Boy that's nice. I never want to have to go without it again. You guys don't have that yet," he says to Peter, "you'll like it when you do, boy is it ever nice!"

"I bet it is," Peter responds a little shyly, swinging a leg back and forth.

Carrie, who's just a little overweight, cleverly says to Rita, "no more sittin on a smelly kettle of stew." Referring to the pot they used to go to the bathroom in. Most people in the area don't have wells dug, and have no indoor plumbing.

"Indoor plumbing, gang, it's the only way to go," Lloyd tells them seriously.

"Oh, maybe someday," Brian tells him, "can't afford to dig a well right now, money's too tight. You know how much they charge to dig a well?"

"I reckon I don't. You could always move, that's what I did," Lloyd presses him. "It was time for something a little nicer. Ma wanted to," he concedes.

"Move? I aint moving nowhere," he snickers, "that was my daddy's farm."

"Not much of a house though," Tom insists.

"Okay, I think that's enough talk about indoor plumbing," Betty, sitting nearby, interrupts them and changes the subject, "Kimberly how's Clay been?"

"He's fine! I'm meeting him later this afternoon, we're going for a drive and then out for ice cream," she says smiling and quickly hunches her shoulders back, happy.

"He's over at his folks now helping with chores."

"How's married life for you two? Evelyn asks her, "I thought we might get an invitation." Evelyn isn't always concerned about being polite.

"Where are you meeting him?" Brian asks.

"At home. I'm gonna walk home in a little while, it's not far," she tells him.

"It's cold out, I hope your dressed warm," Brian tells her.

"You're leaving?" Betty responds, surprised, "I thought you were staying?"

Lloyd gets up and joins Edward and Larry talking in the dining room. "What are you two so quiet about?" he asks them, pulling up a chair and sitting down.

He looks at his sons and they're suddenly even quieter.

"The war," Larry tells him, looking at him, and says no more.

"Lloyd get me another beer as long as you're up," Evelyn says to him.

"I already sat down," he tells her.

"So you can't get up again?" She asks him demandingly, then turns to Betty and asks, "Betty, are you ever going to get Theresa baptized?"

"Yes, we are. We're going to get her baptized at the Catholic Church, here in Lexington," she says brightly. She loves the quaint little church.

"Here in Lexington, huh? I thought maybe you'd join the one in town, where momma and daddy belonged," Brian tells her.

"There's nothing wrong with the church out here," Evelyn tells him, "it's small, but you know all the parishioners better. It's like another family out here."

"Oh, I didn't mean to imply it wasn't nice," Brian responds, "I just thought, with both momma and daddy gone and all..."

"I know Brian, but we're from Lexington, were not from town," Betty tries to explain. "We'd be going to church with our neighbors."

"I know that, but there's more people to get to know, in case things go wrong or a person needs help, there's more people to help out," he suggests.

"People need help out here too, Brian," Evelyn tells him.

"I like how small the church is," Betty tells them, "it's like a small, little community out here. Like we're all apart of another family."

"We're all neighbors out here I know, but I just figured we were part of a bigger community from town,"

Brian says trying to describe his feelings.

"We're our own town," Evelyn tells them.

"Not much of a town," Tom tells them, "there's not even a store here."

"I know, but we have the pavilion and the dance hall, and they carry some canned food and milk and bread, and butter and baking goods behind the bar, and they have gasoline. And there's the other bar," Evelyn tries to convince them, "the Green Lantern. And the lake, town doesn't have a lake. And there's the service station. Why don't you and Peter go outside and play for a while," Evelyn tells Jimmy.

Lloyd comes back with another bottle of beer for Evelyn and an extra one for anyone who wants it, as Kimberly tells everyone she's leaving and is walking home now to meet her husband. Tom takes the extra beer from his dad.

"That's enough beer for you after that one," Lloyd tells his son, as the girls walk into the kitchen to say goodbye to Kimberly.

Betty walks the girls into the kitchen with Blanch, talking to Kimberly whose walking behind them as Gertrude, and Carrie and Rita follow. "I like your new place," Gertrude tells Betty, seeming bored.

"...Don't do anything I wouldn't do," Betty tells Kimberly sarcastically, making her and Blanch laugh. The pun isn't lost on the other girls.

"Like getting pregnant?" Gertrude asks dryly.

"Get pregnant," Carrie repeats waiving her arms in the air, chuckling.

"Get pregnant!" Rita repeats again, trying to be funny, but no one laughs.

"Dress warm, it's cold outside," Betty tells Kimberly.

"It's not bad," she tells her, "It's nice out really. Bye everyone," Kimberly shouts whipping a tan scarf around her neck, and turning to wave to everyone before leaving.

Everybody agrees, there's just something about Kimberly.

"Maybe we should put some snacks out," Edward tells Betty from the dining room table. She walks around the other girls in the kitchen.

"Let's make the announcement first for those that don't know yet," Betty tells him. Most of them already know, but a few still don't.

"What announcement?" Larry turns and asks Edward.

"Betty's pregnant," he tells them all, smiling."

"Well my God, congratulations," Larry tells them, turning his eyes to Betty.

"You're pregnant again?" Gertrude asks her, dropping her chin and rolling her eyes, "oh my word." Some days Gertrude has her hands full with just Peter.

"We're happy for you dear," Evelyn tells her son, as the smile disappears from Betty's face, getting no response from her mother-in-law.

Not noticing, Edward accepts the accolades, "thank you, we're pretty excited about it." He looks up at Betty and notices his mother has made her feel left out.

Evelyn notices too, smiles and says, "What's the matter Betty? Did I make you feel left out? Maybe we should have those snacks now."

Rita finds delight in her mother's disregard for Betty's feelings and starts laughing at her. Evelyn laughs too, "Oh Betty, don't be so sensitive," she tells her. She turns her head, snorting, in disbelief.

Betty feels she's been made the butt of a bad joke, and very, very quietly tells them, "I'm not," and self-consciously starts to fill the bowls she's set out with snacks. She walks around, placing a bowl here and there.

"Betty feels sorry for herself. Poor Betty..." Rita chides her, and smiles.

"You shush," her dad tells her strictly without looking at her.

"Leave the girl be, Lloyd. We were just trying to have a little fun," Evelyn tells her husband, "the girl is overly sensitive," she tells him matter-of-fact. She continues, "I'm sorry Brian, but your sister needs to be more outgoing around people. She can't even take getting a little fun poked at her without sulking."

With both parents' dead, and no one to help guide them now, Brian is speechless, trying to think it over. He knows she was rude.

"Ma," Larry says, trying to stop her from going any further. Edward's sister, Blanch, doesn't stick up for Betty, her friend, and the room becomes awkwardly quiet. Strange glances are made back and forth between everyone.

"Let's change the subject," Edward says abruptly.

"All right, let's have another beer and change the subject," Evelyn says to them. "What should we drink to? Oh! The baby! Silly me."

"Sounds good to me, Betty can I get you a beer?" Edward asks her, trying to get her to change her mood. "Or a soda?"

"No, I'm fine," she says overly loud, sitting down next to Blanch. She doesn't want to sulk, but they're not talking about anything. They're just giving each other a hard time mostly. Clowning around.

"Blanch, how about you?"

Edward asks his sister.

"No, thank you, Edward, I'm fine." She tells him, all being well with her.

"Dad? Larry? Brian? Tom? Gertrude?" Edward asks everyone.

"Evelyn, as long as my sister is happy, that's all that matters to me," Brian tells her. "Whether she likes getting fun poked at her or not." Evelyn looks up at him, and so does Betty. Evelyn, herself, looks away in a huff of self-pity.

"I think we're gonna go home now too," Gertrude tells them. "I'm gonna call Peter in from outside." she adds getting up from her chair. "I have some sad news that I don't know if you all know about. They found Jacob this morning. One of his brothers found him in a mud lake a couple miles north of here. They found him dead."

Gasps are heard from the women and girls.

"Can you believe it? They think he either poisoned himself or drowned, or both. Poor Jacob, I just can't believe it. He had such a hard life with his rheumatism and his ma dying a while back, and now this. I'm having a hard time believing it."

"He's was too young to die," Betty says solemnly. "He tried so hard to live life like everyone else. That's so sad."

"Betty, are you okay?" Blanch asks her, suddenly concerned.

Betty turns her head and looks at her friend and raises her eyebrows, "I guess so," is all she tells her, sighing.

"I'm gonna get going too, I guess," Larry says looking around, and gets up off his chair and leaves. Not one for long goodbyes.

Edward looks around and doesn't believe what is happening, "I guess the parties fizzling out already," he says with an uncomfortable chuckle.

"Lloyd get our coats, whose ever riding with us, we're leaving," Evelyn suddenly tells her children. She doesn't want to be the last one there.

"You don't have to go," Edward tells his mother with conviction, "have another beer. Betty will get over it, won't you Betty."

"I guess," Betty replies, "I'm tired though," she tells them, lowering her head and rubbing her eyebrow. Still trying to be polite.

"I'm sorry, Betty," Lloyd tells her, giving Evelyn her coat, "We didn't mean no harm. Let's go Evelyn. Kids, get

Lexington Glory Days

in the car. Bye Edward."

"I'll talk to you soon Betty," Blanch tells her. Betty raises her head, and tries to smile. The kids tell Edward, their oldest sibling, good-bye, as Carrie says goodbye to Betty. Again being insensitive, Evelyn tries to walk tall and dignified to the door without a word said to Betty. Edward sees them all to the door.

"Goodbye Edward, stop in sometime."

"I will ma," he tells her.

"We'll be going too, soon as Peter has a chance to warm up a bit," Gertrude says.

"No hurry, Gert. Stay as long as you like," Edward tells her, putting his hand on her shoulder for a moment.

"Are you tired Betty?" Gertrude asks, "Is there anything I can do for you?"

"Come back and check on the kids with me," she tells her.

The men are left alone. Not dwelling on what's just happened, Brian remarks, "you got a nice place here Edward. I'm glad for Betty, and for you too. You know Edward, mama and daddy, God rest their souls, didn't raise us kids to talk back. They raised us to be polite and mind our manners," Brian scratches his head while talking, "I wish your ma wouldn't pick on Betty so. There's no reason for it," he explains, purposely trying to stay friendly towards him.

"She likes to say what's on her mind I guess," Edward confesses to him, "maybe a little too much," he says with a wide grin.

Part 2

Neighbors in The Country

"How many families do you think live around the lake?" Evelyn asks her husband, Lloyd, driving the road along the shoreline in early summer.

"Oh, there's five or six roads that come into Lexington." He thinks it over. "One from the north, two from the east, one from the south, and two from the west. For such a small area there must be twenty-five, thirty or more families," he tells her looking around, "the lake's about a mile long and a half mile wide, plenty of people live around it."

"With all the trees around it, it's a nice drive. Do you want to stop at the pavilion for a beer?" she turns to him and asks.

But he continues, "The village itself can't be more than three miles long and three miles wide. Counting houses just a little further out and away, I suppose around fifty families live out here."

"We are like another family out here," she tells him, fluffing up her hair.

"Kind of a lot of people in a small area," he tells her, driving along.

"Looks like Eugene and Sophia are having company over today," Evelyn says looking out the car window as

Lexington Glory Days

they drive past their neighbors' house.

"Mmm, looks like Charlie and Mabel's car," Lloyd says, "that other one might be Leonard and Anna's. There's Edward in that field over there, plowin," Lloyd says, lifting an index finger off the steering wheel and pointing.

They both look up to watch him plow.

"Must be working for the farmer. I don't feel like going home yet," Evelyn tells Lloyd changing the subject, "let's stop at the Green Lantern."

"All right," he agrees, sighing, passing an old truck in the ditch, "I'm gonna stop at the service station first and fill up with gasoline."

"The mail trucks ahead of us," Evelyn notices.

"John Maruski's mowing the lawn at the church," Lloyd says, driving past what originally was a Catholic mission church.

Watching two young boys with fishing poles fishing in the creek, coming up on them a little further down the road, Lloyd comments, "I wonder if they're bitin? This creek runs between the bigger Lexington Lake and this small mud lake," Lloyd tells her, "it'll be covered in green algae most of the summer cause the water just sits there. Aint got no place to go."

"Lets just go home and see what we got in the mail box," Evelyn suggests. "What kind of name is Maruski?"

She wonders.

"Polish probably," he says, "sounds like it might be anyways."

The old mail truck, with its big old wooden box stationed on the rear end goes one way and Lloyd and Evelyn another. The mailman stops and visits with a woman waiting for a letter from her sister who lives in a distant town.

Driving again, he sees the Mitzenski's aren't home, "no cars in the yard anyway," he says aloud, moving along. He passes two young women with dresses down to their knees, out for a walk. They wave to him cheerfully.

He drives his mail truck out of Lexington a mile, the houses becoming sparser with one only every quarter mile, and notices the men out in the flat fields plowing up the land to mix up the soil and its nutrients, hoping for a light rain. A dry, hot spring would hatch the grasshoppers, which would eat the grain the farmers will plant. Everyone's worried about a large hatching.

'This area has the highest grasshopper infestation in the whole southern part of the state,' he says aloud, looking around and noticing the clouds seeming to be getting darker. He gets an eerie feeling, and the hairs on his arms stand on end. He imagines grasshoppers everywhere, like swarms of mosquitoes.

Evelyn and Lloyd drive up the short, steep hill, around the north side of the lake, near the pavilion and their home, and then into their short driveway.

Seeming like the phone's been ringing for a long time, with a sense of urgency Evelyn quickly answers it. It is Gertrude talking rapidly, "Evelyn, Betty's in labor and I need to get her to the hospital but there's no one here to watch the kids and Edward's not home. Can you come over?"

"Sure, I'll be right there. Don't worry, I'm on my way."

Betty's in labor for twenty-four excruciating hours. Edward is there later, patiently pacing back and forth in the waiting room when the first baby, a boy, is born, and just a few minutes later when he has a new baby daughter.

"Twins?" Surprised and suddenly confused, he repeats the nurse talking to him. "She had twins?" Edward stands there speechless, taking in the news.

Three days later Edward takes Mom Betty, who's become depressed, home from the hospital with the new

Lexington Glory Days

babies, Jack and Bonnie.

"I can't believe they're crying again, I just got them to go to sleep." Tired and weary, Betty says, though no one is listening, and gets out of bed for the third time that night. With her eyes closed, looking as if she's asleep she sits between the two baby cribs in her long white and purple flannel nightgown with a hand on each of the cribs, lightly rocking them for a half an hour.

She's so tired that, after the newborns fall asleep, she falls asleep herself sitting up in the chair beside her bed, as her chin falls to her chest.

The dark, dim light from the rising sun begins to permeate through her window and wakes her. She gets up and leaves the room with its dark colored woodwork, hardwood floors and dark green wall paper with large white shadows of white flowers in it and drags the clothes hamper full of dirty cloth diapers to the kitchen and waiting washing machine. She checks the refrigerator for baby formula, then dumps the dirty cloth diapers in the washer. She's so tired she barely sees only what's in front of her.

She walks into Harold's room and gently rubs his shoulders to wake him. "Harold. Harold it's time to get up for school. Hurry up the school bus will be here soon." She goes back into the kitchen to make coffee, and breakfast for everyone.

Edward gets up and walks out of the bedroom and turns on the black and white television set in the living room and lies on the couch in his underwear to watch the news.

Harold walks into the dining room still tired from his sleep and sits in his chair in his pajamas and waits for his breakfast at the table, noticing the shiny metal legs and thick shiny metal trim around it and white and black speckled top.

"You're getting a polio vaccination at school today,"

Betty tells him.

"I don't like shots," he tells her in a raspy voice.

"Like them or not you're getting one. It's like a mosquito bite. You'll barely feel it, and then it'll all be over with before you know it. All the kids are getting them."

"I still don't like shots," he tells her again in a raspy voice, as she sets a bowl of cereal with milk in it, and buttered toast, in front of him.

Betty walks back into her bedroom and picks Jack, whose still asleep, up out of his crib, and gently pats his back until his tiny body wakes up, then walks over to Edward lying on the couch, and hands him the baby boy.

She walks back into her bedroom and does the same thing with Bonnie, only this time, laying the baby girl on the floor, on a blanket, in the living room in front of Edward and the TV. Hoping the twins stay awake.

The washing machine runs through its cycles and she begins to send the diapers through the wringer. As the cloth diapers come through in between the two rollers, to squeeze the water out, she hangs them on a ten row, wobbly wooden, expandable clothesline to dry, above a rug she's laid underneath it to catch the dripping water.

"If I get polio will I be crippled?" Harold asks her.

"You won't be able to walk or run. That's why I want you to get the vaccination," she tells him, putting another diaper through the wringer.

"Don't worry. All the kids are getting it," she tells him, peering into the living room to check on the newborn twins. "What are you doing letting them fall back asleep?" She yells at Edward loudly. "I woke them up so they'll sleep through the night, not during the day. So I won't have to be up all day and all night."

She's been trying to get them on a schedule since she brought them home.

"Well I can't see their eyes, how was I supposed to

know?" He tells her.

"Wake them up, both of them!" she snaps at him. 'I'm making breakfast, doing laundry and trying to get Harold off to school and you're lying on the couch,' she says, more to herself than to him.

Carol walks into the living room, in her pajamas, carrying two dolls in one hand and rubbing her eyes with the other, with Theresa following right behind her carrying a blanket, and sits on the floor next to Bonnie in front of the television.

"I'm so tired. Why won't anyone help me?" Carol says, holding up and pretending to be the voices of the two dolls. "Because you're the mommy and it's your job. No one's supposed to help you," the other doll says back to her.

"But I'm so tired, all I want to do is lie down."

"Not until you feed the babies and change their diapers. Then you have to wash all of the clothes and dishes, make my supper and clean the house."

"Why do I have to do so much?"

"Because I'm the daddy and I work. Now get going."

"But I'm sad; I wish somebody loved me." She throws the dolls down angrily and lies down next to Bonnie and Theresa, with a scowl look on her face, pouting.

"I'm sorry ma poked fun at you at the party we had, to announce you were pregnant, a while back," Edward tells Betty later.

Betty blinks and rolls her eyes away from him.

"That's just the way my family is. They've been like that for as long as I can remember," he tries explaining to her. "They like giving each other, and other people, a hard time. That's how they are."

Betty's off in her own world, thinking about nothing in particular, only that she's not happy; and she doesn't care about that, either.

"I remember one time when I was just a kid, they kept calling me Sally. Made me cry. People are always picking on someone. They don't really mean any harm, they're just trying to have a little fun."

She lets her distorted feelings come to her whenever they arrive in their own time. "That's just what your ma said," she mumbles, barely audible, staring off into the far, far distance, not caring.

"They're all like that, me included, except for Larry and Carrie a little bit. Dad isn't, I guess we get it from ma...." There's no response from Betty.

"I heard they found some poison missing from the Kulik farm. They think Jacob might've taken it and drank it; but they didn't find the bottle where they found his body, so they don't know for sure. But the poisons gone. Something called Carbolic acid...." He waits for a response and gets none.

"There's a new bus line running from Centerville to Merrifield, maybe we should get a babysitter sometime and go up there. We could go with some other people and spend the day up there and have a little fun, sometime. That is if you want to, we don't have to." He looks at her, worried about her silence.

Not much of anything he says interests her; and just the thought of how many different emotions and responses she'd have to come up with to talk to him tires her. It's all become too much for her to handle. "Sometime," she tells him.

"Do you want me to call somebody and have them come over and help out for a little while? Or a doctor?"

She thinks about this and decides she does. "Who would you call?"

"I don't know. Who do you want me to call?" He asks her sheepishly.

"I don't know," she says. Unable to think straight.

"I'll call. Just tell me who and I'll call." He tries to be

helpful.

"Forget it," she tells him, turning her head away from him.

Frustrated, Edward walks over to the wall phone in the kitchen and picks up the receiver. He looks at the phone numbers written on a piece of paper taped next to the phone and dials one.

Brian is coming in from outside, working on farm equipment for the summer, just as he hears the phone ring. "Hello?"

"Hi Brian, its Edward. I got a little situation over here I was hoping you could help me with. Betty isn't feeling too good and I was wondering if Gertrude could come over and spend a few days with us to help us out."

"Sure, I'll ask her. Betty's sick, huh?"

"No, she aint sick, she just doesn't feel good."

"Okay, hold on.... Yeah, she said she had a few things she wanted to do around here first, and then pack a few things, and she'll be over before suppertime tonight. I might ride over too."

"That's mighty nice of her. Tell her 'thanks' for me. So how are things going over there?" The two men talk on the phones for a while longer, while Betty is sitting emotionless in a wooden rocking chair in the living room.

A few hours later Gertrude shows up.

"So you're not feeling well?" Gertrude asks Betty after she arrives, sitting next to her and leaning in close.

"I feel okay," Betty tells her, slowly beginning to move the rocking chair back and forth with one foot. "I just don't feel like doing anything, and I have no energy. All I wanna do is just sit here."

"I think you must be exhausted and need some rest. You've been working too hard. Has Edward been helping you?"

Betty looks off into the distance and doesn't say anything, trying to think.

"That's okay. I can stay for as long as you need me, and you start to feel better. I suppose I better start by making supper. What would you like to eat?"

"Whatever," Betty tells her quietly, shaking her head and lifting her wrists off the arm rests and pivoting them sideways.

Gertrude pats her bare arm before getting up off her chair.

"Edward get me enough potatoes for all of us for supper, and for some left overs. I don't know where they are," Gertrude orders him, and begins looking through the cupboards and refrigerator for ideas.

Without uttering a word, Betty walks into Carol and Theresa's bedroom to check on them and then to her bedroom to check on the twins, and wakes them one by one by lifting them out of their cribs and laying them on her bed to change their diapers. She doesn't say anything.

"Is Harold home?" Edward says aloud, getting the potatoes.

"School bus must be late today," he says to himself when no one answers him. "Here are the potatoes," he tells Gertrude, giving her the whole sack.

"You can help peel them too, if you want to," Gertrude tells him.

"Nope. I don't want to," he tells her with a smirk on his face, and walks into another room and then outside.

A while later he shows up at Brian's, "This isn't the first time this has happened," he tells him. "After Theresa was born, she was pretty upset too. Your dad had just passed on and she missed your ma something terrible."

"I was overseas in the war. I missed a lot of things. I didn't know that, and I don't know what to say. Poor Betty," Brian says seriously.

"You don't have to say anything," Edward tells him. "Maybe you could come over sometime and try to cheer her up a little bit. Maybe she'd like to see Kimberly and

Peter too. I don't know what to do," Edward tells him honestly.

"Sure. Sure we could," Brian agrees. "I was gonna go over later anyway."

"I gotta do something to try to cheer her up." Edward adds.

"Sure. Sure, I understand," Brian, tells him nodding.

From Brian's place, Edward goes to see his sister, and Betty's friend Blanch, whose been living in an apartment in Centerville.

"Maybe you and some of your old school friends could come over and visit her sometime, you know, to cheer her up?" He figures seeing people she loves should help.

"Well sure, I'd be happy to Edward. I didn't know she was so depressed. If I'd have known, I'd have come over sooner," she agrees.

When he gets home, Edward ends up being an hour late for supper.

"Where did you go?" Gertrude asks him, clearing dishes off the supper table. Just being curious, and yet a little annoyed at Edward's lateness.

"I went over to ma and dad's," he lies. "Where's Betty?"

"She went to bed. Poor thing is exhausted. It'd be nice if she had more help around here. How come you haven't been helping her? You should know she can't take care of newborn twins and three other small children at the same time. Plus do all of the cooking and housework."

"I didn't know they were that much work. It seems like they're sleeping most of the time." He knows at least part of what he said is true.

"I don't know about that. I suppose they sleep a lot, but they still gotta get fed and diapered. And bathed," she adds as if he should already know this.

"I wonder if she heard about the newborn baby that

just died, down the road from here. I hope she didn't. She has enough on her mind. Did you hear? The little thing was only three months old. The Tryzinski's baby. Poor thing had pneumonia and heart problems. The wake is in the family's home next week and the funeral's gonna be at the church here in Lexington. I hope she doesn't decide she wants to go, if she finds out. She doesn't need another reason to feel bad."

"Jacob's wake and funeral is next week too," Edward, adds.

"It's not gonna be a good week for anybody," Gertrude says, sighing.

Off in the distance a lowly country church bell is ringing. You could not hear the bell if a radio were turned on and set it to its lowest setting. A lone man is in the choir loft pulling on a sixty- foot long rope attached to the bell. The faint cry of its' echo is summoning people to church.

Betty hears the bell's lonesome call, "I really should be going," she tells Gertrude, "We've known the Tryzinski's all our lives."

"I don't think you should. A funeral for a young child is too overwhelming and emotional and sad, I think it would do you more harm, than good. I'll tell them you weren't feeling well and convey your sympathies."

"I feel bad about not going, but I suppose your right," she concedes.

A little white casket is in front of the altar, in the front of the church, when Gertrude arrives. She sits towards the back with other neighbors;

Eugene and Sophia Latzki, Charlie and Mabel Monisky, Leonard and Anna Polinski, John Haruska, and Francis and Virginia Burns. She sees her aunts, Antoinette and Josephine, and their husbands, Emil and August, another neighbor Louie Glatinsky, Evelyn and Lloyd with Larry, Rita, Blanch and Carrie. Kimberly and

Lexington Glory Days

Clay, Brian, Joe Jr. and Katherine are there. Jigger, Lily, Junior, Shirley and Tom are there too, as are Roman and Edna Kefren, all within a few rows of her. The rest of the churches pews are filled in on both sides, with friends and family, come to offer their help and support for the poor grieving family.

The church is small and the altar area is ornate with brass and gold colored trim around a large wooden configuration that holds the tabernacle, candles and a large statue of Jesus Christ. The men are all wearing black suits and ties and white shirts, and the women are in black dresses.

Everyone is in different stages of their grief and shock, along with the young parents, heartbroken over losing their first born, looking to Jesus and their deep faith to help carry them through this ordeal.

Father Swiley walks out of the sacristy in a long black robe with a white leather banner, with words written in latin on it, around his neck and immediately the organist begins to play slow, solemn notes and chords. Father walks to the center of the altar, his back to the people, bows his head and prays in front of the large statue of Jesus Christ. He begins talking in Latin.

"In the name of the Father, and the Son, and the Holy Spirit," he begins the Mass as he makes the sign of the cross.

Gertrude looks over the heads of the people in front of her trying to see the priest, the altar and the small white casket, and joins her fellow Catholics in prayer and responses during the Mass.

They kneel and pray, waiting for the moment when the bread and wine is transformed into the true body and blood of Christ. "Amen." Father sprinkles Holy Water on the baby's casket, then swings an elegant brass goblet containing smoking incense over and around it. The pungent aroma fills the whole church. Ashes to ashes, dust to dust.

"Amen."

Mrs. Tryzinski, the young baby's mother, weeps openly throughout much of the service. One by one, men in their dark colored suits and ties and women wearing dark colored dresses below their knees and hats with veils covering their eyes walk past the casket to receive communion.

"Amen."

Gertrude looks at Mr. And Mrs. Tryzinski, waiting in line for the Body of Christ. 'I can only begin to feel the extent of their pain,' she thinks, imagining their loss. She accepts the host the priest offers her and lays on her tongue.

"Amen," she tells him and walks around the outside of the pews in front of the whole congregation, to her seat in the back of the church.

The tiny casket is wheeled down the center aisle to the outside doors where six male members of the family pick it up and carry it to the cemetery behind the church where they hold graveside services.

After the funeral Gertrude goes back to Betty and Edwards' place, where she's been staying, her mind full of questions and thoughts, and has a hard time focusing when Betty tries talking to her.

"How are they doing?" Betty asks her, speaking of Mr. And Mrs. Tryzinski.

In her head Gertrude tries defining the words 'how' and 'doing,' and it takes her several moments to answer, "They're sad," she simply tells her.

"I can't even begin to imagine what those two must be going through," Betty tells her. "Must be the worst thing in the world, to lose a child."

"Don't worry yourself so, Betty. Don't over do it, please," Gertrude, tells her, even though her own mind and thoughts are bothering her.

Lexington Glory Days

"I can't tell you how much I appreciate you being here and helping us out this past week," Betty tells her.

"You came when I needed someone the most."

"I'm happy to do it. Anytime you need me, call, and I'll come over."

"I wish you could stay forever," Betty says, making Gertrude smile.

"I bet you do; but it's time. You're rested up now and starting to feel better, I can see that, besides, I think Peter and Brian are starting to miss me now. You need someone to come over once or twice a week for a few hours, to give you a break. Maybe I can help you with that."

"Jacobs funeral is this week too," Betty reminds her.

"That's gonna be sad too. Two funerals in two days; two young people, what's this world coming to?" Gertrude says, pondering the answer.

The lonely echo of the church bell tolls again for the second time in two days, bemoaning all to come and gather. Jacob's body is brought into the church, carried by his friends, Jigger and Junior and four of his cousins. The church is full, with many of the same people who were there yesterday.

"God needed him more than we did," Blanch tells Betty sadly, outside, in front of the fifty year old church. "We just don't know what His plans are for us."

"I guess so. It's been a sad, sad couple of days for everyone, just the same," Betty tells her, walking up three steps, to the inside of the quaint church. She dabs her finger in a fountain of Holy water and blesses herself.

Jacob's parents and family take his passing extremely hard. Not knowing for certain what all happened to him, how he died causing his death, makes it even harder. They sit through his funeral, part numb and yet all too attentive. Their minds occupied on the words of Father Swiley.

"Think not that our brother Jacob no longer exists.

Lexington Glory Days

But that he exists with God, and in our hearts, and in our memories."

When their minds are free to wonder, thoughts of their beloved, good-natured son and brother come to them and make them cry. Visions of him as a child struggling in pain with his rheumatism come to them, trying unsuccessfully so hard to run and play with the other boys.

"God has plans for all of us," Father Swiley goes on, "and part of his plan was to take Jacob home, and bring him out of his pain."

"Amen."

Betty is sitting with Edward in the middle pews behind her cousins and Jacob's parents. She leans over and tells Edward, "If this ever happened to one of our kids, I think I would wanna die." He puts his arm around her.

"Don't be sad for Jacob. The Lord has taken his pain away today," Father Swiley goes on.

"Instead, support one another, talk to one another, love one another. Go on and live your lives like Jacob would want you to. We say this in the name of the Jesus Christ our Lord."

"Amen."

"It's just so sad. His poor family, I just can't imagine," Betty tells Edward on their way home after the funeral.

"It's all a part of life and living. There's nothing you can do about it, or do to take their pain away," Edward says, trying to be helpful.

"That's right. They just gotta go through it like I did," Betty says.

Edward looks at her for a moment, wondering what she means, and thinks about when her ma died, "Yeah, that's a tough one."

He tells her.

Eugene and Sophia, Charlie and Mabel, Leonard and Anna, and Roman and Edna, local neighbors who were at the funeral, stop at the Green Lantern bar afterwards, to offer their support and comfort.

"He was a good bartender," Charlie tells them, reflecting on Jacob's life.

"Yeah, yeah, he was a good bartender," Leonard agrees, laughing with bloodshot eyes.

"He was the best," Roman tells them with a friendly smile.

"Don't forget about all the times he left," Eugene reminds them.

"He was good when he was here, but Gawd Almighty, the kid liked to take off, and go wandering without telling anybody where he was going. I'da been worried sick if he were one of my kids and did that."

"Oh, shut up for once Eugene," Roman tells him. "You always got too much to say. I'm sorry if I'm outa line everybody, but by God we just come from the boy's funeral, and sayin all that aint right. It just aint right."

All the couples are in their thirties, except for Roman and Edna who are in their sixties. They've been neighbors and friends all their lives. Roman doesn't care for Eugene most of the time, he thinks he talks too much. Charlie and Mabel Monisky are religious, Leonard Polinski likes to drink a lot; his wife Anna Polinski does not.

"I'm not trying to say anything bad about him, I liked him. Don't get me wrong," Eugene, continues, "just don't forget he still had faults, like everyone else. You's were starting to make him sound better than even he would tell you he was." He's just being realistic and honest in his own special way.

"Yeah, yeah, you always gotta be sayin something," Roman tells him disgusted and disturbed.

At home, Edward tries to think of ways to keep Betty's spirits up.

Lexington Glory Days

"There's a dance at the Pavilion next weekend, I think we oughta go," Edward tells Betty. "Get out of the house for a while."

"I don't feel like going dancing. Besides it seems wrong to go dancing right away after two funerals," Betty tells him. "It doesn't seem right."

"Well think about it," he tells her.

"Maybe we could invite a few people over to play cards and talk," she suggests.

"Not this weekend though, it'd be too soon."

"What are we gonna do this weekend?" He asks her.

"Watch the kids," she replies in a tired way, "like we always do."

Three weeks go by and Betty and Edward invite the neighbors over.

"Leonard, this is Eugene." He shouts into the phone. "Do you wanna go to the Green Lantern for a few drinks before we go over to Edward and Betty's?"

"I suppose we could," he answers. Leonard drinks at least a few cocktails everyday.

"Do you want me to pick you up, or do you want to meet me up there?"

"No, I'll just meet you there, that way I can come and go when I'm ready."

When they get there, they see Roman and Edna sitting at the bar and they sit next to them. Edna is talking to Roman.

"You remember that?" Edna asks him.

"Remember what?" He asks her.

"That gypsy who was in here a few years back! Sheesh!" She looks at the ceiling, rolling her eyes and shaking her head.

"You don't remember nothing," she tells him.

"Sometimes I think you'd forget your head."

"What? The gypsy? I remember, what about him?"

"Nothing about him, I just asked you if you

remembered him!"

"Yeah I remember him, so what?" He tells her. "That thief stole three dollars from me that time. I remember him."

Meanwhile, Sophia and Anna are on their phones at home, talking.

"I heard Betty's been depressed lately, so when we get there let's try and be in a good mood and cheer her up." Sophia and Anna conspire together.

"That's a good idea, I didn't know that. Why has she been depressed?" Anna asks her, trying to get to the root of her problem.

"The twins haven't been sleeping through the night. She's overly tired mostly I think. I don't know the whole story. I heard Gertrude was staying with her a few weeks ago to help her out."

"Poor thing, with twins I can imagine how hard it must be. Poor Gertrude's been through a lot over the past few years too, what with her pa dying and having to raise Peter."

"I know. Say, I hate to cut you off, but I have something in the oven that needs to come out. I'll talk to you later."

"Okay," Anna tells her politely. "Mm, good bye."

"What are you gonna serve for a lunch?" Edward asks Betty at home, getting ready for their company.

"I have salami, and bread and butter if they wanna make a sandwich. I'll cut up some cheese and put out crackers, and cake," she tells him.

Back at the bar, Eugene is telling Leonard, "I hear they're going to pave the highway."

The road from Lexington to the nearest town.

"I heard that. That'll be nice," Leonard, a short, balding fat man with glasses says, stumbling over his words, spit spraying from his mouth.

"They're letting bids out in a few months, so they can

Lexington Glory Days

do the work next summer and be done with it by next winter," Eugene says.

"We've come a long way in the past twenty years," Leonard says giggling, having already had a few drinks at home.

"The cars are getting better, we have better farm equipment, modern plumbing and electricity in the houses. So, paved roads are next, huh?" He looks at Eugene and gulps some of his drink.

"I guess so," Eugene says, smiling curiously at him. "In a couple of years they plan on paving the road to the East. Pretty soon we'll be able to drive up to the big city, all on paved roads."

"Boy, you aint a kiddin we come along way," Roman interrupts them.

"When I was a kid there wasn't nothin around here but trees! There weren't even any houses! First we had to cut down the trees to get the wood, then we had to build our own house. All the old settlers had to do it that way... What? Now what are you looking at me for?" He asks his wife.

"I didn't say nothin," she tells him, defensively.

"Well, you looked like you were about to," he says and smiles.

Jigger, Junior and Lily walk into the bar.

"Oh, boy!" Leonard sees them and gets excited. "Now we gotta party!" He laughs like a hyena.

"Hey Lily." He waves his drink in the air.

"What's happenin?" Lily shouts at them and giggles.

"Oh, boy," Edna says, letting her head fall in disgust. "I think we should go," she tells Roman. "That woman, my God..." she starts shaking her head, not wanting to share her thoughts on Lily.

"Go where?" Roman asks her.

"To Edward and Betty's! Did you forget we were invited over there?"

"I didn't forget. I'm not as absince...er, absent minded as you think I am."

"Is that right?" She questions him, pretending to be surprised.

"Yeah, that's right. God damn right, that's right," he tells her, and smiles, looking around at everyone.

"Yeah, that's what I said."

Jigger and Junior, both big men though Jiggers heavier, stand at the bar and order a beer and get coins for the pool table, while observing the bar room conversations.

"I'm gonna kick your ass," Jigger tells Junior kidding him, and laughs hysterically. "I'm gonna kick your ass!"

"I wanna play!" Lily tells them, pouting.

"You can play the next one," Jigger tells her and laughs. So she turns and walks over to visit with the neighbors.

"Is everyone chipper and happy?" She asks them sarcastically.

"Oh, boy, let's go," Edna says under her breath, turning to Roman. She rolls her eyes behind her head, giving her own private signal to Roman.

"Chipper and happy! Yeah, tryin!" Leonard tells Lily. "How about you?"

"I'm always chipper and happy," Lily tells him, giggling.

"We'll see you's at Betty and Edward's. We're going. We'll see ya later."

Edna announces to the bar customers.

"I should be going soon, too," Eugene says.

"I drove myself! I just about forgot!" Leonard says smiling and laughing, making Lily laugh.

"I just about forgot," he repeats as if she didn't hear him.

"Sheesh!" Edna says, turning to Roman, "Let's go."

As the guests begin to arrive at Edward and Betty's,

Lexington Glory Days

Sophia enters and says, "You have such a nice home, Betty. I wish mine looked like this," with a whimper in her voice.

"I don't know about that," Betty responds flustered yet flattered, "but thank you."

"Heavens yes. Mine's a pig sty compared to yours," Sophia tells her with a bright laugh, fully aware that everyone knows her home is cluttered and lived in, but not dirty.

"I don't know about that either," Betty smiles. "It doesn't clean it by itself, that's for sure."

Edward walks into the dining room holding four beers for his guests and one for himself, and begins passing them out.

Leonard, I know you're a brandy drinker, so I'll let you mix your own, that way you can make it as strong as you want to. Anna I'm afraid I don't know what you drink." He looks at her, waiting for her to tell him.

"Leonard can make me a brandy," she tells him politely.

"We've set up another card table, so we'll have two tables going. The winners at each table can play the next game," Betty announces happily.

"Where are the kids, Betty?" Edna asks her.

"My brother Joe and Katherine have the three older ones, and my brother Brian, and sister Gertrude came out and got the twins for the afternoon."

"Oh, how nice!" Sophia says, a little surprised.

"I'm free to baby-sit for you too, if you ever need someone," Anna tells her. Leonard and Anna have two children. "I know. Sometimes you just need a break." Anna looks at her knowing all too well what she is talking about.

"I can too," Sophia offers with a knowing smile. Eugene and Sophia have two children.

"I did, but not now," Edna laughs. "We raised our

kids. Besides, I'm getting too old for all that. All that running around..."

"Too old for what?" Roman asks her.

"Watching kids," she tells him, frustration seeping into her voice. She wonders if he's losing his hearing.

"Are the kids coming over?" Roman asks her smiling, teasing her.

"I oughta..." she doesn't finish the sentence, and raises her hand.

"I hear they're building a Ready-Mix concrete plant in town," Eugene starts telling the men. "They already put in forty foot long pilings in the ground, for the footings." According to the local paper.

"I suppose they're hoping to get the bid to supply the cement, for when they pave the highway next year," Edward suggests.

"You could be right, there," Leonard says.

Eugene goes on, "One of the bins they're putting up will hold almost nine-hundred barrels of cement. The weight between the bin and the cement's gonna be about five-hundred tons. They're also putting up bins to hold sand and gravel, which they'll mix with the cement; and a hopper to mix it all together in. Can you imagine the money it's gonna take to pay for all of that?"

"Yeah, yeah, yeah," Roman groans, "are we gonna talk or play cards?"

"Play cards!" Leonard says loudly and laughs.

"Are we ready? Whose gonna play who first? Betty asks energetically.

They all start talking at once and move to find a chair.

They play cards all afternoon, and end the day's fun with the abundant lunch Betty has prepared. "Everything was wonderful." "Perfect," they reassure her.

That evening, with the kids tucked in for the night, Betty dresses for bed in her nicest nightgown and calls

Lexington Glory Days

Edward into the bedroom. Edward sees her in her shimmering pink nightgown and moves to kiss her. She unbuttons his shirt and rubs her hands on his chest. She moves away from him, getting into bed. Edward finishes undressing and climbs in next to her. They begin caressing each other's soft bodies and soon are in the throws of long lovemaking. The first time since before the twins were born.

Part 3

The Anniversary Waltz

Later that summer, with the newly made roads completely paved all the way to the city, Mamie and Ted drive down from St. James, with their two kids, and stop at Edward and Betty's to visit.

"Are you still getting together with the neighbors for cards?" Mamie asks Edward, after hearing about their card parties.

"From time to time. Not too often," he tells her. "I get tired of seeing 'em if we play too often," he chuckles, trying to be funny.

"How's your brother Joe, Betty? I hear he got shot up pretty bad, during the war." Ted, an affable man, asks.

"Seems like he's going to the doctor for something all the time. I don't know for what, exactly," she tells him. "I think he's lucky to be alive."

"I guess Penicillin isn't the "wonder drug' they thought it was gonna be," Mamie tells them. "Everyone had such high hopes."

"If it were, all these kids wouldn't be getting the polio," Edward tells them.

"And Joe would be healthy," Betty adds.

"Kinda exciting about our sister, Blanch, and our brother Tom, both getting married next year," Mamie tells them all, especially Edward.

"I got married ten years ago, I don't know what took 'em so long." Edward says chuckling. No one else finds this humorous.

"They had to find Mr. And Mrs. Right," Mamie tells him, mumbling and snickering, trying to make a joke while smoking a cigarette.

"Time goes by fast," Ted tells them. "Sometimes the days go by slow, but the weeks, months, and years, well, that's another thing."

"We'll be married ten years next year," Betty says. "I can't believe it's been that long already."

"See what I mean?" Ted says, "time flies."

"Time flies when you're having fun," Mamie tells them and chuckles. "Betty, you's got married in 1945, right?"

"Yes, we did. I remember it like it was yesterday, too."

A few months before their tenth anniversary, Kimberly calls Betty, sensing something might be wrong.

"What's wrong, Betty?" Kimberly asks her. "You don't sound like yourself."

"I don't have anything to do besides watch the kids and cook and clean. I don't have anyone to talk to. Edward's never home since he got hired on with that road construction crew. I feel so useless. I feel like a babysitter, or somebody's maid. Sometimes I go days at a time with just talking to the kids."

"Your ten year anniversary is coming up, aren't you looking forward to that?" Kimberly asks her, surprised by her feelings.

"I don't know what's to look forward to? We probably won't do anything anyway. If, he's even home."

"You hang in there kid. Maybe Edward will surprise you with a big night out! He might, you never know. It wouldn't surprise me."

"I won't be holding my breath," Betty sighs in vain.

The day of their anniversary, Edward has arranged a baby-sitter for the kids, and takes Betty out to the pavilion, to a dance that's going on that night.

"I had no idea everybody was coming!" Betty exclaims, seeing all of her friends and family there.

"I had no idea!" She says beaming with delight.

"What a nice surprise, huh Betty?" Katherine tells her smiling, then laughing. Katherine seems to laugh after everything.

"Surprise! That's not the word for it!" Betty tells her overwhelmed with feelings.

"Happy anniversary, Betty!" Blanch greets her, stopping by with her new husband, who is lightly touching her on the shoulder.

The band begins playing the 'Anniversary Waltz,' as Edward approaches her. "Would you care to dance?" He asks her, gentlemanly, holding out his hand.

He waits, watching her as she watches him.

She takes his hand, "I'd love to," she tells him, slowly accepting the hand she knows so well.

The two walk out onto the dance floor, as more and more couples join them, leaving room enough in the center to waltz. They dance like they're floating on air, completely in sync with one another's moves.

"What a beautiful way to start the evening. Look at them, happy as can be. Like they never had a problem in the world. And look, Roman and Edna are out dancing too, isn't that adorable?" Katherine tells Joe Jr.

"How come you don't look at me like that anymore?" Edna asks Roman.

"Cause you're not twenty-nine anymore," he tells her and smiles.

"They can't take their eyes off of each other," Lily sighs, "how romantic."

"Isn't that sweet," Sophia tells Eugene, "look at

them." Eugene looks out of the corner of his eye and spots Leonard.

"Leonard looks shined up already," he tells her.

"You dance real nice!" Leonard hollers at Edward, lifting his head above the music, but Edward doesn't hear him.

"I wanna be just like that on our tenth anniversary," Kimberly tells Clay, motioning to the happy couple. "And every anniversary after that one."

Rita with her boyfriend, and Carrie with her husband, smile and nod at one another as they pass each other on the dance floor.

"Gertrude is trying to teach Peter how to waltz," Carrie giggles as she tells her husband Jeff.

"I'm glad I'm not married with five young brats," Jigger laughs, playfully, watching the dancers while standing on the side with Lily.

"That don't razz my berries."

"I don't like to dance," Larry tells his girlfriend, sitting at a table.

"How come you don't like to dance? I wish you would. I love to dance," she replies with a pout.

"Tom is here with his new bride. Junior and Shirley are unfamiliar with the waltz it seems. They're stepping on one another's toes," Blanch tells her husband with a pleasant chuckle.

"Look how happy they look," Antoinette tells Josephine, while sitting at a table with their husbands. "I'm so glad things turned around for her."

"That's Edwards' aunt over there, and that's another one," Charlie tells Mabel, motioning with a nod of his head.

"Mm, I know. A couple of his uncles are here too," she tells him.

"The 'Anniversary Waltz,' ladies and gentlemen," the singer for the band says over the microphone, as the song

Lexington Glory Days

ends.

"Let's have a nice round of applause for the anniversary couple." Suddenly the drummer accidentally kicks the bass drum, and all these thoughts are interupted.

Edward gives Betty a long kiss on the lips. The dancers applaud for the band, as well as for Betty and Edward and their anniversary.

"We're gonna pick up the tempo now. First up is "Out Behind The Barn," by Little Jimmy Dickens! Then 'Kaw Liga!' by Hank Williams. A one, a two..."

The band begins its up tempo numbers and the dancers either polka, or free style dance. Fast dancing is becoming more and more popular.

Laurie and Peter, a young couple with six kids and another one due, by the way she looks, have arrived, with two other couples, neighbors and members of the church. Steve, who sings in the choir, and JoAnn, a young couple with three kids; and John, one of the bell ringers from the church, and Judy, another young couple with two kids.

They take their time getting acclimated to the social scene, talking with others they meet and amongst themselves, and eventually find their way to the dance area. The musicians begin playing another song.

"*Kaw Liga was a wooden Indian, standing by the door....*" The front man for the band sings, as the drummer beats an Indian tempo.

"I like this song, let's go dance," Steve tells JoAnn. The other couples, John and Judy, and Laurie and Pete, follow them.

The singer, "*He fell in love with an Indian maid.... Kaw Ligaaaa...Woo!*"

"Woo!" everyone shouts, repeating him, clapping their hands, dancing faster to the beat and feeling the music.

The band plays, 'Wild Side of Life,' by Burl Ives, 'It

Wasn't God Who Made Honky Tonk Angels,' by Kitty Wells, and a new song, 'Aint That a Shame,' by Fats Domino. The crowd loves the music, and keeps dancing.

They play, 'Maybellene,' by Chuck Berry, 'Your Cheatin' Heart,' by Hank Williams, and 'The Yellow Rose of Texas,' by Ernest Tubb. A few of the dancers get tired out and go to find a chair. The band finishes their first set with 'Good Night, Sweetheart, Good Night,' and a fast song that's just come out, 'Rock Around the Clock,' by Bill Haley and his Comets, with a jazzy saxophone.

With the band on break, people use this opportunity to get another drink and visit, or use the restroom.

"That Hank Williams sure has a haunting voice sometimes," Joe Jr. tells Edward.

"Pulls right at your heartstrings don't he?" He replies.

"I like Kitty Wells," Betty tells Katherine.

"I do too," she agrees.

"I still like, 'How Much is That Doggie, in the Window...'" Sophia starts singing the song... "How much is that doggie in the window...the one with the waggy tail..." Then she begins humming the song. "Mmm Mmm."

"Sh-Boom, Sh-Boom," Leonard belts out, singing and thrusting his hips out and laughing, "sha-na-na-na-na-na-na...I like that one."

"I like the slower ones," Larry tells them. "'The Great Pretender,' 'Earth Angel.'" Larry has a peaceful way about him.

"I like 'em fast, 'Shake, Rattle and Roll,' and 'Rock Around the Clock,' Steve says, "gets me pumped up. It's crazy, man."

"We don't go out much," John says, "who can afford it? No bread." People are scattered all over the huge dance hall, talking.

"Aint that a bite?" Steve tells him, shaking his head.

"Once in a while," Judy corrects him. "Kimberly, do you see Betty very often, now that you have a family?"

"Not so much. Not as much as I'd like to sometimes."

"Why not?" Clay, a big man, asks her, in a deep baritone voice. "You can go over there if you want to, I don't mind."

"There's too much to do all the time. I cook, and clean, and watch the kids. Sometimes I help with chores. There's not enough time at the end of the day. I guess I'd rather be home, anyway. Are you two planning on starting a family?" She asks Katherine, not meaning to pry.

"A small one. We'll see how one goes first," she laughs light heartedly, and looks around, first at Joe, and then at the other faces in the crowd.

"Are you's two ever gonna get married or just keep shackin' up?" Carrie asks Rita with a little chuckle, the two walking around the dance area.

"Oh, I don't know. Don't ask me," she tells her, perplexed. "I don't know what his plans are," and holds her hands up to her ears.

"Have you's two done the nasty?" Carrie smiles and asks Rita.

"Oh, yeah. It was like trying to find a needle in the hay stack."

"What do you mean?" Carrie laughs.

"We don't know what we're doing," Rita tells her in a very nasal voice, scrunching her nose and snickering. This makes Carrie laugh again.

"Peter, you were waltzing like a pro out there," Jigger tells him. He smiles back, embarrassed. "What? Better than I could do," he tells him. "You're pretty hip for a kid."

Peter feels good about the compliment.

"Gertrude will you dance with me? For some reason no one's asking me to dance, and I feel like it," Lily asks her, rolling her arms and swinging her full hips in four or

Lexington Glory Days

five fluid motions, like a lava lamp.

"Sure, we'll go out when they get back from break."

"What do you think?" Tom asks his new wife.

"I think their all crazy," the young, polite little woman tells him. "All these people, all this noise."

"All that fast music, pop, pop, pop," Roman tells Edna snapping his fingers. "This is what the younger generation is listening to? Bunch of crap."

"I like it," Edna disagrees with him. "Ya gotta keep up with the times, so ya don't grow old!"

She purposely shouts in his ear.

"How are the kids, Pete? Got a dozen yet?" Steve asks him.

The tall blond man smiles, "nope, not yet," he says, a little embarrassed.

"I don't know how you can have six kids," John tells him. "We got two and they drive us crazy," he laughs.

"And one on the way," Pete adds. "We're good Catholics," he says with an honest smile. "Very good Catholics." He winks, and smiles again.

The band comes back from their break and the guitarist strums a few loud chords, getting the crowds attention, and begins playing another new song, 'In the Jailhouse Now.' Lily starts to sing along while smoking a cigarette, "We're in the jail house now! We're in the jail house now!" and starts laughing at the thought of it.

Leonard, out on the dance floor with Anna, slips and falls.

"What a klutz," Jigger says.

At first a painful expression crosses Leonard's face, but then he gets up laughing, "I'm okay, I'm okay." He smiles and points down at the floor.

"What a punk," Jigger says, shaking his head.

"How have you been feeling?" Edward asks Joe.

"I feel okay most of the time, as long as I take it easy," he answers him.

"How have things been going between you and Edward, lately?" Katherine asks Betty.

"He's never home," she says pointing at him. "He's always at work on road construction. There I sit all day and half the night, just me and the kids."

"At least he's making good money," she offers her.

"Boy I like this music," Leonard tells Eugene.

"I can really get out there and shake it up!" He lets out a loud, full giggle, coming off the dance floor.

"I went on road construction," Larry is telling Steve, sitting at the table with his girlfriend and a few of the others.

"There's a whole bunch of us from Lexington on the same crew," he volunteers. "Edward's on it."

"I'm gonna go get something to drink, you want anything?" Edward interrupts Betty and Katherine's conversation.

"Yeah, get me a beer," she tells him, "thank you," and winks at him.

Edward interprets her wink and smiles back, knowing what she means.

"You're gonna get lucky," Betty mouths the words silently to Edward, with a secret grin on her face.

Lily walks by smoking a weed and reads Betty's lips and walks off in a huff. 'Why won't any of the guys ask me to dance, tonight?' she wonders.

The beer flows through them like fish to water, and everyone is feeling its affects, getting buzzed and drunk.

"Hey Roman," Eugene greets him by partially raising his hand, and spilling some of his beer. They're near the bar and front door.

"We're gearing up to go home," Roman tells him.

"Home? He says loudly." "It's just gotten started!"

"This isn't for us old fuddy duddy's, this is for you younger kids," Roman tells him. He turns and looks at the crowd, "Where the hell is that wife of mine?"

"All right. I'll talk to you soon."

"Yeah," He tells him, turning away to go.

"I bought the last round, it's your turn!" Jigger is arguing with Junior.

"You punk, I bought it. You were out dancing," Junior tells him. "Didn't you notice you had a full beer when you came back?"

"I had two beers in front of me all night! I bought the last round," he says meanness seeping into his voice.

With the chatter of people talking and the music playing, Tom decides to walk up and down the dance floor along the booths where people are sitting, and suddenly feels like a stranger, not recognizing as many people as he thought he would. 'Must be a lot of people from out of town,' he thinks.

"What do you mean, I don't love you?" Rita's boyfriend asks her.

"You don't love me!" she tells him again. "You've barely spoken to me, all night!" She walks off mad.

"Wait! Rita!" He yells, running after her.

Lily who is sitting in a booth with Junior, Jigger and Shirley lights up a marijuana cigarette, takes a drag and passes it around.

Edward, Betty, Kimberly and Clay are sitting at a table with a whole group of the others, chatting. "I think I should be getting Peter home," Gertrude announces. "It's getting a little late."

Brian arrives with his fiancé and happily greets the people at the table. "How come yer's not dancing?" he asks them. "This is such a pretty song... 'There goes my only possession...there goes my everything...'" he sings along. He turns to his fiancé, Nancy, "Let's go out and dance." Some of the others pick up on his cue, and go out onto the dance floor again.

Betty and Edward get up, "I'm going to put on my prettiest nightgown for you tonight," she tells him.

"Happy anniversary," he whispers in her ear.

The next day, after church, John and Steve are talking. "Did you see Leonard in church the morning after the dance?" John asks Steve, with a peculiar smile on his face.

"His eyes looked like they were still closed. I think he was still drunk from the night before!" He tells him, suddenly laughing.

"What's everyone doing for New Year's Eve?" Steve asks him.

"We stay home. We don't go in for all that party crowd, usually," he answers.

"It's a few weeks away anyway. We'll probably just stay home."

Betty and Kimberly are out shopping in a bigger town, nearby.

"Look at that hat!" Kimberly tells Betty. "How cute. 'Happy New Year 1956'. I want one."

The women are dressed up still for the holidays, in their nicest long coats with big fur collars and scarves. It's cold, with a mild but bitter wind and it's snowing very lightly. It's been freezing cold all week.

"Lets go in someplace for a cup of coffee and a piece of pie and warm up," Betty suggests. "And get out of this cold for a while."

"Sounds good to me," Kimberly agrees.

The two get their coffee and order two pieces of apple pie and watch the people walk by, through the big window they're sitting next to.

"They have such pretty dresses in the windows," Kimberly says. "I wish I could afford some of them.

I could use a new one."

"Me too," Betty agrees, "but where would I wear it? I never go anyplace."

Kimberly finds this funny. "Me too, I'd have to wear it around the house or outside slopping the hogs," she laughs. "Clay would think I went crazy!"

"Have you told Clay you're pregnant yet?" Betty asks her sister.

"I did. He's happy about it," she says gayly. "He's not bouncing up and down about it, but he's happy. How about Edward, have you told him yet that you're pregnant? What did he say?"

"I told him. 'Oh, that's nice,' is all he said. It doesn't matter to him, I do all the work after they're born anyway. Before and after they're born."

"You think you're the only mom that does ninety-nine percent of the work? Get a grip there, Sally. You're not alone, let me tell you. Every mother I know does most of the work. How's your pie?"

"It's very good. How are your kids all doing?" Betty asks.

"Good! Growin like weeds though. My God I can remember the day I bought each of them home from the hospital. I can't believe the nineteen-fifties are just about over with, can you? My God, we'll be old ladies soon," she snickers at her.

Chapter Five

The Fire

The headline in the October issue of the 1960 local paper read, "Fire destroys family home in Lexington Township." "A fire raged thru the home of Edward and Betty Reich, consuming all of its contents, late Saturday night, local authorities reported. At approximately eight-thirty p.m. a passerby noticed the flames and reported the house was on fire, and it appeared like it was spreading rapidly. Fire trucks were dispatched out to the home, but by the time they arrived the fire had already consumed most of the building. Successful attempts were made to extinguish the remaining flames, but by that time, the entire structure had already burnt to the ground. No one was at home at the time of the fire, so no one was injured. Edward and Betty Reich and five of their seven children were out for the evening, visiting relatives. The family had left for the evening around six o'clock p.m. to visit Edward's sister, Mamie and Ted Rison and family, of St. James. All was well when they left the home. They reported having no problems earlier in the day, which would lead to the cause of the fire. Upon hearing about the fire, the Reich family immediately returned from St. James, around ten-thirty p.m., to find their home and all its belongings completely destroyed. The home and all its contents are considered a total loss."

Earlier that eventful day, while Edward is talking to Betty in their kitchen, suggests, "Let's drive up to St. James with the younger kids, to visit Mamie and Ted, and their kids."

"I suppose," Betty, agrees easily, without giving it much thought.

To Mamie and Ted's kids it feels like the country bumpkins are coming to town when their cousins visit. But it's the difference between big city inner youth meets small town country kids just the same, to both sets of cousins.

Their eventful day started out like any other for them, preparing meals, doing homework and chores around the house. The family left rather casually around six o'clock p.m. The adults were in the Rison's dining room, playing cards, smoking cigarettes, and having a few drinks, and the kids were scattered about watching TV in the living room or in one of the upstairs bedrooms with their cousins, when the phone rang. Ted got up to answer the phone and called for Edward. Edward got on the other end and listened, and grew more and more solemn and calm.

He listens, and whispers, "all right." He moves to hang up the phone. "Betty, Maimie, Ted, there's been a fire. Our home is on fire as I speak. Everyone is okay, don't worry, no one was home. The kids aren't there. The fire departments on its way out to try to extinguish the fire."

"What?" Betty whispers. "Are the kids okay?"

"The kids are all okay," Edward reassures her quickly. "Gertrude found out where they were staying and called them all to make sure."

"You're kidding," Mamie reacts, surprised.

Edward looks at Betty a little teary-eyed, "round up the kids, we need to get home."

Lexington Glory Days

He looks at them all, not knowing what else to say.

"Goodbye Edward," Maimie tells him patting his shoulder, "I'm sorry Betty. Don't worry, at least the kids are all safe," she tries giving her a smile to make her feel better. The family stands around the entrance door – waiting to leave, to see what fate had left for him or her back home.

"All my stuff!" Jack says. "Dad, will they put out the fire and save some of our things? Will we still be able to live there?" he asks him.

"I don't know yet," is all his father can tell them from the information he just received. "I don't think so son. I don't know."

"Where will we go if there's nothing left when we get there?" Bonnie wants to know. "Where will we go then?"

"I don't know." Edward tells her, losing his patients.

"It's not possible there won't be anything left. Surely they'll save some things," Theresa hopes, looking on the bright side.

With Edward and Betty and five of their seven youngest kids in tow, they arrive back home in the dark. They drive up the short driveway, fully knowing a horrible tragedy has occurred.

"There's nothing left. After years of trying to find a nice home for you's kids, there's nothing left," Betty says, in disbelief. "I guess we'll have to go on and keep looking. Our family photos, the piano, our cloths, all gone. The beautiful hardwood floors, the scenic view of the lake. It's as if our lives, previous to right now, hasn't even existed. As if we were some kind of vagabonds or migrants or hobos, arriving at a new place, with nothing to our names besides what we have on us and the clothes on our back. The place doesn't even look familiar." It makes Betty sick to look at.

Edward pulls the car up and with the lights shining on the burnt rubble instructs everyone to stay in the car.

As he gets out, Betty is sobbing and keeps repeating, "I can't believe it, I just can't believe it."

Edward talks to a couple of gentlemen who are there, a neighbor, Joe and his brother Larry. Edward walks around the burnt home, looking around for anything salvageable, and to make sure there are no more glowing ashes that could re-ignite, as if there were anything left to burn.

Larry tells Edward, "You're supposed to all go to ma and dad's they said. I talked to 'em, and they said you's should go over there."

Without a word spoken, Edward puts his hands in his pockets and returns to the car. He drives the two miles to his parent's home, where he finds everyone tired and sad.

Grandma and grandpa are busy trying to make room for seven extra people, and trying to figure out where to put them all.

"As soon as we get there I want to know the two older children are all right, and I'm going to call them," Betty tells her husband.

One by one she calls them even though it's late and nearing eleven o'clock pm. Each one is staying at a different friend's house. She knows all the parents by name, is nervous but polite when they answer. She explains quickly the situation, even though they've already heard the news of the fire. Sadness can be heard in her voice as she asks to speak to her children, and they respectfully oblige. She becomes relieved.

Somewhat comforted, knowing her older children are ok, she settles in on the task at hand; helping grandma and grandpa and Edward get blankets and sheets and pillows, and making up the sofa and even the floor, as there aren't enough beds for everyone. "We're just gonna have to make do," grandma says.

It's been a long, long day for everyone, and soon the

younger children are settling into their spots for the night, and soon sleeping. Betty wipes her eyes with a tissue, sobbing, not knowing what to do first or next. Edward tells her, "Come on upstairs," and follows her up the creaky staircase, "we can worry about it in the morning." And closes the door to the bedroom, in their new home.

Betty's relationship with her mother-in-law has always been strained, and though she doesn't know it yet, she's pregnant. Grandma, a tall and big-framed woman, becomes very strict with Betty's kids, and Mom Betty doesn't like it, but she's all but helpless in trying to change her mother-in-law's behavior.

"I'll borrow you the money, Betty, absolutely I will. A dime for a loaf of bread, a quarter for a quart of milk and fifteen cents for some butter. Fifty cents. Pay me back when you can," grandma tells her, writing down the debt on a piece of paper. Grandma writes down these small loans and fully expects her to repay it, and hands her the money. Two months go by and her bill is up to two dollars.

"Betty is pregnant with her eighth child, she just found out. Their youngest child is Frankie, he's two years old. Patrick is four; the twins, Bonnie and Jack are eight. Theresa is 10, Carol is 14, and Harold is 16. Harold quit school and moved out on his own with a friend of his, thinking it was all too cramped here." Grandma is on the phone talking in the kitchen, as Betty listens curiously, feeding Frankie at the dining room table.

"He started working for a local company that makes pool tables and ping-pong tables. He's doing fine, even with his reckless ways of fast cars and drinking," she chuckles, telling the person on the other end. "The apple didn't fall far from the tree with him," she laughs.

"Carol is their oldest daughter. She's staying with an aunt and uncle, on Betty's side, in town. She walks to school. She's doing well. She comes out on weekends to spend time with us." She continues talking.

With just Patrick and Frankie home on a school day, Edward and his dad talk of the whole family living together one afternoon in the living room. His dad begins, "I know this isn't the ideal situation for you son, but you're welcome to stay here for however long you need to. I know this eighty acre farm came up for sale, and you'd like to buy it, and I think it's a good idea."

Edward tells him, "I know it's cramped, and the kids get under ma's feet a lot, but we try to keep them from getting too out of hand." Edward says.

"They're young Edward, they're about to be mischievous and grandma doesn't really mind, it's just her way. Don't worry about it."

"I know it's hard for everybody," Edward says, "we're all tripping over everybody. The place wasn't meant to hold so many people."

"That's all right," grandpa, says, "it's just temporary, spring will soon be here and the kids can be outside more, and life will be a little easier for everybody. Grandma can get outside and get some fresh air."

Just then grandma lets out a yell from the kitchen, "put that down! You have no business playing with that!" Patrick puts the iron back on the table.

Betty is heard, "You put that back right now young man."

The two men in the living room smile a little bit at one another, and continue talking, the sun shining through the window. "Well, thank you," Edward says, "I'm not sure where we would have gone if we couldn't have come here."

"Your mother and I know how hard it can be sometimes. We're sorry for the fire, and we don't have much ourselves, but were glad to help," grandpa says looking him in the eye. "We needed help too when we first started out."

Edward gets up from his chair, analyzing where his father might be going with this and says, "I know how hard it can be. Times have been tough for a lot of people over the years, it's got a little easier for some, and some are still struggling. We were doing all right, until the fire. I can give you a little money," and pulls out his wallet and hands his dad a twenty dollar bill.

"If you don't need it, I'll take it," grandpa says, "but if you need it for the kids or Betty, you can give me some, some other time."

"Take it," Edward says, "I know there's bills to pay around here, heat, electric, water. We been buying some food for everyone, so we should be sitting fair that way." Grandpa takes the twenty-dollar bill and says, "all right then," not feeling good about it, but also trying to teach him a lesson.

Grandpa gets up from his chair and wanders into the kitchen for a glass of water. Grandma yells at him "use the glass next to the faucet, don't use a new one, I just washed that one! That's what it's there for."

Edward enters the kitchen a moment later to see what everyone is doing, and rubs up against Betty a little. She gives him a cold stare. Grandpa finishes his glass of water, in the newly washed glass, and sets it down near the sink where the other dirty dishes are waiting to be washed.

Grandma lets out a small groan. "Lloyd, we need wood for the wood stove." Lloyd looks around at the small pile and says, "I'll get some in a little bit."

"With the snow last night, looks like the drive way could use shoveling to," grandma adds, matter-of-factly. "We'll get to it," is all grandpa says.

"I need Betty to rinse some cloths in the sink, after were done with the dishes," grandma says to no one in particular, and then turns and faces Betty and adds, "and

Lexington Glory Days

I need them hung up to dry over the stove on the lines, over them pans." She makes two quick pointing gestures with her long index finger, one high and the other low.

Betty is drying the dishes and stacking them in the light colored cupboard and says simply, "all right."

"I'll get you the laundry soap, soons as were done here," grandma adds.

Betty sets the drying towel down on the counter and says, "I've just got to sit down for a few minutes, my legs are tired." She sits and bends over and begins rubbing the tops of her lower legs.

Grandma pours herself a cup of coffee from the percolator, and sits across from her, and asks her, "How are you feeling?"

"I was nauseated earlier this morning, and I keep getting these leg cramps," she tells her, "my ankles are swelled up and my feet hurt. I'm going to lie down for a while this afternoon." Looking up at Edward she says, "You'll have to watch the kids. I just have to get off my feet."

Grandma gets up from her chair and says, "Kids will be fine. There's work to be done today is what I'm worried about not getting done. Lloyd, when are you going to get that wood and clear the driveway?"

Grandpa goes over to the percolator, reaches for a cup and pours himself some coffee.

"We'll get to it. It's early yet," he tells her.

Edward says, "I'll clear the driveway, this morning, so I can watch the kids this afternoon. I'll clear a path big enough to get the car out and I'll run over to Larry's, and ask him if I can borrow his tractor and plow, and plow the rest out with his tractor and loader."

"That's fine," grandma says, "and Lloyd you make sure there's gas in our car, and by the way, how much fuel oil we got for the furnace?"

"There's plenty of fuel oil in the tank for now,"

Lexington Glory Days

grandpa states.

"Check the gas in the car and if it's low Edward can take a tank into town to fill as long as he's out," Grandma says. "How long can we run with what fuel oil we got in the tank?"

"We'll be good till toward spring," grandpa responds.

"Good," grandma says. "Betty let's get these dishes finished up."

Betty is sitting in a chair sideways leaning back with one arm on the back rest of the chair, resting and listening, and says to Edward, "if you go into town, bring me back some soda crackers for my nausea, and remember you have to watch the kids this afternoon," she tells him, raising and lowering her legs, trying to stretch them to ease the cramps.

She waits for a reaction from him but gets none. She gets up from the chair and goes into the dining room to check on Patrick – who's at the table coloring, and goes into the bedroom where Frankie is napping and watches him for a moment, then returns to the kitchen to finish drying the dishes. Without grandma talking, the place is quiet.

Edward is drinking a cup of coffee, leaning against the counter. Grandpa is sitting at the table, while grandma is trying to clean and wipe off the table. "Move your arm, Lloyd, so I can wipe the table off," grandma tells him.

Betty remembers covering Frankie with a blanket, but doesn't remember seeing it on him when she just checked on him a moment ago. "What happened to the blanket I put over Frankie, when I laid him down for his nap?" She wants to know.

"I had a blanket over him."

"It's one of the things I want you to wash out in the sink," grandma says, looking at her. "It was starting to smell like baby formula."

Lexington Glory Days

"You couldn't have left it on him till after he woke up, could you?" Betty says sternly.

"I wanted it on him."

"I've got everything I need washed in the basket," she tells her. "And it's not getting done by itself either," she adds.

Betty gives her a cold stare for a moment, when grandpa says, "you could have left it on the boy till she was ready to wash it, everything else was in the basket that needed be, it wasn't harming nothing where it was."

"I told you I need wood for the wood stove. How come nobody's doing anything I say, nothing going to get done today! We might as well all starve and freeze and wear dirty cloths till spring, is that what you all want?"

"No, that's not what we want," Edward says, taking the burnt ashes out of the stove, and scooping them into a metal five gallon bucket. "It'll all get done, don't worry, we'll do it. We just want to make sure we don't leave something else out that might needs tending to, that's all."

"It better get done, that's all I'm saying," says grandma.

Betty, looking small next to grandmas big, tall frame, finishes drying the dishes and stacks them in the cupboard. She looks at Edward and she wonders what else could be left out, that he might be thinking of. Edward takes the last of the burnt coals out of the stove and puts them in the bucket and sets the bucket by the door.

Grandma gets the laundry soap for Mom Betty to use, and says, "only use a handful of soap and mix it up good with the water when it's running, and use good hot water, and rub 'em down good." She next gets the basket of clothes and sets it on the table near the sink.

Edward starts to put his coat on and Mom Betty says, "You're going out now? Dress warm, it looks awfully cold outside."

Edward replies, "yeah, might as well get started. I'll come back in before I go anywhere," he says looking at her. He turns and walks towards the door, picks up the pail of burnt ashes and goes out into the cold day. Grandpa is still sitting at the table and grandma is making sure there are enough clothespins to hang the clothes and pans to catch the dripping water.

Betty walks towards the sink and begins to run the water and adds a handful of laundry soap and begins to stir it around with her hand. "Be careful Betty," that water can get awfully hot, grandpa warns her.

"I will grandpa," she tells him. Betty watches Edward, through the window above the sink, throw the old burnt ashes out in a snow pile and throw the empty pail toward the front door. "Looks like he's going into the shed to get a shovel," she says. "He's going to the shed for something, anyway."

"About time," comes from grandma.

"Lloyd, you just gonna just sit there all morning?"

"No, I guess not," comes his rapid reply. He gets up and walks into the living room and stares out of the window, thinking. "You know what grandma?" He says.

"What?" Grandma answers him back.

"Get Larry on the phone and tell him to come over with his tractor and loader and tell him we need the whole drive way plowed out. Looks like there's an awful lot of snow out there, and I don't know if one man with a shovel can do it all." It's hard for him to judge just how much snow is out there.

"All right, just a minute, let me finish what I'm doing first," she says loudly.

Betty is at the sink washing out some clothes, and watches Edward start shoveling; and feels a little sad and tired.

Grandpa sits down on the couch, waiting to hear

what Larry says about cleaning the driveway out. And thinks about the twenty-dollars Edward gave him, and feels bad.

Grandma comes out from digging in the cupboard and walks over to the phone and dials Larry's number. "Hello Larry? This is ma. Dad wants to know if you can come over with your tractor and clean up the snow in the driveway? Edward's out there now shoveling, but dad says it's too much for one person." ... "You can?" ... "In a little while?" ... "As soon as you can." ... "I'll tell him," she says, and hangs up the phone.

She walks halfway to where grandpa is sitting in the living room, stopping in the dining room and says, "He has it on the battery charger. He tried starting it up this morning, but it would barely turn over, so he plugged it into the battery charger about an hour ago, doesn't know if the battery is charged up enough yet, but he'll come over as soon as he gets it started and clear us out."

Grandpa nods his head up and down, acknowledging what she said.

Grandma walks around the far side of the dining room table, puts her hand on the radiator to make sure it's throwing off heat, and gives Patrick a light slap on the cheek. She trips over a toy on her way back to the kitchen, and stumbles a little, and cries, "don't leave your toys lying around Patrick, or I'll have grandpa burn them." Betty turns from the sink to see what happened, and everything appearing okay, decides to keep quiet and go on washing the soiled clothes.

"Lloyd!" Grandma hollers, "I need that wood for the stove!"

"All right, I'm going," grandpa says getting up, and walks to where all the winter coats are hung on hooks in the dining room. He picks his out, adds a hat on his head making sure the ear flaps are down, and puts on his gloves and heads for the door. "I'll be outside," he

mumbles.
Little Frankie, awakened by grandma's sudden cries, starts to whimper, but soon falls back to sleep.

Betty says, "Grandpa must be telling Edward, that Larry's going to come over to plow the driveway, they're both heading to the wood pile for some wood, I suppose." She watches the two men outside.

"We need it," grandma says.

"I know we do," Betty replies.

"What kind of vegetables you think the kids would like for supper Betty?" Grandma asks her, tired of green beans, corn, and carrots.

"Oh, how about corn," Betty tells her, "I think we had green beans last night. It looks so cold out."

Grandma starts rummaging through the canned vegetables in the cupboard and pulls out a can, "how about potatoes? Fried, baked or boiled?"

"Whatever you decide," Mom Betty tells her quickly.

"Okay" grandma says, "Don't yell at me if you don't like them." She snaps.

"Oh, I won't," Betty, tells her, dryly. "Here comes Edward and grandpa with their arms full of wood, I suppose I better go open the door for them," says Mom Betty, dropping a piece of clothing in the sink, and grabbing a towel to wipe her hands, she rushes to open the door for the men.

A large blast of cold air floods the room and in come the two men with their arms full of wood. They stack it quickly on the porch, and return outdoors for a second trip, then a third, then a fourth and then a fifth.

Betty finishes up washing the clothes in the sink between trips to open the door, let's the water go down in the drain, rinses the sink with clean water and begins rinsing the soap suds out of the clean clothes.

Grandma begins hanging the clothes on the lines near the stove, as Mom Betty finishes rinsing out each one. The two women watch the men outside near the cars. They do some shoveling around the tires, and eventually start the cars.

"You know Betty," grandma begins, "Grandpa and I aren't fussy eaters, but if your kids don't like some of the meal we make tonight, I don't think they should have anything else to eat after supper."

Betty's eyes begin to roll back into her head, and replies, "We've been buying a lot of food, and anyway, if I want to give my kids something to eat, with the food I bought, I will."

"You don't have to get like that with me, I just meant they should have to eat everything on their plate," grandma says.

"They're my kids, grandma, and I wish you wouldn't tell me how to treat them," Betty says, defending herself.

"I just thought you shouldn't let them leave good food on their plate go to waste. That's all I said. Have it your way. You always do anyway. I can't say anything without you getting mad," grandma accuses her.

She throws the clean piece of clothing down on the counter, and tells Betty, "Hang them up yourself then."

"I will," Betty tells her, matter-of-factly.

"Larry's here with the tractor and front end loader," Betty says.

"Good," grandma yells out from the porch, upset.

Chapter Six

A Cold, Cold Winter

Grandpa and Edward let a cold rush of air into the house, as they come in, Edward carrying the empty pail he carried the ashes out in. Noticing the tension in the room between the two women grandpa says, "Larry is here with his tractor, cleaning out the driveway." "We know," grandma, says, "we saw," not seeming as upset anymore. "Take your boots off at the door."

"The car is a little low on gas, so Edward's taking an empty tank to town to fill up, like you wanted ma," grandpa says.

"I didn't want nothing," grandma concedes, "It all just needs to get done is all. If I waited for you's to come up with things needing to get done, sometimes I think I'd starve and freeze to death."

"I'm just sayin," says grandpa, trying to keep peace in the family.

"Take off your boots and warm up some," grandma says to both men, "I'll make some coffee." She empties the old coffee grinds out of the percolator basket and fills it again. "How's Larry doing out there?"

Betty is busy pinning a pair of the kid's underwear on the clothesline, next to the stove and says to Edward.

"You must be freezing, you were out there a long

time," surprised at grandmas sudden amicable turn about.

"I am freezing," he tells her. "Cold to the bone."

"I'll get the coffee going, that'll warm you up some," says grandma.

"Stand by the fire for a while, let the heat warm you up," Betty tells him, and hangs another pair of kids underwear on the clothesline.

Edward rubs his hands together back and forth over the top of the hot stove while grandpa sits at the small kitchen table. Grandma sets two coffee cups on the table, one in front of grandpa and one directly across from him.

"I told Larry to move the snow as far back and out of the way as he can, in case we get a lot more snow," grandpa says.

"You should have told him to push it over on the north and west side to help block the wind," Edward tells him.

"Too late now, that's good enough for today, anyway, we get it out of the way," grandpa says.

"You'd have been out there all day shoveling," Betty tells her husband, smiling, hanging up a sock to dry.

"He wouldn't have been out there all day," grandma says, oddly laughing, "he was just gonna clear a path so the car can get out."

Grandpa gets up and moves over to the woodpile he and Edward made earlier, picks up a bigger piece and moves over to the stove. He opens the vent a little, opens the door and sets the wood on top of the burning coals inside, jiggles it a little bit, closes the door and closes the damper a little.

"It's going to be real cold today and tonight, and maybe tomorrow and tomorrow night too," grandpa instructs everyone, "we need to keep this stove going for heat, so the water pipes don't freeze. If any of you see its getting low, put some wood in 'er. Keep 'er fired up."

Lexington Glory Days

Everyone watches him.

"Edward, maybe you should think twice about going into town, if it's going to be so cold," grandma tries warning him, "why don't you just go down to the pavilion? No sense in taking any chances."

The nearest town is five miles away, but the bar and dance pavilion keeps a few grocery items in stock and also has one gas pump, just down the road.

Grandpa moves back to the small kitchen table, and sits down with his coffee cup, his coat still on, and grandma pours the two cups of coffee from the percolator. Grandpa has seemed to adjust to the weather easily.

Edward works his way from the stove to the table, and catches Mom Betty looking at him, "How is our car on gas?" She asks him.

"Good, it's over half full," he tells her. And sits down and wrestles to take his coat off.

"I could go down to the pavilion," he says, "for the gas for your car, but Betty wanted some soda crackers," he says looking at the floor.

"You stay away from that Pavilion," Betty tells him, "you know what happens when you go down there, you won't come home."

"Well we need some gas for our car, "grandma says, leaning against the countertop with her arms crossed and folded.

"Why do you need gas in your car?" Betty questions her, "you're not going anywhere. You just said it was too cold to go to town."

"Because it's low on gas and we might need it, that's all," she replies, "watch so them pans stay under them clothes to catch the dripping water," she scolds her. Not wanting to let her get the best of her.

Betty takes a few steps nearer and gives the pans a little tap with her foot, to pacify her.

"I don't see why you need gas in your car, if we need

one we can take ours, it's so blasted cold out, no one's going anyplace anyway," Betty complains, "all I need are some soda crackers for my nausea."

"It's low and I want it gassed up, I don't care where you get it from," grandma demands.

"We don't know if it's gonna get colder, or how long the cold is going to last, or if we're in for a snowstorm. I want to be prepared just in case," she says straightforward and sympathetically at the same time.

Betty hangs a pair of underwear on the clothesline and thinks about this and says reluctantly, "I guess you're right." She then turns to Edward and says sternly, "and you come right home if you go down there. You get gas, some crackers and whatever else we might need, and come right back."

"I'll come right back," he says tiredly, with a little smirk edging up at the corner of his mouth.

"I'll follow Larry home first and make sure he gets home okay I suppose." Betty looks at him with distrust in her eyes and hangs another pair of kid's socks on the clothesline.

"Don't do nothing till after we have some lunch," grandpa pipes in.

"By the time Larry finishes up plowing the driveway, and comes in and warms up some, we'll all be ready to eat something. Evelyn, what are you making for lunch?" Grandpa asks her.

"Haven't ever given it a thought yet," she tells him. "There's not much leftovers in the refrigerator. I got pork steak out for supper. Suppose I could go down the cellar and bring up two quarts of tomatoes and heat that up for everybody. We have bread and head cheese, and I can put a ring of blood sausage in a skillet. That ought to be enough for everybody. Be five of us and the two kids." Headcheese is a favorite among the Bohemian descendants.

"Better fry up some potatoes with onions in it too," grandpa says.

"Betty, finish up rinsing out those clothes, you can peel the potatoes," grandma orders her, looking inside the refrigerators freezer compartment.

Grandma heads toward the cellar door, stops at the cupboards and pulls out a bowl and continues on. Betty finishes rinsing out Frankie's blanket and hangs it on the line, and rinses eight stockings out quickly and pins them to the line. Then quickly washes the sink out with clean water.

They hear grandma coming back up the old wooden steps from the cellar, then the squeaking of the cellar door closing. The creaking of the old floorboards follows her back into the kitchen. She's holding two quarts of canned tomatoes under her arm and against the side of her stomach, and a bowl full of potatoes in her hands and sets them all down on the kitchen counter in one motion.

Patrick has become bored with his coloring, and comes and sits at the kitchen table next to his dad, puts his elbow on the table and his fist under his chin, and looks around the room. Betty smiles at him and he manages a half smile back as she finds a paring knife for peeling the potatoes and sets the potatoes in the sink and begins washing them off.

"Hi, Patrick," grandpa says.

"Hi, grandpa," he replies, sullen.

"Why so glum, son?" grandpa asks him.

"I don't know," he tells him, shrugging his shoulders. Grandpa lightly rubs his hair. "What's everyone doing?"

Edward gets up, and goes over to the coffee pot, and brings it back to the table and fills the two coffee cups on the table, leaves the pot on the table and sits back down. He looks at the boy for a moment.

"I wish I could take you with us, Patrick, I really do. But it's so cold outside and we're gonna be busy getting the drive way plowed out, and getting gas for the cars," his dad tells him.

"I wish I could take you with me."

"That's okay dad, I understand. I'll stay home. Maybe I can go next time?" He asks him, suddenly full of hope.

"Yeah, you can come along next time," he tells him understandingly.

Grandma is busy opening the jars of canned tomatoes, and emptying them into a pan, then gets the blood sausage out of the refrigerator, unwraps the paper they're in, and puts them in a hot, black cast-iron skillet with lard in it on the stove. The fast sizzling of the sausage in the hot lard sends smoke in the air.

Betty, busy peeling potatoes, turns her head toward the kitchen table and tells Patrick, "Go wake up Frankie if he's still sleeping, shake his shoulders a little until he wakes up. Wake him up slowly, don't startle or holler at him, and if he starts crying, try talking to him to get him to stop. Will you do that?" Patrick lets his head fall purposely off his fist, gets off his chair and walks out of the room.

"I wish you wouldn't go down to the pavilion," Betty tells Edward again.

"You always say you'll come right home, but you never do."

"They'll be ok, Betty," grandma tries to convince her, "if they're not back before too long, I'll drive down there, and drag them out of there myself, by their ears. You hear that Edward? Lloyd that goes for you too."

"I hear you," Edward replies knowingly.

Letting this brighten up her mood, Betty looks out the window and remarks, "looks like Larry's doing a pretty good job out there. He's got the yard looking pretty clean." There's a feeling of freedom when the car can get out.

Grandpa gets up and walks to the door, fiddles with

Lexington Glory Days

the earflaps on his hat, puts on his gloves and goes outside. He walks to where Larry is, sitting on the tractor, with Betty watching him through the window, puts his hand on the back of the seat, and pulls himself up onto the tractor hitch and talks to him for a few moments. Larry nods his head up and down, and grandpa steps down from the hitch and retraces his steps in the snow, back to the house.

Grandpa is heard coming in the porch and is soon back in the warm kitchen where he notices a sense of quiet. Grandma has put the radio on and is listening to the funeral notices. Grandpa notices the sound of the radio and stands in front of the stove to warm himself, and listens, his back to his family.

"Betty are you almost finished peeling the potatoes? Slice them into cubes for the frying pan, please when you are," grandma tells her. In silence, grandma is busy at the cook stove adjusting the heat under the canned tomatoes and blood sausage, listening to the radio.

They all listen, waiting for the broadcaster to announce another funeral notice and to see if they recognize the name. "This is the death and funeral notice of Thomas Grat of Redwing. Mr. Grat died peacefully at his home, surrounded by his family, late Tuesday night. His wife Marion, four children, and seven grandchildren survive Mr. Grat. Funeral services will be held Friday, at ten a.m. at Most Holy Sacred Church in Belle River. Visitation will be at Vicks funeral home in Belle River, Thursday evening from four pm to eight pm. Interment will be at Most Holy Sacred Church in Belle River, following the mass of the Christian burial. Mr. Grat was eighty-seven. This completes the death and funeral notices for today February 8, 1961. Stay tuned for the Catholic rosary."

Noises are heard out on the porch, and the stomping of feet and wrestling of the jacket suggests it must be

Larry. Soon a big man that takes up most of the doorway enters the kitchen. He looks like a giant.

"Stand by the stove a while," grandpa tells him, "and warm yourself up."

Grandpa walks across the small room and sits down at the table. Larry walks over to the stove, and leans over it. His big husky frame in the small kitchen makes him look like a giant. A sudden crackling is heard as grandma dumps the chopped up potatoes in the hot frying pan with lard in it.

The kitchen begins to have a strong spicy aroma as the tomatoes, blood sausage and potatoes all begin cooking on the stove.

"I'll set a cup of coffee out for you, Larry, on the table, when you're ready." Grandma tells him. "Lunch won't be ready for little while yet, so warm yourself up good. We're having blood sausage, headcheese, and stewed tomatoes."

Grandma stirs the tomatos in their own juice and moves the sausage around in the pan, and does the same with the potatoes. She speaks to the men around the table, "you's two go into the living room so Betty and I can finish making lunch and setting the table," she tells Edward and grandpa. The two men do as they're told and Mom takes the rag out of the sink, rinses it out and begins wiping off the table. She scrubs hard in two spots, trying to release her tension.

Betty steps out of the kitchen for a moment and peaks into the bedroom where baby Frankie was napping and finds Patrick entertaining him, making funny faces. Larry sits at the table, and sips his coffee, quietly.

Betty begins to get out plates and silverware as Edward calls out from the living room, "Larry, come on in here, bring your coffee with you, and get out of the women's way." Larry enjoys just letting things happen naturally around him.

Lexington Glory Days

Larry gets up smiling, walks into the living room and plops down into an easy chair. Grandpa is in the old wooden rocker and Edward's on the couch, sitting in front of the coffee table, smoking a cigarette.

"So you got all the snow moved?" Edward asks him, flicking the ashes into an ashtray. "You should pile it toward the north, to block the wind."

"I got it all pushed out of the way in the yard, and a big wide swath made to the road, along the driveway," he tells him slowly and deliberately. "Why didn't you come out and help me? You could've told me then."

"I started shoveling it, but it was too much, we thought it was best to get someone over here with the tractor," Edward tells him.

"Why, you didn't have anything to do today anyway, did you?" Larry asks seriously and joking at the same time.

"I gotta get gas for one of the cars, and a few things from the market," Edward tells him, earnestly. "Betty needs some things."

"One of the cars is empty of gas?" Larry asks.

"Pretty low, not empty. It'd make it to town, that's about all, I guess," Edward adds, ignoring the ribbing his brother tried giving him, with a smile.

"Edward's gonna follow you home, and make sure you get there ok," grandpa says, "Just in case something happens. Then he's going to go down to the pavilion for the gas and other supplies. I'm thinking of riding along with him. After lunch. Gotta be careful when it's this cold out."

"I see," Larry says, staring Edward in the eye, "maybe I'll stop down there too, I could use a few things. I'll be okay going home."

"Suit yourself," Edward tells him, thinks about it, and then adds, curiously, "how are you going to carry anything on the tractor?"

"I'll find a way," Larry says convincingly, deadpan. "I'll find a way."

The living room in the old house is sparse of knick-knacks. There's a soft, fading gray couch, a faded flowered easy chair, an old wooden rocking chair, a small coffee table, a radio as big as the cook stove, a small end table with a colorfully flowered kerosene lamp on it, and a fuel oil stove for heat.

An old clock hangs on the wall, and a picture in a frame of some horses and cows around an old barn. A big gray oval rug covers up much of the wooden slats that make up the floor, and there are yellowing shades on the windows, and dull white curtains. The room is comfortable, but bland.

"I went ice fishing the other day," Larry begins.

"Ya did? Did ya catch anything?" Edward interrupts him on purpose.

"I caught some real nice sunny's, a couple small crappies, and a couple bullheads about this long," he holds two fingers apart about eight inches apart.

"I talked to a few of the guys out there and they weren't catching much of anything either. A few here and there, nothing much with size though. I guess a week ago or so; your neighbor over here did pretty well over by the island. He said he got his limit of sunny's, pretty good size too, I guess about a pound, pound and a half. Depends what time of the day you go and where you fish if you wanna catch anything. Guess he was catching them on wax worms. Just south of the island and maybe a little east. We should try it sometime."

"We should, maybe later today even," Edward, suggests.

Grandma interrupts him with a call to the table, "come on and eat now, lunch is ready." The three men get up and walk to the kitchen, Larry continues talking about ice fishing and they sit around the table with Betty,

Lexington Glory Days

Patrick, Frankie and grandma joining them. Grandma, standing, says a few words of grace, crosses herself, and the four begin filling their plates and bowls with tomato soup, fried potatoes, blood sausage, head cheese, and bread.

"How's baby Helen?" grandma asks Larry about his young daughter.

"Good, healthy, anyway," he tells her, a man of few words sometimes.

"And the babies mother, Ruth, how is she doing?"

"Ruth is okay, tired a lot, she's not getting much sleep I guess."

"Does she have everything she needs for the baby? Diapers? Clothes? Blankets? You should tell her to bring the baby out sometime," grandma tells him.

She hasn't seen the baby since she saw her at the hospital.

"She's got everything she needs. She'll come out, when the weather warms up a bit. How are your little ones?"

"Good, Edward," says, "real good mostly," bragging.

They finish eating about a half hour later, and talk turns to getting the gas and a few supplies at the Pavilion. Soon, the men get up away from the table, get dressed in their jackets and hats and gloves. One by one, they leave the kitchen out to the porch and walk outside. Larry gets on his tractor and starts it. Edward gets into the driver side of his car, and grandpa in the passenger side.

The 1949 Ford car turns over and over, slowly, before it spins faster and finally starts. Larry puts the tractor in gear and heads down the driveway. Edward and grandpa, in the old 1949 car, follow him. They travel, at a slow pace, down the snow-covered dirt road to the Pavilion, and pull into the short, sloped driveway and park in front, next to two different old cars.

They walk up the two small steps leading to the

entryway of the pavilion, chilled to the bone, and all three men walk into the bar.

Chapter Seven

Times Gone By

The three big men enter the old pavilion, with its long dark bar and four legged metal bar stools with black padding, all along the east wall, facing the lake. There are a handful of small square tables with chairs around them. They leave their heavy winter coats on and sit in stools nearest the door, next to two older gentlemen sitting two stools further down. Hubert, the sixty-five year old bartender and owner, nods at each of them and greets them by name. "Lloyd, Edward, Larry, what can I get ya's?" he asks. His wide, happy smile belying the brown false teeth behind it.

"Hi there smiley!" Edward tells him. "We just come down for some gas for the car and soda crackers for ma, she's gotta a little upset stomach, but I suppose you can set us up each one. I'll get it." He reaches into a pocket in his dungarees, pulls out six dimes and slides them on the bar. "How are things down here?" He asks friendly.

Hubert pours them each a beer from the tap and sets it in front of them. There's a calendar on the wall that reads February 1961. "Fine as can be," Hubert tells him, smiling.

The two gentlemen dressed for the cold, sitting down from them, lean back in their stools and eye the three men up. "Hey there Lloyd," one says in a high-pitched voice.

"Hey Joe, how's it going?"

Lloyd replies, inquiring.

"Fish aint bitin," is all he says, a man of few words.

Joe's lived in this area longer than anyone can remember, even the old timers, and lives along the lake around the other side. You can see him spring, summer and fall, in sleet, rain and sun out in his boat, fishing, every day.

"Edward," Hubert tells him with compassion in his voice, "people been bringing in clothes and food for your family. They're all in some boxes and bags, over in the corner, by the door. A few of them got to talking, I guess, and thought you's could use a few extra things. Can't tell you who bought what, but it's all right there."

Lloyd and his two sons look back and to their left toward the door and see a pile of bags and boxes almost four feet high and that much around, sitting in the corner.

"No kidding," Lloyd says, "I'll be damned. You mean people brought all that in for us?" turning serious. "Aint that nice. Aint that nice Edward?" He repeats himself, surprised at the generosity.

Edward remarks, "We can use it. Money's tight. Just getting a little from unemployment like I do. It'll come in handy. Nice of people to do that, real nice."

"What's all in there?" Larry wants to know, looking back, curious.

"Food and clothes, like I said," Hubert tells him with a cross look on his face, wondering what he didn't understand the first time he told him, while still bearing a big wide smile.

"Food and clothes," Larry repeats him, "food and clothes."

"No sense in looking through em' till we get home," Edward remarks, "then Betty and ma can sort through it."

"Maybe there's soda crackers like Betty wanted in there," Lloyd says. "Larry, look in there and see if you can see any soda crackers."

Larry takes a drink of his beer, gets up, and takes a few steps and starts looking in the bags and boxes, without saying a word. Lloyd and Edward turn and look towards the bar again.

There are two small windows six feet in front of them that look out at the frozen lake, and the fish houses that have assembled out on the ice. Snowflakes have started to come down. Behind the bar are pickled gizzards and pickled eggs in a large jar, and bags of potato chips and peanuts, candy bars and gum sitting on a small three-tiered, wooden shelf, next to an old cash register. On the far side of the bar is a large chest freezer and four shelves of store items, toilet paper, canned vegetables, and canned soups, flour, and bread among other items.

"Sorry about the fire, Edward," Hubert tells him as sincerely as he can, putting his hands over Edward's hands. "Real sorry."

"Me too, Edward, sorry about the fire," Joe says shaking his head, and chewing on a piece of pickled gizzard. "Terrible thing."

"Thank you," Edward says.

"Terrible thing a fire," Joe's friend adds, looking at Joe.

"Nobody got hurt, that's the important thing." Edward tells them. "We been stayin with my folks. This is my dad, here," he points to Lloyd.

"I know your dad," Joe says, not bothering to turn to look at him.

Joe's friend asks, "What was the last name? I'm not from around here."

"Reich," Edward tells him. "Edward Reich," extending his hand out.

"Reich," the gentleman repeats, "how do you spell

that?"

"R-e-i-c-h," Edward tells him.

"Okay," the man says, thinking. "Edward Reich...Okay...I'm Roy Vleer, from out by Belle River way." He extends his arm and the two men shake hands.

Edward says, "Good to know ya. This is my dad, Lloyd, and my brother Larry," he points back at the two with his thumb. Roy and Lloyd look at each other and nod. Both say, "Hi," and "how do you do?"

Larry keeps sifting through the bags and boxes of clothes and food.

"I see the dance hall is closed off when it's not being used. They divide the bar and dance hall off with cut pieces of plywood hung from the ceiling," grandpa notices and tells everybody.

"No sense in trying to heat the whole place," Hubert tries telling him convincingly as if he were pleading with him. "The bar can be heated with this small woodstove," he tells him."

"That's a good idea," Edward responds positively, "Why heat the whole place if you don't have to?"

"Well that's what I thought," Hubert tells him.

"Look at that glass cooler in the corner, 'Drink Coke,'" grandpa says quietly, "wrote in red letters."

"Inside I have some packages of bacon, hamburger, and pork sausage, along with quarts of milk, butter and egg's, a few essentials," Hubert tells him, hearing him talk about it, his smile gone now. "Just got it put in a few days ago. On the other side I got bottles of Mountain Dew, Coke, Pepsi, orange crush, and grape soda, and twelve packs of beer on the bottom," Hubert adds.

Behind the bar is a sign that says, "No spitting on the floor," and spittoons are scattered about every other barstool. Roy, takes a tin of Copenhagen out, takes a pinch of the tobacco out with his thumb and index finger and pushes it between his cheek and gum.

Lloyd tells Roy, "I recognize the name. I'm from that direction myself, over near Belle River." Roy nods and says, "Mmm." Busy chewing his tobacco.

Larry comes back to the bar, sits down, finishes his beer and orders another. He reaches in his pocket for change and drops it on the bar.

"Any soda crackers?" Lloyd asks him.

"Yeah, there's some in there," Larry responds, in his low voice.

"There is?" Edward states, "I'll be damned."

The old bar smells of stale beer, cigarettes and smoke from the wood and the wood stove, and the odor inside of the old wood floor, walls and ceiling.

"Maybe we should have a shot," Edward says, looking at his dad and Larry.

"You want a shot of something?"

"Hubert, get us three a shot of brandy, take it out of the change I got here," Larry says motioning to his pile of pennies, nickels, dimes and quarters.

"All right, three shots coming up," he looks at them, his smile returning to his face. Efficiently he gets three shot glasses in front of each of the gentleman, pulls a bottle from the rack below him, and fills each glass equally up to the brim, smiling the whole time. "Ninety cents," he tells Larry, counting out the money on the bar. "Twenty-five, thirty, forty, fifty, seventy-five, eighty-five, ninety. Thank you."

He stretches out the word 'you' to sound, yeewww.

The three gentlemen take a sip of their brandy, and begin talking about what's on television with Joe and Roy, while they watch and listen to the portable black and white TV set up towards the ceiling on a corner shelf near the door.

"I seen Milton Berle, Arthur Godfrey and Lucille Ball on the Ed Sullivan show last week," grandpa tells them.

They remark about enjoying listening to the banter.

Lexington Glory Days

"What they don't come up with," grandpa continues, "I like watching it. I don't know who these people are, or why they're on. They're all just on the television I guess. Just to be on. Like a job I suppose. I like that Milton Berle though, what a rascal he seems like. Dressing up like a woman, he comes out. Ugliest woman I ever saw. Ugly! Damn near pissed myself, I laughed so."

"I like Ed Sullivan," Larry says clearly and slowly in his low voice, "he has people on his show, that have their own TV shows. You get to see what they're like besides what they do on their own shows."

"I like that too," Edward says, "You get to see them how they are in real life, and not made up all the time."

"Get us three more beers," Larry tells Hubert.

"I'll get this one, Larry," his dad tells him, reaching in his back pocket for his wallet. "Doesn't take long for the money to disappear, does it?"

"What do you think of Elvis Presley?" Larry inquires.

"Never heard of him," grandpa tells him.

"Yes, you have," Edward tells him. "We've seen him on TV. Nice voice, but you didn't like the way he uses it. He sings too fast! All this new music, fast, fast, fast." Edward says mocking his dad. "I don't like some of it myself."

"I agree with you. It's not good music like we're used to hearing on the radio."

"'The Red River Valley,' now there is a song!" Roy says hitting the tip of his index finger hard on the bar.

"All those good old songs," Hubert says smiling, "The log train," he starts singing. "'Sweatin' and swearin' all day long, shoutin, 'git up there oxen, keep movin along. Load'er up boys cause it looks like rain. I've got get rollin, this old log train,'" he keeps singing the last few words and smiles, "Hank Williams," he tells them brightly, laughing, taking a few steps backwards.

"All them old songs tell a story," Joe says.

"Not like today," Lloyd interrupts him, "today it's all, jibber, jibber, love you baby, love you baby." He says loudly and twists in his chair, with a look of disgust on his face, "it's all crap," and looks away.

"Not to change the subject or seem foolish, but Dwight Eisenhower's still president, isn't he?" Roy questions them.

"Yes he is. It's his second term and last year in office," Larry looks at him questioningly. "Nixon, Kennedy and Humphrey want the job now."

"Franklin Roosevelt, now there was a president," Lloyd says affectionately.

"We'll be in another war yet," Edward predicts. "The Russians want to take over the world. They got the big bomb now and we can't trust them. We can't trust them!" he says slamming his fist hard down on the bar, the brandy and beer starting to have its affect on him.

Bombs are going off in his head, flashbacks from the war.

"Settle down," Larry tells him calmly.

"Do you trust him?" Edward asks mad.

"I didn't say nothing," Larry tells him, staying calm.

"You must have meant something!" Edward remarks, still mad.

"I didn't say nothing," he repeats.

"All right then, you agree with me! We can't trust em," Edward says, his voice settling down, his face turning red.

Roy, put off by the sudden anger in the room, decides to leave. Slips his jacket on, and stops for a moment to tell Edward, "I'm sorry your house burned down, Edward, I hope things work out for you and your family."

"Thank you," Edward tells him, still red in the face from anger, "thank you, Roy..." Roy pats him on the shoulder, turns and nods to Larry and the bartender and walks to leave. Edward turns and watches him for a moment and notices the boxes and bags of food and clothing in the corner and thinks of Betty.

Grandma and Betty, back at the house are both separately wondering what the men are up to, even though they both have a good idea and are correct in it.

"I haven't laid down yet, like I wanted to, and the youngest one Frankie is full of energy and wants attention. I wish Edward and grandpa would come home."

"You'll be all right Betty, just sit with them. If they're not home soon I'll call down there and talk to grandpa. He needs to be getting home anyway."

Betty sits in the wooden rocking chair in the living room to keep an eye on Frankie, as he crawls around. "Frankie, I don't want to have to holler at you when you crawl out of my sight to get you to come back," she tells him uselessly. She gets up and gets him and brings him back into the living room where she can keep an eye on him, and every ten minutes later repeats the exercise. "Why can't you be like Patrick and play nice and quietly with a toy tractor between the living and dining room here, where I can see you?" she talks sweetly to him.

"Frankie, you can play with me, if you want to," Patrick kindly offers him.

Grandma, after washing and drying the lunch dishes is working around the kitchen, wiping off the table and the countertops. She puts wood in the wood stove, and takes the freshly dried clothes and blankets off the line that Betty had hung earlier in the day.

"I'm gonna lay the clean blankets and clothes in a basket and put them on a chair around the dining room table," she tells Betty, "they're there whenever you wanna do something with them. They're your things."

"Okay," she tells her lacklusterly, rocking in the old wooden chair.

Grandma thinks about driving down to the pavilion

and pull the men out of the bar by their ears, or maybe have a beer with them, she's not sure which she'd rather do. She's considering doing both, equally.

Larry gets up from his stool and announces he's going to take a few of the bags and boxes out to the car.

"Fill up the empty gas tank for the car while you're out there," Edward tells him. "As long as you're going outside, I mean."

"All right," he responds, without emotion in his voice.

"It's in the trunk." Edward adds, yelling after him.

Hubert walks over to the end of the bar near the door and flips the switch on to the gas pump, located on the wall.

"Why don't you just put it right in the car?" Grandpa suggests, getting up and walking to the door to tell Larry.

Grandpa opens the door and yells after him.

"You gentlemen want another beer?" Hubert asks them, smiling.

"What do you think, should we have another one?" Edward asks his dad.

"Set us up," Lloyd tells him, "one more, get Larry too. I'll pay for it."

"Coming up," Hubert says, quickly moving his big frame.

"Tell me what the gas comes to, and add it on."

"Okaayy," Hubert says to him, stretching out the syllables. He looks out of the two small windows at Larry and the gas pump. "Larry's not done filling the tank," he says and waits. A minute later he says, "two and a quarter for the gas," and flips the switch to the gas pump in the other direction. He sets the three men up each a beer. "Two dollars eighty-five cents," he says with a smile.

Lloyd hands him three-one dollar bills and Hubert gets him change. "Thank yeewww,' he stretches the syllables out.

Larry comes in from outside a few minutes later,

grabs one of the boxes of food that was donated to them from the corner, stacks it on top of another one, and takes them outside to the car.

By now Edward has settled down some, but the adrenaline is still running through his veins. "People make me so mad sometimes," he says, laughing a little to release his tension. "That ever happened to you, Hubert? People ever make you mad?"

"Once in a while," he states, smiling, "Not too often."

"You gotta just go with it Edward, let it out of your system and get over it. That's all. Let it out of your system, and get over it," his dad tells him again.

"I suppose," Edward says quietly.

Joe decides it's time for him to go and walks out without saying a word.

"Goin fishing, now Joe?" Hubert calls after him, smiling.

He stops and turns, looking at Hubert, zipping up his winter jacket, "Maybe later. Stop at home first and see what the Mrs. is doing," he tells him.

"Okayyy, thank yeww," Hubert tells him, smiling.

Larry comes back in and sits down on the stool he occupied before, and takes a drink of the beer set up in front of him. "Who bought this? He asks.

"I did," Lloyd tells him, picking up his glass and taking a drink of his beer.

"I suppose we better go after this one," Edward says and tips the mug of beer up to his lips and takes a drink.

"Be a good idea," Lloyd says, "we got the gas and crackers we came down for. I want to split some wood for the woodstove this afternoon yet, before it gets dark out, so we have plenty. Gotta keep up with it or we'll get low and I'll be out there splittin all day long someday. Larry, how you doing on wood?"

"I'm doing good," he tells him. "I cut a dead tree down last fall after road construction got over with, and I cut it up and split most of it then too. I should have some left over for next winter even. I got a couple more dead ones that need to come down. Maybe I'll drop them this winter yet."

"If you need or want any help, let me know," Edward tells him sincerely, "we could maybe drop 'em and cut them up yet this winter, I'll help ya if ya want. I don't know, maybe you don't want help. I don't know." Unexplainably, he starts laughing, thinking this is funny. Larry's calm ways makes him a little nervous.

"I'll think about it," Larry tells him. "I am gonna drop one this winter, I know that. You can help with that if you want. I'll think about cutting them up after we get them down."

"Well boys, drink up. Larry, we'll follow you home, and make sure you get there all right," grandpa says looking above the door at the clock on the wall.

"All right," Larry says, "I'm ready."

The three drink up, say their thanks to Hubert, zip up their heavy winter jackets and put on their gloves, grab the remaining boxes of food and bags of clothes and go on their way.

Hubert wipes down the bar and the little mess the men made. He goes to the corner where the bags and boxes of food and clothes were, and straightens out the empty cases of beer there and looks around for anything that might have dropped out. He goes back behind the bar, peers out the little windows and watches Larry as he's plugging along up the hill of the driveway on his tractor, and Lloyd and Edward in the old car, not far behind him. He notices how overcast and dreary it is outside. He brings his attention back inside the bar, 'be a quiet afternoon,' he mumbles to nobody, looking down towards the old wood floor.

The men go chugging down the frozen dirt road to Larry's, about two miles away. The inside of the windshield on the dark-colored car starts to fog up and Edward turns the fan on high even though there's only cold air coming out of it.

"Larry's bundled up good, has the earflaps folded down out from the inside of his hat. With his big winter jacket on he looks huge, even from some distance away," Lloyd notices and tells Edward.

"He's a big guy, that's for sure."

Edward says, driving his dads car.

The two men in the car keep their eyes on the road ahead and Larry in the tractor. They soon pass their house. Both men look in the driveway, "did a good job," Lloyd says.

As they pass each neighbor's home, like clockwork, both men turn their heads and look in the other driveways to see if they've been plowed out. Soon they're nearing Larry's place, and their eyes turn to his house in the near distance, the yard and its outbuildings, and whether there's smoke coming out of the chimney.

Lots of families are related out here in these houses.

The road ahead gets bumpy and Larry starts bouncing up and down in his tractor seat. He's almost at his driveway and Edward lets more room get in between the two vehicles, following at a longer distance.

Larry pulls into his driveway, still bouncing up and down, and speeds up the tractor. Lloyd and Edward pull in behind him and park next to the house and wait while Larry parks the tractor in a shed with no door, out of the wind, and away from where snow could bury it.

A minute later Larry comes strolling up to the car and knocks on the driver side window with his knuckle. "Come on in," he yells at them, behind the closed window. He waits outside for their response, and a moment later the two men reach for their door handles and open the doors and get out.

Larry leads them to the house and goes inside, where

immediately he sits down on a small stool in front of the door to an old cast iron woodstove, with his jacket still on and starts adding wood to the woodstove in the small, dank and dark kitchen.

"Sit down," he tells them. "Turn a light on."

He forgot to open the damper vent on the stove, and smoke starts filling up the cramped kitchen from the open fire door.

"Dammit," he says softly, and reaches up to turn the flap on the chimney pipe.

His face is getting hot from the smoke and heat.

"The rooms in your house are small." Lloyd tells him. "You gotta kitchen, bedroom and living room on the lower level and two bedrooms upstairs, but it's small." Lloyd finds this interesting.

"It's all I need," he tells him, not in the least offended. Larry has a young daughter, but her and her mother live in town.

He walks to the refrigerator and takes out three bottles of beer, and sets one each in front of where Edward and Lloyd are sitting, and one for himself. He walks back to the refrigerator, opens the freezer compartment and takes out a pint of brandy and passes the bottle to Edward. Edward removes the cap, takes a swig and hands it to his dad. Lloyd takes a swig and hands it off to Larry, and Larry takes a big swallow. The men crack their beers with the bottle opener that's lying on the small white laminated table. Each takes a drink, and washes down the brown, strong burning brandy.

The room lacks of light, and the three men are almost in the dark. Larry pulls on a string attached to a small round fluorescent light bulb on the ceiling and a dim gray light permeates around the small room, allowing the cracked plaster on the walls to show through, and the cupboards to appear. Everything looks darker than what it should, becoming a pale yellow. Smoke still hangs in

Lexington Glory Days

the air from the closed off damper and woodstove. Larry looks like a giant in the small kitchen.

"I better call ma," Lloyd says tentatively. He gets up, complaining his stomach is cramping and moves over to the phone hanging on the wall, picks up the receiver and dials his number. Grandma answers right away.

"We're at Larry's now, how are things going over there?"

Larry looks at Edward and asks, "heard anything lately from Rita?"

"Yeah I did. They stopped in a few weeks ago for a bit, her and Bill," her husband. "Weren't up to too much, just drove down for the day I guess."

"How about Mamie?"

"Not since the fire last fall," he tells him, "No, not since the fire."

Lloyd raises his voice momentarily and starts defending himself. "We haven't been gone that long. We'll be home soon."

Edward continues talking to Larry, "Rita and Bill were at Carrie and Jeff's a little while back. Just out bumming around for the day I guess. Spent a couple of hours over there, and then they came over to our place for a couple hours, then went back home, I guess... Had a nice visit with them. They're fine; working, both of them," Edward tells him.

Lloyd gets off the phone. "Talk to Ruth?" Lloyd asks his son about his girlfriend. Grandma, over the phone, made him ask.

"We talk all the time. She doesn't want to move to the country." He tells him, anticipating his train of thought.

"What about Helen?" His daughter.

"I stop in and see her all the time too," Larry tells him.

A few moments go by and Lloyd says, "Well Larry, thanks for plowing up the driveway, you done a good job on it, but I think we better be getting back. Ma's worried about us, and I still want to split some wood yet today, that is if my belly don't quit acting up."

"I'm ready," Edward, tells him, finishing the last of his beer.

The big dark car looks out of place next to the house with all the white snow piled up. They drive the short distance back home, and each grab a box and some bags out of the car, and take them into the house, and come back out for a second and then a third trip.

"What's all this?" Grandma asks them.

"People's been leaving stuff for us at the pavilion, food and clothes," Lloyd tells her. He sets another box down on the floor.

"What people? Who?" She wants to know.

"Hubert didn't say, just that some people thought we could use a few extra things. For Edward and Betty and the kids, because of the fire," he explains.

"We don't need no people's charity, Lloyd," she tells him. "But tell him to thank the people for us anyway."

"You don't want it?" Lloyd asks her, not believing her.

"All right. Just leave it," she tells him, "be rude to take it back."

Patrick, the curious four-year-old, comes into the kitchen to greet his father. "Hi dad," he says smiling. Edward picks up his son and tosses him in the air, "Hi Patrick, how are you boy?" His dad asks him.

"I'm good, dad, I've been playing farm with my tractor. I got it set up so the house is over there, see?" Pointing near the dining room window, "and the field is all under the table, see?" pointing to the rug underneath the dining room table.

"That's a lot of land to be farming, how far along are you?"

"I got it all planted, I had to do some work on the

tractor for a while," he says becoming serious. "The tractor broke down."

"That happens," his dad tells him smiling.

"Did you get the gas for the car?" grandma asks him.

"Yep, we did," Edward, says smiling, enjoying this time with his son, "we sure did. Patrick, where's your mom?"

"In the living room, watching Frankie," his son tells him.

"Tell her to come in here, we got something for her."

"What do you got dad?" Patrick asks him, happy to see him.

"I said go tell her..." His dad says smiling, raising his hand, pretending he's about to whack the boy on the butt.

"Okay," Patrick says smiling, running into the living room. "Mom, dad says to come into the kitchen, he's got something for you." They can hear him tell her. A minute later Betty walks into the kitchen holding Frankie. "What's going on, what do you have?"

"Look, people left clothes and food at the pavilion for us," Edward tells her.

"What people? Who?" She wants to know, confused.

"Don't know who exactly, Hubert didn't say, just people," Edward tells her, "look at it all. Mighty nice of people."

"Oh, my word," Betty says in disbelief, "that's all food and clothes? You got a be kidding!" She says smiling. "Let me see," and sets Frankie down, and starts looking in the bags.

"Betty let's take them into the living room and sit and look through them after supper," grandma tells her. "I'm gonna take the food out now and set it all out on the table and put it away."

Betty says, "okay," but keeps looking anyway. "I'll help you," she tells her, but instead picks up a bag of clothes and takes them into the living room.

Lexington Glory Days

Lloyd walks into the bedroom and lies on the bed for a nap and Edward grabs a bag of clothes, enters the living room and sits in the easy chair. He sees from the window, the yellow school bus gaining speed past the driveway, and thinks, 'it must be four clock.'

A few minutes later Jack and Bonnie, the twins, and Theresa and Carol enter the house. They're happy to see Carol, who's been staying with an aunt and uncle in town. The three girls walk into the living room, and Theresa and Bonnie go straight upstairs to their room. Carol stops and kisses her dad on the cheek. "Hi daddy, I'm home."

"Hi sweetheart, it's sure nice to see you," her dad tells her affectionately, "how have you been? Sit down for a while."

"I'm good daddy. I missed you," Carol tells him.

"I missed you too. Is everything okay at school and at your aunt and uncles? Tell me if it's not and we'll help make it better."

"It's all good daddy, I'm getting good grades. I like being in town, I like it a lot. I live close to my friends."

"It's not forever, now remember, we want you home with us as soon as we can," her dad tells her.

"I know, I miss everyone too," she tells him.

"And everyone misses you too," he tells her.

"I'm gonna go upstairs with Theresa and Bonnie now," she says. "I'll see you later," and kisses him on the cheek.

"Okay, sweetheart," he says and chuckles.

Betty brings more bags of clothes into the living room. Having heard Carol and part of their conversation, she tells her husband, "I can't wait till she's home for good. I worry about her constantly."

"I know you do, she seems fine though, and says everything is going good," he tries to reassure her.

"I know I still worry though. At least it'll be nice to have her home for a few days again, I guess," she tells him, seeming frustrated.

The upstairs bedrooms are small and drafty. The old worn linoleum on the floors is cracked in places and there's fading flowered wallpaper hung on the walls.

The three girls are in one bedroom.

Betty walks up the narrow staircase and follows the sound of laughter to where her girls are and her mood brightens. She is smiling when she enters the room, and sits down on the bed. She listens and watches the girls. They are especially happy because Carol's home for the weekend.

Carol sits on the bed next to her mother and puts her arm around her, and lays her head on her shoulder. "I miss you," she tells her mom.

Betty kisses her forehead, "I love you," she tells her.

Theresa and Bonnie are sitting on the bed playing, their knees knocking into the other ones and back and forth, giggling. "Roll, roll, roll the boat, gently down the stream," Bonnie sings. "Merrily, merrily, merrily, merrily, life is but a dream," Theresa sings, playing the game. Bonnie begins the verse again, and Theresa jumps in when Bonnie finishes with her verse, and the two go round and round, stopping to giggle.

Betty and Carol begin to rock back and forth, holding each other, and begin to sing along slowly. "Roll, roll, roll the boat, gently down the stream..." The four smile and sing. The two younger ones soon lose interest and begin to make funny faces at each other.

"You two are being silly," their mom, tells them, smiling, putting her hand on their knees, and gives them a loving rub. The two small girls look at each other and begin smiling.

"Silly!" Bonnie shouts. "I'll show you silly, and stands on the bed and begins to dance around, waving her arms and legs in the air and starts singing, and spins around and falls, showing off. The other three laugh at the girl's antics.

"Some nice people gave us some clothes," Betty tells the girls, "I don't know what's all in the bags yet, but I hope there's something for everyone."

"New clothes! New clothes!" The two girls start chanting.

"We'll look through them in the living room after supper together, okay?" Betty tells them, standing.

"Yeah!!!" The girls scream. She leans over and gives each one of the three young girls a peck on the cheek and tells each of them, "I love you."

"We love you too," they tell her.

"I'm going downstairs now, don't stay up here too long," she tells them, "Supper will be ready soon. I'll call you when it's time to eat."

"Okay," they tell her, happy to be done with school for the week.

Up from his nap grandpa complains, "My stomach just doesn't feel right. I got an ache in there. Hope I'm not gettin an ulcer."

"Did you eat something that didn't agree with you at Larry's or the Pavilion? Or drink something?" Grandma questions him.

She asks Edward, "How do you feel?"

"I feel all right," he tells her.

She calls Larry and asks him. He feels fine as well.

Betty is putting the food grandma has set on the table from the neighbors in cupboards and is feeling fortunate, with Carol home now.

"Jack came home from school and changed clothes and turned around and went back outside and started splitting wood from the woodpile," she tells Lloyd, trying to get his mind off his pain, and trying to judge it's intensity.

Grandma is worried. Betty can tell by the way she's acting, and doesn't know what to say or do. She keeps an eye on Lloyd sitting at the table, while putting the food away. "Poor, grandpa. The shooting pain comes and goes. The color in his face is getting more and more pale, I think he should go see the doctor. He doesn't look good at all."

"Not yet, Betty. I'm not sold on the idea of doctors anyway. I want him to eat something first and I'll bring him a glass of milk." She quickly starts to prepare supper. She moves around the kitchen carelessly, her big frame opening and slamming cupboards, starts the stove and slides frying pans on the burners. "Betty, I'm gonna go get potatoes, will you peel them for me?" She asks her nervously. She didn't mean it as a question.

"Yes, I'll peel them," she responds quietly, worried about grandpa.

Grandma walks hard going down the steps, and soon her stomps can be heard coming back up, and sets the bowl of potatoes in the sink. She leans over and looks Lloyd close in the face, "How are you feeling, Lloyd?" She asks him.

"Not too good," he strains to tell her, "Cramps are comin and goin. I feel lightheaded I think, like I could pass out."

"Stay sit up by the table," she tells him, "we'll get some food in you just as quick as we can make it. Stay sit up."

Quickly the two women fry pork chops, open cans of vegetables, peel potatoes and boil water. A few minutes later grandma sets a plate with a pork chop and green beans, and a slice of bread on it, in front of Lloyd, "Now eat," she tells him. "Take your time, eat as much as you can."

His hands are shaking, but he maneuvers the knife and fork and manages to cut the meat, and starts feeding himself.

Betty goes around and sets the dining room table for

Lexington Glory Days

the rest of the family. "How's dad?" Edward asks her, coming in from the living room.

She stops and looks off into the distance, and says with a small grimace on her face, "well he's eating. I don't think he feels better though," turning to look at him. "I think you should take him to the doctor."

Smelling the food cooking, the girls come down from upstairs, laughing and giggling. All three sit on the fading gray coach in the dimly lit living room colored orange from the faded out yellow lampshades. They continue to talk and joke with each other, and now with their two younger brothers. "Hi, Frankie," Carol smiles and tells the baby. "Hi..." she sings this and waves to him. Frankie smiles back and flaps his arms at her. "Come here," she slaps her hands together once and Frankie giggles and starts crawling on the rug to her. Patrick comes over to the couch and tries to sit on Theresa, but she raises her leg and he falls on Bonnie, and the two start wrestling.

"I've had enough," grandpa announces. He pushes the plate away, cramps up in the middle of getting up, and walks slowly into the bedroom to lie down, holding his stomach. Grandma finishes boiling the rest of the potatoes and tells Mom Betty to call the family around the table, suppers just about ready.

The family comes and seats themselves around the table and Betty and grandma finish setting the bowls of food in the center. Mom Betty tells everyone to cross themselves and begins to say grace, "thank you, oh Lord, for these thy gifts, which we are about to receive, through Christ our Lord, amen." Everyone quietly says, "amen," crosses him or herself, and digs in. Grandma puts bread on the table, and sits down to join them.

Betty picks Frankie up, sits him on her lap, as she sits down.

Patrick's all talk about his day of farming on the dining room rug today. Bonnie tells him about her day at school. "You two, shush, eat," Betty tells them.

"We had a test in math today, I don't think I did very well," Bonnie announces. "It was hard!"

Hearing this, Betty says, "I want you to bring your math books home, if you haven't already, and I want to see you studying."

"But mom, it's too hard," she recants.

"That's why you need to study it, so it isn't so hard," she tells her. Betty feeds Frankie mashed potatoes and mashed green beans from her plate, and eats some herself. The boy's hungry and doesn't fuss.

Jack says, "dad I split a bunch of wood after I came home from school, that should last us for a few more days, I think."

"There's gas that's in a gas tank in grandpa's car. Pour it in the gas tank in our car, would you?" his dad asks him.

"Yeah, I can do that; is there a funnel around someplace?" he asks.

"There's one hanging on the wall in the shed," he tells him, passing him the plate of pork chops.

"I thought you bought the gas for our car!" grandma says, abruptly.

"We already put gas in your car," Edward tells her, "pass the potatoes and gravy. We took your car to the pavilion and put gas in down there."

Carol tells Theresa about meeting her friends after school.

"We walk each other home. There are five of us and we all live nearby one another. I'm the second one closest, so they walk me home, and then the other three walk home together. I like it that we all live so close to each other."

Theresa listens intently to her older sister's every word; she seems so grown up to her now.

"Jack, how did you do on your math test today?" His

Lexington Glory Days

mom asks him.

"Pretty good, I think. I know I didn't get all the answers right, but I know I got most of them right." Jacks a good student, and good son.

"Good for you," she tells him.

Bonnie says, "na, na, na, blah, blah, blah," and rolls her eyes after hearing this. "You probably didn't do 'that' good."

"You be quiet and eat," her mother tells her.

Jack is a big eater and has his large piece of pork chop half gone, but has a mound of potatoes and gravy and green beans left on his plate. His twin sister has smaller portions and picks at her food, eating slowly.

Patrick asks his older brother, "Can I help you put the gas in the car with you?"

Patrick's anxious to learn how to do things to help out.

"You can do it yourself if you want," he teases him.

"I don't want to do it myself, I said I want to help you do it," he tells him; making a funny face, not recognizing his brother was kidding him.

"Okay, okay, you can help," Jack, says, smiling at him.

Grandma is talking to Edward, about grandpa. "He really doesn't look good," she tells him. "He was shaking terrible when he tried to eat, and pale as a ghost. Do you think we should take him to the doctor?"

"I'll look in on him after supper," he tells her.

"Tell me, what he tells you," she says, "you sure you's didn't eat anything today? Sounds like some bad food got in him."

"He didn't eat or drink anything me or Larry didn't have," he tells her. "We didn't eat anything," he suddenly tells her. "We had a few beers and a shot of brandy, and that was it. He wasn't complaining about his stomach then. Well, he said it hurt when we were at Larry's, come

195

Lexington Glory Days

to think of it."

"What's wrong with grandpa?" Carol asks, cutting her pork chop.

"He's complaining he's having stomach cramps," Betty tells her.

"Is he catching the flu?" Theresa wants to know, putting a forkful of potatoes in her mouth. "I know kids in school are sick with it."

"Could be, we don't know. He just started complaining before supper," Mom Betty tells her. "I hope it isn't the flu. Or anything serious."

Grunts are heard from the bedroom and grandpa is vomiting.

"Are you okay, Lloyd?" Grandma hollers from the table.

"I'm sick," he says back, barely audible.

The kids look around the table at one another, with a sense of seriousness. Betty speaks, "after we get done with supper, you girls can do the dishes up and then we'll look through the bags of clothes we got today."

"Do we have to do the dishes?" Bonnie whines.

"Yes, you do," her mom tells her. "And I want to see you studying your math book tonight, too," she adds.

Jack tells Patrick, "I'll be heading outside soon, if you still want to help."

"Yeah," he sings, "I do. Wait till I'm done. Don't go out without me. Ok?"

"Okay," he tells him, "I'm not done yet either."

"There's cake," grandma says getting up hurriedly, and brings a white cake with chocolate frosting back from the kitchen. "Eat everything on your plate, and you can have a piece," she announces.

Patrick quickly eats the last of the food on his plate and says, "I'm done," and holds his plate up for his piece of cake.

"Theresa, give your brother a piece of cake, would

you?" Grandma asks her, handing her the cake pan.

"Sure," she says, taking the dessert. "How big a piece do you want?"

"Put one on my plate too would you?" Bonnie asks her. Theresa gives them both a piece, and sets the cake pan back down. The other girls, their dad, grandma, and Betty, aren't finished yet and keep eating.

"Carol, how are things going at Joe and Katherine's?" Jack asks her.

"Fine, school is going good, and I like living in town."

"Are there any cute boys in your class?" Grandma asks.

"There's a couple," she replies smiling, shyly, looking at her mom. Betty looks at her husband, and rolls her eyes without Carol seeing.

"And what about your teachers?" Grandma asks her.

"I have three teachers this year. Sister Mary is nice, but the other two are rather strict. One sister hit a boy in my class on his hands, hard, with a ruler."

"They're strict for a reason, dear," grandma says, not telling her what the reasons are. "Some kids don't have long attention spans."

"I know," Carol tells her. "He probably deserved it."

Jack and Patrick have gotten up and have gone to the porch to put their boots on. "It's cold out, Patrick, dress up good," Jack tells him.

"I'm gonna go check on dad," Edward says rising, as more vomiting noises come from the bedroom. "I'm startin to worry myself."

Betty has finished feeding Frankie, and takes him into the living room and sets him on the floor, setting some toys next to him, and comes back to the table for dessert and takes a piece of cake.

Grandma is telling a story about her childhood, and the girls listen only passively. Betty finishes her cake, takes a drink of water and tells the girls, "finish eating now and have your cake, and then clear the table. I'll start in the kitchen, to help you. And we'll look in those bags of clothes when we're done."

"Okay mom," the girls chime in together.

Edward comes back to the table and tells his mother, "Dad wants to go in and see the doctor. He wants you to call him first – to make sure he's around," he tells her. "He said his stomach feels knotted up inside."

Startled, grandma quickly jumps up off the chair and heads straight to the phone in the kitchen. She looks up the phone number in the book hanging on the wall, trembling and begins dialing, and soon gets an answer. She explains the circumstances to the doctor and quickly hangs up. Edward is in the kitchen doorway, and grandma tells him to help her get Lloyd ready.

The doctor can see him. "We're supposed to come right in. Did Jack put the gas in the car?"

"There's plenty gas," he responds. "Lets go get dad ready."

Theresa volunteers to help with grandpa and Carol gets up and begins to clear off the table, "Bonnie take your time finishing."

Edward and grandma go into to the bedroom and help Lloyd get ready, putting on his boots. Soon he is up, sitting on the edge of the bed, grandma on one side and Edward on the other. "Help me get his jacket on him Edward and help him stand and walk him to the door," grandma says.

Betty stands next to Edward, "call me if you're going to be long."

I will," he tells her and kisses her on the cheek, as the three start to walk out the door. Grandpa looks very weak.

Betty watches the old car out the window as its engine comes to life, its headlights get turned on, and slowly begins to make its way suddenly down the

Lexington Glory Days

driveway. She says a silent prayer before returning her attention back inside the house. 'Please Lord, don't let it be anything serious.'

"Where are they going?" Jack wants to know, coming in from outside with his little brother.

"They're taking grandpa to see the doctor," Betty tells him, then adds, "Patrick, will you go into the living room and play with Frankie?"

"We'll both go," Jack answers for the both of them, glancing quickly at his younger brother, nodding at him.

"Thank you," she tells them, still thinking about grandpa.

Betty and the girls quickly get the table cleared. The leftovers are placed in the refrigerator, and they start on washing and drying the dishes. Soon they are all sitting around in the living room. Betty is sitting in the rocking chair surrounded by bags of clothes and the children on the floor. One by one, she picks out an article of clothing and hands it to someone. "Jack, hold them up and see if they're too long. You can always roll them up for the time being," she tells him.

They sit for an hour, looking through the used clothes, discussing who should get which articles of clothing, when the phone interrupts them. Betty gets up to answer it. It is grandma, "Doc Boyd wants to take grandpa to the hospital to keep an eye on him and run some tests," she tells her. "We're on our way to the hospital now. It'll be getting late by the time Edward and I get home."

"Does he know what might be causing the cramps?" Betty asks her, compassionately. She listens for her voice on the other end.

"He thinks it might be his gallbladder, but he's not sure. He wants to take x-rays at the hospital. I need to get going; Edward and I are taking him ourselves, and we're ready to go. I'll call you if anything comes up. Goodbye."

With that grandma hangs up.

"Goodbye," Betty says slowly, and hangs up the phone.

Back in the living room, the kids are going through more of the used clothes. "How's grandpa?" Carol asks her when she returns. "Grandma and your dad are taking him to the hospital for x-rays," she tells her.

"X-rays? Is he going to be okay?" Jack asks.

"I'm sure he's going to be fine," their mom tells them, trying not to worry them.

"Look, a couple of dresses and slips for Carol and Theresa," Bonnie tells them, rummaging through the bags quickly. "Jeans for Jack and Patrick, button-down shirts, sweatshirts, sweaters. A couple pairs of dress slacks and blouses, two dresses for mom, oh my, look mom, some dresses for you! Work pants and shirts for dad, good heaven knows he can use them."

"Okay everyone, decide what you want and put them on a pile in your bedroom," Betty tells them, "and I don't want any fighting. We'll wash them and then you can wear them," she pauses, "I think it's time you's get ready for bed now, so go get your pajamas on and we'll watch some TV for a while."

One by one they come back into the living room with their pajamas on. Much later, they each become more and more drowsy in front of the black and white television. Some get up, tired, say "good night" to everyone and go to bed. Others have to be woken up and coaxed into going to bed. About eleven o'clock p.m. Edward and grandma arrive home, with everyone in bed sleeping, without Lloyd.

The next morning most of the family is down for breakfast early for a Saturday. Still in their pajamas, the first ones down get fed right away.

"I'm going back to the hospital soon as possible. Edward's volunteered to go with me," grandma

Lexington Glory Days

announces sharply, "we have to leave about eight o'clock."

About nine-thirty a.m. the phone rings. It is grandma from the hospital. "Betty, Doc Boyd wants to remove Lloyd's gallbladder. They took x-rays and there's swelling inside. They want to operate right away."

At the hospital Lloyd is already on a gurney and getting wheeled down to the operating room. They give him anesthesia to put him under and he quickly becomes unconscious. Doc Boyd is there with two nurses and an anesthesiologist, and they begin operating.

In the waiting room grandma is nervous, "I want to call all the kids and let them know about the operation."

Edward says to her, "I'll call Betty. She can call a few of them, and they can figure out who to call next." Grandma, fidgeting, decides that will work.

But suddenly in the operating room, a panic sets in as there's too much bleeding and Doc Boyd can't stop it. A hasty decision is made to slow the bleeding as much as possible, and to transfer him to hospital in Merrifield to get him more expert attention.

They tell grandma about the unfortunate and unexpected situation

Edward has been on the phone with Betty and is hanging up just as grandma rushes up to him. In tears, she explains to Edward what has happened and Edward goes to the nurse's station to get the name of the hospital and directions to where they're taking his dad.

The doctor and nurses stabilize the bleeding as best as they can, and prepare Lloyd for the transfer. Quickly an ambulance is brought around to take grandpa for help. He is put on a stretcher, taken from the operating room, and loaded into the ambulance on a gurney.

Two men enter with him. The rear doors close, the sirens are turned on, the lights begin flashing and they begin the hour-long drive. They rush him through the small town, out into the country, and are soon on their way to the better equipped, bigger hospital in the city.

Edward calls Betty back, quickly explains the developments to her, and that he and grandma are going to drive to the hospital in the city. Betty nervously calls two of her sisters-in-law, with the upsetting news, and explains what is happening.

First she calls Blanche. "He went in last night and spent the night in the hospital. He was complaining of stomach cramps around suppertime. And he was throwing up. First he saw Doc Boyd..."

Blanch interrupts her...'He spent the night at the hospital?'

"Yes, he did. Edward and grandma went in this morning about eight o'clock to see him, and grandma called and said they were gonna operate right away, to take out his gallbladder. I just talked to Edward and he said there was a lot of bleeding, so they're transferring him to North Memorial."..... "He had really bad stomach cramps right before supper."....."They operated this morning, just not long ago."...."I don't know how many times he threw up, it was a few times anyway."...... "That's right. Edward and grandma took him into see Doc Boyd after supper last night, and Doc Boyd wanted him put in the hospital to run tests."...."He's on his way to the hospital in the city now by ambulance, and Edward and Evelyn are following them in their car."...."Okay, I'll call you if I hear any more. Goodbye."

Before hanging up, Blanche tells her to call Carrie and they'll call everyone else then. Carrie takes the news with difficulty and struggles to finish the call. Mom Betty feels sad and is worried about grandpa and now, Carrie. She tells the kids about what is going on, and the kids feel sad now too. It was just two hours ago they started the operation, but in the ambulance, poor grandpa is losing more and more blood and is getting weaker and weaker.

Finally, the ambulance arrives at the hospital. The

Lexington Glory Days

two men exit the rear of the vehicle and are met quickly with other people from the larger hospital. They exchange words and all enter the hospital. Ten minutes later, the two men climb back into the rear of the ambulance and close the doors. With no lights flashing or sirens going off the ambulance pulls out of the driveway, and with no sense of urgency, begins to make its way back to the small town from where they came from. Grandpa died along the way.

Grandma and Edward arrive at North Memorial hospital about a half hour later, and after some confusion a nurse approaches them and breaks the bad news. Grandma wails in emotional pain and disbelief, and cries hysterically. Edward puts his arm around her and says, "Come on, let's go home."

The pair arrives back at the local hospital, and grandma asks to see Lloyd.

"He'll be in the hospital morgue until morning, when the mortician will pick up the body," a nurse informs her.

They oblige her wish and ask her to prepare herself. The nurse leads the two into the cold hospital morgue, up to a body that's covered head to toe in a plane white sheet, spotted with bloodstains, and lifts the sheet back far enough to expose his face.

"Oh Lloyd!" She exclaims and immediately breaks out crying hysterically. She touches his cold face and kisses his lips, cheeks and forehead. Tears streaming down her face.

Edward watches this, himself crying, and finally tells her again for the second time today, putting his arm around her, "come on, let's go home." She pulls away from him coldly and slowly walks towards the door, wiping away tears.

The two pull into the driveway at home, where everybody's been waiting since morning for some word about grandpa. They get out of the car and Edward walks behind his mother up the steps and into the house.

Grandma goes into the dining room and sits down at the table, places her crossed arms on the table, and lays her head on them, sobbing. Some of the kids come in from the living room wondering what's going on.

"Grandpa died," Edward tells them, trying to be strong, "grandpa died."

The following day, Sunday, all of Lloyd and Evelyn's children show up at the house. Blanche, Mamie and her family from St. James, Larry, Tom, Rita and her husband, Carrie and her husband, and Jim, who moved to the city and is staying with Rita and Bill.

Betty and Edward's kids congregate upstairs by themselves for a while. The day's emotional for everyone, with people crying. The families who live nearer by invite those who live further away to stay with them.

The wake is held on the following Tuesday and all of Edward and Betty's kids are there. Carrie, the youngest daughter, completely loses control. She places her hands on her dead father's chest in the casket, lays her head on them, and openly weeps, time and time again.

Now a widow, Grandma tries to remain strong.

His death and funeral notice gets broadcast over the radio and many friends and relatives show up to pay their last respects. Beautiful bouquets of flowers are placed alongside the casket. Dressed in a dark suit, white shirt and dark tie, his family grieves for him.

The funeral, the following day, is at the little country Catholic Church in Lexington, at ten o'clock a.m. The hearse brings his body back from the funeral home in town and the Mass for the Christian burial begins.

The priest holds incense over the casket and waves the gold plated pot in the shape of the sign of the cross, as incense floats toward the heavens. "In the name of the Father, and of the Son, and of the Holy Spirit," the priest continues and begins the High Mass.

Lexington Glory Days

An hour later, the pallbearers carry his body and the casket to the cemetery behind the church, where he will be laid into the ground, the family following behind them, crying.

The priest says gravesite prayers and the family huddles together closer, for warmth. Afterwards they make their way back to the church basement for a small luncheon then slowly disperse until the church basement is empty and echoes from the hollowness of it all.

On the way home from the funeral, a song plays over the radio in Edward and Betty's sturdy old car, that when heard again later on would always remind them of this day and the funeral.

"I don't like those things," Patrick tells no one in particular of the funeral, sitting in the front seat with his mom and dad, "everyone wears black suits, and the girls wear black dresses, and everyone is old. I don't like dead bodies either. It smells," he says, as if in a trance. The song on the radio makes him melancholy.

The other kids in the back seat watch the processional of cars leaving the church, quiet, filled with questions and mixed feelings. They travel along the dirt road towards Lexington, around the lake and Pavilion and their home.

Betty turns and looks at the children in the backseat, dressed in their Sunday best, and stares at Edward for a moment. He looks different in his black fedora hat, she thinks. Everyone is quiet.

She wonders, with the sudden death, what it might mean for her and her family, and how it will affect them and particularly her husband.

She rubs her stomach and thinks about her unborn baby inside of her.

She thinks of her other children and their ages, and her responsibilities to them. She wants to say something to her husband, but decides to finish the ride in silence, and stares instead out the side window of the car at the winter landscape passing her by.

Chapter Eight

A Farm House and Eighty-Acres

"The next number called is B-6. B-6," Eugene calls out.

"Bingo!" A wiry teenage girl sitting with her parents shrieks. "I'm so excited, I can't believe I won! I won!" She quickly gets up out of her chair and stands looking down at her card, in the basement of Lexington church.

"That game was for fifteen dollars and twenty-five cent. Come up and claim your prize," Eugene tells her, appearing as if he's enjoying his job.

Down the narrow, steep staircase Leonard and Anna make their way to the basement of the church, hanging onto the hand railing for dear life. The basement, with its low ceiling and lime green painted cement walls, was added underneath the church in 1947 after they lifted up the main structure.

Leonard and Anna make it down the stairs and join fifty other people from the Lexington church and other surrounding churches, already there.

"Get a bingo card and find a place to sit," Eugene tells them.

The ladies in the kitchen are busy making ham and butter sandwiches, and slicing cakes and delicious bars they made and brought from home.

"I won Gertrude!" The teenage girl tells her, waving her hands in the air.

"Good for you," she replies smiling, half-heartedly, sitting with her boyfriend. "How come you can win and I can't," she tells her seriously then busts out laughing. "God, I just can't get nothing," she says seeming discouraged.

John, one of the bell ringers and a considerate young man, figures as long as someone has Gertrude's attention, now would be a good time to talk to her. "Gert how's Peter? I haven't seen him in a long time," he asks.

"He's fine," she acknowledges, "he's probably at home working on the farm equipment, getting ready for spring planting." She tells him flatly.

"I heard you're engaged," John's wife, Judy, asks her, standing between her and her husband, smiling. Not meaning to be nosy.

Gertrude holds her hand up to reveal her engagement ring and smiles. She quickly points her fingers towards her neck and flutters them back and forth, and bats her eyelashes. "What does this tell you?" She asks them, smiling.

"That's beautiful. Congratulations," Judy tells her smiling.

"Thank you."

"Have you met Eli?" Eli nods his head a little and grunts, smoking a pipe. "Hi," he says, coughing and choking on the tobacco smoke.

Anna walks over to the kitchen counter, hoping to get a bar, when she see's Mrs. Tryzinski, the woman who lost her baby several years ago. "Mrs. Tryzinski, how are you? I see you all the time, I know, but I haven't had a chance to talk to you. We're always so rushed after church to get back home."

"I'm doing okay. What else can I do? I could complain but no one wants to hear it anyway," she tells her curtly, with the smallest hint of a smile rising on one corner of her mouth. "Isn't that what people say?"

"We're about ready to start the next game," Eugene announces. "Is everybody ready?" People nod their heads and look around.

In the kitchen, Sophia asks Betty, "How are Katherine and Joe?" Both ladies are working in the kitchen making the sandwiches and cutting the bars.

"They're doing all right," Betty tells her, appearing happy. "They had a baby girl…"

Sophia's mouth drops open and a gasp comes from her lungs.

"They did?" She interrupts her, "I didn't know that."

Betty thinks for a moment, "She must be… about six months old now, I would say." Neither women are paying attention to the bingo game.

"Well for Pete's sake. And Kimberly and Clay, how are they? It seems I never get to see anybody anymore," Sophia tells her.

"Well, Katherine and Joe joined the church in Centerville, and Kimberly and Clay belong to the one in Le Prarie," Betty tells her.

"So that's why I don't see them anymore," Sophia says, nodding her head clearly up and down.

"And how are they?"

"Good. Good as far as I know. Kimberly's busy raising her own kids and works at the canning factory over there in Le Prarie."

"She does. Well good for her. When does she find the time?" Sophia asks Betty, starting to laugh loudly.

"I don't know." Betty starts smiling. "I wish I knew."

Around the bingo tables, a little chatter is heard.

"Lost another one," Edna tells Roman shaking her head in disbelief.

"Can't win all the time," he tells her smiling.

"All the time! I'd be happy to win one!" She tells him

with her eyes bulged out. "Say, when are we gonna get to sample those bars," she slyly asks Judy.

"Here we go," Eugene, announces rolling the small white balls with numbers painted on them, in a small cage. "O-68. O-68," he repeats.

"Should we go play bingo at the church?" Jigger asks Lily, outside at his camper trailer, sitting on the motorcycle he's purchased. The two are dating.

"I wanna go frickin ridin," Lily tells him, wearing a bandana around her forehead. Ever since Jigger bought the motorcycle, Lily's turned into a bitch. She thinks chicks that ride motorcycles are supposed to act that way.

"Let's go for a ride around the frickin lake and stop at the pavilion for a beer, and then go for a long ride over to Belle River or someplace," she tells him. "I don't wanna sit in no stinkin church basement playin bingo. It's too nice out today."

"Get on. Let's go then," Jigger tells her, ready to roll.

They ride through the campgrounds next to the pavilion, down to the boat landing and see boats on the lake. "I wonder if they're bitin!" Jigger hollers off to his side to Lily, sitting on the back. He makes a circle to turn the bike around and they ride towards the pavilion again. Gunning the engine.

Let's go to the Green Lantern instead," Lily yells into his ear, "maybe there'll be more people there," noticing only a few cars at the pavilion.

They ride the shore line the short distance on the road and park the bike and go inside," What the hell happened to you?" Jigger asks Junior.

"I was in a fight. I know I look bad, but you should see the other guy," he tells him suddenly bursting out laughing, and then turns serious, black and blue bruises and cuts covering his face, "it hurts to laugh." He says.

"Who was the fight with? I hope you beat him up as much as he hit you," Lily tells him.

Lexington Glory Days

"Holy shit, you look terrible."

"I don't really wanna talk about it," Junior. tells her, looking straight ahead across the bar at bottles of booze, and of himself in a large square mirror. "I do look pretty bad, though don't I?" he grunts, trying to laugh.

They have a beer and talk with Jr. and then take off again on the bike.

"That's where Edward and Betty are moving to!" Jigger yells to Lily.

He takes his hand off one of the handlebars and points to a farmhouse their passing by, a mile away from the Green Lantern.

Inside the farmhouse Betty and grandma are talking.

"It's been six months today since grandpa suddenly passed away," Betty says, with her youth gone and age creeping into her face, to grandma, in the kitchen of the families' new home.

"Although it's been hard on me at times, having Edward and you and the kids living with me eased my burden greatly, Betty. Even though having another woman in my house hasn't been easy for me, having you's all around since Lloyd's death has been a great comfort to me."

Betty's heart sinks upon hearing this, and thinks she'd never thought she'd hear her talk to her woman to woman, not to mention kindly.

"While the younger kids tend to fight and get unruly from time to time, and get under my skin, they provide at other times a great distraction from endlessly thinking about Lloyd. I know your nine months pregnant, with your eighth child, Betty. I know you need a place of your own."

"All the paperwork has been signed for the eighty-acres, home and farmstead, and we can move in at any time. More cleaning and a little painting needs to be done first, along with purchasing a few more beds and some furnishings," Betty tells grandma.

"Edward is back working on road construction and the job is nearby enough where he can be home every night."

Grandma tells her, "Larry's going to move in with me, to save us both money and for the company, and since Ruth refuses to move into the country with their daughter. She grew up in town, and is determined to stay there, I guess." Ruth and her daughter live with her parents.

"The kids are out of school for the summer and Carol has moved back in with us, to my great relief," Betty tells her sighing.

"The family has seemed to put the house fire behind them. Although it's been a tough winter for everyone, they seem excited about having their own place again." Evelyn looks her in the eye, staying connected with her.

"They are. Edward's looking forward to farming the land and raising livestock," Betty says, "I just want to have the baby, and a safe place where we can all be together. I'm hoping the luck for my family's well being has turned a corner. And I hope the baby doesn't come until after the move."

"I know you do dear," grandma tells her in a moment of graciousness towards her. "It must be hard, with the moving and being pregnant."

"We've spent two weeks working on the new place already, washing walls and floors, sweeping, and mopping. I even help as much as I can, doing the best I can," Betty admits. She's in a hurry to make the transition.

Grandma tells her, "Being that school is over for the summer months all the kids can chip in to help too, and they should."

Occasionally Edward comes in with another bed frame or piece of furniture, eyeing the women and surprised they seem to be getting along. "God damn it Harold, watch what you're doing. You just put a big chip into the doorframe!" Edward hollers at his son, who let the coffee table hit the wood.

It isn't too long before the house is cleaned top to bottom. More painting, it's decided will be left for another time.

"What are you thinking about? Pay attention to what you're doing, Christ almighty!" Edward continues scolding his son. "I don't know what I'm gonna do with you."

"Set one bed frame up in each of the three bedrooms upstairs," Betty tells Edward. "We need one in Carol's room, which she will have to herself, being the oldest, put one in the adjoining bedroom that Theresa and Bonnie will share, two in the bedroom across the hall, one for Jack, and one for Patrick and Frankie, we have one for the downstairs bedroom for us. The crib for the baby will be set up in our room, next to the bed along the wall. Finding enough sheets, pillows and blankets for all the beds has been a challenge, but thanks to you, and mine and Edward's brothers and sisters there's suddenly enough to go around."

"I'm glad I could help. Glad you let me help," Evelyn tells her politely.

"Edward and Harold are coming in with the used brown couch and matching chair we bought, I better get the door for them," Betty says, trying to get out of her chair.

"Now be careful this time, and watch what you're doing," Edward tells him.

"Where do you want it?" Edward asks Betty, shuffling his weight around under the load of the couch.

"Anywhere for now, just set it down," she tells him. The men place it over the golden colored carpet along one wall in the living room.

A used refrigerator and electric stove has been bought and kitchen table and chairs have already been purchased and moved in. The house is all but complete. Betty and Edward decide, "It's time to move in."

"With just a few more trips from the new house to grandma's and back, mostly for clothes, we can start to settle into our new home you've been waiting nine months for," Edward tells Betty, proud of himself.

"There's no running water except for the pump in the kitchen sink?" Grandma asks looking around. Surprised Betty would agree to it.

"Nine or ten pumps of the handle and water starts to pour out of the mouth of the pump. The bathroom is the outhouse in the middle of the yard about sixty feet away," Edward tells her, "There's a small room off the kitchen with a pot in it if you need it," Edward explains to his mom with a bit of humor in his voice.

Larry comes in carrying a used black and white TV with Jack, while the girls are helping out in the kitchen. The kitchen is serving as the control center and kids come in with questions and comments, and leave, as grandma and Carol try to organize the pantry, and figure where to put plates and silverware, bowls and cups and glasses, and the pots and pans they got from neighbors, friends, and family members.

"Well, I have to be going," grandma, tells them, looking around the kitchen. Carol keeps working as grandma says good-bye. "K grandma, bye."

The kids are happy as can be and it rubs off on Betty and Edward. They've been spending time together, walking around the yard, the barn, and the other out buildings, "What's that in the corner?" Betty asks him curiously.

"I think we've discovered an old rocking chair," in what used to be a granary, he tells her. They dust off the chair and Jack and Patrick struggle to carry it closer to the house for a good cleaning before it's brought in for Betty to use with the new baby.

"The days going by so fast soon it'll time to turn in for the night," Betty tells them. They sleep well and sound, content in the way things are turning out, in the first night in their new home.

The next day is a busy day for unpacking, phone calls and well-wishers.

"A few months ago, Edward bought a tractor, plow and disk and planted the crops in the field," Betty is on the phone, the next morning, talking to Kimberly, whose married and has six kids of her own now and lives just eight miles down the road. "I've got drapes and shades for the windows and hung pictures, clocks, shelves and knickknacks to brighten up the walls. You's will have to come over and see it sometime."

"We sure will," Kimberly tells her with conviction, insisting.

Two weeks after the move, in July, Betty has the baby. It's a girl, and they name her Jennifer. A week later, Kimberly calls her again.

"I'd been having contractions for a few hours and about eight o'clock p.m. decided to go into the hospital, I had to have Carol drive me. Edward was at the bar with his coworkers drinking, he didn't bother to stop at home after work. He didn't know I was in labor," Betty continues talking with Kimberly. "When he got home, Theresa told him I went into the hospital to have the baby. But he was so drunk, all he could do was manage to find a little bit of something to eat, and go to bed to pass out," she tells her half heartedly laughing, then turns serious.

"I was so embarrassed and mad when I found out, but I'm used to his irresponsible ways when he's drinking, and nothing was going to stop the baby from coming anyway, I thought."

"Well, the summer months should go by well enough for everyone," Kimberly tells her. "For the kids there's a garden to tend and weeds to pull out, that in the fall I suppose you'll can vegetables, mostly cucumbers and tomatoes, I suppose," Kimberly tells her.

"I hope to. Edward bought a few pigs and some heifer cattle and put them in the barn the other day and now they need to be fed and watered every day. We even got some chickens, both for their eggs and butchering," Betty tells her, and continues. "Edward puts in long days at his road construction job, and doesn't have much time to do any drinking, besides a little, occasionally on the weekends, but not much really. As far as me, I think, 'it could be worse,'" they both laugh. Kimberly knows what she means.

Kimberly tells her seriously, "And you know that's the truth too, it could be worse," and smiles. Betty agrees.

"Okay then, I should let you go. I'll call you soon," Kimberly says.

"Mmm, bye now. Talk to you soon."

"Seemingly as quickly as it started, summer's almost over. September's just about here already. Soon it'll be time for the kids to go back to school," Betty is telling Edward. "I don't mind them all being home, but I'm looking forward to all of them being in school again," she says with a slight laugh. "Patrick will be starting first-grade, and I can spend more time with Frankie and Jennifer." Edward listens patiently to every word.

It's a beautiful, fall, mid-September day in the Minnesota countryside. It's hard to think there could be any place any better or nicer in the world. The kids are now in school and Edward is at work. The two littlest kids are down for naps, and Betty, in her apron finally gets one of her rare and very infrequent times to herself, and is in the kitchen, preparing to bake a cake. She very much enjoys this time by herself. She puts a little bowl of milk with some breadcrumbs crumbled up in it for some cats that seem to have called this place home, outside the door. She doesn't mind, 'good mouse catchers' she thinks, and likes their quiet ways.

She has time to call her sisters and brothers and friends, without anyone interrupting her. Three of her siblings live nearby, but like everyone else, they are busy working and raising families of their own.

At just thirty-four years old and having just had her eighth child, often times it seems, "all I ever do is cook and clean," she thinks.

After moving from place to place, five times in the fifteen years she's been married, she prays this one works out for them. It's certainly no mansion, 'and I wouldn't want one anyway. All I need is a home for the kids.'

… Lexington Glory Days

Part 2

Angels Among Us

Betty walks into her bedroom and peeks in on Jennifer, sleeping in her crib. She watches her and thinks how precious she is, how helpless she is, and how much she needs her. And how much work she's going to be. She smiles a little to herself for thinking that, but she knows it's the truth. She watches Frankie sleeping on her bed, next to the crib, and remembers when she was pregnant with him, and how much he's grown already. She takes a step back and watches both of them for a moment, and captures the picture in her mind and quietly returns to the kitchen.

She's only lived in the house for three months, and this the first time she's been able to look at it and feel it, in the peace and quiet, alone. Feel its presence; and wonder, 'how many families before mine lived here?' 'Whose hands put up the wallpaper in the bedroom?' 'What were the people like?'

She envisions another family living here in a previous time. She watches them in the kitchen. The Mrs. of the house cooking something on the stove, the men sitting around the table, kids underfoot, the family eating together.

She thinks about the unhappier times the family may

have experienced. The loss of a parent or perhaps a child, she hopes they were happy, overall.

She walks around the house, stopping to look out the window and feels the warm air, with just a hint of coolness in it, coming in from the open window. She turns her head and notices lots of scratchings around the wood in the window frame in one spot, and wonders, 'what was someone doing to cause all the scratches?' She wanders into the living room and gives it a once over, satisfied with how nice it's become to look.

She sits down in the old rocking chair they found in the granary, letting the warm breeze from the open window hit her, and watches the dainty and delicate lace curtains flow in the breezes trail, and thinks back and reflects when she was younger. The dances her and Edward would attend with her sister, or one or more of his brothers or sisters. How carefree and uncomplicated things were then. She misses her mother and father.

She looks out of the window and sees how bright it is, and is reminded just how beautiful it is outside. She leans back in the rocking chair and closes her eyes, and starts rocking herself, and tries to not think of anything else and relax. Try to enjoy the moment, without the kids fighting or a child crying.

A car goes by on the dirt road outside and she opens her eyes and watches the dust trailing behind it for a moment and closes them again. Without realizing it, she notices how tall the corn has gotten in the field. She hears birds chirping from the open window. This relaxes her.

Her eyes close, and memories wade through her mind, stopping for just the briefest of the seconds, before moving on, until the next one comes along and goes, and then the next one, and the next. So many memories.

She's remembering, as a child walking to school with her sisters and brothers, along the old dirt road just down the road from here, to the little country schoolhouse, with its old wood stove for heat. Kids in her class, some of the girls and her friends and some of the boys and her teachers, still live close by.

Her parents, she's remembers, early in the morning and later in the afternoons and evenings, and of doing homework at the table by the light of the kerosene lamp, and of eating supper around the table with them. Sitting around the living room listening to the words of the storytellers on the radio, as a child, fondly watching her dad ride his horse. Listening to her dad play the fiddle, while helping her mom with the baking in the kitchen. She breathes in deeply, thinking she can smell freshly baked bread.

With her eyes still closed, her grandmother's face is in her mind, she sees her helpful ways and remembers she outlived her own mother by three years. Memories of her ten aunts and uncles come to her, some alive and some now deceased. She sees some of her twenty first cousins and some of her second cousins. The first time she saw Edward appears in her conscious, and for the first time she sees the faces of each of her children after they're born.

Flashes of baptisms, first Communion's, confirmations and birthdays for the kids come to her. She's thinking about which kids like what foods and which ones they don't, what each one is good at, and whether they have a lucky number. She thinks of their favorite color, if they have one, their shoe size, and what flavor their favorite soda is. She knows and remembers, everything, about each one of them. One thought about them leads to another, and then another.

She sits there, with her eyes closed, worrying about the unknown. Things she knows about that aren't going well, she can try to fix, but things going on around her that she doesn't know about can hurt her. With her family, she tries to read between the lines, catch all the messages and signs she can from them. And hope she doesn't mess up too badly when she misreads something.

She's thinking of herself and her own instincts and feelings now, and the hopes that she follows them. She's thinking of God, and may He truly take care of her and her family. She recites a prayer to herself, her lips move slightly.

Without Betty knowing about it, there are angels in the room with her, at least two of them, maybe more. They're both tall, dressed in white and shades of light blue. You can't make out the shape or color of their faces or hands but your sure they are not faceless or without hands. They have wings, down by their sides touching the ground, like you hear and see so often in all the stories and pictures. Their gowns reach down to their feet and they all appear to have womanly features. They look lovingly and content. One looks compassionate, the other more friendly. They're standing around her living room, watching Betty. One occasionally speaks to the other, in very short, brief sentences. Soon one smiles after communicating with the other one. It is not sure what the Angels want, just that they are here, in peace, for God. And Betty is happy they are.

She begins praying to them, not knowing they are so close to her. She believes in them, in God and angels. She is praying for the Angels to help her in her daily life and challenges. That she may do God's work and live a good Christian life. For her children and her husband's health and well being; for the Angels to watch over them, and keep them safe. To protect them from harm, and all hurtful things.

She begins praying for her husband, that he may come home safely to her every night, and that they help him control his temptations, his anger, and forgive his faults. She adds a pray for her deceased parents, their souls and that they may be with God, forever in His kingdom. There are so many things she can think of to pray for, people and children in need.

She asks the angles for guidance and strength, wisdom and humility.

She meditates, trying to free her mind of all thoughts and let the spirits in. Let the answers come to her. Let them enter her mind freely, quietly, clearly, when they are ready to.

The Angels watch her, translucent and glowing at the same time. Perhaps they are reading her thoughts and will take her prayers up to God in heaven. It is impossible to know their full realm of abilities. Maybe they will steer someone out of harms way today – or help Betty find something she thought was lost. Were they sent by God? Are they part of the Holy Spirit? Do they already know what she needs?

There are so many questions.

Betty feels safe in her prayers, and knows things will be okay. A sense of comfort comes over her and she sinks into a deeper level of slumber, releasing all of her tensions, and feeling at peace.

She becomes slightly startled. Betty thinks she hears a baby cry and listens with her ears for a moment, but the baby she hears is not hers, and she drifts off to sleep again.

The face of a man she does not recognize enters the dreams in her mind. There's a group of men standing around, smashing bottles with the liquid inside spraying out all over. She sees people dancing in a dance hall, smiling and having a good time. A car drives off to somewhere in the night, with its headlights on. And then she sees nothing from it.

Then there's a man getting out of a car dressed in a white suit and hat, but this time it's light outside. He gets out of the car and looks friendly and has a smile on his face – and suddenly, she sees his face, close-up. He turns a little and she sees him take a cigarette from his mouth. He begins to walk around the front of the car. He looks around the land, laid out before him, and she follows his gaze. A little spot in the distance catches both their eyes, and soon she is whisked to a field next to the spot she had just seen. She is in a field with green grasses up to her eyes as if she were little. The grain and grasses are so high, she can't see beyond them, but notices a clearing with a nice house and a kept yard and a car and outbuildings. But it appears to be abandoned. There is no one around. It seems strange to her, but she stays there for a while waiting for some form of life; a person, a bird, a cat, something, even a breeze, but there is just nothing.

Now, she dreams of a man in dark clothes and a hat, riding a horse in a pasture. He bounces up and down with every step the horse makes. Suddenly the horse lifts its front legs high in the air, like he was getting ready to charge at something, or became spooked. The man lifts something long, into the air.

Suddenly there are loud noises all around her, booms and crashes, as the man on the horse disappears. In its place there becomes flashes of light and dark and pieces of both colors intertwined in strange shapes, and the noises continue. Like she was caught in a car accident, and the cars rolling over and over, but she doesn't feel like she's getting tossed around or hurt. Like she was caught in a war zone and had gone blind, but could still see the flashes of light and dark from behind her eyelids. The noises are still going off and popping all around her, as if she was standing in front of a huge fire, but she could not feel the heat, but the blaze was blinding her. And the booms and pops were the crackling of the fire and things inside of it exploding. It startles her awake.

Her eyes quickly open, her heart is racing and she's breathing deeply. She rubs her bare arms with her hands, trying to warm them, sitting in the rocking chair for a moment and realizes there's a knocking noise coming from the bedroom.

'It must be the two-year-old doing something,' she thinks. She gets up to check on the children. Frankie has gotten out of bed from his nap. And is pushing the crib, with the baby in it, up against the wall and back, and forth again, laughing. The baby is awake, but not crying, and instead, is watching him.

"What are you doing?" She whispers loudly to him.

He looks up at her, smiling and laughing, and continues hitting the crib against the wall. Betty picks up the infant, carrying her, and takes Frankie's hand and leads him into the living room, and sits back down in the rocking chair with the baby on her lap, and Frankie by her side, sitting on the floor.

The three spend quality time together, in peace and quiet, giggling and making baby talk. She sits Jennifer in her baby chair on the floor, and Frankie follows her baby sister, and keeps her company, trying to talk to her. "Ba ba ba."

"I might as well darn socks and catch up on some sewing," she says aloud. Attaching buttons, and adding patches to holey jeans, she can sew and watch the kids at the same time she figures.

She sits and sews, enjoying watching Frankie speak his baby talk to Jennifer. He rocks her chair and talks to her. 'If it were this easy all the time,' Betty thinks to herself. She relishes how well the two get along. "Ba ba ba," Frankie tells her. The baby giggles with delight.

Betty sings, "Twinkle, twinkle little star," hoping Frankie will catch on and sing with her and to the baby, and he does. "How I wonder where you are..." He doesn't know yet how to say the words. "How wa wa wa...wa wa wa."

Soon the serene afternoon is over, the afternoon autumn sun is quickly falling and the house becomes full of kids again, home from school.

Edward gets home, from work, quite a bit later. He's obviously had a few beers or hard liquor drinks, and is not in a good mood. The pressures of working and raising a big family and now the big mortgage on the farm are getting to him.

He's been putting in a lot of overtime at work and needs to combine the ripe corn sitting out in the field. The old combine he purchased over the summer isn't working and he doesn't have time to find out where the problems are so he can fix it. He's sitting at the kitchen table complaining about it to Betty.

"I might have to hire someone to fix it, God dammit, I don't know what else to do. If I had the time I could do it myself. I should get Harold out here to help me is what I should do, but he probably won't. Damn kid. I gotta get it done, and soon, the corn'll be ripe in another week. Damn – it – anyway."

"Do you want me to call him and see if he'll come out and help you?" Betty asks him. She wants to help, sometimes he won't let her.

"Yeah, call him up, let me talk to him," he tells her, disgruntled.

Even though it's getting late, she walks over to the phone and dials his number from memory and quickly gets an answer. "Hello, Harold? This is your mother talking." He listens to her, and starts talking.

"I just walked in the door, hi. Is everything okay?" He says to her

"We're okay," she tells him, "How are you?"

"Doin alright. I just got home. I was gonna change clothes and meet some of the guys up town for a beer." He was at a friend's house, working on his car.

"Well I won't keep you," she tells him "your dad wants to talk to you. Come out and visit sometime." She finishes listening to him.

"What does dad want?" he wants to know, feeling trouble coming on.

"I'll let him tell you, here he is." Betty hands Edward the phone.

"All right," Harold grumbles.

"Yeah, this is your dad, say I need some help fixing the combine. I was wondering if you'd come out and help me. It's too late tonight, but soon, sooner the better. I'd appreciate it if you could."

"Why, what's wrong with it?" Harold asks, not wanting to help him.

"I don't know what's wrong with it, if I knew what was wrong with it, I'd be fixing it. Can you come out sometime and help me or not? Maybe tomorrow?"

"I suppose," Harold says, feeling a sense of obligation, "tomorrow night, after work I'll come out," he tells him.

"Tomorrow night. All right, I'll see you then. Don't forget. I gotta get that damn thing running. I can't wait any longer. So make sure you come," his dad lets him know. Edward listens to hear what he has to say.

"Yeah, okay, goodbye," Harold tells him and hangs up on him.

"All right, remember, don't forget now," His dad says and hangs up, then adds, "damn kid." He turns to Betty, "What have you got to eat?"

The next evening just like he said he would, Harold, tall with black hair like his dad's, arrives with his girlfriend, Laura, in tow. The two walk towards the house, with its white paint chipping off everywhere and open the screen door to the small porch. They walk into the house that enters into the kitchen. Betty's at the table feeding Jennifer in her high chair, and the other kids are in the living room watching TV.

"Well, hi," Betty greets the two pleasantly.

"Hi," Laura greets her, "I thought I'd come along for

the ride," she tells her, smiling. "I hope you don't mind."

"No, not at all, come on in, the more the merrier," Betty tells her, with a little roll of her eyes and a slight smile.

"Where's dad?" Harold asks her sternly.

Betty tells him, "he hasn't gotten home from work yet."

The two pull out chairs from the table and sit down.

"I thought maybe he'd be home already," he tells her, relaxing.

"He usually gets off work early on Fridays, he should be coming," she tells him. "I don't think he'll be too much longer."

"If he doesn't stop off at the bar and starts drinking," her son tells her.

"No, I don't think he will, he wants to get the combine fixed so he can start combining the corn," she tells him, feeding Jennifer baby food.

"He better get here, I'm not waiting all night for him," Harold says to her defiantly. "I got better things to do than sitting around here waiting for him."

"He'll be here," Laura chimes in. "We just got here, give him a little time."

"I'm just saying, with him you never know." He offers his little finger to Jennifer and the baby takes it and Harold moves it around in circles, feeling the baby's grip. "Hi, Jennifer," he says in a higher than normal voice, "Hi! How are you?" he says, raising his eyebrows and smiling, making the baby smile and giggle. "Hi. Hi. Your such a good baby..."

The baby's stomach gurgles and she spits up.

"Now what did you do that for?" He tells her and wipes up the mess.

"Betty, how are you doing?" Laura asks Betty.

"I'm doing okay," she tells her, "what choice do I have?" And laughs.

"And the baby? Does she sleep good at night?" Laura asks her.

"She sleeps all night through," Betty tells her with a hint of happy conviction in her voice.

"Don't you?" She asks Jennifer, making a little funny face at her, "don't you sleep all night long? Yes you do! Yes, you do!" She brings her head closer to the babies, and backs it away, brings it closer again, and backs it away a second time. She's a contented baby.

"That's good," Laura tells her, looking around the kitchen.

"Tell me about it," Betty says seriously, with a little chuckle, bringing out a laugh from Harold.

He gets up from his chair and says, "I'm gonna go see what the kids are doing in the living room." He goes in and sits next to Carol on the couch and wraps his arm around her neck and squeezes and jerks it gently a few times.

"Stop it," she tells him and pulls away. He lightly pinches her outer leg and she slaps his hand away. "Quit it," she says, amused and irritated by her older brother, and begins smiling. "What are you up to?" she asks him. He tells her about the combine and relaxes a little, stretching his legs out. "You don't know anything about combines," she teases him, bumping her shoulder into his.

"I know everything, don't you know that?" he tells her conceitedly.

Theresa tells Bonnie, "come upstairs with me and lets listen to records on the phonograph together. Theresa walks towards Harold.

"Hi Theresa," Harold greets her, "how's school?" he asks. She stands over him, near the couch and sits on the armrest.

"I have a lot more homework this year compared to last year." Harold pats her on the back. "It's nice to see my friends again, though, you know I haven't seen them all summer," she tells him. "If it weren't for all the classes and homework we have to do, it would be fun," she says kidding him, smiling.

"That's what I thought about it too," he tells her, "wait til you're a little older, they start teaching you geography and science, stuff you'll never use after you graduate. You might as well take an art class or Phy-Ed for as good as it does."

"Don't listen to him, Theresa," Carol tells her, "if you want to be smart, you have to know all that stuff. And if you want to be a nurse you have to know all that stuff. You can't be a nurse without it." She explains to her.

"I know. That's what I think too," Theresa tells her. "Do you want to come upstairs and listen to records with us?" she asks Harold, knowing he'll decline.

"No," he tells her, "I'm waiting for dad to come home."

"Okay then, come on Bonnie, let's go upstairs," she tells her little sister.

Betty and Laura are talking in the kitchen. Betty likes Laura; "your wiry and you've got spunk. I wish I had a little more spunk sometimes," she tells her.

Laura is from a very small town about ten miles away. She waitresses at a diner and interestingly, she met Edward before she met Harold.

"Look ma, Harold and Jack are play fighting on the floor in the living room." Soon Patrick joins them. Betty hollers at them from the kitchen.

"You's be careful in there, I don't want anyone getting hurt." They hear her and continue playing, now acting like the guys on All-Star Wrestling, running into fake turn belts and giving each other fake body slams.

Laura is smiling, watching them from the kitchen and shakes her head. "Like a little kid," she tells Betty, "I'm dating a little kid, Betty!" She exclaims laughing.

"Look at them in there," she says, then quickly gets up and runs into the living room and begins wrestling with them on the floor. She maneuvers her legs around Harold's and takes Jack and Patrick around by the arms and jumps up and announces she's the winner. Straightens her shirt by pulling it down at the ends and watches the three still wrestling and laughs. She returns back to the kitchen with Betty.

"You're pretty good in there," Betty tells her smiling.

"It was nothing," she says hamming it up, straightening her hair.

Carol enters the kitchen from the living room. "You want to wrestle now too?" Laura asks her with a straight face, and then smiles.

"I don't think so," comes her reply, Carol says smiling and giggling, "besides I don't wrestle, it's unladylike," she says rolling her shoulder.

"Well I'm a lady and I wrestle!" Laura says loudly. Carol sits at the table between them. "Wanna arm wrestle?" Laura kids her, putting up her arm.

"No...Is Harold your boyfriend?" Carol asks her.

"We're just dating, but I suppose you could call him my boyfriend if you want to," she tells her. "I guess so." She tells her, not wanting to scare him off.

"How long have you been dating?" Carol asks.

"We started dating just this last summer," comes her reply.

"What do you do on dates?" Carol wants to know.

"Well, let's see," she rolls her eyes towards Betty, "sometimes we go to dances, sometimes I just go over to his place and watch TV, sometimes we go see a movie, or come out here. You can do lots of things, or go visit people," she tells her. "You can go bowling, or go for a walk, lots of things."

"You mean you're on a date right now?" She asks.

"Yeah, kind of, well, sure we are," she says,

occasionally looking at Betty.

"Kinda," she laughs at herself.

"That's cool," Carol says brightening up. "I can't wait to start going on dates, it sounds kind of scary though."

Betty doesn't know what to say. Carol has talked about boys before, but never about dating. Betty hasn't really thought about it either, what with all the smaller kids running around, and realizes her little girl isn't so little anymore. She decides to tell her, "Pretty soon, a cute, nice boy will ask you out on a date," she says. Hoping that'll be the end to her curiosity for today.

"Really, mom? You think so?" Carol asks her excited.

"Yes I do, and he might want to kiss you," she adds, teasing her a little.

"I've never kissed a boy before," she says trying to be mature.

"If he wants to do anything else. You tell him, 'good girls don't do that,'" Laura tells her, strictly. Carol gets a smile on her face, not knowing why.

"Don't do what?" She wants to know.

"Let him touch you below your belly button," Laura says, plumping up her boobs, smiling slyly and laughing, trying to see Betty out of the corner of her eye. She wonders if she's said too much.

"Laura! Shame on you!" Betty says smiling coolly.

"She wanted to know," Laura tells Betty laughing. "You'll be fine," Laura tells Carol when her laughter subsides. "I didn't know how to kiss either, but it's easy, you just purse your lips together and the boy leans up to your face, and you put your lips on his, and move em' around a little bit, and that's about it," she says pursing her lips together. "Don't worry about it. Everybody has to have a first kiss, and everybody's nervous the first time."

"Okay thanks," Carol tells her smiling, getting up. "Thanks mom." The young lady walks out of the room, and goes upstairs to her bedroom.

Lexington Glory Days

Betty and Laura start to look at each other and Laura starts laughing, Betty looks worried. "She'll be okay," she tells Betty.

Upstairs, Carol is lying on her bed in her bedroom, watching Theresa and Bonnie dancing around and singing into hair brushes in their bedroom. Their phonograph can play one, 45-rpm record at a time. When that one gets done, they take it off and put on another one. You can hear crackles and hisses from the needle. Occasionally a scratch in the record gets so deep the needle can't play over it, and the song keeps repeating the same words; '...*you ain't nothin but a, you ain't nothin but a, you ain't nothin but a, you aint nothin but a...hound dog...crying all the time...*' With a little push of the needle the rest of the song plays itself. They keep dancing and gyrating around, Carol, though amused, gets tired of watching them and goes over to the mirror and begins to brush her hair, and daydreams of boys and kissing, and dating.

Back downstairs, the boys become tired from wrestling and are laying on the floor watching television. Betty and Laura begin preparing supper in the kitchen, and Harold's in there snacking on a raw carrot from the garden. "Did you have a good garden this year, mom?" Harold asks her.

"We did," she tells him, "we had loads of everything, tomatoes, cucumbers, onions, radishes, green beans, yellow beans, lettuce. We had it all."

"And weeds...," Laura adds chuckling, washing her hands in the sink.

"How many quarts of tomatoes did you can?" he asks her.

"Oh, about forty quarts of tomatoes and about that many quarts of pickles too," she tells him.

"Can I have a quart of each one?"

"You can have two if you want," she looks at him and

tells him with an affectionate smile.

"I'll take two then, thanks," he says looking at her.

He sits down in a chair and lifts his head and chin in the air as he talks. "I sure wish dad would hurry up and get here, so I know if he's coming or not. I don't want to be working on this thing until midnight."

From the kitchen Betty yells into the living room, "Patrick, will you go out into the garden and pick some onions for us so we have some for supper?"

"Okay," he yells back.

Patrick walks out into the garden, picks the onions, cleans off the mud that came up with them when he pulled them out of the ground and is back inside the kitchen, with the others, a short time later.

"Dad just pulled into the driveway," Patrick tells them from the porch, walking back into the house. The screen door snaps shut behind him.

"About time," Harold says, fidgeting in his chair.

"See now; you had yourself all worried for nothing," Laura tells him.

Chapter Nine

Running Bulls

Edward gets home from work and walks into the porch and opens the door to the kitchen and walks in, without a 'hi' or 'hello' to anyone sets his lunch pail down on the table and asks Harold if he's ready. "Let's go see if we can fix that combine," he tells him. Without a word spoken by either of the two, they walk out the door, outside to where the combine is sitting in the middle of the yard.

"I'm gonna hook up the power take off from the tractor to the combine and start it and wait to see what works and what doesn't, so be careful and stay away from it, don't get your hands or shirt sleeves or anything caught in it," Edward warns his son. "It'll rip your arm right off, if you do."

"The cutters aren't moving," Edward notices and looks around the machine, after engaging the power take off. Part of his job working on road construction is fixing the big, heavy machinery. so he knows what he's doing. He looks a little closer at the combine, "The bearing is spinning, but it's not doing anything. Cut the power to the combine, and kill the tractor switch, Harold."

Edward tries turning the bearing with his hands. It moves freely and shouldn't because of the load that's placed on the other end of the shaft. He looks further inside the machine, "Dammit anyway," he says, "The shaft is broken. We gotta take the whole son – of – a – bitchin thing apart. Son of a bitch. We might as well start taking it apart right away. Go to the back of my truck and bring me my toolbox. God damn it anyway."

Harold does as he's told, and brings the toolbox back and sets it down near where his dad is kneeling beside the combine. "Hand me a three-quarter inch socket," his dad tells him. Harold flips through the assortment of tools and pulls out the socket his dad wants and hands it to him without speaking.

Edward tries the socket but it's too small, and asks Harold for a larger size, "give me a seven-eighths inch," he tells him, handing him back the wrong socket. Harold rummages through the tools again and finds the seven-eighth inch socket and hands it to his dad. Edward tries the socket, and this time it fits.

He puts pressure on one of the bolts that's holding up the shaft and bearing, trying to release it. "Get me a seven-eighths inch wrench out of there."

He reaches around the shaft with the wrench, feels for the nut on the other side of the bolt and places the wrench on it. "Hang onto the wrench while I try to unscrew the bolt from the nut." Harold obediently complies.

Harold climbs under the combine and tries to get a firm grip on the wrench and nut. Edward puts pressure on the bolt but it doesn't turn. "Your gonna have to take the nut off from your side," he tells Harold, "I can't get it." Harold tries loosening the nut but it won't turn.

"Dammit," Edward says, "hold on a minute, I got a find a piece of pipe, I'll be right back." Harold waits, impatiently, tapping his foot.

Edward walks over towards the windmill, where he's placed various sizes of pipe and picks one up. He brings it back and hands it to Harold, under the combine. "Put the pipe over the end of the wrench and then try turning it by prying on the pipe." Using the pipe as leverage, Harold puts all the strength he's got onto the pipe and wrench and nut.

"Aagh! It won't budge," Harold tells him, exerting himself.

"Try harder," his dad, tells him. "It should loosen up."

"Nope, it aint gonna go," Harold tells him. "Now what."

"Let me try it," his dad tells him. The two change places and Edward crawls under the combine and Harold holds the bolt attached to the combine from the outside. "I can't get it either, it won't turn. Dammit anyway," Edward says starting to get mad. "Get me a hammer out of the toolbox."

Edward begins pounding on the pipe and starts to pound harder and harder and the nut still won't turn. "Get off of there, you bitch. Go in the back of my truck and see if there's a can of WD-40 in there," Edward tells him sternly.

Harold comes back with the can and Edward starts spraying the lubricant around all the nuts. "We gotta wait for a while to let it soak in," he tells Harold. About a minute goes by and Edward tells him, "let's try it again."

Harold climbs under the combine on the hard gravel and starts pounding on the pipe with the hammer, harder and harder; swearing at the nut, "Get off of there," he says to it. Finally he gives up. "I can't get it."

Edward tells Harold, "we'll have to let the liquid seep in some more, I guess, I don't know what else to do." He sprays more of the lubricant around all the nuts, and works his way out from beneath the combine, "we might as well go in the house while were waiting. Maybe ma's got supper ready. We can eat and try it again after supper."

The two walk toward the house and enter, supper isn't nearly done and Edward tells Betty, "well hurry up we don't have all night!"

"Oh, all right," Betty, says flustered, in front of Laura.

"We just got to boil the potatoes and fry the meat," Laura tries soothing him. "Ten, fifteen minutes and we'll be ready. It's all ready to go, we just gotta turn on the burners," she tells him matter-of-factly, smiling.

Edward walks over to the refrigerator and takes out a beer and uncaps it and takes a drink.

"Did you get the combine fixed?" Betty asks him.

"No we didn't get it fixed, we just started working on it," Edward tells her condescendingly, setting the bottle of beer down on the table.

"What's wrong with it?" She asks him, flustered. More often than not she's unsure of his attitude and this confuses her when she tries talking to him.

"The shaft from the bearing is broken, and we gotta take it all apart."

At least now she knows and maybe can be of some help to him.

Laura looks at Harold and tries to read his face to see how he's doing. He seems in another world to her. "Everything going okay out there, Harold?" She asks him gently. The tension between the father and son is noticeable.

"I guess," he tells her, unattentatively.

The older kids have all come down from upstairs and everyone is in the living room watching TV, or reading a textbook from school and doing their homework. Some gaze into the kitchen to see what's going on.

Their dad says, "I'm gonna have to take it all apart. I don't know if I can get it all done tonight or not. If we don't we'll have to try again tomorrow. After that I'll have to take it into town and try to get it welded back together,

Lexington Glory Days

or find a used one, and I don't think I'll be able to find one that will fit. God dammit, anyway. Can you come back tomorrow after work and help me some more if we don't get it taken apart tonight?" he asks Harold, standing up.

"I suppose," he tells him, feeling inferior.

"I don't know if you can or not, if you can't let me know, so I can find someone else," he tells Harold.

"Yeah, I'll come back and help if we don't get it out tonight," he says, starting to feel anxious. "I'll come back out."

With the smell of the food cooking on the stove in the air, "What are we having for supper, you got enough for everybody?" Edward asks Betty.

"Pork steak and potatoes and a vegetable," she tells him.

"How many pork steaks you got?" Edward quizzes her.

"Ten," she answers. Poking the meat with a fork.

"Is that gonna be enough?" Edward likes to have plenty for everyone.

"It should be, it's one a piece," she says, wishing she could hit him with it.

The pork steaks get fried and the potatoes boiled and the whole family, plus Laura, sits down for a late supper. Afterwards, Betty, Laura, Carol, Theresa and Bonnie clean up the kitchen. Theresa and Bonnie wash and dry the dishes, and Jack goes outside and does the chores, feeding and watering the cattle, pigs and chickens. Edward and Harold start working on the combine again. It's slow going trying to get the nuts off.

Two hours later, with a lot of muscle and torque the nuts come off, stubbornly, one by one. They pull the heavy shaft out and lay it in the back of Edward's truck. "Tomorrow morning I'll take it into town and see if it can be welded together, hopefully I can start combining the corn tomorrow afternoon. As for now, it's time to call it a

Lexington Glory Days

day and go into the house and cleanup. Let's go."

The two men try to wash all the grease off their hands and face and dry off. "Do you want a drink before you leave?" Edward offers both of them.

"We can have one, I guess," Laura tells him, "huh, Harold?"

"I suppose," he moves quickly and sits down, as Edward pulls a quart of brandy out from the pantry.

"You wouldn't make me a sandwich, would you Laura?" Edward teases.

"I'm not working right now, come to the restaurant tomorrow and I'll make you all the sandwiches you want," she tells him, amused by his comment.

They both enjoy sparring back and forth. Giving each other a hard time.

Laura likes to talk and tell stories of customers she's waited on, or about herself and her friends or her family, and this keeps everyone in a good mood.

"I should have made you work harder when you were younger," Edward tells Harold. "You'd be stronger and you might have been able to break those nuts loose." He says in all seriousness.

"You couldn't get 'em loose," Laura interjects, "why would expect Harold too? Maybe you should have worked harder when you were younger."

Edward likes to stir up trouble with Harold, but tonight Harold's not buying into it, and Laura puts a stop to it when she can.

"You tell him," Betty tells her, looking at Harold smiling.

Mom Betty is thankful for the company of other adults. She likes Laura and is extra happy to spend time with Harold.

"We got it out, that's the main thing," Harold tells them.

Early the next day before work, Edward takes the

shaft into town to get welded. Harold comes back out after his job is done at the pool table and ping pong factory to help him put it back in. By seven o'clock p.m. the shaft is put back in and ready to try out. Edward makes a test run in the cornfield with the combine to make sure it is working properly. He comes back into the house and tells them, "I think it's going to work." Everyone is relieved.

The following Saturday, Edward announces to Betty, "I'm going out combining. I'll need you to take the big truck into town once the wagon is full of corn to get it unloaded. I'll come back in a couple of hours and tell you when it's full. It's gonna be a couple hours, so no hurry."

He tells her what she needs to do and she competently agrees. Farming is one of the few things they spend time doing together, something outside of the house and without any kids. Betty enjoys this part of her life, being outside in the fresh country air with just her husband, being a farmer's wife.

Part 2

Among The Harvest

'It's beautiful out here with all the rows of gold colored corn. It's meaningful, productive,' Edward thinks to himself. 'There's nothing like farming. It's me working with the land. Raising something from the dirt. There's something fundamental and basic and instinctive about it. Man going out to get food for his family.' "As long as the tractor stays running and the combine keeps working," he says out loud. He just began combining the eighty acres of corn.

Images of his father being a bit of a curmudgeon enter his thoughts. His dad wasn't opposed to getting physical with his sons from time to time when they were younger. He had his own temper to deal with, 'but he was a good man just the same.' Edward realizes now. Traits that get passed from one generation to the next, and this case is no exception. He chuckles at this, remembering the times he got physical and pushed Harold around, and sees humor in it. He drives down a row of corn.

'Things were different in the old days. You listened or you got whipped. That's the way it was.' His dad was born in 1890 and his mother was born in 1894. 'A long time ago,' he thinks.

Edward and his eldest brothers, Larry, and Tom have

Lexington Glory Days

reputations for being tough fighters and big men.

'You don't mess with us,' he realizes. Every town has big brutes and in this case, it's them, and he knows it.

'We're friendly, and quick to joke along right with you, but don't piss us off. We're quick to stand up for ourselves.' He revs up the tractor's engine and sees Eugene across the field combining his own fields.

'Oftentimes the trouble starts with a smart ass, or misunderstanding while drinking,' he thinks to himself. Loud voices and cursive stares follow, if the offender did not quickly back down, the argument would escalate into accusations, then to swinging fists. The boys didn't lose very often.

Edward gets nostalgic and a little sad thinking about his dead father and his mother, still grieving for him. He thinks of his own family.

'It's a lot of responsibility,' he thinks, driving the tractor and pulling the combine and wagon. 'Keeping the wife happy, and raising and feeding all those mouths, keeping the money coming in, and maintaining my own sanity and thoughts clear. It isn't easy,' he thinks to himself. He's feeling sorry for himself.

He continues mulling over life and its circumstances. 'I know the pressures get to me, and I know I don't always handle things as well as I could or would like to, but I'm human. There's outside forces I can't control, that quickly need a response, that come at me from out of the blue, that I'm not prepared to deal with at a moments notice. On top of it all, I need to take care of myself and enjoy myself once in a while.' That includes drinking and living it up.

He slows the tractor down momentarily, letting the combine catch up decobbing the corn stalks. 'I try the best I can. I know I could do better. I know I don't try as hard as I could, but I try plenty hard. It can all be so overwhelming. I don't have it so easy either.' Edward works all day out in the field, way past dark.

The following day is another absolutely beautiful fall day in October in the country. It's windier than the day before. It's a dusty job, picking the corn. When the wind is just right, it blows all the dust away from Edward, and he can breathe fresh air for a while again. But it isn't long and it's right back in his face.

He begins thinking about Betty. 'Oh, how she can aggravate me,' he reflects on her and thinks of all the little things that bother him about her. 'The way she questions me about things she wouldn't have to know about. The way she sometimes takes the kid's side over mine, the tone in her voice, her complaining about my drinking.' He wonders how sometimes these things can seem so small and at other moments seem so important, all at the same time.

'I know things bother her, especially when I'm not forthcoming with a better answer, and I know she thinks she's right.' He realizes she's just doing what she thinks is best for them.

'I love her though. I'd do anything for her and the kids. I know she loves with me. I know I could be nicer to her; show her more understanding and affection. It's a tough relationship, especially with all the kids. She's not going anywhere.' He gets tired from all his thinking.

He looks back and sees the wagon behind the combine is getting full of corn. So he decides to combine the rows closer to the house, where he'll unhook the wagon once it's full from the combine, then hook it up to the big truck, that he'll need Betty to take to the elevator in town to get unloaded.

Working until well after dark tonight, and all day tomorrow, and tomorrow night, 'It should take about two weeks to get all the corn picked,' he predicts.

Monday he comes home from his job working on road construction and picks corn until close to midnight, when both wagons are full again.

Tuesday, Betty runs them into town so he has two empty ones to fill again the next night. He goes out again after work, picking corn till close to midnight for the next week.

Gertrude baby sits two-year-old Frankie and baby Jennifer, as long as the older kids are in school and until Betty is back with both empty wagons.

On the following Saturday he's out there from early morning till after dark.

Edward's combining the corn near the house, trying to get the wagon as full of corn as he can, without any spilling any onto the ground, as the wagon will get moved around and taken into town.

Betty is an obedient follower in times like these, when it comes to the farm and farming. 'She's a good farm wife, I love this about her.' But she's apt to do things her own way, and he needs to keep an eye on her, in case she starts to do things differently than how he wants them done.

He revs the engine again, giving the tractor more power. 'I get mad just thinking about her doing things her own way. I know my way works, don't change it.'

'It's not a bad little place,' he thinks, looking around the yard, driving near the house in the field. 'The two-story barn is in good shape and the upstairs loft will hold plenty of hay for the cattle to feed on. The one long corncrib and three other outbuildings are nice and sturdy enough and will hold some of the corn crop or serve as storage sheds for something else.'

He looks at the house, 'the paint is peeling and flaking off all around and everywhere on it, but besides that it aint bad,' he thinks. Not having indoor plumbing enters the back of his mind. 'That would be nice.'

His thoughts turn to the yard, 'It's nice with plenty of pine trees for a windbreak for the house, and a big lawn

Lexington Glory Days

for the kids to play. It's got all kinds of shrubbery and even a plum tree,' he thinks satisfied.

He makes a couple of more passes in the field and pulls up and stops where the field meets the yard, and kills the tractor and walks the one-hundred or so yards to the house, where Betty is.

"I got the wagon full again," he tells her, getting a drink of water. "I'm gonna take a little break before I go back out. So no hurry."

"I'm ready whenever you are," she tells him, waiting.

"All right. Let's go then. We'll get those wagons switched around, and you can head into town with the truck and wagon."

They walk outside and get in the big truck and drive the old vehicle down to the field to switch the wagons. "Now take your time. There's no reason to be in any hurry," he tells her. Hoping she'll be careful.

"I've driven it before, I'll be okay," she tells him, trying to reassure him. He looks at her for a few moments, judging her mood.

With no further instructions, Betty climbs back into the big truck and heads into town to the elevator to get the wagon unloaded. He watches her drive the old truck until she is out of eyesight. Satisfied, hopeful and a little nervous.

He sees Eugene again in his own fields trying to get his crops out and waves. Eugene reaches his arm high out into the air and waves, and starts to make his way over to where Edward is, driving his tractor. "How's it going?" Eugene asks him. "I'm going along pretty good."

"All right," Edward tells him, "I was just thinking about my boys," he stands there, looking around the field, contemplative.

"What about them," Eugene asks him. "Everything okay?"

"Yeah, as far as I know. It's just I want them to be

strong, in their minds and physically. Sometimes I wonder if I'm too hard on them. I just don't want them to have to put up with other people's bullshit. "

"Of course not, no one does. You care about them," Eugene tells him.

"I'm just looking out for them. I know they don't understand this, they don't have to. It's about teaching them to stand up for themselves, and not letting people walk all over them." Edward tells him with conviction in his voice, smiling.

"I know, Edward, your preaching to the choir. I don't want any of my kids, the boys or girls, to grow up thinking life owes them anything. If they want something, they're going to have to work for it. Like we did."

Edward wants them to understand life isn't fair or easy. He looks over his land, to the far, far end of his field where his land meets up with his neighbors. Back there far away from the house, is a beautiful small meadow. He's fenced it in for the cattle to graze on the grasses. It has a ravine and a couple of dozen mature trees. Harold and Jack have been back there to shoot squirrels and an occasional rabbit. He looks back at Eugene, who's watching him.

"I guess I better get back at it," Edward tells him. "How's everything going for you?" Eugene has fifty more acres to combine than Edward does.

"Good. No trouble at all," he tells him happily.

"I better get back at it too if I want to get it done. I'll talk to ya later."

Edward climbs back on the tractor and goes back out into the field.

The combine and tractor jerk suddenly and he is startled from his thoughts, and wonders if he ran over a rock or if something on the tractor or combine broke. He notices his body starting to feel tense.

He throttles the engine down and moves along

slowly, keeping an eye on the combine for any noticeable problems. He takes a pint of brandy out from under the seat and takes a large swallow and drives along slowly for a few minutes and decides everything appears to be working all right so he throttles the engine back up and keeps going.

He combines the corn down by the meadow, going up and down the rows the short way, leaving a large square area that he won't combine it all, for the pheasants and deer and other wildlife to feed from and use as cover this winter.

After an hour he sees the wagon is little less than half full and decides to get closer to the house, and heads out for the other side of the field, but instead makes one path all along the outside rows around the whole field. He likes how the field looks, with a bunch of the middle rows already picked and gone, and having the end rows picked makes it look like he's really gaining headway.

The tractor jerks again a second time and he looks back to make sure the combine is still working. It jerks again, this time with so much more force that his head and body lurch forward from the seat. He looks behind him and sees the combine has quit running and he begins cussing. "God dammit, now what."

He sees Betty is back from town and has parked the old truck and the empty wagon back on the field. He reaches for the pint of brandy and takes another big swallow. He gets down from the tractor and goes around to look over the combine.

From the corner of his eye, he sees Betty driving the car down the dirt road. She pulls over, parks halfway in the ditch and halfway on the road nearby where he is broken down, and starts walking towards him. 'She's always there when I need her," he thinks.

"What's wrong? Did you break down again? She asks him. "Here, I bought you some ice water in a thermos."

Lexington Glory Days

He takes the thermos from her and takes a long drink.

"Something happened, I'm not sure what yet. How did everything go taking the corn to town?"

"It was a long wait, but I made it," she tells him feeling close and good about their relationship.

He asks her, "Why don't you drive me back to the house, so I can get the truck with the tools in it and take a little break. Its so God damn dusty out here."

The two walk to the car side by side and Edward asks her, "What are the kids doing?"

"Jack and Patrick are outside monkeying around…"

"Monkeying around?" he interrupts her. "Monkeying around with what?" He wants to know.

"I don't know, I didn't look. And the girls are in the house watching Frankie and Jennifer. It's such a nice day." She says freely.

"Not a nice day to have a breakdown," he grins a little at her.

"You want me to call Harold and see if he'll come out and help you?"

"Nah, wait a while, I'll see if I can fix it. First I got to figure out what's wrong with it." They pull into the yard and Edward tells her, "Park over by the truck so I can make sure my toolboxes are in it."

"Let's go in the house for a bit," Betty tells him. "Are you hungry? Do you want me to make you something to eat?"

"No, I'm good." They get out of the car and walk towards the house and Edward notices Jack and Patrick near the cow pen, and decides to go see what they're doing. "I'll be right in," he tells her.

He walks closer to the boys and sees them throwing rocks at the cattle, and the cattle are getting jumpy and frightened. He's afraid they might break down the fences keeping them in if they get too wild.

"What the hell are you doing?" he hollers at the boys,

Lexington Glory Days

"get the hell out of there and quit throwing rocks at them cattle! Or I'm gonna start throwing rocks at you and your gonna feel it too!" he warns them. But it's too late, a few of the cattle have busted through the gate and the rest of the cattle are about to stampede out of the broken fence.

Edward quickly jumps over the fence into the pen and runs along the side of the barnyard to the gate, and starts waving his hands in the air to get the cattle to turn around, and stay in the pen. He manages to scare most of them back in and they retreat, but they're still very jumpy. There are four that got out and are in the cornfield, eating up the golden grain.

He yells at the boys, "Run in the house and get ma!"

Betty comes running out and Edward orders her to stay by the gate and chase any cattle back that might try to get out, while he gets some lumber and nails and a hammer to fix the gate. All the while he's getting the supplies, he gets madder and madder at the boys and cussing about the loose cattle.

"I gotta fix the God damn combine! What do you think I got all the time in the world? What were you's throwing rocks at the cattle for anyway? God damned kids, I'll fix you's! I'm mad, and I am! You're gonna get it too. When I get done fixing this gate. You's better hide because when I find you's, I'm gonna beat you! I got four cattle out now because of you brats, and the combines broke down and I gotta fix that! I gotta fix this gate first, then I got a go round up them cattle that just got out! Jesus Christ I'm mad now!"

He finds the lumber he needs and the hammer and nails and goes about repairing the gate, cussing the whole time. Bonnie and Theresa, hearing him from inside the old farmhouse come out to see what's going on, and he starts hollering at them. Directing his anger anywhere he can.

"What do you two want? You gonna start throwing

rocks too now? So more cattle get out? How come you weren't watching your little brothers? You's were in your bedroom I suppose, listening to your records! I'm gonna throw that phonograph out is what I'm gonna do! Find those two little brats for me, cause when I'm done here, fixing this fence, I'm gonna beat their asses till they can't sit down, that's what I'm gonna do!"

Poor Betty doesn't know what to say or do. If she's quiet, she won't be able to settle his anger down, and if she speaks up, she knows he'll turn his anger towards her. She's never seen him so mad.

She decides to speak her mind, "Oh, just fix the gate and leave the kids alone." She looks unsure about how he's going to react to her words.

Edward mimics her, "Oh, just fix the gate, just fix the gate. Why don't you just fix the gate? Then you can go round up them cattle that are out! And then you can go fix the combine! And then you can finish combining the corn, before it snows or rains. Just fix the fence. God damn it I am fixing the gate!"

Betty knows he hasn't calmed down at all and tells Theresa to tell Jack, Bonnie and Patrick to hide in the cornfield right here behind the house, and to stay with them. Betty wants to go into the house and tell Carol the same thing, and pick up the baby and take Frankie by the hand and join them, so their dad won't find them until after his temper flares down. She's afraid of him.

"Now go! Hide!" she whispers.

Betty has never seen her husband so angry and is afraid of what he might do to the kids if he gets his hands on them.

She sees the kids wander into the cornfield and waits until Edward's occupied elsewhere and rushes to the house to get the other children, and meets the other kids out in the cornfield.

"Everyone stay together," she tells them quietly. In

their tattered, worn clothes, their young innocent faces looking up at her, belying the possible dire circumstances. They all have scared expressions.

"Don't think I don't know where you are," he hollers in the air. "I know right where all of you are, and when I'm done, I'm coming in there after you," he says to them, as they watch him nervously from behind corn stocks in the field.

After realizing how afraid his family is of him, his anger subsides a little, but not much. Betty doesn't know if he's serious or just trying to teach the kids a lesson, but she's just as afraid for them, and herself, either way.

"Kids be quiet now," she warns them. A half an hour goes by and Betty decides she should talk to her husband and see if he's calmed down at all.

She appears out of the cornfield. The mere image of her emerging is strange. She crosses the yard and approaches Edward, and he sees her coming. She purposely tries walking nonchalantly and Edward notices.

"It's okay, you can tell them to come out now," he reassures her, "then come back, I gotta have you open and close the gate when I bring those four cattle up." Most of his anger has subsided.

She walks back into the cornfield where the kids are and tells them, "it's okay you can come out now, but you's better behave," she scolds them, "or he'll get mad at you's again. And stay by the house too, all of you!"

Betty helps Edward get the four cattle back in the pen, and then watches him get into his truck and drive down the road, out onto the field to the combine.

Back at the broken down combine, Edward sees it's a broken chain that's caused all of the problems and can be fixed without too much trouble. He fixes the chain and has good weather to finish picking the corn. 'What a day,' he thinks, confessing to himself honestly, 'some things went well and others did not.'

The first snow of the season falls in mid-November, and the family settles into the house for their first winter together in a year. The nights come early, with the darkness coming down before supper. The place is warm, almost too warm sometimes. The dim lights all around the house, except the kitchen, keeps a low glow through the frosted windows from the outside, like some obscure Norman Rockwell painting.

The mid 1960s passes by the family, far removed and mostly unaffected by much of the political turmoil, with the slaying of President John F. Kennedy, the war in Viet Nam and the civil rights movement.

Betty and Edward, even with all the trouble in the country, still have mouths to feed, kids to care for, babies to diaper, meals to prepare, arguments to settle, cattle to water, land to till and bills to pay.

They aren't oblivious to the news, on the contrary they watch it every night on TV, but other than the older kids discussing the news of the day at school, as for Betty she worries and thinks, 'what is this world coming to.'

Edward watches, sometimes saddened, sometimes puzzled, by the cruel actions of the governments, including his own. Thankful he's finished with his military service obligation. Yet he still has a wife and kids to raise.

It's a minute-by-minute, day-by-day life for them. Just keeping up with his family and the farm, and keeping his head above water is much of all he manages to do.

Chapter Ten

Quiet Footsteps

"What's wrong mom?" Patrick, eight, asks her softly. Trying to compose herself, she tells him, "Oh, nothing, I'll be okay," and places her hand on her lowered forehead, and begins sobbing. Patrick walks back into the living room, where most of the other kids are and tells them, "something's wrong with mom, she's in the kitchen, crying." Betty has just gotten off the phone. Her eyes are red and full of tears. She sits down in the chair below the phone hanging on the wall, and sobs uncontrollably.

The other kids turn and look at each other, and the ones that can see her from the living room, watch her. "I've never, ever seen her cry before, oh my God," Theresa says. A sullen shadow falls over the group, knowing something's happened, not knowing what.

Theresa and Bonnie get up and look at her through the doorway momentarily, and both walk towards her and ask her, "What's wrong mom? Why are you crying?"

"Something's happened. I don't want to talk about it right now," and straightens up, looking them in the eye, drying her tears with a tissue that's already damp.

"Mom, what is it?" Bonnie, thirteen asks her, starting to cry, shaking her hands out in front of her.

"It's okay, you just go back into the living room," she

Lexington Glory Days

manages to tell her. Bonnie jumps up and down, crying and runs into the living room.

"Are you sure everything's okay mom? Is there anything I can do for you?" Theresa, fifteen, asks her.

Betty stares blankly in front of her and says, "I suppose I have to make supper soon, would you mind going down into the basement and bring up some potatoes, enough for everybody, and peel them?" Wiping the tears from her eyes rubbing her nose.

"Sure I can," she tells her, lingering to watch her for a few moments.

The phone rings and Betty stands up to answer it. "Hello," she says with a weak, crack in her voice.

It's Harold, "Hi mom, how you doing over there?"

"Oh I'm doing, that's about all," she tells him, disgruntled.

"I know of a couple places here in town that are for rent. There's a three-bedroom and then there's a four-bedroom," he tells her.

"How much do they want for them?" She asks.

"They're both sixty-five dollars a month, you pay for gas and they'll pay the electric, on both of them."

"Are they nice? And clean?" She asks him.

"They're not too bad, I went over and looked at both of them, and they're both pretty good."

"Well, tell whoever I'll take the four-bedroom one. Thank you Harold."

"Okay, I'll be talking to you soon. Call me if you need anything."

"I will. Bye." She hangs up the phone, her hands shaking.

Betty walks into the living room, "Where's Carol? I need to talk to Carol," she tells the children.

"She's upstairs," they all tell her, quietly worried.

Betty walks up the narrow staircase into Carol's room and tells her, "Carol I need you to keep an eye on the kids, especially Jennifer and Frankie. Will you do that for me?"

"Sure mom. What's wrong, you look like you've been crying?"

"I don't want the younger kids finding out yet, but I'll tell you. We have to move to town. We have to move."

"Why?" She asks surprised.

"I just can't talk about it right now, I have to lie down for a while, I'll tell you more later. If you really want to know, you can call Harold and ask him about it, he knows. Don't tell the other kids though, okay?" She turns and looks at her again, "It'll be okay. Keep an eye on the kids for me, while I lie down," and leaves the room.

Carol leaves the room right behind her and follows her down the steps and enters the living room looking for Jennifer, Frankie, Patrick and the other kids. Seeing they're all here, she walks into the kitchen, noticing Theresa peeling potatoes. She picks up the phone and dials Harold's number. She gets Harold on the phone and talks to him in a low voice so no one else can hear, and in a few minutes hangs it up.

Theresa looks up at her from peeling potatoes and asks her, "So what's going on?"

"I'm not supposed to tell anyone," she tells her teary-eyed.

"Did someone get hurt?" she guesses.

"No, and I don't want to say anymore, okay? You'll find out soon enough."

"All right then," Theresa tells her.

Carol walks into the living room and sees everyone sitting around, and returns to the kitchen and begins helping Theresa with supper, and sets the table. "The kids are so quiet," Carol tells her.

"They all saw mom talking on the phone and crying, and sobbing with tears coming down her face," Theresa tells her, "you were upstairs in your room."

"Who was she talking to?" Carol asks.

"I don't know, she didn't say. I asked her if everything was okay and if there was anything I could do for her, and she told me to start peeling potatoes for supper. Something must be going on."

"There is something going on," Carol tells her, "and you're not going to like it. None of us will. But it can't be helped I guess," she says with tears in her eyes, not knowing the full story, looking confused.

Bonnie comes into the kitchen and sits down and lies her head down on the table, "What's mom so sad about?" She asks them.

"She has a problem with something," Carol tells her.

"What kind of problem? She presses her.

"I'm not supposed to say," Carol tells her, "I guess mom wants to tell you herself, when she's ready."

"She okay?"

"She will be," Carol assures her.

The phone rings again and Carol walks over and answers it. "Hello... She is, but she's lying down." 'Tell her it's Katherine, and if she wants me to call her back later I will.' "Okay – hold on." Carol walks into Betty's bedroom and leans over and quietly whispers in her ear and gives her the message. She tells her, she'll get up and answer it. She walks into the kitchen, dabbing a tissue at her eyes, and picks up the phone. 'Hi Betty, it's Katherine, how are you doing?' "OK, but miserable, but what can I do?" 'You hang in there. I'm here for you, for whatever you need.' "Thank you, that's nice of you." 'If there's anything I can do, to help you with the move, let me know. Did you find a place yet?' "Yeah, Harold found it for me in town." 'Do you know when you are moving?' "I don't know yet, I guess I'll find out sometime tomorrow." 'Let me know if I can do anything, anything.' "I'm gonna need some mattresses for the kids to sleep on, maybe at the very least. I don't know if I should take all of the beds or what," she tells her sister-in-law. 'I'll ask around. You take care now.' she tells her. "I'll try. Good bye." 'Bye Betty.'

"You girls finish making supper for me, will you? I'm gonna sit down in the living room."

"Okay mom," they tell her. Betty has a lot of thinking to do. She needs to decide what, if anything, to take from this house to the new house she plans to rent in town.

An hour later there's a knock on the kitchen door, and the girls see its Laura, through the window, and they wave her in. Laura is in a little bit more of a serious mood, than usual, but cheery nonetheless. She makes small talk with the girls before asking where Betty is. She walks into the living room, and some of the kids look up from the TV, or their schoolbooks and tell her, 'hi'. She sits next to Betty on the couch and the two begin talking. "I'm so sorry mom," she tells Betty, taking her hand in her own.

"Thank you Laura, I don't know what I should do," she tells her.

"What are you thinking about?" She asks.

"For starters, if I should take the beds and mattresses, or just get different mattresses and lay them on the floor for now. Did you talk to Harold? Did we get the house?"

"Yes you did. And you can move in whenever you're ready," she tells her. "When are you thinking about going?"

"I don't know for sure when the best time would be or how I should do it," Betty tells her.

"I could pick the kids up after school tomorrow, or whenever you're ready, and drive them over for you," Laura tells her.

Betty stares at Laura in the eyes for a moment, the reality of the situation sinking in further, and tells her, "I don't know if I'm ready, what would the kids sleep on?"

"There are two mattresses there, that the people who used to live there left. The owner of the place just left them there, in case someone could use them. I'm sure between Harold and I, we can find two more used ones someplace."

"How about their clothes? Blankets? Sheets, towels, pots and pans? Food?" Betty wants to know, "What do I do about all that?"

"A little bit at a time, maybe," Laura tells her, "I could take some stuff tonight even."

"I don't want the kids to know yet, though. I told Carol part of it."

"So she knows? Maybe we can tell Theresa, and they can help us take some things out to my car."

"I just don't know," Betty, says discouragingly, "I suppose you could tell Theresa too. I just don't have the strength."

"Sure, I will. They're both in the kitchen now. Hang in there, we'll get you through this." Laura walks into the kitchen and slowly, piece meals the story together in small chunks that the girls can comprehend and absorb slowly. Theresa takes the news sadly; tears begin streaming down her face. Laura hugs the girls and tells them to be strong.

"Everything will be okay," she tries to reassure them, being tough. "Mom doesn't want the younger kids to know yet. Are you gonna be okay Theresa?"

Theresa nods, trying to be strong, "I'm trying."

"Okay then, I'm gonna take some pots and pans out to the car, Carol, why don't you see if there's any extra blankets you can find and put them in my car. Get as many as you can and leave enough so everyone stays warm tonight. Theresa, maybe you should keep working on supper. Carol, after the blankets, take a few pairs of pants, some shirts, sweatshirts, socks and underwear, for each of the kids and I'll help you."

"Okay," Carol tells her.

The three begin their jobs slowly, not entirely sure what to make of the situation. Betty has picked up

Jennifer now, from off the floor and is trying to hold her. The child fusses and wants to get down. She looks at the other children, Jack and Bonnie, now thirteen, and wonders if she should tell them. She decides she will tell them, at least parts of it, tomorrow morning, if there's a good opportunity. She looks at Patrick, now eight, and decides the same thing. Frankie, four, is too young to understand.

She gets up from off the couch, slowly walks into the kitchen, and sees Laura with pots and pans stacked on top of one another and tells her, "Take some food if you have room."

"I have lots of room, we can take lots of it," she tells her, optimistically.

Betty pulls a kitchen chair out from under the table and sits down, her elbow on the table, her hand on her cheek, she stares at the speckles in the white tabletop and sighs. Within an hour, Laura and Carol have the car full of essentials, enough to get the family started.

"Harold and I will unload the car and put the things in the new house for you, when I get back to town. I'll tell Harold to get the key from the owner and we'll make sure the place is locked up after were done," Laura tells her future mother in law.

Now for the question Betty knew was coming and isn't sure about yet, how she's going to answer it. Laura prepares to leave, and gives Betty a long hug and asks her, "You want me to pick the kids up from school tomorrow and take them to the new place? It's up to you. I will though if you want me too."

Without thinking Betty tells her, "I suppose you might as well."

"I can come out and pick you up too if you want me to, before I pick up the kids," she tells her.

"No, I want the car," she tells her, "Tell Harold to come out though, maybe you could come with him," her thinking is disoriented.

"You want me to come out too? Okay I'll tell him. We'll be out then..."

"Wait," Betty interrupts her, "You pick the kids up from school, I'd like to be at the new place when they get there. I can load some things in the car myself tomorrow morning, and if Harold wants to come out, about noon, I suppose that'd be all right, but I don't want him to get into any trouble with his job."

"I'll tell him and he can decide what he wants to do. Maybe he can take a long lunch, he won't get into any trouble. So, Harold will come out about noon and I'll pick the kids up at three-fifteen p.m. from school, don't forget to tell them. Have Carol or Theresa remind them or tell them at school tomorrow. I'll see you at the house then."

"Thank you. I don't know if I could have done this without you."

She gives Betty another long hug, "I'll see you tomorrow, call me if you need anything before then."

"I will, thanks again."

"Okay," Laura tells her, then turns and leaves.

A minute later Betty gets up from the chair and tells Carol and Theresa, who have been in the kitchen listening, "I better help make supper. Thank you girls for helping, you can go now if you want, I can finish making it."

"It's okay mom, we can still help," Carol tells her, speaking for herself and her sister. "We'll help with supper, or keep an eye on the kids. Whatever needs to get done."

"Thank you girls," Betty tells them, and gives them each a kiss on the sides of their cheek. "Maybe you could set the table and watch Jennifer and Frankie for me. I'll fry some hamburgers. If you want to, put water in a kettle and boil the potatoes and watch them. Supper should be ready in about a half-hour, you can tell the kids."

As promised supper's ready and everyone is around the table eating the hamburgers and potatoes. Everyone has his or her own place. Carol and Theresa and Bonnie sit on one side. Jack, Patrick and Frankie sit on the other side, across from them. Betty sits on one end, and Edward, if he were home from work, would sit on the other.

Still sensing something wrong, the younger kids eat their meals quietly, and don't fuss much. The older kids make a little small talk in their direction, just to lighten the mood, for their sake as well. Betty isn't eating much; she has no appetite. The kids finish their meals and one by one get up and leave the table and go up to their rooms or back into the living room. Carol, Theresa, and Bonnie help their mom clear the table and do up the dishes. Afterwards they go back into the living room and help keep an eye on the younger kids.

Betty tiredly walks into the living room and sits down in the rocking chair and watches TV with the rest of the family. About an hour later, the sounds of quiet footsteps out on the porch are heard.

The front door to the kitchen is opened then closed. Footsteps around the kitchen make the old floorboards in the house creek in places. The sounds of someone rustling with their jacket can be heard. The refrigerator door is opened, and glass bumps into glass making a 'tink' noise, as plastic bowls and leftovers are moved around to see if there's anything good to eat. A glass plate slides on the kitchen table, and bowls tumble across it, as if someone were carelessly cleaning out the refrigerator. More footsteps are heard walking around the room. The cast-iron skillet is put on the stove with a light bang. The smell of cooked food is soon in the air and metal against metal can be heard as the food is stirred around in the pan. Another glass plate slides on the table, with the tinkle of silverware next. More footsteps that make a few short

Lexington Glory Days

strides then stop, a few more short strides, and they stop again. A few more and they stop for a longer time. All that can be heard is the crackle of the food frying in the pan, and the occasional spoon hitting the sides, stirring it around.

The only other sounds in the house are the voices coming from the TV in the living room. It is eerily quiet. You hear the little noises a house makes on its own. The wood in the walls cracking from time to time, from the house settling down on its foundation, or from the cold. The tick tock of a clock, the quiet whirl of a motor from the refrigerator starting or stopping, the wind against a window, the gas in the furnace igniting, (whoumph) making fire. The floorboards in the upstairs, or the steps leading to the upstairs, occasionally creaking, from the weight of the house, sounding like somebody's walking around, a tree branch scratching the outside of a window beating the wind, the faint sound of a car driving by, that is barely detectable, the cats and dog, bumping at the front door, wanting to get fed, or let in, as if someone were trying to get in. The gurgle of a drain, or the drip... drip... drip of a leaky faucet. It can play with your mind and make the weakest and the strongest jumpy and paranoid.

In the kitchen, the sound of metal scraping the bottom of the cast-iron skillet, and then the skillet being set back on the stove is heard. A plate is moved a very short distance, and silverware is rustled together, and a knife, spoon, or fork is dropped. A chair is slid a short distance on the floor, and a 'hissss' sound is heard, as air is released from one of the chair cushions. Then, all that is left is the sound of the metal silverware lightly touching the glass of the plate, about once every twenty seconds.

A few minutes go by, and then a scruffy, older man's voice is heard. "Isn't anybody gonna talk to me or what? I suppose everybody's mad at me," he grumbles to himself.

"I suppose, you're mad. I know you're mad." A mere few seconds or more goes by without any more words spoken, and then, fairly quietly, "Jesus Christ, I had to make my own supper, and now nobody will talk to me. I come home and nobody will talk to me. That's the thanks I get. I suppose." Speaking louder now, "how come I didn't get any supper? God dammit, when I come home I expect supper to be on the table." He calms down a little all of sudden, and mumbles, "Supper should be on the table by six o'clock. What time is it anyway?" He says and looks up at the clock, "it's after seven, that shouldn't make any difference." He starts getting madder; "You should keep it warm for me until I get home. You put everything away just because I'm late? Oh, what's the use, nobody's listening anyway. I might as well be talking to the wall. Did anybody feed and water the cattle and sows today?" he hollers.

Jack, now thirteen gets up and walks into the kitchen – living room doorway, stands there and tells him, "I fed and watered them when I came home from school."

"You did? Good, thank you. You know those cows and pigs gotta get fed and watered every day. You eat and drink every day don't you? Well they're no different. Every day like clockwork, when you come home from school, change out of your school clothes, and go out there and feed and water them. Every day."

"Okay," he tells him, unaffected by his demeanor, and returns to the living room.

"Maybe Patrick can start helping you," he continues, just to have someone to talk to, "maybe you can show him what needs to get done, and he can start helping you with it. You gotta keep an eye on him though, don't let him get hurt. Christ don't let him get hurt. Don't let him get in the pen with the cattle either, they could trample him or step on him. And keep him out of the pigpen after he's done feeding and watering them. Make sure he stays out of the

Lexington Glory Days

pens. Are you listening? Kid! Did you hear me?"

Jack walks back into the kitchen – living room doorway again, looking at him, "yeah, I heard you. I'll take him out there, and show him what has to get done and he can help me. I don't mind doing it, but I'll show him what I do, and I'll keep an eye on him," he stands there for a moment. The two look at each other, and he returns to the living room without any more instructions or comments.

"You're a good kid, Jack," he tells him, "better than that god damn older brother of yours, I'll tell ya that much. What's mom doing? Is mom home?" he asks anybody that can hear him. "Woman! You in there? Answer me if you are!" He says loudly. A few moments go by with no answer, and he tries it again. "Woman! God damn it if you're in there answer me!"

"I'm right here," Betty tells him from the living room, visibly upset, her eyes full of tears and small. "If you'd of looked instead of hollering you'd of seen me," she tells him, putting him off, trying to stay strong for the sake of the children.

"You are. Why didn't you answer me the first time I asked you then?" No response. "Woman! Answer me!"

"I'm right here in the living room," she tells him, straightforwardly and loudly.

"I said, why didn't you answer me the first time I asked you?"

"I think you know why," she tells him.

"You think – I know? How am I supposed to know? You think I can read your mind? I want to know why you didn't answer me the first time I asked you."

"And I told you, I think you know why," she tells him again.

"Oh I see, you're mad. I can understand that," he says sympathetically. "I know, I know you're mad. You're mad. Do you want to talk about it?"

"No, I don't want to talk about it," is her reply.

"So what, your just gonna stay mad? Well stay mad then. See if I care. Stay mad," he tells her grudgingly. "I'll go someplace else then. I'll go someplace where they'll talk to me."

"Good. Go! Good riddance!" she tells him.

"Good riddance?!! Good riddance?!!" He mumbles something uninterpretable under his breath. "I'll go, I will too. I won't come back either."

"Kids, I want you's all to go upstairs. Carol and Theresa, you take Jennifer and Frankie up with you and watch them." Betty suddenly tells her children.

Questioningly, and on edge, the children go. Carol and Theresa pick up the littlest ones, and everyone else follows them.

"What did you send the kids upstairs for? They can hear this. This is life, maybe they can learn something from it."

"I don't want them hearing this," she tells him, "this is nothing kids should hear."

"So are you gonna come in here and talk about it, or do I have to come in there?"

"I told you I don't want to talk about it," she tells him.

"So you just gonna stay mad then, okay be that way. Stay mad then."

"You're damn right I'm mad," she tells him.

"Well, what are you so mad about? So I had a little fling, big deal, is that what you're mad about? You're mad that I was with another woman? You're mad just because I made love to another woman?"

"You're damn right, that's what I'm mad about. Your family is here, not down the road, you had no business going over there," she says, tears welling up in her eyes.

"I know, I know, I'm sorry."

"You're sorry all right," she tells him indignantly.

"You're a lot more than sorry."

"Well, what does that mean? There's nothing I can do about it now," he tells her.

"You should have thought about that before you went over there."

"I said I was sorry, what more do you want? Jesus Christ, I made a mistake, get over it, will you?"

"I can't get over it. I'm mad as hell, and you want me to just get over it. Well I can't."

"Well, what do you want me to do? Tell me!"

"There's nothing you can do, you never should have went over to that bitches house in the first place."

"Oh, so now she's a bitch?"

"She's a bitch all right, and you're the dog that went to see her."

"Now, I'm a dog?"

"You're a dog all right, you're worse than a dog."

"I suppose," he reflects, "you're right. I had that coming."

"You had that coming and a lot more than that."

"I suppose," he says, reflecting.

The two sit in separate rooms without speaking, each contemplating their own personal situations and their situations together. Edward knows he's gotten himself into a fix that isn't going to be easily resolved but he believes life is going to go on, no matter what happens. He doesn't want Betty to be mad at him, but he doesn't want to put up with all the arguing that's sure to take place, or all the looks, or the comments Betty might make, that's all to certain, to be misconstrued and misinterpreted by him. Still, he realizes she has every right to be mad.

He hates to think about what people will say about him, and the gossip that's sure to ensue, and the black mark now on his reputation. He knows he's made a mistake, and will have to deal with the consequences. He

Lexington Glory Days

just wants it all over with, and life to return to normal, like it was before, as soon as it can.

Betty walks upstairs to see how the kids are doing, and makes a point to talk to each one. Carol has got Frankie in his pajamas, and she tells everyone to go to bed, so they can get up for school in the morning.

"But mom, it's only seven-thirty!" they whine.

She tells Carol, "make sure Theresa, Jack and Bonnie, and Patrick go with Laura after school tomorrow, she'll be picking you all up. I'll tell the kids myself during breakfast tomorrow morning that Laura will be picking them up after school." She doesn't know most of the kids already know.

She kisses her oldest daughter on the forehead, and looks lovingly at her with tear drops in her eyes for a moment and strokes her hair. She picks up Jennifer from Theresa and Bonnie's bed and takes her downstairs and lays her in her crib for the night. She takes a pillow and blankets from her bed, lays them out on the couch in the living room, and lies down. Edward grumbles about there not being any blankets left on the bed, but doesn't pursue it. The two drift into sleep, later than sooner, with so much on their minds, a restless, worrisome sleep.

The next morning the alarm clock goes off at five o'clock. Betty hears the clock in the bedroom and gets up, and hollers at Edward four different times before he hears her, and even then he's apt to drift back off to sleep again. She hollers at him a fifth time, and this time he awakens and stays awake. He gets cleaned up and dressed while she makes him breakfast. She lays back down on the couch while he eats without talking to him. When he's finished he walks into the living room, and tells her, "I'm going out now." She does not answer him, and he leaves the house without a goodbye, to feed and water the pigs and cattle and go about his day.

She tries to get some rest before she has to get the

kids up for school at six-thirty. When it's time to get the kids up, she hollers up the staircase at them, making sure they all respond to her, with some type of verbal communication that they've heard her. Once they are cleaned up and dressed, Betty has breakfast waiting for them.

'This is the time', she thinks, 'while they're all around the table eating, and Edwards outside.' "Laura is going to pick you all up from school today. I want you all to go with her and not make any fuss about it," she tells them. "And don't tell your father," she scolds.

Muted 'okays,' and 'all right's' are heard around the table.

'That went about as well as it could have,' she thinks.

Soon, the school bus picks the kids up for another day of school, with the exception of four-year-old Frankie and two year old Jennifer. She quickly cleans up the breakfast mess, puts everything away and even washes the dishes and dries them. Nervously, she spends most of the morning as usual, taking care of the two youngest ones. When Jennifer goes down for her nap, she packs bags of clothes for each of the kids and puts them in the car. She'll make lunch for herself and the kids, and Edward if he comes home, and she plans leave sometime in the afternoon.

Suddenly realizing she doesn't have a key to the new house, she calls Laura, "I'll meet you there whenever you're ready, with the key," she confirms.

Betty decides she'll meet her there about two o'clock pm. Nervous and in a panic, she feels like she's breaking out of prison, with people watching her, and she mustn't get caught. She doesn't know if Edward will be back are not.

She realizes she's been so occupied making sure the kids have clothes to wear, that she hasn't packed a thing for herself, and this makes her wonder what else she might be forgetting.

'Should I take some pictures? A calendar? A waste paper basket?' She packs her clothes, and decides to fill the wastebasket with a few nonessentials, and a jar with change in it.

She wonders if she should leave Edward a letter and decides against it, but thinks someone should tell him something so he knows the kids are okay, at least, and decides to call Katherine.

Katherine tells her, "I can call some people and let them know, in the course of the conversation; just so it won't seem so much like that was the only reason I called."

Betty tells her, "That's good enough. But don't call them until after I leave, which is gonna be about two o'clock. I don't want anyone coming over, just as I'm ready to go, especially Edward." Katherine agrees, and Betty thanks her, and the two hang up. Lunchtime comes and goes, and there's no sign of Edward.

Alone, Betty stands by the phone on the wall next to the door, looking sad and confused thinking it over, and decides it's time to get going. She carries a few more things out to the car, and comes back in for four year old Frankie and two-year-old Jennifer.

She holds Jennifer in her arm and holds Frankie by the hand and looks around the kitchen, remembering all the good times the family spent here.

Weeping, she glances into the living room, with its gold colored carpeting and brown furniture and remembers the day it all got moved in. She sees her family huddled around the room in her mind's eye. More tears come to her eyes as she turns and leaves the home she so desperately craved. The screen door slams closed as she walks away from the life she waited so long to get. The life she waited for since her first child was born. The life she always wanted.

Chapter Eleven

A Home in Town

"I'm a nervous wreck," Betty explains, trembling. "Jennifer and Patrick put that down. I'm miserable and mad as hell," she tries explaining to Katherine and Joe Jr. "I'm scared to death of what Edward's gonna do when he finds out I took the kids and left him." Betty's at Katherine and Joe Jr.'s home in Centerville, the same town she's rented a house. "I don't know what he's going to do."

"You poor thing," Katherine tells her compassionately, "Come in here."

Betty's entire body is shaking out of control. Katherine puts her arm around her, and walks her to a chair. "Sit down, Betty. Awe, I feel so bad for you."

"Someone should stay with you until things settle down," Joe Jr. tells her.

"There's not enough places for us to sleep, where would someone else stay," she tells him.

Her elbows are on her knees and her face is in her hands.

"You can stay here if you want," Joe Jr. tells her. "He wouldn't dare try anything with us around."

"I can't. Laura's bringing all the kids to the other house after school, later."

Katherine and Joe talk to her long enough to settle her nerves down.

Scared of the unknown and that she might not be capable of living alone with the kids, she soon pulls into the driveway for the first time; at the house she's rented for herself and the kids. She's expecting Laura to be there, but she isn't.

She tells the kids, "Let's go inside Jennifer. Come on Frankie." She looks at him. They get out of the car, Betty takes their little hands in hers, and walks up the sidewalk to the front door to see if it's unlocked. It is.

Wearing blue jeans and a green and white long sleeve flannel shirt that looks like it might have been Edwards she opens the door and walks in.

A shred of comfort comes over her as she walks around the main level and bare rooms. "A kitchen, living room, dining room and bedroom." All brightly lit with plenty of windows. Timidly she walks upstairs, the kids trailing behind her. "A bathroom, good," she says and checks it closer for cleanliness. "A tub. I hope there's hot water in there," she says aloud. 'That'll be nice,' she thinks, feeling empty inside. A white toilet sits in the corner.

The small sense of comfort she felt earlier returns to her again when Frankie speaks. "Mommy, why are we here?" Frankie asks her, fidgeting.

"We're gonna be staying here," she tells him. Hearing his voice calms her nerves.

She walks into each of the three upstairs bedrooms and notices the two mattresses leaning up against the wall in two of the rooms.

"Why mommy?" He looks up at her, the kids still in their winter jackets.

"Because we are," is all she can think of to tell him, starting to walk back down the stairs. She looks down and almost doesn't recognize him with all she's been going through, 'he looks different,' she thinks.

She looks around the living room, at the boxes and bags Laura has already brought over. "I'm gonna see if I can find the blankets and sheets," she says aloud, watching the two kids. She thinks about putting some pots and pans away and lethargically begins tinkering around the house. Her eyebrows are squeezed together and she looks mad. Her mind is on everything but the task in front of her.

She walks upstairs again and makes up the two mattresses she lets fall to the floor, with sheets and blankets. "The kids can carry their own boxes and bags of clothes upstairs," she says.

Among a hundred other things, she wonders for the kids sake mostly but some for herself, if she's doing the right thing. She suddenly misses Edward. The love she feels for him makes her stomach ache, as a pain twists inside of her.

"Knock, knock," someone yells from the entryway door. It's Laura. "Anybody want any kids?" Laura looks around, wondering how she's doing.

Betty walks downstairs to the front door. Among the kids' quiet, idle small talk and confusion, "Hello everyone," she tells them. "Your clothes are in boxes and bags down here, find them and take them up to the bedroom your gonna be sleeping in, so whenever you want, you can go and find them. Carol, Theresa and Bonnie, your gonna have to share a bed till I can find another mattress. Jack and Patrick the same goes for you and Frankie. And I don't want to hear any fighting." The kids walk in, take off their jackets and look around.

"I brought a radio so you'd have something to listen to," Laura tells her, holding it up in the air for a moment. "Just a little something to do."

"Where are you gonna sleep?" Theresa, asks her concerned.

"On the floor, where do you think?" Her mother frowns and tells her strictly. "There isn't any other place."

"You can't sleep on the floor," Laura tells her. "It's too uncomfortable. You'll get a back ache and you won't be able to sleep much."

"Where else is there?" She stands there, asking her, looking crabby.

"Harold and I will find something for you. You need two or three more mattresses, a couch and some chairs, for starters," Laura says.

"For starters," Betty repeats her sarcastically, turning away.

"And a kitchen table and chairs," Laura tells her. "That's all you really need, everything else you can get whenever it comes along. You're doing good." Laura says trying to be encouraging.

"Good or not, it'll have to do," Betty tells her. "We'll have to eat off the floor like dogs." She looks through boxes containing kitchen supplies.

"Maybe for tonight," Laura tells her laughing a little, and then a thought occurs to her. "No. You's could all come over to mine and Harold's house tonight for supper."

She wants to suggest having one of the kids spend the night on her couch, but she decides against it.

"We're not going anywhere tonight," Betty tells her, certainly.

"No? Okay then, I offered. You can still come over if you change your mind. In the mean time we'll look for mattresses and a kitchen table and chairs and couch for you's and ask around, maybe we can find one tonight yet. Okay? Is there anything else we can do for you, or that you need right away?" Laura asks her. She's never seen Betty so uptight.

Betty thinks for a moment and waves her hands in the air and says, "No, you've done enough. We're just gonna have to make do for tonight."

"If you need anything, just call us, me or Harold, were both here for you. We'll stop back later, okay? I gotta go. I gotta work for a few hours this afternoon." Laura says.

"Okay," she tells her plainly, not looking at her, or thinking to thank her. All she can think of is Edward, and how he's going to react to the news

"Okay. Bye kids." Laura leaves with a worried expression on her face.

"I don't know what you're all gonna do, but standing around watching me isn't gonna get anything done," Betty tells the kids.

Betty is left alone in a strange house full of kids and barely any furnishings, except for the two mattresses left there by the previous renters. She plugs the radio in, that Laura brought over, and turns it on. The kids aren't sure what to make of the situation, or what to do, and Betty senses this.

"I'm going to take Jennifer and go outside and sit on the steps," she tells the kids. Frankie follows her in his little faded bib overalls and sits next to her.

"Mom, is there anything you want me or Theresa to do for you? Carol asks her. Her mom's unusually mean demeanor scares her.

"Like what? There isn't anything to do," she tells her, flatly.

"Well, I don't know..." she says hesitantly.

"There isn't anything to do," she tells her again, cutting her off.

The weather's turning warm for this time of year and the temperature is in the lower fifties. It isn't long before all the other kids are outside, sitting on the steps with her, or standing nearby, not knowing what else to do.

"Is this where we're gonna live now, mom?" Bonnie, asks her.

"I'm in charge of everyone now, for the first time in my life, and I'm not sure what to make of it, only that I know I don't like it," she tells her. And yes, this is where we're living now."

She snaps at the kids quickly, making her even unhappier. And the circle of feelings go around and around. Her rage fighting against her fear and unhappiness, and feeling numb inside, and her sense of total abandonment.

"It's weird living in town," Jack tells them, looking around at the other houses and a few people outside. "What do people do? They don't have chores to do. What do they do?"

"It's like we moved in with a whole bunch of other people," Carol notices.

"I'm gonna wave and say 'hi' to these people as they walk by," Bonnie says, trying to be friendly.

"You just mind your own business," Betty growls at her. But she does it anyway.

Patrick is quiet and taking in the new surroundings, listening.

"I just can't be standing around here, I'm going to go up to the room and sort out some clothes or something," Theresa tells them.

"I know your dad is gonna end up on this doorstep some time before the day is over, and he's gonna be mad as hell. I want you kids be careful, you know what his temper is like when he gets mad, be careful and stay away from him," she warns them.

Bonnie wants to say something, but is hesitant. "We all have friends from school that live in town, it's just a matter of time until we find out where they live," Bonnie announces loudly, looking for something to do.

"You're not going anywhere. School and home," her mom scolds her. "I know people too, but I'm not going anywhere and neither are you."

"I don't like the unfamiliarity of everything. The strange new house, no furniture, new neighbors," Carol, says, thinking about their situation.

After tryinging for so many years to find a home for all of them, Betty's situation is contrary to what she's always envisioned her life to be. Contrary to her very being and very soul.

"This isn't the way my parents raised me. And I had a good upbringing too. None of this, kids picking on each other all the time. We got along with each other. And we didn't complain either," she tells them.

Carole King, the singer, comes over the radio singing melodically, *'Tonight your mine - completely. You give your love - so sweetly. Tonight - the light of love is in your eyes. But will you love me – tomorrow...'* Betty hears the words to the song, and sadly wonders if Edward will ever love her again.

Betty thinks back to this morning and the last time she saw Edward at breakfast, before he left the house. It seems like years ago and at the same time, seems like it never happened at all. All her feelings of anger and contempt and abandonment, and loathing, fairness and love mesh together. She doesn't want to see him and there's nothing she wants to tell him. She wants to yell at him, loudly, and tell him how big of a jerk he is, and how big of a mistake he made, and a thousand other things, and hit him. But not talk to him.

Edward shows up a few hours later as Betty is in the kitchen trying to put something together for supper. He's mad and drunk. He walks in without knocking. This is the moment she's been fearing.

"What the hell are you doing here? Get your stuff together, get the kids together, and get in the car right now!" He yells, slamming his fist down on the kitchen counter. "What the hell do you think you're doing?"

"I'm making supper for the kids," she mumbles, not

looking at him, her body starting to tremble.

"And you can just get the hell out of here."

"I don't care. Shut off the burners, get the kids and get your ass in the car, like I said! I'm not fooling around!"

"I'm not going anywhere," she tells him, then adds, "especially not with you. Not with a jackass like you."

The sweet enchanting music from the radio, in the background, the beautiful lyrics and lovely melody, is a sharp contrast to the glib foray going on all around them.

'...*Will you still love me, tomorrow...*' paradoxically she sings.

"Your gonna make it hard for yourself, huh? Okay. See if I give a fuck."

He turns to leave and Betty says, "I know you don't give a fuck."

He turns, startled and looks at her, he's never heard her swear before.

"You rented a whole fucking house? Why do you have to leave? Why can't we work it out at home?" He asks her shouting, angrily, his eyes glaring.

"We don't have a home!" She cries, yelling at him, "now get out!"

"I'll leave, but I'll be back, you bet your ass I'll be back," he tells her.

"Don't bother, why don't you stop at your girlfriend whores place instead."

"My girlfriend whore, that's all you got in your head, I ought to take something and beat you over the head with it."

He approaches her near the stove as she tries to make supper. "I said shut off the God damn burners, get the kids and get in the car, right God damn now!" He flips the switches on the stove off. "Right now!"

"Get out of here!" She tells him and tries pushing him away from the stove and turns the burners back on.

Lexington Glory Days

"I said get in the car! You'll get in that car if I have to drag you out of here!"

"I said get the hell out of here, you lay one hand on me and so help me I'll knock you out with something if I have to do it with my fists. You broke up our home and I'll be damned if your gonna break up this one too."

He's like a bomb ready to explode; the stare in his eyes makes him look possessed and she has no idea what he's capable of doing. She's frightened.

The radio continues playing sweet music, *'Tonight with words unspoken... You said I'm the only one...But will my heart be broken....When the night, meets the morning sun...'*

"Be that way, God damn be that way, I hope you fuckin burn yourself. Where are the kids? You can stay all you want, but I'm taking the kids back with me."

"The hell you are, over my dead body."

"Kids! Kids! Come down here," he marches to the entryway and opens the outside door, "kids get in the car, I'm taking you home."

Betty rushes to the door after him, "kids don't listen to him," she yells, standing behind him. "Don't listen to him, don't get into the car, you're staying right here with me."

"Get the hell out of here!" he yells at her. "Kids get in the car! Let's go home. Were gonna go home now!"

"Don't go kids."

"God dammit, shut up!"

"You need to go, you need to go, you leave, leave now, go, go on, get out of here, go, before I call somebody and they'll throw you out. Get out! Get out of here, I said!" She screams.

"I'll get out of here all right!" He pushes the screen door open so hard it breaks off the top half of the hinges, and hangs there, practically on its side.

"I'll get the hell out of here all right," he storms out

of the door, where the screen door used to be and bolts down the steps with a heavy pace.

"Kids stay away from him so he doesn't take you. He's mad!" She yells at the children. "Get back, stay back away from him!"

"Now you turn the kids against me!" He turns and faces her, standing in front of the car. "Turn the God damn kids against me, that's the way you are. You better watch out, I'm telling you."

"Just go! Leave already!" She pleads to him, crying, "just leave!"

"God dammit!" he hollers. He turns and kicks the car, denting the doors side panel. "I'm taking this car too," he yells back at her, "I'll be back. I'm coming back for the kids and I'm taking the car too! You wait!"

He gets in his truck and starts the motor. He's got a disgusted look on his face as he drives off and he's talking as he drives away and yells something out the window, but it's inaudible.

"Kids, come in the house, come on, it's just about supper time." She rushes back to the stove, to see what she can save for supper.

The kids come in as emotions are high and tense and Betty's heart is racing. The kids are scared, just as scared as she is, but she has to carry on. She has to. Jennifer is crying, and Frankie looks as if he's about to, when the older girls pick them both up. "Sh sh sh, it's okay," Carol tells Jennifer. "It's okay."

"Mom are you okay?" Carol asks her, rocking the three year old.

"Just....leave me alone for a few minutes, I can't think right now," Betty tells her, tears streaming down her face.

The kids come in from outside, and the heartbroken family tries to make do as best they can for the night. Full of questions, confusion, sadness and despondency.

Betty and Jennifer sleep restlessly on the floor. The next morning, Betty is up and makes breakfast for the kids before they go off to school. She spends most of the day with Jennifer outside on the steps, as it's the only place to sit. During the latter part of the afternoon Laura stops in.

She talks low key, "Good news. We've found another mattress and a couch for you. Katherine got a hold of me, and told me to relay the message to you. She found them. Harold volunteered to borrow a truck and bring them over, after he's done working today at about three-thirty."

"That's good, cause I need all the help I can get right about now," she tells her, emotionally drained and exhausted from it.

"Did Edward show up last night?"

Laura asks her, carefully.

"Did he ever," she replies, bitterly. "And the jackass was mad as hell."

"Tell him to quit seeing that other woman, and quit drinking," Laura tells her. Katherine feels the same. She stops in mid-sentence to see how she's reacting. "Then tell him you'll not talk to him until that's done, not before."

"Harold is here," Patrick hollers, after getting home from school with the other kids, "He has a mattress and a couch in the back of a truck."

Piece by piece, Betty slowly gets the things she needs for the kids and the house. One thing at a time, just like her life.

Betty meets him at the door, "The mattress gets hauled upstairs and the couch can get set in the living room," she tells him. "Jack! Get down here!"

"Its good enough to sit on or another place for somebody to sleep," Laura tells her. "It didn't cost anything."

Betty, Harold and Laura talk after moving the

Lexington Glory Days

furniture. "'You know who,' was here yesterday. I don't know what I'll do if he comes back again, as mad as he was. He could barely control himself. He wanted to take the kids! He kicked the car so hard he put it a dent in it! He broke the screen door. He was like a madman, like he was possessed." She breaks down and cries.

Laura makes a suggestion, "Maybe Katherine could make some phone calls and have someone talk to him to calm him down."

"Get a phone put in," Harold says, "if he comes back like that again, call the police. Let him sit in jail for a while, that oughta calm him down."

The next day she does just that and by late afternoon the phone is connected. The line to the outside world brings her a sense of relief.

Patrick spots him staring into the house from the outside.

"Mom, dad's standing at the door, he's just standing there."

Betty goes to the door, and eyes him up through the window, her nerves are so frazzled, she freezes. A half a minute goes by with the two of them staring at one another.

"Open the door, I want to talk to you," he says through the glass, next to the screen door he broke the day before.

"What do you want?" she asks him with the door still closed, not wanting to let him in. "I got nothing to say to you."

"Open the door, I want to talk to you."

"I'll open the door, but I don't want you inside."

"Open it."

"Are you gonna stay outside?"

"I suppose."

Reluctantly, she opens the door a few inches. "You come back to break something else? Or act like a wild man again?"

"I want to know what you're planning on doing?"

"I'm doing what I plan on doing," she tells him.

"What about the kids?" He asks her roughly.

"The kids are staying with me, you don't think I'd let them go with a maniac like you, do you?"

"God dammit, I need help out there, the animals need feeding and watering, and someone's got to take care of the house."

"There's staying with me," she tells him again and begins to close the door.

"Get your whore to help with the rest of the animals."

"This ain't over," he tells her, "those kids are half mine and I need some help." She shuts the door without saying anymore, and watches him for a moment through the glass, until he turns and steps away.

Every moment with him is a roller coaster ride of emotions for her. Not knowing whether she can believe him at all, or if he'll come out swinging, or if he'll deal with all this in some sort of rational manner. It takes all of her efforts to deal with him. No other thing exists when he's around. Nothing. He's that empowering; that forceful of an entity to her. Like a bull, temperamental and unpredictable.

"How are you doing Carol," Theresa asks her concerned, "you doing okay?" The older kids are upstairs talking, and Carol looks upset.

"I'm trying to settle in as best I can," Carol tells her, "mom's the one who needs help. I'm fine," she snaps back at her.

"Living out of boxes and bags, sleeping on mattresses on the floor, eating standing up, and no TV? You call that living?" Patrick tells them, standing nearby.

"This is stupid. Why don't we get someone to help us."

"Things are going to be tough for the first few

Lexington Glory Days

weeks," Jack tries explaining to him, "there's no need for you to talk like that. We'll be okay."

"Mom's never in a good mood anymore," Bonnie complains to Theresa. "She 'gets through' the day, and that's about it."

"You don't know how hard it is for her," Theresa tells her. "She makes us breakfast before school, sees us off to school, watches Frankie and Jennifer all morning, makes them lunch, watches them again all afternoon, makes supper for everyone when we get home, makes sure our homework is getting done, make sure we go to bed on time."

"You don't know how hard it is to watch two small children," Carol tells her. "You have to know what they're doing all the time."

"She goes to bed, and gets up and does it all over again," Theresa adds.

"It's all becoming too mechanical for her," Bonnie tells them. "The loving, happy person inside of her can't find its way out."

"She's withdrawn, unemotional, distant and crabby most of the time, no question about that. She takes care of the things that need to get done, with us kids and the household chores, and then goes to bed." Theresa says.

"She doesn't take time off for just herself or anything else. Even when we were living on the farm the only other thing she was involved with was the Ladies Rosary Society, at the church," Carol explains to them.

"We need to help her more, and be more patient with her. Stop complaining about everything Patrick."

"I hear stories about dad from Uncle Larry and Uncle Brian that he's seeing some woman, that he's dating her." His mood turns sour. "And that he's been drinking a lot. Getting loud, and into fights. I don't think he wants us back," Jack tells Carol and Theresa.

"Dad hasn't been over in two weeks. He's forgot

Lexington Glory Days

about us," Bonnie tells them. "Mom's probably worried wondering what kind of trouble he's getting into."

Jigger and Lily, though Lily's skeptical, are doing Edward a favor by trying to arrange a meeting between Betty and him. Betty's waiting at Jigger's trailer when Edward walks in, and immediately he approaches her.

"You stay away from me. I don't want your hands anywhere near me," Betty tells Edward.

"Come on, you know you want to," Edward tries tricking her, to seduce her, to get her back and tries grabbing her again.

"I said get away from me before I find a cast iron skillet and knock you out cold with it. You said you wanted to talk to me, well I'm here, start talking," Betty tells him, impatient and mad.

"What do you want? You got one minute." She looks at him with disdain.

"I wanted to see you. I thought maybe we could talk a little bit and sort through this," he tells her, trying to come up with a way to get her back.

"That's it? I came out here and left the kids for this? Drop dead." She walks out of Jiggers trailer.

"Betty wait," Lily, says, walking after her.

"What's this bitch's name he's been fooling around with? Where does she live?" Betty asks Lily in a fit of anger outside, next to her car.

Lily looks taken aback, "Betty, I, I, I…"

"Never mind, I could care less, anyway," Betty tells her.

"Betty wait," Lily tries getting her attention. "I'm sorry, I know it's none of my business, and you have every right to be pissed off, but he does miss you."

"Big deal," Betty tells her, getting into the car.

Lily walks around the car to the open drivers side window.

"Lily, it's no use. I've been waiting twenty years for

284

Lexington Glory Days

Edward to grow up, and I'm sick of him. You should have been around when my folks were still alive. My father would never dream of treating my mother this way. He can go to hell." Betty starts the car and drives away.

"She's pisssed at you! Sorry Edward, we tried," Jigger tells him, inside the camper.

"God damn it, what am I gonna do? What am I supposed to do? She won't even talk to me," he tells him.

Lily walks back into the camper. "She's really pissed, Edward, and I don't blame her. All you men are pigs. I want you to leave, now!"

Edward gets up and shuffles his feet and walks out without saying a word.

Edward goes home, and the quiet in the house is piercing to his ears. He fumbles around the kitchen and makes himself something to eat. The silence is so loud he doesn't hear the cupboard door he just closed, or the other noises he makes. It's as if he's watching himself in his mind. He sees his arm reaching for the loaf of bread on the counter, and for a moment thinks it could be someone else's. Frustrated for a distraction he calls Larry.

"Larry, what are you doing? Why don't you come over, we'll have a beer." Edward tells his brother and talks to him on the phone, trying to convince him.

"Maybe I'll ask Jigger, or Leonard or Eugene over too. We'll play some cards and drink beer."

On her way home, Betty decides to visit her priest at her church in Lexington. She hasn't been taking the children to Sunday masses and that has been bothering her, too.

"I struggle everyday just to keep it all together, Father," she tells him, "just to get through the day. The kids will be out of school for the summer in a few months, and then what am I supposed to do with them? How am I gonna keep track of them all then? I can barely do it now. I'm trying to keep everyone busy and out of trouble and keep them from picking on each other. It's all I can do to keep myself from wanting to haul off and swat them sometimes."

"I know you have no idea how this is going to turn out, but the thoughts still keep coming at you, don't they? The kids won't be out of school for a few months yet, no sense in worrying about that now," the priest tells her, "and don't forget to Pray. Ask God for his help."

"These thoughts I have about my husband are so unchristian of me, father, I wish he were dead sometimes. I don't feel right about going to church while I'm thinking all these bad thoughts," Betty confesses to him.

"These are the precise times you need church and God in your life," he advises her.

"Let Him, and us, help you."

Part 2

Living Without Edward

"Come on in. Don't be bashful. Take your jackets off and anything else you want," Edward laughs drinking a beer, as Lily, Shirley, and Shirley's friend Becky walk into Edward's house on the farm. Jigger and Larry are already there. "Come on in. Grab a beer out of the refrigerator, or I can get you one, whichever," Edward tells them. "Lily's here, I thought she was mad at me," he turns to the side and tells Larry.

"Yes, I'm here," Lily, announces upon hearing him. "Let's have a shot and party! I want to drink and get fu-huh-ked up!"

"Come on in, and take your clothes off. I mean your jackets," Edward says chuckling a little embarrassed, obviously intending to misspeak.

"Ooo, all right," Shirley says, smiling at him pretending to drop her shirt off of her shoulder. She gives Edward a sexy look.

Becky smiles and acts shocked, "What did I walk in to?" And quickly makes herself comfortable. "Hi, everyone." She smiles at them.

"The beers in the fridge. Make yourself at home," Edward tells her.

Becky walks over to Edward and he puts his hand on

her butt. "Boy that feels nice," he tells her. She smiles at him.

"I wanna do that," Jigger says and laughs, watching him.

"You have mine to squeeze. You can squeeze them all you want," Lily, tells him. "I don't want you playing with somebody else's."

"Okay," he feigns being apologetic, looking as if he's about to throw a tantrum, like a child. "I'm sorry," he whines.

"What about mine?" Shirley asks them. "Doesn't anyone want to feel mine?" She's kidding, trying to include herself.

"I'll squeeze them," Larry tells her with a sly grin.

"Okay, maybe later," She tells him and giggles, satisfied with the attention.

Lily lights a small pipe filled with marijuana and passes it around. "I think we should all go to the pavilion," Lily tells them, "and play games and have music. I feel like doin something. I don't wanna just sit around."

"What's your hurry? You just got here," Edward tells her.

"Yeah, let's stick around for a while," Jigger tells her.

"Let's go outside then, and start a fire and sit around out there," Lily tells them.

"How does that sound?"

"That sounds like fun," Shirley tells them. "I'd like that."

The group picks up and take what they need and go outside.

"It's kind of chilly out," Becky comments. "Where are we gonna find the wood for the fire?"

"I'll help," Lily volunteers. "Edward where's your wood?" She giggles.

"There's sticks all over the yard. Spread out and look

Lexington Glory Days

around," Edward tells them. "I've got some bigger pieces on a pile, back of the house."

Larry comes back with a big arm full of twigs and by the time everyone returns, there's a big pile of kindling. Edward comes back with an armful of larger pieces. Lily crunches up old newspapers she's found in the porch and puts them in with the kindling, and Larry lights it.

"Nice fire," Jigger says, after Larry gets it going.

"Now that the work is done, let's all have another beer," Lily tells them.

"It's a perfect day for a fire." Becky comments. "The heat will feel nice." I'll help you get the beers, Lily."

The two women walk into the small porch that leads into the kitchen. "Becky, I have something to tell you. Jigger and I set up a meeting between Betty and Edward last week at Edwards' request. I'm just letting you know," Lily tells her. "You can make of it, whatever you want."

"Is that supposed to mean something? Or tell me something?" She looks peculiarly at her and starts laughing.

Lily takes six beers out of the refrigerator, and Becky helps her take them outside for the others. Lily looks skeptically at her.

"Let's go look at the animals in the barn," Shirley suggests.

"Go if you want to go. I don't want to," Jigger tells her.

"Do you have a bull, Edward? Let's get the guys to ride a bull," Lily tells Shirley and makes the motion of roping a calf like a cowboy, and then giggles.

"I don't think Shirley's seeing anybody," Edward tells Larry. "You should try and hook up with her. She's a cutie."

"I'm not looking for anybody," Larry tells him. "I got Ruth in town, that's all I need. I got my daughter, Helen, to think about."

Edward looks at him momentarily, judging his character.

Jigger's found a poking stick, and is moving the wood around in the fire. "I wish the sun would come out a little bit. It's too cloudy."

"Anybody want to do a shot? I brought some blackberry brandy," Shirley tells them slowly, in her manner of speaking.

"I could do a shot of blackberry," Larry tells her. The rest agree.

The group hangs around the campfire for most of the afternoon, drinking shots of blackberry brandy and drinking beer, talking and enjoying the fire.

Later in the afternoon they decide to go to the pavilion.

When they get there, they sit at the bar.

"Bartender, get us all a beer," Edward tells the man.

"Let me finish telling you about the time me and Becky took a road trip to a bar," Lily tells them. "The bartender kept bringing Becky drinks. No one was ordering them. She got so shined up." Lily tells them, laughing. "She was fu-huh-ked up."

Shirley's unusually talkative and brings Becky into the conversation. She laughs, "I remember seeing Becky on many occasions, all drunked up. Of course I'm one to talk," she admits.

Becky tries defending herself.

"No, no, don't even," Shirley, tells her adamantly about telling her story.

"I remember you screwing guy after guy in front of everybody." Shirley starts giggling. "Yeah, that was you."

"And I missed it," Edward says, "I mighta liked that," he turns and tells her.

"So what, Shirley? So what if she did?" Lily asks her.

Becky sits next to Shirley, and puts her arm around her.

"We've all done things. It doesn't mean we're bad people," Lily tells her.

"You're right," Shirley agrees. "You are. You're right."

Becky's hand brushes against Shirley's breast and lets her hand troll back and forth against it a few times.

"Goll!" Shirley laughs, brushing her hand away. "Do you want to make out or what?" She looks over at Edward.

"I wouldn't mind seeing that," Edward says.

"Do it! Do it!" Jigger says, laughing loudly.

"I would," Becky tells her. "Maybe not full out making out, but maybe some touching and stuff," she tells her innocently. "I would," Becky tells her friend, feeling shamed. Edward watches her.

"Do it then, quit talking about it," Edward tries encouraging them.

"Come with me," Shirley tells her, standing up and walking off towards the bathroom. Shirley has a wide smile on her face.

"I want to come too," Edward tells them. "Let me come along."

When they get back, they're both giggling. "If you'd have let me come, we could've all had some fun," Edward remarks to them.

Becky and Shirley, still giggling, sit at the bar next to the others. Edward's hand reaches out and starts fondling Becky's breasts. "Those are nice, mmm..." He grunts. He rubs and squeezes them in front of the others.

Edward gets up, walks behind Becky and stumbles, swaying side to side, feeling the affects of the alcohol. "What are you looking at?" Edward fiercely tells a man sitting down the bar from them. "Keep your God damn eyes to yourself, or I'll knock 'em out with my God damn fists."

"You think you're so tough," the man tells him, unafraid of him.

Lexington Glory Days

"You want me to show you how tough I am?" Edward asks him, getting mad. He walks over to the man and shoves him hard. The man falls off the bar stool and lands on the floor. He gets back up and takes a swing at Edward, landing his fist on his chin. Edward's head bounces back, and he quickly throws a punch back at the man, hitting him in the eye. The man stumbles backwards and trips over a chair, and lands on the floor for a second time. Edward follows him, leans down, and grabs him by the shirt and pulls him up. He punches him in the face, again and again.

"Edward, stop it!" Lily rushes up to him, trying to get him to stop.

Becky and Shirley are screaming. "Oh, my God!" "Look out!"

Lily pulls on Edward's shirt and he throws her off of him. He keeps hitting the man in the face, again and again. Lily comes back, "Edward! Stop it!" She tries pulling him away again.

Edward stands up, "That oughta teach you. Now who's tough?" Edward walks away with the man groaning in pain, stumbling and trying to get to his feet, with Lily there trying to help him. "God damn it Edward, what did you have to do that for? Shirley, somebody, get me damp cloth."

"Give me a shot of blackberry," Edward tells the bartender, and throws the shot down quickly. Everyone around him is quiet, looking at him. "Get him cleaned up and get his ass out of here and let's get this party started," he demands. The whole fight took less than five minutes.

Shirley gets Lily a damp cloth, and Lily wipes the blood from the mans face.

"It isn't too bad," Lily tells him. "You've got a nice cut above your left eye. I think you should have that stitched up by a doctor."

"So you like to drink?" Edward asks Becky. "And you

Lexington Glory Days

like getting naked and screwing in front of other people?" He chuckles a little and puts his hand on her leg. She responds by putting her hand on his.

Two couples sitting at a table decide they no longer like the atmosphere in the bar and leave.

"Edward, I told you I don't want any fighting in here," the bartender tells him. "It's bad for business."

"What did you want me to do?" He exclaims! "The guy was smarting off!"

"I don't care about that. No fighting." The bartender tells him again.

"You're just a mealy mouthed punk like he is," Edward tells him.

"Keep talking like that, and I'll kick you out of here," he tells him.

"Go to hell," Edward tells him, turning to talk to the girls again.

"It was so nice, sitting around the campfire this afternoon, and now this," Lily says to Shirley and Becky. "Edward you're a jerk."

"I want to go. This sucks," Shirley tells her.

"Go! You want to go?" Edward tells her, hearing her. "Go then. See if I give a damn," he says, turning away. "Get the hell out of here then."

"Edward, you know you can be a real ass sometimes," Lily tells him. "Come on girls, let's go." Becky and Shirley get up to leave with Lily.

Edward turns to Becky, "You're leaving too? I suppose. Go then, get the hell out of here. Who needs you."

The girls leave, and it's just Larry and Jigger left at the bar with him. There's another couple at the far end of the bar that's been quietly listening and watching them, minding their own business. Occasionally they look over at Edward, but quickly return their gaze, afraid he might see them.

"What did you let them leave for?" Jigger asks Edward.

"I didn't let them do nothing," Edward tells him.

"Jesus Christ, what's wrong with you?" Jigger asks him.

Larry, as usual, is quiet and takes it all in. "It wasn't his fault. They left."

"Bartender!" Edward hollers. "Set us up each a beer, before I come over there and start punching your lights out too."

The bartender sets them up, giving Edward a pathetic look. "I told you, you better watch your mouth."

"We were having a good time, what did you have to go and get into a fight for?" Larry asks him calmly.

"I don't know. It just happened," Edward tells him.

A group of people come in and soon the fight, and the girls, are forgotten. The mood suddenly becomes jovial. Edward turns and looks at them and says, "Who are these ass holes now?"

Jigger tells him, "Settle down a little bit. Geez, you're gonna chase these people off like you chased the girls off."

The group comes in talking and the ladies are laughing. "I haven't been down here in ages," one of them says.

"You haven't?" Edward says, suddenly turning around and talking to them, trying hard to be friendly. "What brings you folks around?"

"Well, howdy stranger. I was just telling Frankie here, 'Let's go to the pavilion.' It's been years since we've been down here."

"We're glad you did," Edward tells them, slurring his words.

"Well, we are too," the lady laughs. "Frankie, go to the bar and get us a round of beers," she tells her husband, as the others sit around a table.

"I wonder where the girls went," Jigger tells Larry.

Lexington Glory Days

"Who gives a shit," Edward replies, turning to look at them. "Let 'em go."

"Whose been doing your chores for you?" Larry asks Edward.

"I do, when I get home," he tells him.

"It's almost five o'clock, what time do you feed them?" Larry asks him.

"I told you, when I get home," he answers him snarly. "Jesus Christ I just told you that." Larry looks him in the eye, expressionless.

The three couples at the table are lively and talkative. "My God, this place hasn't changed in forty years," one of the ladies says.

Edward turns again to face the couples, enjoying their banter.

Hours go by and several people have come and gone and the place is busy. Edward is downright drunk. He's at the bar drooling and mumbling to himself. His hands and arms are on the bar, and his head is inches away from them bobbing up and down. Jigger looks at Larry and shakes his head, with a disturbed look on his face.

"Let's get him home," Larry tells Jigger. "I'll take him home in his truck, and you can follow me in your car and pick me up at his place."

People stare at them as they practically have to drag him out of the bar. His legs and knees are buckling as he walks, one arm around Larry's shoulder and the other around Jigger's.

The next morning, Monday, two of Edward's co-workers stop by and pick him up to go to work. They have to wake him, and get him out of bed. He's hung over and has an occasional beer throughout the day to take the shakes away. After work, he gets dropped off at home, does chores, and then goes back down to the pavilion for more beer.

"Hi Edward," Leonard greets him. "Sounds like you

got pretty pied eyed yesterday," he says laughing. "Got into a little fight, did ya?" He giggles.

There's quite a few men there, having an after work beer.

"Give me a beer," he tells the bartender. "Yeah, so what if I did? I don't really remember." He tells Leonard.

One beer leads to another, and soon it's ten o'clock, and he's still there. "I gotta go. I gotta get up in the morning," he tells the last of the bunch to go home.

"One more," they tell him, trying to get him to stay, laughing.

"One more and that's it," he says lighting a cigarette. "Why the hell can't I ever get out of here at a reasonable hour?" He asks them.

"Cause you don't want to go home," a neighbor tells him.

They continue talking, whiling away their time.

"I hear Roman's painting his house," the neighbor tells him. "The guys eighty years old, up on a ladder and painting his two story house." They all laugh. "Can you believe it?" They laugh at the thought of it.

They talk a while longer, but soon Edward's had enough and decides to leave. "See you guy's, later," he tells them, with thoughts of home.

"I've got to get going." He gets up, walks slowly to the door, and leaves.

The next day, while Edward's at work, Laura and Harold are over at the rented house, trying to help piece together Betty's life.

"They're nice really," Laura tells Betty. "Don't you think?" She sits on one of the kitchen chairs her and Harold have just brought over, trying it out. "There's a few tears in some of them, but that doesn't hurt anything."

"They're fine," Betty tells her. "It's a place to sit."

"I like the color." Bright yellow. "It cheers the place

up," Laura tells her.

"Heaven knows we can use all the cheering up around here we can get right about now," Betty replies.

"It's a place to sit down while you're eating your oatmeal in the morning," Harold tells them, "You're not decorating the Taj Mahal."

"I need to go to the market for some milk and things, will you's stick around?" Betty asks the two. Besides spending money she can't afford to part with, she doesn't mind going to the supermarket. It's easy to find another woman there to talk to, to ease the congestion in her feelings.

"No, we gotta go," Harold, tells her.

"Where?" Laura asks him, thinking she's forgotten about something.

"Home. I'm tired," he tells her. They all walk outside together and leave.

At the store, Betty meets her old neighbor, Sophia.

"Carol is a senior in high school this year, she'll graduate this spring," Betty tells her. "I feel terrible having to drag her away from home like I did, and put her through all these feelings and changes. That damn husband, I'd like to wring his neck. She should be out enjoying herself, life should be fun and carefree for her right now." 'She's growing up so fast,' she thinks to herself.

"Don't forget, you and I both know how hard life can be. We didn't always have it so easy either!" Sophia reminds her.

"There's many a times we had to scratch and dig to come up with the rent money every month."

"I know," Betty responds feeling sorry for her daughter. "I wanted things to be nice for her." She can barely control herself from breaking down and crying.

"It isn't your fault, don't take it out on yourself. How about you, Betty, how are you doing?"

"Not so good, but what can I do? I take one day at a time."

"Stay strong, Betty. Everything will work out in the end."

Talking to Sophia changes something inside of Betty. A force tells her that she's the one in charge, 'I take all the bumps and bruises, the chief, cook and bottle washer,' she thinks.

"Your right, I guess. I can't afford to be soft. I need the kids to listen to me when I tell them something, without putting up a fuss. I need them to know, my word is what goes. There's no room for giving in. I need to get off my butt and stop feeling sorry for myself. The kids need one good parent anyway, and I need to keep a clear head to do it all."

"There ya go, sister," Sophia tells her.

Betty begins to feel stronger emotionally. First she talks to Laura and Harold, and then she becomes stricter and less patient with the kids.

"I want you and Laura to come over for Sunday dinner," Betty tells Harold, early in the week. "Maybe we could all go to church for a change." It'll be like someone saying to the kids, 'everything will be okay.'

She looks at him desperate, hopeful he says yes, before she has to tell him flatly, 'You're coming and that's that.'

"I'd like to, but I'll have to ask Laura, first," he tells her. "I don't know what her plans are. Our wedding is coming up in only a few months, and we might have something we have to do for that."

Betty persists. "We'll spend the afternoon with the kids, maybe go for a walk. They deserve a nice time. Everything's been so hard on them." 'It'll be like a weight being lifted from all of us,' she thinks.

"It's been a long time since we've all been together for a whole afternoon," Betty tells him, strongly hoping he says yes. She wants to make him come, but she can't order him to, he's too old for that.

"It'd mean a lot to me if you did," she finally tells him.

"All right," Harold tells her. "I'll tell Laura you want us to come over and I said yes. If she has something to do, we can go earlier or later, I guess."

"Thank you," she tells him and kisses him on the cheek.

Later that week Betty talks to Gertrude for the first time since her separation. Gertrude's married now and lives an hour away.

"Edward's only been by to see us once in the past three weeks, Betty tells Gertrude, over the phone. "I don't know if he misses us or not. He must've finally lost his rage over me taking the kids and moving out, but you should have seen him when he found out. Things have settled down, and thank God they have. Emotions aren't running quite as high as they had been," she tells her, "even the kids are doing better."

"Good. I've been so worried about you. I get bits and pieces of how you're doing from Katherine, and I meant to call sooner, but I didn't have the phone number. I'm doing okay."

"I'm so glad to hear that. It's so nice to hear your voice and to talk to you." Betty tells her.

"It's not the same as being there in person. I'll have to come down and visit. I wish I could come over today, but I can't."

"It'll be so nice to see you again, we have a lot of catching up to do. I haven't seen you in ages."

"I know. Are you taking care of yourself?" Gertrude asks her.

"Who else is here that would?" she tells her, dumbfounded.

"I wish I could be there more for you, kid. On the

bright side, the weather will be turning nicer. Soon you'll want to be spending time outside and opening the doors and windows and letting in all that fresh air. Maybe the spring rains and flowers will wash your problems away. Everyone feels a little reborn and renewed this time of year." Gertrude tells her.

"Oh, I hope so. Thank you, I needed that." Betty appreciates her encouragement.

"Hang in there! I'll be down to see you soon."

"I will, bye now." Betty hangs up the phone carefully and slowly, wondering how Gertrude truly is, hoping things are going well for her.

Meanwhile, Evelyn decides to pay Edward a visit.

"This is quite a sight," she tells him. "Middle of the afternoon and your in bed. How come you're not at work? Haven't you gotten up yet today, or are you drunk already?"

"Neither," he tells her lying there. "What do you want?"

"I come to see how you're doing, and I think I already know."

"What's that supposed to mean?" He mumbles.

"The place is a mess, it smells like a brewery in here, there's beer bottles everywhere, and you're in bed in the middle of the day. What would that tell you? What are your plans for today, anything at all? Or are you gonna spend the whole day in bed?"

"You're looking at them," he tells her.

"That's some attitude. Maybe you could at least clean the place. Have you talked to Betty or seen the kids lately?"

"Not for a couple of weeks. They don't want to see me," he mumbles.

"In the shape you look like you're in it's no wonder," she tells him. "Have you been eating, or just drinking your meals?"

Lexington Glory Days

"I eat. Leave me alone."

"I'll leave you alone all right. Do you want Betty and the kids back or don't you?"

"They took off and left me. I think the question is, 'do they want me?'"

"You better straighten up, whatever you decide. What are you trying to do, drink yourself to death? That's right. I know all about staying at the bar all night, and every day. You could clean yourself up once in a while and go see the kids at least."

"Then I'd have to see Betty, and she doesn't want to see me."

"After what you did, and the way you've been carrying on I don't blame her for that. I have to leave now, but I'll be back later. You better start getting yourself together." Evelyn warns, and leaves the house.

The next weekend, Katherine goes over to Betty's, and the two share different pieces of news about Edward.

"He went back to work last week, but he's still drinking," Katherine tells Betty. "He's drinking more now, than he ever did. I'm beginning to wonder if he can go without it at all."

"He called a couple of weeks ago. He had a few beers in him then too, I'm sure. He said he wants me and the kids to move back home," she tells her.

"You're not thinking about going, are you?" she asks her.

"Heavens no! He said he knew what he did was wrong and promised, if I take him back, it'll never happen again."

"You'd be crazy to go back before he quits drinking." She tells her seriously, trying to help.

"I know that other woman has to be out of the picture too, but for as much as he drinks, he should quit."

"I know. He said he's sorry he hurt me and forced us to move out and go through all this, and that he misses us."

"After what he did! Be careful there woman, remember what he put you through." Katherine's a good source of reason and support for her.

A week after Katherine's call, Edward comes to visit her. He tries reasoning with her.

"You're pregnant, and you belong at home. I want you to move back. I want you and the kids to move back. There I said it. I know you want me to quit drinking, and I will. Tell me you'll come home, and I'll quit."

Betty tells him, "Before I do anything, I need to know you're through with that woman, and you quit drinking. Then we'll see. You have to show me you can do it first. I'm not putting up with that nonsense ever again. Ever. If you start up again, I'll leave you. Your drinking changes you too much. You become a jerk. And if you ever cheat on me again, I'll leave you for good. This time forever. I shouldn't even have to tell you that"

"I'll never cheat again, I swear. And I'll quit drinking, I promise, I will."

"You told me that before, but yet you're still at it."

"I know, I know." Tears of shame start flowing down his cheeks. "I know, I will. I promise, I will." He wipes the tears from his eyes.

"When? When are you gonna quit?"

"Right now. Right now," he says quietly.

"Good. Good for you. I know you're trying now, at least. I've been waiting to hear you say it. You know you're a much better man without that slop. It makes you ornery and stubborn, and sometimes downright mean, without it your level headed and good-natured. Nobody could love the person you become when you're drinking. The kids included. They shy away from you when you're drinking, they're afraid of you."

"Afraid?" Tears still in his eyes. "My own children, afraid of me?"

"You lash out at them, instead of talking to them. You have a quick temper when you're drinking. You don't even know what you're like!"

"I don't want the kids to be afraid of me. I didn't know. Where are they?"

"Upstairs or outside with their friends. They'll be coming in soon. They know they have school in the morning. They have to be home before dark."

"I wanna see them." He tells her, feeling vulnerable.

"You should, it's about time. You can stay until they have to get ready for bed and they have to be in bed by nine o'clock. Do you want a cup coffee?"

"No, it'll keep me awake and I got a get up for work in the morning. How are they all doing? Are any of them in any trouble of any kind?"

"Not that I know of, they better not be." She tells him.

Carol, now eighteen, is the first he sees. She enters the room with an air of sophistication and naivety. "Hi mom," and less enthusiastically, "hi daddy." She's surprised to see him and notices her fathers disheveled appearance.

"Hi sweetheart, come here and give your dad a kiss. How are things going, is everything okay?"

"Everything's hunky dory. I started dating," she tells him sarcastically, wondering what kind of response he's going to give her.

"You have a boyfriend?" he asks, unaware and surprised.

"He's not my boyfriend, were just going out on dates. He's a boy in my class at school, he drives a red Mustang, I like his car."

"I hope he's nice to you," Her dad tells her, not knowing what to say.

"He is. When we go out for burgers, or to a movie, he almost always pays for me."

Lexington Glory Days

She exaggerates her responses because she doesn't like talking to him. She's mad at him. Taking a closer look she thinks he looks terrible. "How are you?"

"I been better. Has he tried kissing you?" Her father asks, wanting to know too much too soon.

"Daddy, that's private, I can't talk about that."

"Oh I see, I'm sorry then." He apologizes, not knowing what for, exactly.

Theresa, fifteen, and Bonnie, thirteen, both arrive at home, and come in at the same time. "Girls, come say hi to your father," their mother tells them.

"Why, what's going on? I was at my girlfriend Margie's, studying," Theresa tells them, wondering if something has given in between the two.

"I was out riding bikes with my friends," Bonnie adds.

"Where were you riding at?" He starts with an easy question first for Bonnie, the one who might forgive him more easily.

"We rode around the school, and around the block. There's like a thousand cars and trucks at school for some reason. We stopped and talked to an old man and his wife, who were sitting on their porch."

"I see. Theresa, what were you and Margie studying?" Her father asks her, and for the first time in a long time he really listens and cares about someone's answers.

"We were doing our math and chemistry homework." She tells him coldly.

"Did you get it done?" He asks her, beginning to miss them all more and more.

"It was a little hard, but we got it," she tells him, standing looking over him.

"Bonnie, how's school going for you?"

"Okay." She does not elaborate.

"Tell him the truth," Betty corrects her.

"Not so good, it's all too hard for me. It doesn't make

any sense. Why do I need to know where all the countries are? Why do I have to dissect a frog? Why do I have to do all the math problems? I know how to add and subtract and multiply and divide, that should be good enough."

"Maybe you could study a little more," her dad suggests.

"She's gonna be studying a whole lot more next year," Betty says.

"Is school is over with for the year?" He asks. Without the kids at home coming and going he's lost track, even though Theresa just told him she was doing her homework.

"Oh she will be, no ifs, ands, or buts about it," Betty tells them.

"It's too much! It's too hard!" A frustrated Bonnie raises her voice and tells them.

"Don't talk back either, or I'll send you to summer school, and maybe I will anyway, just to teach you," Betty tells her.

Patrick, eight, comes striding into the house like he's in a hurry.

"Patrick." His dad says roughly, beginning to smile.

"What?" he says in return, looking at him, but keeps walking.

"Come in here," his mom tells him.

"Why, what do you want?" Patrick walks into the room, caring only a little his dad is there.

"Come in here and talk to me," his dad tells him.

"I suppose," he says. "Why are you here?" He asks him.

"I came to see you." Edward tells him.

"Why?" he asks him.

"To see you, I've missed you. I'm glad to see you," his father tells him, trying to become something meaningful to the boy again.

"You are? How come?" He knows his dad doesn't

show a lot of honest emotions when he's drinking. Before Edward has a chance to answer, Jack, 13, walks in and sees everyone in the living room.

"Hi dad, how are you?" And shakes his hand.

Jack has always been a good kid.

"I'm okay. How is everything with you?" On some level, Edward relates to him the most, for his plain talk and easy ways.

"Good," Jack tells him. "Going good."

"Jack's been working at the gas station in town," Bonnie tells him. Bonnie talks about everything she hears and sees.

"You are? What do you do there?" his dad asks, surprised by the news.

"I work on lawnmowers, and small engines, and stuff. I like it. It gives me a little extra spending money for myself and for around here."

"You're a good kid. Good for you. I'm glad to hear that." Edward finally begins to feel the full weight of his emotions.

"Yeah, so, I got a little reading to do for school tomorrow, so I'm gonna head upstairs now, it's good to see you though, dad."

"You too son, it's good to see you too," he tries to say politely.

He spends an hour talking with his family, and then decides he should be leaving. It's a painful reminder for him, to see all the kids, so well adjusted in their new surroundings without him. It reminds him of how interesting the kids are, the way they interact with one another, and how much they all mean to him. His past indiscretions seems so ridiculous now, so frivolous and irresponsible.

"Good bye kids, I'm leaving," he hollers up the stairs, near the door. They all yell, "Bye dad," without coming downstairs to see him.

He leaves with parting words to Betty, "I promise, no more drinking. And I'll never cheat on you again, ever, I swear." He turns and looks quickly at her one more time, and leaves, downtrodden, having hit rock bottom.

She watches him leave, and lets a deep sigh of air escape from her lungs. "Kids," she hollers up the stairs, "time for bed."

Two weeks pass, and good to his word, Edward hasn't taken one drink of alcohol. He's feeling and looking better already, and Betty is growing larger everyday with the new baby.

Upstairs, Jack is telling his sisters, "He has to quit drinking for six months before she'll take him back. That'll give him enough time to figure out how he wants to spend his time, without alcohol and his bar friends, I heard her telling Katherine."

Three more weeks pass by and Edward's going on one month without drinking. One night in June he comes back to see her, to ask her to move back home with him again.

"I can't yet, Edward," she tells him, "I need to know you can really do this. Just because you quit drinking for one month, doesn't mean you can keep from it. I told you, there's no way I'm going back if you're drinking."

"I did quit! How much time do you need?" he questions her, "I'm not gonna wait forever," his anger starting to surface.

"I'll let you know when I'm ready. And when and if I do, so help you, if you start up again, I'll be out that door just like the last time."

"I want you back now!" He tells her, his anger getting closer and closer to the surface.

"I don't want to wait any longer!"

"Well your gonna have to and that's all there is to it. I can't help it. You can do it. You've already shown yourself you can get by without it."

"Jesus Christ woman, I'm going stir crazy in that house all by myself! There's no one to talk to!" He's quickly pacing back and forth.

"You can stop over here as often as you want to if you need company. Company. And that's all." Edward senses a hidden message in her words.

"Just company, huh? No hanky panky?" He tries to get her frisky.

"Don't get smart with me," she warns him.

He likes this, "I suppose then, just company."

She looks, but does not grin back. "Don't start thinking about it either," she tells him, "that especially won't do you any good."

Part 3

Harold And Laura Get Married

In a quiet moment of reflection, among all of his jitters and anxieties, Harold looks at himself in the mirror. Dressed in a white tuxedo with black pants he stares at the man in the mirror, trying to figure who the man is and how he feels about getting married. Laura is at the church getting ready and the ceremony begins in less than an hour.

"Who do you see in there?" Peter, a young man of twenty-two and groomsman in the wedding asks him, jokingly.

"A guy who wants another drink," Harold tells him.

"I think we've had enough until after the ceremony. We still have to walk down the aisle," Peter tells him, "and we can't be stumbling," he laughs.

"I'm sure Laura's having another one," Harold tells him, fairly calm.

"We gotta get going anyway, we can't be late, Laura would kill us," Peter says.

"All right, let's go then and get this over with."

They arrive at Laura's church, twenty miles from Lexington, and stand around outside visiting with the wedding guests.

Betty arrives with all of the kids, ranging in ages

from three to eighteen. Carol has brought a date.

"There you are," his mom tells him. She places both of her hands on his cheeks and gives him a kiss on the lips.

"That ones for good luck." She kisses him again, "That ones for all my best wishes and a happy life."

Inside the simple church, the ushers are seating people and soon the pews are full of relatives and friends from both families. Edward arrives alone looking clean and sober, in a black suit. He motions Harold off to the side. "It's a big day in your life and Laura is a wonderful girl. You're lucky to have her. She's a good woman. You'll be fine."

Harold is humbled and stares at the ground as his dad slaps him on both shoulders, and then enters the church. But he doesn't sit with Betty and his kids.

The ceremony is an hour long with both Laura and Harold lighting candles and saying their "I do's." Laura looks beautiful in her long white wedding dress, but different with a short wavy haircut that does nothing to change the spunky gal underneath.

"I'm so glad you's could come," she tells everyone with Harold by her side, later at the packed reception being held at the pavilion in Lexington.

"You did it! Congratulations!" Peter says, beaming, kissing the bride.

"Now to get through all of this," Harold tells him, less enthusiastic.

"Just have fun," Laura's father tells him, drunk and happy.

"Don't have too much fun, you still have the wedding night!" Laura's mom tells him, also drunk, but serious.

"The wedding nights the most fun!" Edward adds, making them all laugh.

Betty tries being friendly, but her whole heart just isn't in it.

"Whose Carol with?" Harold asks Gertrude.

"I don't know. This is the first time we've been down in months."

"Carol, who's your friend?" Kimberly asks her.

"This is Chris. A boy I graduated high school with last spring, and have been dating." She tells him starting to get embarrassed.

"Theresa, when are you going to get married?" Harold teases her.

The mature thirteen year old tells him curtly, "Whenever I'm ready."

The old dance hall is filled from corner to corner with well-dressed guests, drinking to celebrate the new newlyweds. The beer and whiskey is flowing as fast as the conversation. People are laughing and have a wonderful time all afternoon, into the evening, and well into the very early parts of the morning.

Later that night, Betty thinks back on her own wedding and how hopeful she was and the dreams she had. In contrast, she imagines what life would be like now, with Edward, but without the booze and alcohol in their lives. She would have the life she's always wanted. Their home would be stable instead of chaotic, full of love and not bitterness. They would still have arguments and disagreements, but they would get sorted through, and become repaired. Her house would again become a home, with all and everything good that comes with it. And then she remembers come September, whether or not she decides to go back to him, the two will have another baby.

Chapter Twelve

Is It Cold In Here, Or Is It Just Me?

It's six o'clock a.m. on a snowy, cold winter morning five years later, in 1968. Timmy, the youngest of Betty's children, is 5 years old, and not yet old enough to go to school with his older brothers and sisters.

"I made oatmeal for the kids going to school, Timmy, you can have as big a fit as you want to, but you're not getting any until the older kids get theirs," Betty tells him. "I'm feeding the school kids first." She loses her patience.

"I want to eat breakfast with them!" He hollers at her, running off mad and whining, wanting to be a part of this 'thing' they call school, then he mopes back in.

"Everyone upstairs in their bedroom getting dressed and combing their hair, come on down, breakfast is ready I told you!" she shouts from the kitchen. Quickly, five kids come tumbling down the steep staircase.

Carol and Theresa no longer live at home. Theresa graduated from high school and is away at nursing school about thirty miles away. Carol got married a few years ago and moved up north.

Edward suddenly appears in the doorway, "Is it cold in here, or is it just me?" he asks them, in the old four-bedroom farmhouse.

"I'm boiling water on the electric stove for you

enough to fill the tub. I want you to take a bath, you're starting to stink," Betty tells Edward.

"The tub is barely big enough for the smaller kids. You mean you're gonna take a bath in there?" Bonnie asks him, "I'm too big to fit in there, how are you going to fit?" Her hair is wrapped up in a towel, wet from having washed it earlier, every bit the sixteen-year old girl worried about her hair and clothes.

The rest of the kids come down one by one for their breakfast of oatmeal and chocolate milk. Betty is in her kitchen, with the walls painted a few shades too dark, navy blue.

"I'm setting the table now, are you kids coming?" She hollers again. They walk into the kitchen, as she's setting bowls and spoons and glasses around the table, stirring the oatmeal, getting out napkins, and pouring milk.

"Timmy, go into the living room and watch cartoons until after the older kids have had their breakfast and leave for school," his mom scolds him one more time.

"Go on, get in there, and I mean it."

After breakfast the kids wait for the big orange school bus outside at the end of the long driveway to take them to school for the day.

"It's starting to snow," Jennifer, nine, the youngest of the school aged children announces, as Jack, Bonnie, Patrick and Frankie stand at the end of the long gravel driveway, waiting for the bus to pull up with its red and orange lights flashing. It all seems so exciting to Timmy, inside watching them.

The snow is beautiful as it putters down from the sky, accumulating on their stocking caps, and winter jackets. Timmy can see them through the window, and he sees the tree house, "someday soon, I'm gonna be old enough to climb that, maybe next summer," he decides. But for now it stands there, taunting him through the glass, inviting only the snow to play with it.

Lexington Glory Days

Betty walks into the living room with an upright oil burner stove in it, "the living room, is toasty warm," she tells Edward, "It must just be you."

"There's two oil burners, one in the living room and one in the kitchen and they have to heat the whole house. Are you sure there both giving off heat?" Edward asks her.

"There's no ductwork attached to either of them, like in newer houses. Just the heat it's giving off has to circulate throughout the whole house," Edward tells her.

"I know, and that round hole in the ceiling just above the heater in the living room, and the one above the heater in the kitchen allows the heat upstairs," she adds. "Along with what goes up the stairs."

"It gets cold up there in the wintertime," Edward tells her "crawling into bed between those cold sheets is like going to bed with a bag of ice between your legs," he tells her and laughs.

"There's plenty of blankets on the beds," she tells him.

The front door has a beautiful window that takes up the whole upper half of the door, with etchings carved right into the glass. "Patrick," twelve years old and tall for his age, "uses the tank as a chalk board, to write on," he chuckles.

Betty, her dark, neat short hair getting puffy and long, is busy in the kitchen, cleaning up after breakfast. "I wish this kitchen were just a little bigger. There's too much stuff in here. I spend a lot of time in here, preparing meals and people sit in here when we have company over, around the table when we play cards," she explains, "It gets a little cramped."

Edward goes and takes his bath in the small metal tub, the water now luke warm and Betty cranks the handle on the pump to bring up more water to put in a kettle, to warm up on the stove, so she can do up the morning dishes.

"Timmy, your breakfast is ready," she tells him. Moody, he eats his breakfast of oatmeal and Ovaltine, as he sits at the table quietly, alone, as Betty washes the dishes.

Edward comes out of the room that doubles as the bathroom, "Do you want some breakfast?" Betty asks him.

"No. I'll eat later," he tells her.

"What are you gonna do today?" she asks him. Being the winter months, Edward is laid off from working on road construction.

"I'll start by feeding and watering the cattle and pigs and chickens. And make sure things are all okay in the barn. I've got a heifer cow in there right now ready to have a calf any day now." The vet has been out a few times in the past few weeks, checking on her.

Betty takes the kettle of hot water off of the stove and pours more of it into the sink, along with a few squirts of dish soap. Dressed, Edward walks out of the front door to the barn. Timmy lollygags at the table, finishes eating his breakfast, and starts to horse around, and Betty yells at him, "hurry up and finish eating already, so I can do up the dishes. Then you can go outside if you want to."

The school bus has come and picked up his older brothers and sisters and all the good cartoons on TV that he wants to watch have already been on. So he decides to find his coat, and stocking cap and mittens, and boots and checks out what he can do outside.

"Take out the pot as long as your going outside," Betty says to him.

"I don't wanna take that thing out. Why do I always have to do it?"

"You can take it out, there's no reason why you can't take it out. We don't have running water or a working bathroom so someone's gotta do it."

"I hate taking out the pot. It stinks." He traipses into

the room where the pot is, the same room they take their baths in, and puts the lid on it. He lifts the handle on the pot and carefully lifts up the pot and its contents. He holds his breath a little and walks outside onto the newly fallen snow. He opens the door to the outhouse, a two seater, and dumps the contents of the pot into the hole.

He takes it to the barn, rinses it out good and then trudges back to the house and puts the pot back in its spot.

"You can't let the pot get too full, or your butt will get wet," his mother tells him, "and the last thing you want to do is to have to run out to the outhouse in the middle of the night in winter. Thank you, Timmy," she tells him.

He cautiously walks back out to the barn where his dad is, because the animals in there are a lot bigger than he is and they scare him a little. The barn is divided into two sections with a hallway in the middle. The hallway has hay on the floor. In one half are all the cattle, where they can come and go from the outside and go out to the meadow to feed, walk around the yard, and drink from the big stock tank. Here in the barn is where they're fed hay from the hayloft. The old rafters, turned gray by time, look as if the whole barn could come tumbling down at anytime. They're strong, but their look is deceiving.

The other half of the barn is divided in half again. There is a sow and some young piglets in one compartment, and the heifer that is about to give birth is in the other section. She is lying down on a bed of hay, with a pan of corn feed and a dish of water nearby. She is bellowing loudly and Edward is in the stall with her.

"Is she okay, dad?" Timmy asks.

"I don't know," he tells him honestly.

Timmy walks through the barn, smells the mix of odors of corn dust and hay, feed, and cow and pig dung, and decides it's safe to enter, and walks along the hallway. He sees his dad bring the water dish closer to the heifer, as he starts climbing the ladder to the hayloft. In between the steps, chickens have roosted and laid their eggs. He checks a couple of nests and finds three eggs and checks another. One of the chickens quickly pecks at his hand. It startles and scares him and he quickly climbs up another few steps, glances around the huge hayloft full of baled and stacked hay bales, and quickly descends down the ladder, past the chickens as fast as he can.

He walks confidently back down the short hallway, places the eggs carefully near the entry door, on some soft hay, and walks back down the short hallway again, past the cattle gnawing on hay and snorting their visible breath high into the air. He approaches the stall where his dad is, still with the heifer.

"Is there something wrong with her dad?" he asks.

Standing up and giving the heifer a few gentle strokes along her neck he says, "No she'll be okay, but I might have to call the vet out again. Let's go to the house and warm-up little."

"Not much hay in the cows trough," Timmy notices, "Jack will have to feed 'em extra tonight," he says.

Timmy looks around the barn, trying to check things out a little closer and walks toward the door. He swings open the bottom half of the door, picks up the eggs he had left there, takes one more deep breath for good measure, smells hay, and ducks under the top half of the door, turns and closes both doors and latches it.

He sees his dad down by the watering tank. There's an electric heater in there that keeps the water from freezing, but it isn't working. There is ice building up in the tank where the cattle drink. He sidles up next to his dad, to help him assess the situation and his dad says, "The tank heaters not working it looks like, we'll have to get that fixed today. Come on, let's go to the house and warm-up."

Realizing his hands are getting cold, Timmy decides

this is probably best, and heads toward the house, following his dad's footprints in the snow.

They get to the house and Timmy decides to make one more stop before going inside. He walks to the side of the house, and peeks inside the doghouse, and sees there's plenty of hay on the bottom for Whitey, their dog, to lie on. The flap that he uses to enter and exit the doghouse looks like a good size, it doesn't let any more cold air in than possible. He has freshwater, and food in his bowl.

'Good.' Satisfied with that, he turns around and walks towards the porch. He looks around once more, 'where is that dog anyway?' he wonders.

When they get into the house, Betty is sitting at the kitchen table looking at recipes and she and Edward begin talking. Edward is at the sink washing his hands.

"The tank heater for the cows is broken. I gotta figure out what's wrong with it and fix it so the cows got something to drink."

"Timmy, take your coat, mittens, gloves and boots off at the door," his mom tells him and he goes into the living room and stands next to the oil burner that's as tall as he is, to warm himself. Betty is at the kitchen table looking through a cookbook, and Edward is already on his way back out the door, to figure out why the tank heater quit working.

Timmy's nestled himself into the living room and turns the TV back on and sits on the floor in front of it and begins watching Captain Kangaroo, his favorite show. A few minutes later he thinks he hears the car driving down the driveway, 'dad must be going to go get a part or something for the broken tank heater,' he thinks to himself.

The early morning sun is peeking out from behind clouds just a little, and it looks very bright out against the newly fallen snow. "Timmy," his mother calls him to the kitchen, "go down into the basement and get me some potatoes would you?"

"I hate going into the basement. It's dark and full of cobwebs."

"Pretty please," she tries sweet-talking him. It only has a dirt floor, and the first step is a long step for someone with short legs.

"All right," he bows his head and succumbs to her.

He turns on the light switch and heads down the creaky steps. "It's cold and dark down here," he hollers back up to her. There are home canned tomatoes, green and waxed beans and pickles on shelves, a huge burlap bag full of potatoes and a basket full of onions. There is something in the far side corner of the one room basement, he doesn't know what it is, and thinks it might be an animal. He doesn't go near it, but keeps the corner of his eye on it just in case. He puts a bunch of potatoes in the container Betty has given him and quickly heads back upstairs, where the sun is now shining through the kitchen windows, brightening up the room.

"Put the container of potatoes on the table for me, and sit down and I'll give you a glass of milk and a cookie." He does what she asks and waits patiently; looking up at the windows, and notices just how bright it is inside and out.

"The windows look as bright as the sun, it's blinding me," he tells her.

"Then don't look at it," she tells him.

'It's brighter than I've ever noticed it before,' he thinks. It makes his eyes hurt a little. He tries looking at it again, and it blinds him.

"Here's your glass of milk," his mom pours it half full and sets the milk carton down and comes back, "and here's your cookie," then she puts the milk container back into the refrigerator.

Edward walks in, letting in some cold air, and he

takes off his gloves, "the tank heater is fixed." He pulls out a chair from under the table and sits down, as Betty is ready with a cup of coffee for him. She gets another cup, and fills it with coffee for herself and sets it on the table, pulls out a chair and sits down in front of it, next to Edward.

Edward begins, "Well son, your ma and I got something we want to tell ya," he looks down smiling at him. "It looks like your gonna have a little brother or sister to play with around here pretty soon. What do you think about that?"

He shrugs his shoulders, meekly and says, "I don't know."

"It's pretty exciting really. You'll be able to play with the baby. You can teach the baby things. Once the baby gets old enough you can take him or her outside and play together. What do you think?"

"How soon is the baby coming?" He wants to know.

"In a couple of months," Betty chimes in, "by next summer the baby will be here."

She carefully watches his reactions.

"I'm not sharing my toys with it!" he suddenly says angrily."

"You won't have to worry about that for a long time. It'll be a long while before the baby is old enough to play with your toys," his mom tells him.

"Finish eating your cookie and drinking your milk and get dressed and you can come with me," his dad says.

"Where we going?" Timmy asks.

"Oh just for a ride," he says, "Ma has things to do."

When they get back, Edward heads straight to the barn with Timmy in toe. When he gets inside the barn, he sees the heifer is lying down and bellowing in discomfort and pain. Edward squats down to check out the heifer and finds she doesn't look good and tells Timmy to run to the house and tell ma to call the vet out right away.

"Mom? Mom! Something's wrong with the heifer. Dad said to call and get the vet out here right away!"

Quickly she races to the phone, and looks up the number in the phone book. She gets the vet on the phone, tells him who she is and why she's calling.

"Timmy, run back out to the barn and tell your dad the vet will be out here right away. Quick, run!" He turns and races back out to the barn and relays the information to his dad.

"Dad, he's on his way out!" he shrieks, all excited.

Soon, Betty comes into the barn with her kerchief on her head and her old coat unbuttoned but wrapped closed with her hands. She approaches Edward. Mom Betty bends down and starts rubbing the cows neck and forehead. She looks into the birthing heifer's eyes and asks Edward how he thinks she is.

"I don't know," is all he tells her.

"Timmy, go back into the house, and listen for the phone, just in case the vet calls back," she tells him.

"We'll find out when the vet gets here, I guess," Edward tells her.

Timmy gets back into the house and takes off his coat, mittens, and boots and huddles up to the kitchen stove to get warm. After a few minutes, he looks out the kitchen window to see if the vet has come yet. Nothing. He looks up at the phone and wanders into the living room. He doesn't ever remember being alone in the house before, and doesn't know quite what to make of it. Everything looks more real. He starts to notice things he has never noticed before. The square wood work at the top of the corners of the doorways, the gold color of the carpet. He walks into his mom and dad's bedroom off the living room, and notices there's a baby's crib in there. He walks past the upstairs staircase and notices the plasters coming off the wall in one spot and wooden lats are showing through. There is a door that goes outside, from the bathroom; he's never seen before.

Betty walks into the kitchen from the outside and the barn, and Timmy winds around the house, back into the kitchen to meet her and asks her, "How's the cow doing?"

"She looks uncomfortable and is going to need the vet to have the calf. That's all I can tell you. I hope they're going to be okay."

"Can I go back out there?" he asks her.

"No, you better stay in the house out-of-the-way," she tells him. Just then the vet pulls into the driveway and the yard and drives another sixty feet closer to the barn. He parks his truck, gets out and walks towards the barn and goes in. He and Edward are in there for hours and hours before any sign of them are seen again. By then Timmy had begun thinking everything was okay.

Edward walks into the house and tells Betty to boil some water. "We're gonna have to bring the calf into the house," he says, "at least for the night, and maybe for a couple of days. It's too cold out for him to be out there, and the heifers not suckling him, so we're gonna have to try and feed it too."

Betty exclaims, "Oh, not in the house! You can't bring it into the house. It's all dirty and it's gonna get everything else all dirty!"

"Well, what else do you want to do with it?" Edward asks her, "it can't stay outside, it'll freeze to death!"

"Oh I suppose. Bring it in then," Betty says dishearteningly.

Betty goes to the pump and starts to pump the white handle, waiting for the water to come up to fill a kettle, so she can boil the water. Edward turns to go get the calf, to bring it into the house and says, "Put some rugs down, we'll keep it in the kitchen."

Betty quickly finds some old rugs and puts them down near the sink, complaining. When Edward comes back into the house, he's holding the quiet newborn calf

Lexington Glory Days

that occasionally kicks his legs around quickly. With both arms close to his body he lays it down where Betty has laid the rugs. He walks back out to the porch and brings in some fence gates the vet has put there, and tries to set the fence gates around the calf in case he gets up or starts jumping around.

The telltale sound of the school busses motor is heard through the open door, speeding up and moving down the road. Soon Jennifer, wearing red, white and blue striped pants, enters the room quietly, and behind her Frankie, ten, walks in. Looking around he asks puzzled.

"What's going on? Why is there a calf in the kitchen?" And keeps walking. Patrick walks in behind them.

Edward tells Patrick, "change out of your school clothes and come back down to help me set up these fence gates better around the calf. Jack should be home shortly." Jack and his twin sister, Bonnie, sixteen, share a car and drive back and forth to school. "Jack can help me then."

Patrick and Frankie go out to the barn to do chores and throw hay bales down from the hayloft for the cattle to eat and make sure the water tanks are full.

"We had to bring it inside," Edward tells Betty, seeing her frown.

The vet leaves and passes by a farmhouse two miles down the road with a sign out front that says, 'eggs for sale.' He decides to stop to get a couple of dozen. 'Nothin like farm fresh eggs,' he thinks to himself.

He lets his truck run and walks up to the door. A woman behind a curtain peers out from the other side. "I'm here for eggs," he shouts. He points at the sign, "eggs!" He hollers. The curtain falls and soon a small middle aged woman is at the front door.

Looking timid and frail the woman responds as if she hasn't seen another living soul in years.

"Yes? May I help you?" There's a small girl clinging to her mothers dress.

"Yes 'mam, I'd like to get two dozen eggs, if it's no bother."

"Come in," she tells him. There's egg cartons and dozens and dozens of both cleaned and dirty eggs spread along the kitchen counters, and in bowls. The room is cluttered and warm. There's newspapers spread all around the floor.

"No bother, a'tall, let me just wash a few and put them in a carton for you." She turns her back to him and washes the eggs.

The little girl stays close to her mother, "I'm six," she says and quickly hides behind her mother's dress.

"Here you go," the woman, says, "fifty cents…You're the veterinarian, aren't you? I thought I recognized you."

"Yes, 'mam. I was just down the road at the Edward Reich farm helping with a heifer having trouble birthing. Everything turned out fine," he tells her.

"How is the family?" she asks him turning slowly, looking him in the eyes. "My daughter is dating their son, Jack."

Chapter Thirteen

Spring In The Country

Like all holidays before this one, two years later, Betty and Edward have invited their ever expanding family over for supper, for Easter Sunday. "But come over anytime," they tell everybody. "Anytime after two."

"I'll always have an evening meal during the holidays," Betty is telling Kathy, Jack's new wife, talking to her on the phone. "This gives you's time to spend with your families during the day, and whenever you're done over there, you can always come out here whenever you're ready," she explains to her. Betty has this worked out with her in-laws.

"Oh, that's nice to know," Kathy tells her, pleasantly surprised.

It's Sunday and the kids have gotten up early, excited to eagerly find out where the mysterious Easter Bunny has hidden their Easter baskets full of jellybeans, chocolate rabbits, and hard-boiled eggs. Jennifer and Timmy find theirs easily, behind the television and couch. Some have to look harder.

"I can't find it," Frankie tells his parents, embarrassed, smiling a little.

"It must be around someplace. Are you sure you looked everywhere?" Betty asks him, as Edward walks

Lexington Glory Days

around the house looking suspicious.

"There's no eating an hour before mass, Patrick. You can have some when we get back." Patrick looks at her and puts down the jellybean.

All the kids and Betty are dressed in their nicest Sunday clothes. "You can look some more when we get back," Betty tells Frankie. "We have to get going or we'll be late for church."

"Happy Easter, Sophia," Betty greets her neighbor, in the quickly warming morning air, with all the kids in tow. "Good morning."

"Good morning. Happy Easter. What a beautiful day," Sophia tells her.

"Morning, Leonard. Looks like winter is finally over." Roman says friendly.

"Morning Roman, morning Edna." John, the bell ringer, greets them. "Happy Easter."

The parishioners arrive dressed up more than usual, especially the little girls, in cute pink and yellow dresses and bonnets. The windows are cracked open in the church, allowing for a much needed fresh breeze, after a long winter.

After Mass, back at home in the kitchen, Betty makes lunch for everyone.

"What's Timmy doing?" Edward asks Betty, "I worry about him. Ever since I let him stay at home by himself a couple of years ago, I don't know, he's just not the same." Edward's just come in from outside.

"He's only six years old, he probably doesn't even remember it." Betty tells him, working around the kitchen.

"I can notice a difference. Where is he?"

"He's out in the back lawn playing, make-believe farming. He's got his tractors and wagons out there. He's pretending the mowed grass is the hay, and he's going around driving over it pretending he's baling it."

Lexington Glory Days

Edward goes to look out of the window from the downstairs bedroom he and Betty share and watches him, carefully. "What's everyone else doing?" he asks Betty, returning to the kitchen, unsure of what to make of Timmy.

"Jennifer's upstairs in her room and Frankie went fishing with the neighbor boy for a while. I don't know what Patrick's doing, he's outside someplace," she tells him." None of the older children, besides Bonnie, live at home anymore.

"I just came from out there. He's washing Dr. Pescokiv's truck." The head of medicine at St. Mary's hospital in Merrifield has a cabin on the lake just down the road from them. The doctor has an old truck he uses to haul things in and keeps it in one of Edward's shed, and Patrick takes care of it.

"On days like these when the kids are out of the house, it almost seems quiet in here," Edward tells her, "I kinda like it."

"It's pretty quiet, that's for sure. And It better stay that way," Betty agrees, the sunny, peaceful afternoon agreeing with her, spending time in the kitchen baking bread.

"What are you doing?" She looks up and asks him.

"I'm not doin nothin," he says as he pulls a kitchen chair out from under the table and sits down. "I been thinking. Maybe we should build a pole shed."

"What do you want a pole shed for?" she asks him, looking at him, "you've already got sheds out there."

"Yeah, but half of them are too small to use to put things in, and a couple of the other ones are ready to fall down. In a pole shed we can park the car and truck in if we want to, keeping it out of the winter and the snow off of it. And we can store other stuff in it too. The place could really use one. Joe," Theresa's husband, "builds sheds now doesn't he? Maybe we could do a lot of it ourselves, if he helps us."

"Oh, I don't know, I suppose. Ask him and see what he says. If he'll help, and it doesn't cost too terribly much, go ahead." The sweet aroma of the fresh baking bread in the oven is starting to fill the air in the room, and Edward's belly starts to rumble.

"I'm taking the car uptown tomorrow night to do laundry," she tells him, as shadows from the clouds outside begin to cast the room in a darker glow.

"Must be clouding up outside. Is it suppose to rain?" He asks.

"I don't know, but I'm taking the car uptown tomorrow tonight to do laundry. Or did you hear me?"

"I heard you. Weren't you out last night with the kids? Can't you stay home once?" He's teasing her, but she doesn't realize it, and turns feisty.

"I took them to catechism classes at the church! It's not like I went out to a party. If you don't like it, take the clothes to town yourself and wash them," she tells him adamantly.

"I was just kidding," smiling, he tells her. "Take them in."

Soon the front door to the outside opens, "Happy Easter!" Laura says, walking in with Harold and their two kids, full of energy. Greeting his parents when they come in, they quickly get comfortable and take off their light jackets. Theresa and Joe walk in a few minutes behind them.

"Happy Easter," Betty and Edward return the greeting, happy and smiling. The young kids are eager to start playing with each other.

A half hour later Carol and Chris arrive with their two kids. "Happy Easter!"

Carol greets everyone, walking into the kitchen, smiling.

"Happy Easter," Chris says, serious and friendly.

"Happy Easter. Help yourselves to drinks or beer," Edward tells them.

Jack and Kathy arrive a short while later.

"How do you like having dad home all the time?" Laura asks her mother-in-law, referring to Edward retiring from road construction, once she settles in.

"Oh, it's all right I guess," she says with a small grimace on her face, "sometimes I wish he wasn't around quite so much," she looks at her and chuckles.

"And I hope 'and pray!' he doesn't start drinking a lot," she tells her, already feeling like he's let her down. "He does enough the way it is." Edward quit for six years and then started again, to Betty's chagrin.

Just then a large roar is heard from the men playing poker in the living room, someone has just won, and someone just lost, a large pot. Chris looks interested and wanders into the living room.

"Does he have enough to do to keep himself occupied?" Carol asks her.

"He keeps busy," she continues, her eyes gazing into the living room, "but when he's not busy, he goes out and has a few beers, sometimes he comes home pretty shined up. He's been bringing home little bags of candy for the younger kids, especially Timmy, I think, to make up for the time he left him alone. You know Timmy, still is a little distant towards him, and that happened over a year ago already.

"Why, what happened?" Kathy, Jacks wife, says seriously, wanting to know.

Theresa tries filling her in. "Dad was babysitting Timmy and told him he was going out for a while, and he'd be right back. He left him alone in the house. (I think he went to see that woman he had the affair with a long time ago)," she whispers off to the side. "Timmy got really scared and left a note in the mailbox, saying he needed help, hoping someone would find it and come rescue him," Theresa explains. "Nothing happened and he was fine, but he was really scared. Anyway, he never really forgave dad for leaving him. You know, on the inside."

"Oh, that poor kid." Kathy empathizes, "he must have been scared out of his mind, and now he doesn't trust his own dad, how sad."

In the living room Jack is telling a story to the men, while they play poker.

"Bonnie was sitting at the front end of the empty hay wagon, just behind the tractor, when we hit a bump. She fell off and ended up underneath one of the tires. She was shaken up pretty bad. One of the neighbors saw us and came out to make sure she was okay and took us to the hospital to get her checked out. She wasn't hurt, but she was scraped up pretty good," Jack explains to them.

"I might have had a few car accidents," Harold chides him, "but I never ran anybody over before," he says laughing loudly, teasing him. "Get out of the way," Harold calls into his folded hands and laughs.

"She's lucky it wasn't worse," Joe tells them seriously.

In the kitchen, the women are talking and Bonnie asks her mom about her being pregnant. "How far along are you mom?"

"Four months," her mom tells her. "Four long months." She chuckles looking at them, sitting around the table, visiting with them.

"Laura, how far along are you?" Carol asks her sister-in-law.

"Two months," she tells them. "Two months and counting," she chuckles.

The talk of being pregnant, leads to talk of families and weddings.

"Everyone was shined up before our wedding ceremony even started." Laura says with a smile. "We'd been drinking all morning." She laughs. "We're lucky we

Lexington Glory Days

could still walk down the aisle without falling, or tripping." She laughs again, thoroughly enjoying the others' company.

Jack hears this from the living room, and ribs his brother good naturedly about it, "Is that the only way you could get up the nerve to walk down the aisle Harold, was all shined up?" Jack mischievously smiles at him.

Harold tells him, "God damn just about," he says under his breath, laughing. "No, I was ready, I wanted to get married." He says, turning serious.

"Maybe we should have another drink, "Edward suggests. The men all agree. "I'll get the bottle and soda and bring it in here," Edward tells them, getting up.

"Chris and I had a big formal wedding," Carol tells them, although everyone already knows. "And no, we weren't drinking. I wasn't anyway." She stops and thinks for a moment, "I don't think Chris was." She wonders.

"Both Laura and Carol had beautiful, white wedding dresses, attendants, a social hour, big dinner, and dances afterwards. The whole nine yards," Theresa adds, holding a drink in her hand.

"And both were held at small Catholic churches," Bonnie shares with them, noticing the similarities. "Laura's church, in a small town ten miles away," she adds, "and Carol's, the country church, here at Lexington," the church Betty takes the kids to, religiously every week for Sunday mass and catechism.

"It was a beautiful day I remember," Carol says. "It'll be four years ago this January. I had such a nice time, I wish I could do it all over again," she giggles.

"Four years ago," Betty repeats, "where is all that time going?"

"And you and Joe eloped," Carol says to her sister Theresa, "what made you decide to elope?" She asks with genuine curiosity.

The men are listening in the living room and Jack

responds, "Joe was probably afraid when the priest asked, 'if anybody knows of any reason these two should not be married,' everyone was gonna stand up and start telling him," Jack laughs out loud hysterically, with Harold and Chris laughing along.

Joe smiles a little, not embarrassed or amused.

"We didn't want a big, fancy wedding," Theresa tells them. "We just wanted the two of us and the justice of the peace. Just something quiet and personal," she tells them. "Something simple. We were happy with it. I'd do it again the same way if I had to do it over again. I would too."

"Me too," Carol agrees. "I'd do mine the same way."

"And Kathy," Bonnie goes on, "you and Jack had a nice church wedding."

"It was small, but it was nice. We didn't want anything really big either," Kathy tells them. "We just wanted something small. Small and intimate."

"You didn't wear a traditional wedding dress either, you wore a short dress," Theresa remembers.

Betty delights in hearing them tell their wedding stories and getting along so well. She listens and watches contently.

"Yeah, it was just a simple dress I had bought especially for the wedding," Kathy tells her. "I liked it." Kathy isn't a quick talker like her sisters-in-law.

The house is especially warm now, with the food cooking in the hot oven all day, and the door to the oven now opened to remove the ham.

"Theresa, how's married life?" Bonnie asks, changing the subject.

"It's good," she states matter-of-fact like, her eyes darting back and forth as her head nods up and down. "I won't say it doesn't have its ups and downs, but things are good. Very good."

"What kind of ups and downs do you mean?" Carol asks her slyly, raising and lowering her eyebrows suggestively.

Theresa takes a swallow of her drink and begins laughing at the same time. Some of the drink goes down her windpipe into her lungs, interrupting her airflow, causing her to cough. Soon she's wheezing heavily and can't catch her breath. She walks over to the sink, her face turning redder and redder.

Gasping for air, both of her hands are holding onto the porcelain basin, and her head tilts up and down with each attempt at trying to breath. Panic sets in across the room.

"My God she's choking!" Bonnie screams startled, jumping up. "Somebody do something! She can't breath! Quick, somebody do something!"

Bonnie stands, frozen in time, afraid, not knowing what to do.

Betty rushes over to her daughter and begins patting her on the back, and Theresa reacts by pulling away. The other women are scared, and talk quickly and loudly. "What should we do!" "Dad, come in here, quick!"

Wondering what to do they yell for their brothers and husbands in the living room. "She's choking!"

The clatter from the kitchen brings the men's help, as they rush in to help from the doorway, like wild horses. Theresa sits herself on the floor, beginning to black out and lays down, feeling faint and not wanting to fall. Harold rushes in and helps her lay on the floor, face up, and starts holding her arms and hands down, as she weakly struggles to free herself.

Edward and Chris kneel down beside her, trying to help.

Anxiously, Harold tells her, "Take long, slow, deep breaths." Theresa tries, slowly struggling for air, her wheezing gets better and she starts to settle down. Every breath she takes is forced. She inhales with all the energy she can muster, and gets only a small amount of air each

Lexington Glory Days

time, getting a little more in the next breath, and then a little more still.

"Tell her again," Edward orders him.

"Theresa, listen to me. Take long, slow, deep breaths," he repeats.

With a look of fright in her eyes Betty tells them, "Sit her up now! Sit her up! Her breathings better, maybe it'll go down now if we sit her up!" She hopes this will help.

Still laying on the floor, they help her sit up. She tries to take a deep breath, but can't.

"Try taking deep breaths," her dad tells her soothingly.

There's a searing pain, right below her chest and she lifts her hands to rub it. Her eyes are watery and for the first time in ten minutes she glances up and looks all at once to all the family members watching her. She lets out a weak cough, and brings her hand up to wipe her eyes, still wheezing and struggling to catch her breath, but getting better in small increments.

Betty rushes to wet a washcloth and kneels nearby her and begins to pat her forehead and cheeks, frantically. Theresa takes the cloth from her, and begins wiping her eyes and dabbing at her face. Harold and Mom Betty take her by the arms and help her to her feet. Her knees buckling like a doll.

The four stand, and nervously Edward asks her, "are you all right?"

Shaking her, dazed and unresponsive, she lets out another cough, "I think so," and walks, weakly towards the kitchen table to sit down, with everyone helping her.

"Just let me…" Cough. "be for a…" Cough. "minute."

Carol brings her a glass of water and sets it in front of her, and instinctively Theresa picks it up and takes just a small sip, and sets it back down. She speaks in a low moan, "that was a tough one," and immediately starts coughing again. "I think I'm gonna make it." She barely

Lexington Glory Days

gets the words out before she starts wheezing and coughing again.

With the crisis over and people's hearts racing, they begin to settle down.

"Oh my word," Carol says in disbelief. "Are you sure you're going to be okay?" They all look at her and watch her head slowly nod up and down.

"It's getting better," she tells them, still wheezing. Beads of perspiration are all around her face, and she lets out another cough. "It's better."

Betty tells the men, "finish up your card games in the living room if you's want," hoping to put the episode behind them. "I think we should eat. Bonnie, go outside and round up all the kids and bring them in now."

The men walk over to the table and they each make themselves a whiskey drink, Jack has a beer, and they go back into the living room.

"It's time for the kids to come in anyway. They've been out there long enough," Laura says.

"You sure know how to put the scare into everybody," she tells Theresa. "I'd hate to imagine what would have happened if it didn't go down. Oh my word, my heart is still pounding." She looks around seriously.

Betty and the other women start to tend to the food on the stove and in the oven. Bonnie goes out the door, rounding up all the kids, as they set the table and start to dish the food out.

In the tromp, their moms get up and get their jackets off as they all talk at once and laugh and stumble over their words as they try to relive every detail, from the past two hours. Their happiness is contagious and everyone begins to talk and laugh amongst themselves and their kids. Even Theresa, after almost having choked is beginning to feel better, and the place suddenly becomes lively again.

Betty announces to everyone with a smile, "supper

will be ready soon, so don't anybody go anywhere." Supper is served in shifts, as only so many people can fit around the oval kitchen table at one time.

"So, what are we having?" Chris asks, cautious about leaving Theresa. In case something else should happen to her.

Betty tells him, "We're having ham and turkey, a big roaster full of dressing, big bowls of mashed potatoes, gravy, corn, hot fresh biscuits from the oven, coleslaw, my own canned pickles, radishes, canned beets, and apple and pumpkin pie for dessert."

Age has slowly crept into Betty and Edward's faces. They celebrated their 25th wedding anniversary last fall. Gone are those youthful looks, without wrinkles or cares. They are still young enough to remember how each of them looked when they were younger. The scent of young love still fresh in their minds; but still in the past, never the less.

Edward is losing his hair, and Betty has kept a nice figure, even after having nine children. She has retained much of her natural beauty as when she was younger. Her up and back, off her forehead curly black hairstyle is the same, but her curls have lost some of their spin. Her chic, frameless glasses have been replaced by something more sturdy and practical. They both have, without giving it any thought at all, become older.

They are happy today, glad in the moment. They will always be happiest when the whole family is together.

Their party is as much a celebration for them, thrown by them, as it is a reason to get the whole family together. Not that the real reason for Easter, Jesus Christ, is ever forgotten in their mix. They all know, today He has risen. It's been engrained in them, after all those years of going to catechism classes at church. First He died, then He was buried, and today He rose from the dead.

Betty and Edward are a proud pair today. With all

their problems, they did a good job raising the kids. It is seldom either one of them can be seen today without a grin stemming from ear to ear.

Carol snaps their picture with her camera. "Say cheese," she tells them.

In the picture, Edward's arm is around Betty's neck and shoulder. She looks nice in her knee length grass colored dress with a gold colored circular broach pinned above her left breast. Edward's hand is dangling in front of her. Betty is holding onto his little finger. They're in front of the oil burner heat stove, with its croaked chimney pipe going outside, in the kitchen painted just a little bit too dark of blue, smiling, happy, and in love.

They walk away from the kitchen and reminisce between themselves.

"Twenty-five Christmases, Easters, Thanksgivings, and anniversaries. I can't count how many birthdays and birthday cakes, five high school graduations, four weddings..." Betty says, recounting back in time.

"And we're only half done, baby," Edward says, finishing for her. The two kiss, a short familiar kiss. Then Edward tells her, "I'm gonna get a drink."

Harold, Jack, Chris, Joe and Patrick have begun eating at the table. Frankie and Timmy are hanging around the kitchen; Frankie so he can hear what the men have to say and Timmy because Frankie is there.

"So dad," Harold asks, "are you putting the farm up for sale?"

"I guess so," he replies. Thinking to himself, 'what do you care? I can't get you out here to help with anything anyway.' He's starting to turn belligerent from the alcohol he's been drinking.

"I guess we have to. Timmy can't be around all the pollen and hay, with his hay fever," Betty answers for him, trying to avoid an argument.

Betty leaves Edward's side to help Laura, Carol,

Theresa, Kathy and Bonnie, who have been filling the food bowls with the delicious dinner.

"Yeah, we gotta. We got no choice, we got to get him out of here," his dad replies, feeling obtrusive. "Not that you'll miss it," he tells Harold.

"Then what you going to do?" Harold follows up. "Move far, far away I hope." The two still have had many unresolved differences to settle.

Edward sneers at him, "I don't know yet, maybe move to town. I hear Arizona's nice," he tries hiding the anger building up in him.

"Arizona? You wouldn't move all the way to Arizona would you?" Jack asks surprised, looking at him to see if he can tell whether or not he's serious.

"That'd be far enough away for me," Harold says, laughing. The alcohol he's been drinking is also starting to have its effects.

"What the hell do you mean, 'that'd be far enough away?' You're startin to piss me off," Edward tells him. "You better watch what you say, I'm telling you."

"It's not like you never pissed me off," Harold says combatively.

"We don't know what were gonna do yet. We got time to think about it. We don't even have it listed yet," Betty intervenes again, trying to stave off a fight.

"Huh, no kidding," Jack chortles in disbelief, still surprised.

"The only reason I ever pissed you off, is because you were such a screw up," Edward tells Harold, getting mad and starting to lash out.

"Stop it now," Laura says to both of them.

"The only reason I was such a screw up is because you were such a lousy dad," Harold tells him, his voice getting loud.

"I'll show you how lousy of a dad I was," Edward says, approaching him.

Lexington Glory Days

"Well don't move by me," Chris kids him, making a few of them laugh.

"Bring it on," Harold tells him, sweeping his chair away from the table and standing up, bumping into him. Edward quickly swipes him around the neck, trying to put him in a headlock.

"Oh, no" Laura says aloud, "Not again."

Harold tries pushing him off, and swings his arms, hitting him in the back.

The other men at the table slide their chairs away from them, so they don't get hit. Edward takes Harold around the stomach from the front like he was going to lift him up, and Harold pushes him with all of his strength, making Edward stumble backwards, into the table filled with food. Still hanging on to the back of his shirt, Edward pulls him away from him, and throws him on the floor. Harold gets up madder than before, and rises up on his tiptoes making a fist, ready to hit him the face.

"Stop it! Stop it!" Betty rushes between them to break them up, supporting a hand on each of their chests.

"Harold!" Laura hollers at him, trying to get him to turn around.

"So I was a bad dad, huh? Now I know what you really think," Edward sneers, yelling at him, walking away. "God damn, good for nothing kid."

"Shut up!" Betty hollers at him. "You go over there, and you go over there," she tells Harold. The small kids and women are frightened, watching timidly from the living room. "Both of you, sit down and shut up and eat. The foods getting cold." They both sit on the far opposite sides of the table, as far away from one another as they can get. They both mumble something.

Betty quickly makes the sign of the cross and begins to say grace, "Bless us, oh Lord, for these thy gifts, which we are about to receive through Jesus Christ our Lord.

Amen. Now eat," she tells them. "Come on everyone, sit back down. Come on." Slowly the men resume their places at the table.

Bowls are filled again and again with either the tender meat of the pig or turkey, or the mashed potatoes, dressing and gravy. Slowly, uncomfortably, people resume their conversations.

"Sit down and eat Kathy. Laura you too, girls eat," Betty tells them, trying to lighten the mood.

The sky begins clouding up, and for two hours, a nice slow soaking rain falls from the sky. The sky is dark blue, but not threatening, late in the day. The color is unusual and after the rain finally stops an enormous rainbow appears over the dark tilled soil that Edward has churned with his plow in the field. Betty stands, staring out of the window admiring its presence and soon, others come and stand around her.

With the sun starting to set, it peeks out one last time for the day. The suns brightness reflecting off the tops of tin sheds and a few white clouds in the sky, in contrast with the mostly dark blue sky, with the low hanging rainbow is breathtaking. Betty admires it one last time with her family. "Isn't that beautiful?"

Part 2

A Styrofoam Bell

"It's been a blustery God damn cold, snowy winter so far," Harold says, walking idly from room to room. "It's been snowing so much, the damn piles along the sides of the road are reaching ten feet high!" He tells them talking with his hands, "and it's just the beginning of January!" He laughs a little, his dark black hair slicked back.

He's at Betty and Edward's with other family members, in the old two-story farmhouse his mom and dad have owned for the past ten years, with the same gold colored carpeting and old brown couch and matching chair. The family has all come together to go to the annual ice-fishing contest at the lake and pavilion at Lexington.

"Down every road there isn't any more room to plow any more snow into the ditches. I don't know where they'll put it if we get much more," Jack says, his politeness and slightly smaller frame, compared to his brother and light brown hair suggest the differences between the two.

"Harold married Laura in 1962 and the two have three children," Betty is explaining to Jennifer, who's eleven, with the family all around them.

"Mom and I were pregnant at the same time, twice!" Laura says to the others and lets out a big laugh.

Timmy is no longer the youngest of Edward and Betty's busy family. Two years ago they had another son, Mathew.

"Carol met a very nice man from a nearby town and married him 1965, and moved up north. You know that, you've been to their house," Laura helps Jennifer fill in the pieces, "and the two have two daughters and Carol is expecting again." Carol and Jennifer both nod their heads up and down.

"Theresa eloped out to Mount Rushmore three summers ago, and Jack married his high school sweetheart a few years back, and they have a baby girl," Carol finishes explaining, her dark hair dyed blonde. Jennifer, shy with short brown curls in her hair, sweetly smiles at them.

"With everybody's wives and husbands and kids, there's about twenty people here," Jennifer tells them quietly in the kitchen. "I counted them."

Jack walks into the kitchen a little while later, "Carol and Laura have their cameras out and are in the living room taking pictures of the kids sitting around the Christmas tree," that's still up from the holidays in the corner between two windows, "if you're wondering what they're doing," he adds.

"The tree has an assortment of brightly colored bulbs on it, mostly blue, red, and purple. A white, one-dimensional Styrofoam bell, with 'NOEL' written on it with red glitter," Theresa's husband, Joe, says out loud, amused, watching the kids around the tree fidget and get their picture taken.

"It has a cardboard Santa Claus half inside a red chimney; a baby reindeer made of cloth, and lights," Laura says, "It's very pretty." Trying to get all the kids to settle down and get in the picture.

"Christmas cards are still on top of the television and a few opened gifts are still under the tree, a book, a box that contains a shirt, and a Monopoly game," Bonnie tells them, her thin lanky body twisting as she speaks.

"Jennifer...We need you in the picture," Carol shouts.

Harold's oldest daughter is eight and the same age as Timmy. She's smiling ear to ear and is sitting on the floor and has her younger sister, 2, sitting on the floor in front of her, her arms are wrapped around her tightly. Haold's middle child, a son, is sitting on the floor next to them, and is holding a big, light blue and white teddy bear that's as big as he is.

Jennifer is smiling and sitting on her legs on the floor, sitting next to him, dressed in a prim white shirt and short hair, she's holding Carol's oldest daughter, 3, who's dressed in a blue dress with white trim and ruffles. Jack's baby daughter is in front, in the middle, smiling brightly with a head full of bright red hair.

Timmy is sitting cross-legged on the floor, smiling just a little, in front of them. Frankie is behind them, smiling a big smile, standing on his knees.

Carol's second daughter is in the center of the picture, in the front row, with Matthew, the youngest of Edward and Betty's children. "Carol make some funny faces and say something to get them to smile," Laura kids her.

"Say cheese everyone. Smile, look here," Carol holds her hand above her camera and clicks her fingers hoping to make them smile, and get a good picture. "Hey, over here!" She quickly bellows, trying to rattle them to look.

"If they'd stop fidgeting for two seconds maybe you could take it," Harold says laughing. The kids are always turning to look one way or the other.

"While the kids are in the living room getting their picture taken, this would be a good time for the men to sneak into the kitchen where it's quiet," Jack tells his brother, Harold.

"Good idea. Let's get out of here." Betty's in the

Lexington Glory Days

small kitchen, talking with Theresa, Bonnie, Kathy and Edward, as Harold, Jack, and Carol's husband, Chris, and Theresa's husband, Joe, walk into the kitchen with them. "Come sit down," Betty tells them pleasantly.

"There's herring, vegetables, dips, chips, pickles, crackers and cheese and summer sausage to snack on, and whiskey or beer, and water or soda to drink," Edward announces, "help yourselves, I'm not going to wait on you."

Everyone indulges in the beer or liquor and makes themselves a drink except Betty, Kathy and Carol, who's pregnant.

"It's so nice to see everyone again," Theresa tells everyone, outgoing and friendly, holding her drink in her hand, "How is everyone? And the kid's, how are all the kids? What has everyone been up to?" She says, clearly missing everyone. Jack is talking about days gone by, when they were younger.

"Remember the time when we all had to move in with grandma and grandpa?" Jack adds.

"After the fire, yeah... I liked living there," Theresa tells them, "I didn't mind it one bit."

"Grandpa died while we were living there," Mom Betty remembers.

"That's right," Harold tells him, "I almost forgot about that."

"I hated living there," Bonnie tells them, walking towards her mother.

"Why?" Theresa asks her.

"I thought the place was haunted." She tells her.

"Haunted? Why would you think that?" Theresa asks, snickering.

"Carol was telling ghost stories in her room, and we all had to wait in the hallway for our turn, and it was dark. Well, while I was waiting for my turn in the hallway, and I swear there was this little midget that came up to me and

Lexington Glory Days

started tickling me!"

"What?" they all question her and laugh. "A midget?" Harold says loudly and starts laughing, "har har har."

"No, really?" Carol asks her, surprised.

"Really!" Bonnie tells her, "I didn't like it there one bit."

"Well, no wonder," Kathy, Jacks wife, tells them and laughs coyly.

"Timmy is eight years old, and Matthew," Mom Betty and Edward's youngest child, "is two." Theresa is educating her husband, Joe, about the family history. "It's not uncommon for a devoted catholic woman to have so many kids," Theresa tells him. "They can't use birth control, it's against her religion."

Laura and Carol come back from taking their pictures from the living room and join the group in the kitchen. "What are you talking about?" Carol asks Theresa. "Those kids, they just can't sit still." She tells her, chuckling.

"Matthew was born with really bad asthma. He had to spend many weeks in the hospital when he was first born, with the doctors trying to keep his lungs working," Theresa continues talking.

"Mom had to stay up all day and night, watching over him, making sure he kept breathing," Carol tells her. "I remember her telling me that," she adds with an air of concern. "I had already moved out by then."

"Me too," Theresa tells her.

"When are we going to the ice fishing contest?" Laura asks, curiously.

"Soon," Harold says, defiantly.

"His asthma is under control now with medicines, but it's always a worry. With all the hay that's baled around here, and the dust and pollen in the air in the summer, they gotta be careful around him, for his sake," Theresa tells them.

"I remember Edward talking about moving the

family to Arizona at one time. But I don't think he would up and move everybody that far. Do you?" Laura asks them.

"It's still up for discussion. Another option for them is to just move to town, at least they'd get him away from some of the dust and pollen," Carol suggests.

"Anybody wanna play a few hands of penny ante poker around the living room coffee table, before we go to the ice fishing contest?" Harold asks the guys. "Five card stud, five card draw, no peek, jacks are wild," he mentions some poker games, "and no cheating!" he adds seriously, but in a joking way.

"Yeah, I'll play," they all agree.

"I suppose, get the cards," Edward tells him.

"Get the cards. Get the cards, it's your house, you know where they are, I don't." He looks around on top of the hutch and freezer door.

"Ma, where are the cards?" Edward asks Betty.

"They're already in the living room, on the coffee table," she tells him.

Sitting in the sofa and in folding chairs with the coffee table between them, and Patrick and Frankie on the floor, they deal the cards. "What did you guys think of the astronauts landing on the moon last summer?" Chris, Carol's husband asks them, starting the conversation.

"Whoa! Isn't that something?" Jack tells him, flabbergasted.

Theresa's husband, Joe, starts shaking his head, "I can't believe it. It's just amazing. Do you know how 'far away' the moon is?"

"Yeah, it's a lot further away than it looks up in the sky," Chris tells them.

"That was just incredible," Jack states, "and watching them come back through the atmosphere and landing in the ocean? Incredible."

"That 'was' something else," Harold says seriously,

Lexington Glory Days

"everybody in the whole God damn county is still talking about it." He's standing between the doorway of the kitchen and living room.

"President Kennedy predicted it," Edward tells them, "I remember listening to him on TV, telling the whole nation, by the end of the decade they were gonna do it, and by God, they did."

Betty comes in and hands them another deck of cards, "Maybe this one is better," she tells them.

The women and girls spend time in the kitchen visiting and telling their own stories, and keeping watch over the kids. "Hey, how come we get the kids?" Laura says to the men leaving the kitchen.

"Cause we don't want them," Harold tells her, smiling, and keeps walking.

The children are close enough in age to keep each other occupied and company, while Frankie and Patrick opt to play penny ante poker with the older guys, Edward, Harold, Jack, Chris and Joe.

"Well, 1970 is over," Jack, says reminiscing. "Richard Nixon was president. The National Guard killed four students at Kent State for protesting, and the Vietnam War is winding down. It's been an interesting year."

Chris weighs in on his thoughts, "The average price of a home is $26,600 dollars, and the average household income is $8,734. Gas is $.36 a gallon."

The music lover, Bonnie, hears them and shouts from the kitchen, "The Partridge Family and 3 Dog Night had big hits, and Simon and Garfunkel's, 'Bridge Over Troubled Waters,' won song of the year."

"Nixon wants 18 year olds to be able to vote," Edward tells them, looking around at them. Wondering what they think about it.

"White people in a southern state tried to prevent black kids from going into a white school system," Joe says, he is the closest thing the family has to a hippy.

"We watched Markus Welby, Here's Lucy; Bonanza; Gunsmoke; Mayberry RFD; My Three Sons, Hee Haw and Laugh In," on TV, Patrick chimes in, getting into the spirit of nostalgia, for the old year.

IBM introduced the floppy disc for computer data storage.

"There was Super Bowl five." Chris says, not sure what else to add.

"Love Story and MASH were big movies," Carol calls out from the kitchen.

"Janis Joplin died, and so did Jimi Hendrix," Joe tells them.

Inside the house are the sounds of people talking and laughing. 'It's good to be home,' everyone thinks.

"Did you guys go to midnight mass at Lexington for Christmas, Betty?" Kathy asks her mother-in-law.

"Yes we did, and it was so nice. It was snowing lightly and the church looked so pretty with all the flowers on the altar, and the Christmas music and the choir singing. It's such a wonderful thing. It's so special."

"Did all the kids stay awake?" Laura asks wryly, smirking.

"They were pretty tired, midnight is awfully late for them and I made them lie down and try to take a nap before we had to go," Betty tells her, "but it's so nice, all the lights inside the church were dimmed and the choir and organist were playing Christmas songs, and they had candles lit. The church was decorated with strands of garland. It was really beautiful."

"Were there a lot of people there?" Carol asks.

"It sounds really nice," Kathy tells her.

"It was so full you couldn't even hardly find a place to sit down," Betty tells her, "there were a few people there I didn't recognize, not many though." Betty prides herself in knowing a lot of people.

"Probably friends or relatives of someone's," Bonnie

says, scrunching up her nose. "Cousins or aunts or uncles."

"What about you guys, Carol, did you make it to church?" Kathy asks her sister-in-law. Kathy likes it that the family is the same religion as her own.

"We went with Chris's folks on Christmas day, how about you?"

"We went to 5:00 p.m. mass in Centerville. It was packed too," Kathy tells them. "You couldn't hardly even find a place to sit down."

"I'm glad it's all over with," Carol says to the group, "all the Christmas shopping for the kids and the grown-ups, you never know what to get anyone, and there's all the wrapping and sending out Christmas cards, and the parties, it's too much."

"It's not so bad," Laura chimes in, "it's all what you want to make of it."

"That's right," Theresa agrees, "if you want to spend all that time doing that stuff then that's up to you. I don't even send out Christmas cards."

"How have you been feeling Carol?" Laura asks her about being pregnant.

"Well pretty good. A little morning sickness, and then it goes away. My legs cramp up sometimes, not cramp but tingle and ache and itch, like all at the same time."

She leans over and begins rubbing them.

"Is that common?" Kathy wants to know, "I didn't have that."

"Anything can happen when you're pregnant, just ask your mother-in-law," Laura cracks up laughing, "she went through it ten times!" Everyone laughs.

"And I wouldn't trade any one of them for anything in the world," Betty tells them. She looks up at them, from feeding two year old Mathew in his high chair and smiles at them.

"Oh, of course not," Laura says looking around,

turning serious.

"So how are your kids, Laura?" Kathy asks her. "Good, they're doing good, now that they're getting a little older and I don't have to change their diapers anymore. A lot better," she says with a laugh.

"You've got it easy nowadays, with the disposable diapers. I had to wash and dry the cloth ones all by hand," Betty tells them, "what a dirty job that was."

"I'm glad I don't have to do that," Carol tells them.

"Boy your not a kidding," Laura adds.

"You's all went through a lot of those cloth diapers too, let me tell you" Mom Betty says, smiling. "I wish I had a nickel for everyone I washed."

Her daughters look at her, not knowing what to say. "Well, thank you," Carol finally tells her, laughing.

Sitting in the living room, Harold asks Jack, "Are you gonna go out fishing? Down at the contest?" He means the ice fishing contest.

"No, I think I'm just going to go down to the pavilion for a while. Kathy's staying here, so I won't be there too long anyway," he tells him. "Are you?"

"I don't know yet, I might." Harold tells him. "Dad, do we have to have our own bait and jiggle stick?"

"You have to have your own jiggle stick. I got some around here somewhere. Patrick do you know where my jiggle sticks are?" Edward asks him. "I had them just a few days ago. Was anybody using them?"

"I think they're in your truck," he tells him.

"You can use one of mine," Edward tells him. "Or anybody else that wants to use one for that matter. I want them back though. I think the sportsman club provides the bait. I'm not one hundred percent sure on that."

"Chris? Joe? Are you guys going fishing?" Harold asks his brothers-in-law.

"Yeah, I'm going. Theresa has to work, but I'm going," Joe replies.

"Work? What do you mean work? It's Sunday," Jack asks him.

"She's waitressing at the pavilion today for extra money," he explains.

Chris gets an arrogant look on his face, "I'm not going either. I'm going to go to the pavilion for a few hours and have a few drinks and come back here and pick up Carol and the kids and go home," he tells Jack.

"So, who's all going?" Jack asks. "Are Patrick, Frankie and Timmy going?" He looks at Patrick.

"I'm going out fishing, I don't know what you guys are dong, or Frankie or Timmy," Patrick tells him.

"I suppose they'll ride down with me and ma," Edward tells him. "I think Jennifer is staying here."

"Yeah, she is. I just heard mom ask her," Patrick tells him.

"Are your kids going down?" Jack asks Harold.

"Hell no, it's time we left them with somebody else for a change," he says.

Bonnie is unusually quiet today, but attentive, smiling and listens to the others, but is just not her outgoing self. Her hair, like Laura's, is piled on top of her head, like a beehive. A new style.

"What's new with you Bonnie?" Kathy asks her old classmate and sister-in-law.

"Not much really, working at the nursing home."

"How do you like that?" she asks.

"I don't, but it's okay. Cleaning up after some of those older people is pretty disgusting sometimes," she says leaning forward, "Aacckk!!!" she says as she pretends to throw up. This makes Kathy laugh.

"I bet," Kathy says still chuckling.

"And how about you, how have you been?" Bonnie asks her.

"Oh good." Kathy tells her.

"As good as can be I guess," she adds.

Lexington Glory Days

"And the baby?" Bonnie asks. "How's the baby?"

"The baby is doing just fine. Growin like a weed," she smiles at her.

Laura, Carol, Betty and Theresa have been talking about their husbands and how they've been personally and about their work, but drop the conversation and begin talking with Bonnie and Kathy about the baby.

"Do you have everything you need?" Laura asks Kathy, "I might have some baby clothes you can have."

"Sure, I'll take them," Kathy tells her, "yeah, thanks. Otherwise I think we're good. I think we have everything we need," she says, a bit unsure.

"You'll be fine," Laura reassures her.

"What you don't have, you get," Mom Betty says, "That's all there is to it."

"How about you, Carol? I might have some maternity clothes left if you need any," Laura tells her.

"I've got plenty from the first two kids, but thanks anyway," she acknowledges. "If I need some more I'll call you."

"You don't really need that much," Betty tells them, "besides baby bottles to feed them, clothes, a crib to sleep in, and diapers to shit in.

The women laugh from the way Betty said this, and Laura repeats it laughing, "bottles to feed them, a crib to sleep in and diapers to shit in!" she laughs even harder at hearing it again a second time.

Carol nods her head, "that's about it too."

"I'm glad I don't have to worry about it all," Theresa tells them.

"You don't want kids? Laura asks her.

"Oh maybe someday – but not right now," Theresa tells her confidently.

"Oh, you're gonna wait?" Kathy says, surprised.

"We're in no hurry. We gotta get ourselves more situated first. Decide where we want to live, talk some things over, that kind of stuff."

"That sounds like a good idea," Kathy tells her, "a really good idea."

"You're never really ready for them," Laura tells them, "you think you are, but you're not, not really."

"Why not?" Kathy wants to know.

"Because they need so much attention, and take up all of your time," Laura tells her. "You have to constantly be watching them."

"That's the part I like the most, spending time with her," Kathy tells her.

"That's good. Because you'll be spending all of your time with her," Laura tells her laughing. "And I mean 'all of it.'"

"I don't think I'm going to mind that," Kathy says.

"How about Jack," Bonnie asks excitedly, "does he like being a daddy?"

"He's pretty quiet about the whole thing. He doesn't get too excited about anything." Kathy tells them, straightforwardly.

"He must get excited once in a while, you did have a baby after all," Theresa says, smiling, making a joke.

Kathy laughs, embarrassed, "Yeah he gets a little excited then!"

"Ohh!" Bonnie exclaims. "And Jack, he likes being a mechanic?"

"He hasn't said anything about finding a different job. He likes it I think," Kathy tells her. "He likes working on cars."

"Let's go to the fishing contest already. Enough of this," Harold, tells them all. "Are we gonna go or what?"

"Yeah, let's go," they all agree.

The women start to bundle up the kids in their winter coats, hats and mittens, and the men step outside to warm up the vehicles. Everyone but Kathy and Carol, who's pregnant, are going, and are staying back to watch the smaller kids with Jennifer.

Betty stands by the door, making sure each one gets a hug before they leave. She stands there almost breathless, with love in her eyes, waiting for the next child to leave. Laughs are heard outside as Betty and Edward say goodbye as they walk to their cars. "Bye now, come again soon," Edward calls after them, even though he'll see them again in a short while.

"We'll meet you's down there. We'll be there shortly,"

Betty hollers out of the door at them, laughing and smiling. "Bye," she tells them one last time, waving.

Chapter Fourteen

Tickets, Get Your Tickets!

With the sun shining so brightly it hurts your eyes to look reflecting off the white snow on the frozen lake, snowmobiles are whizzing by with their high-pitched engines, screaming one, two, three, four at a time. A cluster of them has just ridden in from a town sixty miles away. Forty of them are already parked on top of the snow covered frozen grass along the side of the pavilion.

"Looks like people are coming in from all over to go to the ice fishing contest," smiling, Larry tells Theresa, whose waitressing for extra money inside the pavilion.

"There's people here from all over the county," he says. "I heard someone say they drove over an hour to get here." A man in a black snowmobile suit carrying a black helmet quickly walks past him, bringing with him a trail of cool air and the smell of gasoline.

"It's a big fundraiser for the Sportsman's Club and, as usual, there's a big turnout. There's a lot of people here," she tells him, setting a tray of empty glasses on the bar, "and more coming in all the time. You couldn't ask for a nicer day for it. The contest out on the lake hasn't started yet, has it?"

"Starts at one," he tells her. "But all the prizes are given away inside the pavilion here."

"A good concertina band should be starting up any time now," Theresa tells him starting to dance a little bit, down by the bar area which is crowded with people, gathered around drinking and socializing.

Gertrude and Kimberly walk in, cold and shivering. "Hi," Theresa tells them, happy to see her aunts. Jack and Chris walk in behind them.

"It's cold out there!" Kimberly tells her, smiling from ear to ear, rubbing her hands together. "Feel my hands." She puts one against Jacks ear.

"All these people, my God," Gertrude, says, disbelieving. "Look at all of them. I see old friends and neighbors already," mingling in the crowd, she says to Kimberly. "It seems like just about everyone is wearing a snowmobile suit."

"It's cold out," Jack and Chris agree, telling her, taking off their gloves.

The place is packed with people and busy and the mood is lively. It is early afternoon, one o'clock, 1973.

"It looks like there's a lot of people out on the lake," Theresa tells Jigger at the bar, looking out a small window. "How come you're not out there?"

"I might go out, I haven't decided yet," he tells her, sounding serious.

"Isn't it a nice day?" Lily says, sitting next to him at the bar, drinking a beer. Suddenly she gets excited, "I'll be right back. I see some people I want to say 'hi' to." She gets up and quickly disappears into the crowd of people.

"It really is a nice day. Bright, crisp and sunny," Theresa says.

"And cold," Jigger adds seriously, and then laughs.

"The fishermen, some of them as young as three and some as old as ninety are crowding around holes drilled in the ice by the sportsmen. If you're going to go, you better get out there. Looks like it's about to start," Theresa tells Jigger, still looking out of the window. The bartender

Lexington Glory Days

comes over and Theresa gathers her notepad and pen and then walks away with a tray of full of beers in plastic cups.

"Excuse me," she says, as she makes her way around the bar.

"Tickets! Get your tickets! Winner every time!" A jolly Eli, Gertrude's husband, is shouting, selling raffle tickets.

"First prize is three hundred dollars in cash. Second prize is two hundred dollars in cash; third prize is a hundred dollars in cash. The grand prize is a new, child's snowmobile, made for the kiddies," he shouts above the clatter of the crowd.

People are walking around the bar, eating hot beef sandwiches and chips, or bratwursts and sauerkraut, and most of the crowd washes it down with a cold beer right out of the keg. The crowd is constantly in motion and people are always walking from one place to another, mingling to see who all is here.

A man yells loudly across the bar, "It's starting! The contest is starting!"

Harold and Laura walk into the bar, with other people from Centerville.

"The lake's been making good ice for three months now, and there's almost a solid two feet of ice out there," Eugene is telling Sophia and Larry, as they walk in.

"That's a lot of ice!" A man brushes up against him, on his way to the bar. "I been out there fishing all winter but I never measured it 'til today."

"Is that right?" Larry responds, interested. "I didn't know there was that much." Sophia doesn't care and her eyes wonder over the crowd.

Harold sees Peter and walks over to him, "Hi Peter. I didn't know who I'd all see here today. It's cold outside, only ten degrees. How have you been?" He starts laughing and shakes his hand.

"You have to have warm clothes and a jacket on.

Otherwise it aint too bad. I'm good," Peter tells him, smiling. "I haven't seen you in a long time. How are you? Hi Laura." Like everyone else here, they catch up with old friends and relatives and find out how their lives are going.

Bonnie is here and walks in with a group of friends.

"Better have your long johns on or you'll freeze to death," Gertrude tells Laura. "I'm cold," she wraps her arms around her waist and starts laughing unexpectedly.

Bonnie tells her, "It's only cold outside, it's nice in here." She seems happy. There's people huddled around inside near the entrance door who have just arrived, looking for room to sit or stand, waiting to get in. Two young men in brightly colored snowmobile suits walk past them.

"Hi guys," Lily greets them, "I was wondering if you's were coming."

"Hi Lily," Kimberly and Gertrude greet her. Gertrude presses her jacket closer to her body.

She looks at Bonnie and starts laughing again.

A cluster of friends and relatives begin to seat themselves around a large table up on the dance floor. Theresa walks up to the table, joking around.

"Can I get anyone anything?" And stays to mingle with her family. "With all the chatter in the background and all the people talking all at once, it takes all my focus to pay attention when somebody is ordering something," Theresa smiles and tells them. "There's 'so' many people here."

Peter's talking to Harold and Laura about his life on the farm, "I'm out there by myself, but it's good." Suddenly he says, "God Almighty it's loud in here."

"It's just going to get louder," Laura tells him. "Wait 'til the beer starts kicking in," she laughs. "I'm going to go to the bar and get a setup, do you have the whiskey?" She asks Harold. He pulls a bottle out from an inner coat

Lexington Glory Days

pocket.

"All the booths are full," Bonnie is pointing and telling the group of friends she's with. "It's early yet and there's already no place to sit."

The dance hall has a forty-foot high, tall ceiling at its peak, and all the walls and ceilings are covered in wood. People have occupied all the sitting booths and there's a large overflow crowd in the middle of the dance floor, standing around and talking. They can feel the old floorboards slightly swaying up and down from the movement of all the people. "Can you feel that?" Jack asks Chris, sitting at the table, trying to stay still.

Both sections, the lower area where the bar is and the upper section where the dance hall is, are both full of people, and there is a sixteen gallon keg of beer just at the top of the three steps between the two rooms.

Small kids of all ages are wandering around with their parents in their snowmobile suits. It's a great family outing and a tradition for many of them. "I wouldn't miss it," Brian and Clay say smiling, walking around visiting with people.

On the table sits two pitchers of beer and a small stack of empty plastic glasses, turned upside down. Mamie and Ted's daughter, Susan, and her husband, Danny, are sitting at the table with Jack and Chris and others. Susan is Carol's age and a friend and first cousin, Edward's niece. The couple are a lot of fun and full of laughs. Susan has a quick smile and wit and is always ready with something to say. Danny and Susan have strong ties and loving affection for Betty and Edward.

Rita and Carrie, two of Edward's sisters, are sitting with them. "I enjoy sitting around hearing the family's stories," Rita says laughing.

Mamie and Ted's son, Ron, Susan's brother, is also there. Ron has on cowboy boots and a cowboy hat, and it gives him a kind of country air, even though he's lived in

Lexington Glory Days

the big city, just across the river from downtown St. James most of his life. People are passing by the table and all around it, walking in all directions. Harold and Laura come up and seat themselves at the table.

"Hi everyone," they greet them happily.

Betty and Edward enter the already packed building. They walk in talking with two other couples and Betty sees her sisters and smiles and waves.

Seeing there's no room in the main bar area, they walk up the few steps to the dance floor and spot the people around the table. "Oh my God, look who's here!" Susan shouts at them, in a nasal voice. Betty and Edward smile. "Pull up a chair!" Susan tells them. "Come sit down. There's room over here."

They walk up the stairs with Kimberly and Gertrude, and Lily and Larry walking up behind them, while other people are walking back down.

Betty waves, wiggling her fingers and says, "Hi everyone!"

'Hi' they happily greet her. The six stand close to the table, talking.

"Well, did you's catch lots of fish?" Kimberly asks Betty, snickering.

"Heavens no," Betty responds smiling, "you wouldn't catch me out on that ice." A family with kids walks past their table.

"I know, I know," Kimberly says scrunching her face muscles, "me neither," she laughs again.

"I don't like fish that much," Gertrude says, trying to be serious.

"How about you Edward? Did you catch any fish?" Lily asks him.

"Nope, I wasn't out there," he tells her. "We just got here. Just rolled in."

"Here you go Edward, you better have a beer," Chris says, and sets a full glass of beer from the pitcher in front of him.

"Well, sit down, sit down," Susan persuades them.

"Thank you," he tells him. "Just what the doctor ordered." He chuckles.

"Mom, do you want a pop or something? I'll get it for you." Jack tells her.

"I'll have a Pepsi, as long as you're going to get up and get it." Betty tells him and smiles.

"Sure, I'll get you one," Jack says happily, and makes his way into the crowd, down to the bar. "S'cuse me, S'cuse me," he tells a dozen people.

"Hi Ron," Betty greets Edwards nephew from across the table, "how are you? You're looking good." She sits facing the stage and can see all the people sitting in the booths and standing in the middle, around the dance floor.

"Thank you. I feel good," he says holding up his glass. "I got a cold beer and good people around me, what more is there?" He says smiling from ear to ear. "How about you, Betts, how have you been?"

"I'm doing ok," she tells him. "What other choice do I have?"

She smiles a little bit, looking good. Her gaze turns to all the faces in the crowd.

"Can you believe all the people here? My God, everyone from four counties must be here," Susan, says to Betty.

"There's quite a crowd, isn't there?" she responds looking around.

"I think I see some people I haven't seen in forty years," Susan says laughing. "My God there's people here."

Rita is on the other end of the table, talking to Carrie. "I was on my way to work and my wheels started spinning. That snow bank must have been...ten feet high," she exaggerates, in a very nasal voice. "I thought, oh my

God here I go," and puts her elbows on the table and her hands over her ears. "So I tried rocking it. I put it in drive and go forward a little bit, then I put it in reverse and go back a little, then forward, then reverse," she gets flustered and shakes her hands in the air. She looks up at someone walking by.

Carrie is eating popcorn and is amused at this.

With all the noise and commotion going on around them, Jack and Harold talk about work and better jobs, while the women sit around and visit.

Edward and Ron start talking.

"So, Edward," Ron asks him in a deep baritone voice, "what have you been up to?"

Ron fits right in here in the country with his cowboy hat on.

"Nothing, drinking," he tells him. Edward likes Ron, with his drinking and guitar playing and country ways, even though he's from a big city.

"Drinking?" Ron says sarcastically, "not you Edward."

"Yup, I know it's hard to believe, but someone's got to do it."

Ron laughs. "What have you been drinking?"

Ron's a heavy drinker too.

"Beer. Beer mostly, a little brandy sometimes."

Edward admits this a little sheepishly.

"Beer and a little brandy. That's a rough combination – even for you." He tells him smiling. "Are you sure you can handle it?"

"That's up for discussion," he tells him, almost proudly with a small grunt.

"He can't handle it, that's the whole problem," Betty interrupts them.

"You're just going to have to stick to beer," Lily tells him, smiling.

"I suppose," he tells her. Not wanting to continue the

conversation.

"So what did you do?" Carrie asks Rita, continuing their conversation.

"What 'could' I do?" Rita says. "I kept trying to get out! But there I sat, forward and back, forward and back, forward and back. I was digging such a deep hole in the snow and the tires were going deeper and deeper and deeper." She snorts and laughs. Carrie thinks this is funny.

"So you had to have Edward come and pull you out then?" Carrie asks, laughing at her. She moves to the side letting someone through.

"I did, but I didn't want to call him myself, so I had someone else call." Rita says, a little embarrassed.

"Why didn't you want to call?" Carrie asks, obviously amused.

"I didn't want it to seem like I was starting any trouble!" she replies, getting excited. Rita likes attention and doesn't have much time for Betty's more polite ways. Betty feels the same about Rita.

"What have you been up to?" Edward asks Ron, sitting across the table.

"Drinking, same as you. Drinking and playing the guitar," he says.

"What have you been playing?" Edward asks him.

"Oh, some Willy, some Waylon, and Johnny. Gotta play Johnny. You know Johnny Cash? 'I Walk The Line,' 'Folsom Prison Blues?'"

"I've heard of him," Edward remarks jokingly, teasing him.

"You've heard of him." Ron thinks this is funny. "What have you heard about him?" Ron thinks Edward is a bad ass and likes him a lot.

"He's a good singer," Edward says. There's movement and noise around the stage area and there's a concertina band setting up to play.

"The band is here," Ron, says, "maybe they'll play us some Johnny Cash!" He laughs. Instead, they play the 'Beer Barrel Polka.'

Everyone is talking around the table, and having a good time. Once the band begins to play, everyone joins in and starts singing along. "Roll...out the barrel...Roll out, the barrel of beer...Roll out the barrel...Roll out, a barrel of fun."

By three o'clock, the party's in full swing. The ice fishing contest out on the lake has gotten over with, and Peter walks up to the table and Clay comes over from a different side. The chatter of people talking gets even louder with the influx of the fishermen coming in from the lake and the high ceiling makes everything echo even more. Peter starts talking with Harold.

"I hate to ruin the fun, but I have to be getting back and pick up Carol and the kids," Chris tells them, looking around the table.

"I do too," Jack adds. "It's been fun, bye Ron, nice to see you again."

"My old drinking buddy! Take care Jack." Ron says stoutly, smiling.

Old friends and family members continually stop at the table to visit.

"I'll be around for a little while yet, I'm gonna go walk around," Jack says.

Clay stops and pays for a pitcher of beer from the keg, and brings it to the table, "I thought you guys could use another pitcher of beer," he says in a low toned voice, loudly over the noise of the partying crowd and the music.

"Peter, have a beer," Clay tells him, setting the pitcher down on the table.

"I'd love a beer," Kimberly tells her husband, while talking with Betty.

"Well, thank you," Susan tells him, "We were getting pretty low. And I hate running out..." she lets it linger. A child suddenly starts crying in the background.

"No, that would be a crime," Laura says, laughing, making herself another whiskey drink. She looks up quickly to see if there's anyone standing around nearby that she knows.

"Hi everyone isn't this fun?" Edna suddenly appears with Roman, and says enthusiastically. She makes one wave with both her hands in the air. "Where did all these people come from?" She says deliriously, looking around, her arms swaying in a big circle behind her. Betty, Kimberly, and Gertrude laugh at her antics and begin talking with her.

"Sit down," they tell her.

"Thanks for the beer!" Peter says loudly to Clay, and fills up his cup.

"You're welcome," Clay tells him, and turns to walk over to him.

"Hi everybody," Joe, Theresa's husband, says walking up to them, back from lake and the ice fishing contest. "How's everyone doing?"

"We're fine," Betty says, smiling at him. "Pull up a chair, sit down. How did you do fishing? Did you catch any fish?"

"Some small crappies, that's about all. Thanks, but I'm going to walk down to the bar and find Theresa. I want to find out how late she has to work, and if the tips have been any good. I'll be back up, though," he tells her animatedly. "I saw you's up here and I just thought I'd come over and say, 'hi.'"

"Eugene!" Edward exclaims over excitedly, exaggerating his words.

Eugene walks up and nods his head at everyone, "Hi, everybody! You should have seen all the fish the fishermen caught." Clay, Peter and Harold listen to him as he looks around the table. "There must be 'a lot' of fish in this here old lake."

Lexington Glory Days

"You would know," Roman tells him sarcastically, not looking at him.

Edward, what do you know? What's the good word?" Eugene asks.

"I don't know anything, just here like everybody else. What do you know?"

"We were out on the ice, fishing. People was catching some nice fish."

"You were? Did you catch anything?" Edward asks, pretending to be more interested than he is.

Harold, Clay and Peter continue talking.

"We caught some crappies, but nothing big enough to win any of the prizes, I don't think," Eugene tells him, barely able to control his enthusiasm.

Jigger, still a bachelor, drunk and shined up appears, leans his hands on the table next to Edward, and says to him, "Edward you old son-of-a-gun, what do you know?"

"Everything, what do you want to know?" Edward asks him, looking down.

"Ha! Everything! Shit, you don't know anything, do you?" Then he lets out a short, big laugh and looks around the table. He turns serious and says, "Hi Rita, my love, how are you today?" Theresa walks by them, looks and smiles, delivering a pizza to a group of people sitting in one of the orange booths.

"I'm just fine," she tells him, scrunching her nose up at Carrie, laughing at him. Rita's husband died unexpectedly several years ago, and Jigger wants to date her. Rita has serious doubts about it.

Not getting the response he was hoping for from Rita, Jigger stands up almost soberly and says to Betty, "Betty how are you?" Dragging the 'you' out a little too long.

"I'm good Jigger, nice to see you, how are you?" Betty says to him.

"I'm fine, Betty. You know me. Everyone knows

Lexington Glory Days

Jigger!" He shouts. "No, Betty, I'm fine, I'm always fine," he says tiredly. "I better go down to the bar and get a drink," then he turns and starts to leave. "Nice to see everybody," he waves without looking and walks away, staggering.

The concertina band plays another polka as couples dance around the big room. It's crowded up front near the band as small kids jump around to the old time music, some never having seen a band before.

People at the bar area tap their feet with the beat of the music, and people around the dance hall clap their hands, as the already packed bar and dance hall begin filling up even more, with the last of the fisherman and spectators from off the lake coming in, stretching the capacity of the building. People are elbow to elbow, shoulder to shoulder.

The door to the outside is opened and closed all day long, each time letting in the brisk Minnesota winter air. This time a group of eight people come in, with matching snowmobile suits and helmets. Everyone looks to see who they are, and when they take off their helmets, they raise their hands to acknowledge their friends. Folks around the table murmur, "It looks like Katherine and Joe Jr. and Wayne ...I can't see who the other ones are...Well it's Blanch! I haven't talked to her in such a long time. I wonder who they're with?"

Eli walks by them shouting, "Tickets! Tickets! Get your tickets! Winner every time!" He smiles every time he says it. "Last chance for tickets!"

Patrick and Frankie see the group at the table, and walk up to join them.

"There you are," Betty says, relieved to see them. "You must be frozen!"

"We're okay," Frankie says smiling. His cheeks bright red and rosy.

"Bonnie!" Betty says loudly across the table, rubbing

Frankie's ears, motioning her over to her. She whispers something in her ear. "I think your dad is drinking too much." And getting loud and unruly. "Tell Harold and Jack for me, and tell them to come over and talk to me." Bonnie disappears into the crowd of people and comes back with them. "I think I should get him home before he gets too drunk," Betty tells her sons. She knows if she says anything to Edward, he'll whine about it for hours. "I'll never hear the end of it," she tells them.

"We'll keep an eye on him for you," Harold tells her. "It's early yet. When we think he's had enough, we'll let you know. In the meantime, don't worry about it and enjoy yourself." Betty looks unsure, but goes along with them anyway.

"You deserve an afternoon of fun," Jack tells her. "He'll be okay."

Just then Carrie gets up and walks around the table, and Betty catches her and asks her where she is going. "To the bathroom," she leans into her ear and tells her. The others around the table notice the two whispering to each other. "Wait just a minute and I'll go with you," Betty tells her.

"Well, hurry up," Carrie tells her jokingly, bending at the knees a few times, smiling, "I have to go..."

They work their way through the large crowd of people, down the steps and down to the far end of the bar, to the bathrooms. On their way there and back they exchange brief 'hello's' with friends of theirs; people who live in trailer houses in the campgrounds, a nephew of Betty's; neighbors; relatives of Edward's; friends of their kids; men and women from the church; Betty's aunts Josephine and Antoinette and their husbands; an elderly, neighbor woman they visit from time to time who lives alone in a camper trailer in the camp grounds; and some of Carrie's or Betty's nieces and nephews.

Winners of the ice fishing contest and raffle tickets

are starting to be announced and the crowd suddenly gets mellow for the first time all afternoon.

"Can I have your attention?" Eli yells. "We're gonna start announcing the winners of the fishing contest. The winner of the biggest fish, goes to John Bruzinski," Eli calls out.

"Ring the bell!" Lily shouts out from the table. Rita just about spits all of her beer out, laughing.

"Ring the bell," Rita repeats laughing. He's the bell ringer at the church. "Ring the bell!" People around the table laugh hysterically.

"The oldest fisherman prize goes to Roman Kefren." The people applaud and cheer for him and then Eli announces the winner for the smallest fish and then the winner for the youngest fisherman, "Jeremy Pike. Come up and get your prize, Jeremy."

"That's our oldest brother, Wayne's, grandson," Kimberly tells them. "I didn't know they were all here." Gertrude looks up to see him.

"Okay, we'll do the raffle ticket winners next." Bottles of wine and booze, gift certificates, free oil changes, a cooler and cash are given away. Twelve packs of beer, a free car wash, almost fifty prizes are given out.

Eli announces the winners and the prize they won. "Come up and claim your prize," he tells them. "Laura Reich. Is Laura still here?" Eli shouts.

"I won!" Laura exclaims. "He called my name!" She gets up from her chair to claim her prize. "I don't know what I won, but I won!" Lily giggles.

"Betty Reich," Eli calls out. "Betty you won a ten dollar gift certificate."

Other cheers can be heard over the crowd getting louder. "I won!" "I won!"

"And the Grand prize...The winner of the kids' snowmobile goes to... Eugene Latzki. Congratulations Eugene, and thank you everyone for coming out and supporting the Lexington Sportsman Club."

After the drawing the crowd starts to thin out, as families go home.

Laura has come back from claiming her prize, and Betty and Carrie are back from the bathroom and seat themselves back around the table, as the bright sun from earlier in the day quickly begins to set, and it starts to get dark out.

"Betty did you hear your name being called? You won a gift certificate!" Kimberly tells her enthusiastically.

"I did," she responds smiling and happy and waves it in the air.

Carrie and the other women begin chatting with Carrie's daughter, Mary. Mary and her husband have decided to have another baby, and Mary's pregnant.

"Well congratulations," Mom Betty tells them both, happily.

"He's wanted a boy for the longest time," Mary goes on; they have three daughters. "And he better get one this time, cause there's no more after this one coming out of me. This is it. I'm done. Somebody else's turn." She says laughing. "I've had three and this will be my fourth, I'm getting old!" she says, dragging the word out.

"Oh, you're young yet," Betty tells her.

"I'll be thirty this year," Mary tells her. "I'm no spring chicky chicky anymore," she says smiling. Carrie and Betty and Kimberly and Gertrude look at one another and laugh over her thinking thirty is old. "I'm not old," she admits, recognizing her gaff.

Her dad, Carrie's husband, sits and listens to them, smiling proudly.

There's plenty of open space for elbowroom now as more people have left, and the band keeps playing its old time music, still enticing many of the country dancers out onto the dance floor with its lively waltzes and polkas.

Peter comes up to the table, animated and obviously

Lexington Glory Days

inebriated and asks if anyone wants a beer. "I'm buying! I won a gift certificate to the Lexington pavilion!" He stammers, laughing. His laugh sounds like a stutter.

"Sure get me one," everyone says, turning to look at each other, nodding.

"I'll get everyone one," he turns around, thinking about how much a round for the whole table is going to cost him.

The last keg, near the table, has run dry and Harold tells him to bring a tray from the bar, "Put on as many as you can fit on a tray," he tells him.

"All right," he grumbles, worried about the bill. The gift certificate isn't going to cover the whole thing.

"Well he asked, he shouldn't be mad," Bonnie says. "For crying out loud."

"I'm hungry, I'm thinking about getting a burger, you want one?" Edward asks Betty, grumpy.

"Sure I'll have one," she says. "I won't have to cook supper that way," she looks at Laura and laughs. Laura nods and smiles, agreeing.

"What do you mean you won't have to cook supper?" Edward asks her, turning belligerent. "You don't think one hamburger is gonna fill me up do you?"

"Well get two then! I can't have one day off from cooking?" Betty tells him quickly, getting slightly embarrassed.

"I don't want two! Damn it, woman!" Edward tells her, seriously.

"Oh, I'll make supper, don't worry about it." She tells him quickly.

"You better," he says, getting ornery. "You know I've got to have supper."

"Make your own damn supper, that's what I'd tell you, Edward," Lily pipes in, half serious, but smiling, waiting for his reaction.

"I would too," Laura tells them, "Let 'em make their

own."

"Edward you just can't win," Ron tells him, laughing.

"I suppose," Edward says and turns to get up to get the hamburgers.

Lily turns to Betty, laughing and says, "I hope I didn't make him mad, I shouldn't have said that."

"Don't worry about it, he gets mad every time he drinks anyway. Over nothing, I don't do anything and he gets mad. He's mad about something all the time." Betty confides in them.

"Really?" Carrie says surprised, "he's usually in such a good mood when I see him. He's always happy and jolly..."

"You don't see him when he gets home," Betty tells her, trying not to stare at her in her eyes. "He's not happy and jolly all the time, let me tell you."

The band has played its final polka of the day and someone has put money in the jukebox. The singer, Kenny Rogers' and his song, 'Lucille,' is playing.

When the entertainer gets to the verse, where he sings, '...you picked a fine time to leave me Lucille, with four hungry children and a crop in the field...' the crowd at the table sings along, but changes the words. '...You picked a fine time to leave me Lucille, with four-hundred children and a crop in the field," and everyone laughs, and keeps singing along, happy and amused.

It's Sunday night, and most people have to work in the morning, so the remaining crowd keeps thinning out. If people start leaving, the rest will follow. The group decides to take their beers and sit at the tables below, down by the bar.

Betty and the others decide they've almost had enough and talk of heading for home. Harold tells Ron, "Go get your guitar for a while."

"No, I don't think so," he replies, eyeing the remaining crowd.

Lexington Glory Days

"Go on bring it in, we'll clap and sing along with you," Lily adds, clapping her hands and stopping her feet. "Go on, it's early yet!"

"Well, all right," he gives in, rubs his hands over the tops of his jeans, gets up, puts on his coat and moves towards the door to get his guitar from the car.

Edward comes back with the hamburgers, wrapped in plastic wrap, one for him and one for Betty. He sits across from her at the smaller table by the bar, and lightly tosses hers across the small table. "Here's your hamburger," he tells her easily, noticeably drunk and still grumpy.

She gives him a quick look, and begins to unwrap the sandwich and comments, "Oh, this smells so good." She looks at Kimberly and chuckles.

"It does, it smells very good. Clay! Clay! Go get me a hamburger would you? Get yourself one too," Kimberly tells her husband quietly. "I'm not making supper tonight either." She laughs.

"What? Why can't you get your own hamburger?" He asks her slightly annoyed in his deep voice, "They're right there!" Talking about the bartenders.

"No, you have to get it for me. Edward got Betty one, so I want you to get me one," she says smartly, teasing him.

He stammers, starting to complain, "What the hell..." Then just gives up and says to the bartender, "Make me two of those, would you please?"

Ron comes back in with his guitar, and sets the case down behind where the group is sitting and takes it out. "Now were going to hear some music!" Lily says, annunciating the 'now' and 'music' more forcefully.

Ron sits down, and places the guitar along his knee, and gives it a few strums. Ron has a deep, baritone voice when he sings, and starts playing 'Folsom Prison Blues,' a Johnny Cash tune. People listen and tap their feet and enjoy his music. Laura gets up, extends her arms to Lily whose standing nearby, and the two begin to dance, and sing along with the song. '...Well if they free me from this prison and that railroad train is mine, you'd bet I'd move it on a little farther down the line....far from Folsum Prison...' The strums on the guitar get hard and softer. '...that's where I want to be...'

Ron plays song after song, each one a Johnny Cash song, or Willie Nelson or Waylon Jennings song. 'Walbash Cannon Ball,' 'Good Hearted Woman,' 'Old Shep,' 'Home of the Blues.'

Edward speaks up, "Well, it's been fun. Ron you sound good. Very good. But I suppose we should get going," he tells them.

"You're leaving Edward?" Ron asks him.

"I guess so, ma has to work in the morning, and I gotta get up to take her," he replies. Ron begins playing, 'City of New Orleans,' on the guitar.

"How come you don't have to work in the morning?" Ron asks him.

"I don't have to," he tells him, "I already made my money," he laughs.

"Bye, Betty," Kimberly and Gertrude tell her, "it was fun spending the afternoon with you."

"Bye Edward, don't do anything I wouldn't do," Lily laughs.

"It was fun talking to all of you's too. I can't remember the last time I had so much fun," Betty tells them, standing, putting on her coat. She notices peanuts shells and a small amount of garbage spread around on the old wooden floor from the day's events.

"Bye Betty, Bye Edward," Carrie tells them, smiling.

"Until next time." Ron says, holding up his beer glass.

"Bye everyone," Betty tells them, waving her hand at each one, "It sure was a good time." They all agree and tell her good bye again.

Betty walks to the door and opens it, waiting for Edward, but he's still talking. She closes the door, and Edward begins walking towards her. He bends over in the corner next to the door and picks out his coat off of a pile of coats and suddenly remembers how years ago in the same spot, with the clock above the door, the TV in the corner, and the empty beer cases stacked up along the wall, himself, Larry and his dad picked up bags of clothes and boxes of food people donated for his family, after their house burned down in 1960.

He turns around and looks at the old familiar pavilion and the small crowd left there, and thinks of this kindness of his neighbors and relatives. He smiles a little, fortunate, thankful and grateful, and he and Betty walk out the door. The same way they did nearly fourteen years and a million problems ago. The same way they did a thousand times before. The same way they always will.

The End

Made in the USA
Middletown, DE
14 April 2015